REVELATIONS

Horror Writers for Climate Action

Edited by Seán O'Connor

REVELATIONS

Horror Writers for Climate Action

Edited by Seán O'Connor

STYGIAN SKY MEDIA
Houston, Texas
www.stygianskymedia.com

Copyright © 2022
All Rights Reserved

ISBN: 978-1-63951-005-4

First Edition

The stories included in this publication are a work of fiction. Names, characters, places and incidents are products of each author's imagination or are used fictitiously. Any resemblance to actual events or locales or persons living or dead is entirely coincidental.

Without limiting the rights under copyright reserved above, no part of this publication may be reproduced, stored in or introduced into a retrieval system, or transmitted, in any form, or by any means (electronic, mechanical, photocopying, recording, or otherwise), without the prior written permission of both the copyright owner and the above publisher of this book.

Interior Design by Kenneth W. Cain

For Earth

"There is no going back — no matter what we do now, it's too late to avoid climate change and the poorest, the most vulnerable, those with the least security, are now certain to suffer."

– Sir David Attenborough,
February 2021

TABLE OF CONTENTS

INTRODUCTION

Sadie Hartmann

The authors you'll see in the Table of Contents for Revelations need no introduction. I was invited to do just that by the editor and my friend, Seán O'Connor. How do I introduce Ramsey Campbell to horror fans? Clive Barker anyone? Ever heard of him? How about this, Tananarive Due? I heard that Stephen King guy can write his way out of a paper bag.

This is a joke I could easily run into the ground, and I think I've made my point. The table of contents is a guest list like no other and I am incredibly honored to be typing these words. I've enjoyed hours and hours of reading words penned by this lot; visited many fictional worlds from their imaginations and fell in love with the characters they have created.

Between them all, I'm sure every literary award you could think of has been won – more than once. So, what I will attempt to do is set the stage for the purpose of this anthology and then introduce the stories represented here by doing what I do best,

Sharing my thoughts, pulling quotes, and urging other readers to join me.

I thought a lot about this introduction sitting in a wicker chair on the porch of a beach house called Wit's End. When I was a kid, my parents booked a week in this house every year for our family's one vacation. My sisters and I used to talk about how our classmates and friends took family trips to Yellowstone or Disneyland and how our family just went to Dillon Beach, California every year but honestly, I don't think we missed out on anything.

This year, my sister and I left our own families at home to crash our parent's vacation at Wit's End. We both left California and moved to Washington and neither one of us had been to Dillon Beach since my sister's bachelorette party over a decade ago.

Flying over California, we could see a wildfire. Brownish, gray plumes of smoke mixing with the clouds and on the land below, a clear line of demarcation between the blackened, charred landscape and the wildlife anticipating certain destruction.

Climate change is one hundred percent why California faces a worsening wildfire season every year. The summers are hotter, the drought conditions longer, and the plant life is dryer making the landscape extra flammable. Most California fires start from lightning or downed power lines during high winds. But people are responsible too.

Fireworks during backyard celebrations.

A cigarette is carelessly thrown out of a car on the freeway.

Campers leaving a fire unattended at a campground.

Growing up in a rural, Northern California town, we never canceled school every year because the air quality was dangerous due to smoke. The power company didn't schedule power outages during windstorms. We didn't live under the threat of an evacuation every summer. But these things are common practice now and for the last several years. California is seeing the very real consequences of climate change. This is the way California is now. It will likely get worse.

Everywhere.

Nationally.

Globally.

Unless we do something to radically change our course.

My vision for pulling my favorite quotes from each story serves two purposes. One, to entice you, and two, to create an atmosphere similar to the Academy Awards during the ceremony when clips of nominated movies are shown to the audience. A few lines of greatness to highlight the quality of the film. I hope you enjoy these as they pertain to the theme of our anthology.

"The late State of California had yet more dying to do."
CARRIERS by Tananarive Due

"Haven't you noticed that most of the woodland birds are already gone? No chickadee concerts in the morning, no crow music at noon. By September, the loons will be as gone as the loons who did this. The fish will live a little longer, but eventually, they'll be gone too. Like the deer, the rabbits, and the chipmunks."
SUMMER THUNDER by Stephen King

"Among the corpses on the beach, and amidst the audible splinterings of bone behind the seawall of rubble, she understands that this is the way of things here, in this time. This revelation is the worst thing of all."
CALL THE NAME by Adam L.G. Nevill

"Things in the City were deteriorating rapidly. There were riots. Disease had taken hold of the lower levels. Famine threatened. Political unrest and misinformation was rife."
FIELDS OF ICE by Gemma Amor

"As they walked down the hill Michael smiled a little to himself. Not a happy smile, you understand, but a resigned smile of one who knows what is about to happen, and who also knows that he may do nothing about it."
THE WOOD ON THE HILL by Clive Barker

"The question is, do you want to live to see a curtain call. You're the heroine and if we're following the original plot, you have an unpleasant reckoning in your near future."
FEAR SUN by Laird Barron

"Just now writing something other than his story might well be a trap. He donned sandals and shorts and unbuttoned his shirt as he ventured out beneath a sun that looked as fierce as the rim of a total eclipse."
NO STORY IN IT by Ramsey Campbell

"Of course, when a series of dark and mostly unexplainable events occur in the same spot over the course of many years, and most especially when these events occur within the confines of a small town, the spot is inevitably said to be cursed or even haunted – and the old water tower was no exception."
THE TOWER by Richard Chizmar

"Hesitantly, Eva looked back toward the beach between the rocks and the water, the imbedded footprints of her and Bryce's path still evident. The sand was crawling. All of it."
THE GUARDIAN by Philip Fracassi

"She slept better in the morning. During the night, when she was alone with the dark, she heard screams coming from the hills above. Could be coyotes. Could be worse. The whispering city never gave clues."

LOW HANGING CLOUDS by T. E. Grau

"Somehow it's easier to imagine the ghost of a tree than it is the ghost of a man."
DEAD-WOOD by Joe Hill

"Rather rude, don't you think? Destroying a person's home? I can't fathom anything so devilish as that."
THE MAID FROM THE ASH
by Gwendolyn Kiste

"It's a watery place, teeming with all manner of strange fauna."
INUNDATION by John Langan

"I used to be so into the zombie apocalypse. I figured I'd be this hero in a society risen from ashes. Me, the phoenix of the new world order. But the real thing sucks. Because I'm going to die, and I can't figure out which is more cowardly; resigning to that fate, or fighting it."
LOVE PERVERTS by Sarah Langan

"It isn't your wound that aches you, makes you want to die, it's the war."
IN THE COLD, DARK TIME by Joe R. Lansdale

"We're a long time ago, and you'd barely recognise the people who live here right now. But even in its earliest days, humankind was interfering with nature."
THE EVOLUTIONARY by Tim Lebbon

"A cool gig, the coolest he'd ever heard of; a man with a paperback and a bunch of dead bodies, if that doesn't thrill you nothing will . . ."
TEENAGE GRAVEYARD WATCHMAN
by Josh Malerman

"Crawling her winding flow along the contours of our village, Black Queen was as beautiful as she was terrifying."
BLACK QUEEN by Nuzo Onoh

"The snow still falls. I can feel its purpose, and I think that if I close my eyes a little, I'll see the colors hiding in it."
SNOW ANGELS by Sara Pinborough

"He's been given to Maw as a gift and Maw will give us the sea's bounty in return."
MAW by Priya Sharma

"All our apartment buildings, libraries, markets, salons, and restaurants were crammed together, like space was something to be shared intimately with everyone."
MEAN TIME by Paul Tremblay

A charity anthology donating its proceeds to climateoutreach.org seems so small compared to the scale of the problem. But coming together under the banner of horror fiction in a gesture of unity for the sake of awareness and contribution to a solution is better than not doing anything in all. Climate Outreach is dedicated to research, correcting misinformation, educating the public, and centering the climate change conversation around people, not politics.

It's really important that we keep the dialog about climate change at the forefront of everything we do. Thank you for joining us in making that happen by buying, reading, reviewing, and talking about Revelations.

–Sadie Hartmann
November 2021

FIELDS OF ICE

Gemma Amor

In the Northern Reaches of a dying land that was once prosperous, a vast glacier sprawls along the floor of a valley between two distinct mountain ranges. The largest mountains in each range sit on either side of the glacier like guardian sisters. One is called Old White, and the other Old Red, named for the colours that burn on their peaks at sunrise and sunset. Old Red has a distinct geology, one composed mostly of sedimentary Ironstone, the surface of which has oxidised and now glows a brilliant shade of crimson when the sun hits it just so. Old White's peak is perpetually capped with snow. She is taller, and has a more pronounced summit, one that thrusts up into the sky like a dagger jammed between a man's ribs.

Not much is known of the territory that lies beyond the mountains. The barricade of ice that has piled up over centuries between them has prevented the few scientific and geographic teams that have ventured this far north from making much progress in the region.

Those teams did not count Hayder amongst their number.

Hayder does not travel as part of a team. Hayder travels alone. She does not enjoy responsibility. Expeditions that involve more than one person automatically imply an obligation: to protect the well-being and safety of that extra person. This onerous duty interferes heavily with her ability to do her job. Which is, simply, to find things. Hayder is very good at finding things, but only when she is left the fuck alone to do so. She is an archaeologist, one of the few left in the world, and glad for that. Academic scarcity means that she is valuable to the Minister, and valuable to the Keep. Being valued as a person in this day and age is not a common conceit.

At this present moment in time, Hayder hangs from two ice picks jammed hard into the side of a steeply curving wall of diamond-white ice, about two miles in on the swooping, crenelated surface of the glacier. Her boots are wrapped with leather straps that have wicked metal spikes attached to them: crampons. Her toes are bleeding from the impact of jabbing her spikes into the ice wall over and over again. The fortification she is scaling is starting to crumble in the midday sun. She must get to the top before the ice becomes too mushy to let her climb. If she fails, she will spend another cold, miserable night stuck in a deep, cobalt-blue crevasse, and she does not want that. Crevasses are natural traps, and Hayder has heard movement on the glacier at night. She is fairly certain it is a bear, and a hungry one, and she does not wish to present herself as an easy target by spending any more time in the fissure than she has to. Hayder is not enough of an idiot to think that she can fight a fully grown ice-bear and come out of the encounter unscathed.

Hayder adjusts her goggles, grits her teeth, and drags herself higher up the wall. Her foot slips, suddenly, and she finds herself cheek to jowl with the glacier. It is not a gentle dance partner. She hangs there for a moment, too tired to do much else. Her weight is taken by a rope around her waist. The rope is looped through an iron hoop hammered into the ice wall above her head. As she makes progress, she hammers in new hoops and ties the rope off fresh to each one, anchoring herself to the wall. It's a laborious process. Her arms ache. In fact, Hayder's whole body aches, and she feels as if she has been pummelled flat against an anvil by a heavy hammer. She is getting too old for solo expeditions, she knows this. But Hayder is stubborn, and motivated.

Because at the end of all this, there lies a prize. The Minister has given her a commission.

Once she has fulfilled it, she will be free.

As she recovers her breath, something in the ice by her cheek catches her attention, a discoloration in the intense blue that she has not noticed until now. She squints through her goggles, trying to see what it is. It is something stuck in the ice, something huge, and brownish in colour. It is frozen in place about five hand-widths away from her face, embedded into the glacier like an air-bubble in a pane of glass. The frozen mass is too distorted to be visible clearly, but she thinks she can make out legs, insectile, clawed. Lots of legs, in fact, and a blurry, distorted sort of head, or maybe it is a carapace, or maybe just a rock. Whatever it is, or was, alive or dead, it has been stuck in the ice for a long time and therefore doesn't concern her at this present moment. The only thing she is concerned with is getting out of this crevasse and on with her commission. She has many miles of glacier left to cross, and as intriguing as the frozen object is, it is a distraction she cannot afford.

Hayder takes a deep breath, kicks out away from the wall. On the backwards swing, she jams first one foot, and then the other, into the ice, and pushes up. She throws her right arm back, and sharply hammers her ice axe into the wall. She checks to see that the axe has held, steadies herself, and repeats the motion with her left arm, making sure to swing vertically, rather than down. The trick is not to try and dig a hole with the axe, but to drive it in, like it's a nail being driven through wood. Like most things, it's about rhythm. Once a person masters the rhythm, the rest is simple enough. It's also about keeping as close to the wall as possible, to distribute body weight evenly. *Easier said than done,* Hayder thinks, dragging herself higher. She wonders what the Minister would think of her if he could see her now, red-faced and raw, clinging to a slope like a tick on a goat, short hair drenched in sweat beneath her hat, face already bruised from slamming into the ice. He would most likely find it highly amusing, because he seems to find most things about Hayder amusing, indulging her as one would indulge a favorite pet.

Hayder can put up with his indulgence if it keeps her alive.

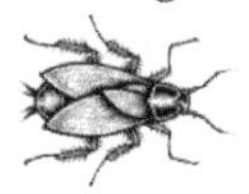

The Minister summoned Hayder in the early grey hours of one morning three weeks ago, to his private quarters, which Hayder was not too comfortable with. She went anyway, because the Minister was difficult to say 'no' to. She hoped he would not try to seduce her again. The last time he had, both of them had come out of the encounter feeling sickened. She had allowed him to paw her a little, but made it clear that she was not in any way enjoying the encounter. He had continued to paw at her despite this, his small, sweaty hands seeking a confirmation that didn't exist, before eventually giving up, acknowledging that her mind was somewhere else entirely. Afterwards, Hayder had told him, gently, not to be offended.

'I do not find pleasure in other people,' she said, carefully avoiding eye contact. 'Only in my work.'

And her dedication to her work was one of the reasons he kept her around, instead of having her executed. The Minister had a soft spot for Hayder, and probably thought that in time she would see sense, give into his advances.

Hayder was more realistic. She knew what refusal could do to a man, and she knew the Minister's soft spot could freeze over at any time.

She thought about this as she entered his quarters, situated on the top floor of the Keep. It was with some relief that she found the Minister pacing, fully clothed, back and forth, back and forth, up and down, wringing his hands with impatience, a preoccupied frown upon his lightly powdered face.

'Where were you?' He snapped, when she cleared her throat to make her presence known.

'Sleeping,' she replied, calmly. One had to be calm at all times with the Minister. His temper was legendary, and Hayder was very well acquainted with it. His tantrums could last for days, with devastating consequences. Once, a key report from the Keep's Chief Climatologist had been delayed by an hour due to a malfunction in one of the four massive solar pillars that cornered and powered the City. The Minister had executed the Climatologist by locking him in an air-tight glass cabinet he'd had purpose built for such an occasion. He forced the entire staff of the Ministry to watch as the climatologist suffocated, publicly. Then, he hunted down the dead man's family, stripped them naked, and strung them up around the four pillars by their ankles. Hayder would never forget the sight of the climatologist's eight year old son, his pale, skinny body twitching and screaming as he hung upside down a thousand feet in the air and tried to fight off a starving carrion-bird as it tore strips of flesh off of him. The bodies hung above the city until the bones were picked clean, and it was at that point that Hayder began to consider, seriously consider, the fragility of her situation.

The Minister grunted, waving away her missing apology. Despite her careful neutrality, not many people spoke to the Minister the way that Hayder did. Most people bowed and scraped, but Hayder had never been one for subjugating herself. While she was in the Keep, she remained courteous and professional, without giving much of herself away. The Minister seemed to respect her for that. It helped that Hayder had made him a lot of money over the years, bringing him the spoils of countless expeditions and excavations without demanding too large a cut for herself. The Minister respected money more than anything on this earth. It was the only thing he thought about, from the moment he awoke to the moment he laid his head upon his fine silk pillow. Money. Riches. Wealth. Resources.

All of which were fast running out. Not just in the City.

Everywhere.

Which, Hayder knew, was why she was here.

She was about to be given a new commission.

And not a moment too soon, Hayder thought. Things in the City were deteriorating rapidly. There were riots. Disease had taken hold of the lower levels. Famine threatened. Political unrest and misinformation was rife. From the Minister's window, she could see thick plumes of smoke coiling into the sky. The smoke came from funeral pyres. Every morning, at first light, the City burned its dead. Mass cremations were becoming problematic, however, acting as a focal point for an already strained population's ire. She could hear the distant cries of assembled protestors jostling around the pyres, beating their drums and chanting angrily as their loved ones burned to ash.

'Rise! Rise! Rise!' They screamed. Hayder knew it was only a matter of time before they did, surging up through the layers of the City like a tide, flooding the streets and eventually swallowing the Keep whole.

In short, Hayder wanted to get out, before the City imploded.

'The Pyres will soon become unfeasible,' the Minister said, following Hayder's eyes. 'I do not know what we shall do with our dead then. Our burial grounds are all full.'

Hayder kept quiet. She knew where a good portion of the dead would go: into the Keep's kitchen, or at least, those bodies that tested as disease-free would. This meant the remains of the elderly, the young, and the malnourished would be recycled, for want of a better word. The meat stripped from the bones and dried, the bones ground to make compost for the Keep's arboretum, one half of which was given over now to crop production- but only to feed those who lived inside the Keep. Not for the plenty, the starving masses down in the City. How could the Ministry govern if they were as hungry as their citizens? The Keep's integrity must be protected at all costs, and if that meant cannibalizing the wider population for the survival of an exalted few, then so be it.

It was the main reason Hayder had been eating only freeze-dried synthetic protein packs for the past six weeks. It played hell with her digestion, but kept her conscience clean.

Yes, a commission was just the thing. And, once she was out from beneath the delicate, groping hands of the Minister, she had no intention of ever coming back. Soon enough, he would have more important things to think about anyway, such as the collapse of an empire.

Hayder waited, as was her way.

The Minister stopped pacing, and turned to her. His eyes were enormous and haunted in the low morning light. They were the eyes of a zealot. Hayder remembered a different time, when the Minister had thought of things aside from his own fiscal legacy. When the Minister had valued culture, and history, learning and art, and not just his own skin.

'I found it,' the Minister said, interrupting her train of thought.

'You found what, Minister?' She asked, cautiously. But Hayder knew very well what. She just wanted him to say it out loud.

'The Vellum,' he replied, obligingly, and a slow, boyish smile spread across his features.

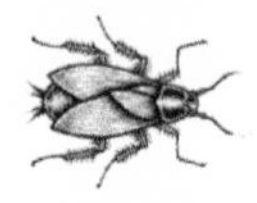

Hayder reaches the top of the ice wall, drags herself over the lip of it, and rolls onto her back in relief, arms and legs now screaming with exertion. Once she gets her breath back, she sits up, taking off her crampons so that she can stretch out her sore feet. She unties the rope from around her waist and groin, and looks around, working out some kinks in her neck. Everything is blue and white and brown upon the glacier, and Hayder grudgingly admits that ice is a good deal more interesting than she's given thought to, before. The shapes and colours are extraordinary, and she has to remind herself that, no matter how static the huge stretch of frozen mountain water seems to be, it is in fact in a constant state of movement. Like molten lava pouring down the sides of a volcano, glaciers creep forward constantly. She knows this, but it is hard to comprehend when sitting upon something that feels so *solid.*

Because this glacier moves quite fast, as glaciers go, it is dirty, much of its surface covered in rock dust and sand that has worn away from the mountains it grinds past. It moves at different speeds in different places, creating ridges and fells, folds and tunnels, caves, crevasses and cliffs. Despite the gravelly top dermis, it is spectacularly beautiful, like an ancient painting Hayder once saw of a melting clock hanging loosely over a naked tree branch: weird, fluid, and improbable. She scans this display with tired, watery eyes, and then freezes. She sees movement to her left, or at least, she thinks she does. It is hard to tell with the way the sun is angled. Hayder frowns. If a clever person was to follow her across this glacier, it would make sense to walk with the sun behind them, so that they could not easily be seen. Hayder's skin prickles. Who would be following her across the ice? Perhaps it is not a person. Perhaps it is the ice-bear she thought she heard before, tracking her through the night.

Hayder discards this idea quickly. Her instincts tell her otherwise.

She removes her goggles, peering through lowered lashes to try and get a clearer look, but the glare is too great. She puts them back on again. Waits, still as a statue.

There! Definitely movement. The sun obligingly vanishes behind a fleeting cloud. Hayder makes out two shapes, dark against the ice. One tall, one small.

Not a bear. Two people. Trekking across the glacier, following the same path she had before falling into the crevasse.

She is being followed. She chews her lip. *Has the Minister sent assassins for me?* She muses. *Has he learned of my plan?*

Hayder is not scared of any would-be death merchants. She has survived four assassination attempts prior to this one. Rivalry and jealousy are rife throughout the Keep, and Hayder's position as one of the Minister's pet academics makes her a target for other people's ambitions.

Hayder is strong and fast, however, and has reasons to live.

She does not think these shadows are assassins. Assassins do not tend to travel in pairs, and they also travel light. The smaller figure seems heavily burdened. Neither of them are particularly nimble upon the ice, nor are they particularly quiet. Hayder can hear clunking and scraping noises as they walk. Assassins do not generally announce themselves quite so noisily.

So who is it? Innocent travellers? Someone from the Keep?

Either way, Hayder does not want to meet them unprepared. She has her ice-axes, but those are only useful for close combat. She much prefers something of a long-range nature.

She crouches, and peers back down over the lip of the crevasse, looking for her pack, which she has left at the bottom. It was too heavy to climb with, so she secured it with a separate rope, meaning to drag it up the slope after her once she'd reached the top.

Hayder clenches her hands, which are sore and bloody from the axes. She starts to haul on the pack rope, pulling the heavy bundle carefully up the wall she has just climbed. Her rifle is in the pack, the barrel of it peeking out of the top flap. It is an antique, like most of the things she owns, but in perfect working order. She learned how to make her own bullets years ago, manufacturing them in her apartment in the Keep as a way of trying to wind down of an evening. She has bags full of cartridges in her pack, and is glad now that she has.

Hayder looks over her shoulder. The couple are much closer now. The weird icy sculptures on the surface of the glacier have warped her distance perspective, making things appear further away than they really are. She curses under her breath, figuring she has maybe five minutes before the couple are close enough to be a threat.

She redoubles her efforts, yanking hard on the pack. Too late, she remembers that she has taken off her crampons. Her feet slip on the ice. Hayder cries out, falling backwards, landing hard on her back and sliding dangerously close to the edge of the crevasse.

Not again! She thinks, frantically, and let's go of the pack rope, not wanting to be pulled back into the deep blue fissure. The pack drops heavily, landing with a thud. Hayder feels her body slip closer to the edge. She tries to sit up, but the sun has melted the ice further in the time that she has been sitting on the lip of the crevasse, and everything is now glossy and wet under her feet and hands, which scrabble for purchase, failing to find any. In slow-motion, Hayder feels herself slide inexorably over the edge of the large crack in the glacier, gliding over the ice like a wet fish slipping out of a fisherman's hands. She yells in frustration, twists her body, and grabs the only thing she can in the split second she is given before tumbling back into the crevasse. One of the iron hoops, hammered into the side. Her right hand hooks over it, the sleeve of her jacket catching fast over the hoop's edge, and she is brought up sharp, one arm stretched out above her head, the other trying to find a hold in the ice wall she is now so reluctantly familiar with.

And this is how Morgan Halligan finds her.

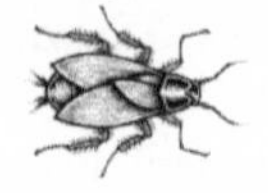

Two faces peer down at Hayder as she hangs uselessly by one hand from the small metal hoop. She is stuck. If she lets go, and slides back down into the crevasse, she will not be able to climb out without her crampons and axes. She is, however, dangling in such an odd way that she cannot lever herself up, even though the top of the crevasse is reasonably close. The situation is not sustainable. Her right hand is quickly growing numb, and her grip is starting to fail. The fabric of her sleeve is similarly unable to take her weight, and very shortly it will rip.

The faces above see this, make surprised noises. They belong to a man and woman. Hayder realises she knows the man.

'Morgan? What the fuck are you doing here?' She pants, angrily.

The man blinks, and an insufferable smile spreads across his downturned face.

'Saving your life, it would seem.'

His hand reaches down, grasps the back of Hayder's jacket, between her shoulders. Another hand clasps around her snagged wrist. Two more hands seize her free arm, and Hayder is pulled to safety. She collapses in an exhausted pile at the feet of the couple. Before saying anything else, she reaches for her crampons, and straps them back on her feet. She has learned her lesson twice over now: never take off your crampons, not while you're on the ice.

Then she says: 'I would have fallen barely twenty feet, don't flatter yourself.' Her arm aches, having been almost wrenched out of its socket by her fall, and she winces, shrugging and rotating her shoulder in an effort to bring some circulation back. It is a diversionary tactic while she tries to think about what to do next.

Morgan dusts ice crystals off ungloved hands, which look blue from the bitterly cold wind that blows across the surface of the glacier. *Why isn't the idiot wearing gloves?* She thinks. That is just like Morgan: to assume that the rules of play are meant for others, and not for him.

'You're welcome,' he says, dryly.

Hayder considers her situation. It is clear that Morgan has been sent by the Minister to spy on her. Morgan is the City's Chief Geologist, and has crossed paths with Hayder more than a few times throughout her career. They trade barbs frequently in academic council meetings. She considers him a flamboyant arse and a sycophant, but he is also a necessary evil. He, like herself, has the ear of the Minister. It is therefore better to have him on her side than not, in the spirit of keeping friends close, and enemies closer.

Hayder doesn't have friends, anyway.

She swears inwardly. This is not something she has planned for, but she realises that she should have, because the Minister likes nothing better than to pit his employees against each other. Morgan is here because the Minister doubts her loyalty. This is not a good thing. The Geologist has been tasked with keeping an eye on Hayder in case she disappears with the Vellum.

I knew it was too easy, she thinks. She curses her naivety in thinking the Minister would allow her to carry out this expedition alone. He had merely indulged her request to do, so in order to persuade her to accept the commission. Not that refusing was ever an option, anyway. Refusal means death. Those terms are hard to argue with.

Hayder takes a good, long look at Morgan's companion while she collects herself. She is an aged, short, stooped woman with a massive pack strapped to her back, although the obvious weight of it does not seem to bother her. Morgan himself carries only a small day-pack. The old woman has bare feet, which on closer inspection are covered with thick, scaly skin, so thick it looks as if she has hooves at the ends of her weathered legs. She does not appear to feel the cold through those rigid soles, and Hayder assumes she is local, a native to the region. One of the elusive Niton tribe, maybe. Or perhaps Clintu. Either way, she is definitely not of the City.

'Who is this?' Hayder asks, rudely. 'A slave? Slavery went out of fashion years ago, Morgan.'

Morgan smiles and shakes his head, unperturbed by Hayder's sarcasm.

'She is not a slave. She has a name. She is called Pamuk, and she is an Ice Sherpa. I hired her to be my guide. She knows this ice field like no-one else. Her family have been crossing it for many generations, guiding the occasional travellers safely along. It is a fine livelihood. Who am I to deny her an opportunity to earn a living?'

'Oh good, a *salaried* slave,' Hayder says, rolling her eyes. Her hostility comes from one place: anger at herself for being caught out. Hayder hates feeling as if she is standing on the back foot.

Pamuk says nothing, patiently waiting for the foreigners to begin moving again.

'Aren't we all?' Morgan says, smiling.

'You might be,' Hayder replies, squinting. 'I prefer my job title: Archaeologist.'

'*Senior* Archaeologist.' Morgan makes a dig at Hayder's age. He is younger than her by only five years, but for some reason, in their society, a man is allowed to grow older with considerably less challenge than a woman is. 'Your reputation precedes you, Hayder.'

'Yours doesn't,' Hayder says. 'And I'm not the one asking an old lady to carry my shit around for me.' As if to illustrate this point, she turns to pull her own pack up the slope once more. Morgan and Pamuk wait close by, their intentions clear. They are joining her solo expedition, whether she likes it or not. And, short of murdering the pair, she cannot see a way of saying 'no', especially not if Morgan has been personally tasked by the Minister. Giving up on her would be tantamount to signing his own death warrant, she knows that. This makes her feel as if she is stuck between a rock and a hard place, and Hayder does not like this one little bit.

For now, I will let them follow me, she thinks, watching as the reassuring shape of her rifle's barrel gets closer and closer, along with the pack.

For now.

'I found the Vellum,' the Minister repeated, and Hayder had to forcibly swallow her own excitement.

'Where?' She breathed, eventually, feeling as if fate were suddenly in the room with them.

'I've had a team of archivists working in the Library, renovating the eastern alcoves. A water pipe behind a wall burst several weeks ago. We were at risk of losing over a thousand manuscripts, so I had them remove every single one, dust them off, and re-file once we'd fixed the leak. An intern found it in a box stuffed with absorbent crystals. It's been here in the Keep, all along, Hayder. Imagine that, eh? The irony of it.'

Hayder didn't know or care much about irony, only authenticity. The Minister was educated, but hardly as versed in antiquities as she was.

'How do you know it's really the Vellum?'

'Because of the seal on the box,' the Minister replied, pulling a folded square of paper from a deep pocket in his robes. He handed it to her without further explanation, and Hayder saw a rubbing. Someone had scribbled charcoal across the paper whilst it was pressed to a hard object underneath. It displayed a circle, within which two items were crossed:

an old-fashioned telescope, and an ice-axe, the sort used for climbing and mountaineering. Around it were the words, in Old Latin, *Imperium Sine Fine,* which translated to 'Empire without an end', the official motto of the early days of the Keep, several hundred years past.

It was the sigil of an explorer.

Hayder felt a deep thrill race down her spine.

Only one expedition party in the history of the Ministry's exploration records had ever been known to have made it beyond the far reaches of the massive ice-field in the North, some time in the middle of the Oil Age, a little over two hundred years ago. The leader of that expedition was a man called Horatius Hecht, and he came back from his excursion alone, all twenty-five other members of his party having perished, or so the story went. Hecht may have lost his crew, but he did bring back a map, a map that quickly became an object of myth and gossip, and after a time, was referred to as 'The Vellum'. This is not because the map was drawn upon deerskin, or parchment. The Vellum was indeed a map, but the map was coded onto a long-obsolete device a little like an electronic tablet, only smaller, sturdier. 'Vellum' was the rather whimsical name of the operating system the tablet ran on. It was solar-powered, and Hayder had once read somewhere that a rudimentary kind of GPS was built into the device, meaning a course could be plotted that would take the owner of the Vellum across the ice-fields, beyond the mountain ridges that were so hard to scale, and to a distinct location somewhere in the lands that lay beyond.

Legend had it, that location was a seam, a huge, untapped seam of a precious substance known only as Ore.

Before airplanes and helicopters had become an extinct form of travel, this hadn't really mattered to anyone. The Vellum had held little importance to a regime convinced its oil reserves would last.

But now that those reserves had been exhausted, well.

It was a very precious object, indeed.

'Ore is a myth, Minister,' Hayder said, trying not to get carried away. 'There has never been, in the entire history of the Ministry, anything to prove or suggest that Ore deposits are real. Even if they are, we have no certainty that we can exploit it or use it to our advantage, and certainly no indication of whether or not we could convert Ore into any meaningful energy source, even if we could mine it somehow.'

'Pshaw.' The Minister waved her concerns away. 'My Geologist tells me otherwise, Hayder. I know you two rarely see eye-to-eye, but I trust his judgment in matters of this nature. When it comes to digging up the past, there is no-one on this earth who is your equal, Hayder. But I am running out of choices. Our solar pillars are degrading at an alarming rate, down to fifty-five percent of efficiency, and decreasing every day. We can no longer manufacture new panels with any degree of consistency. It is too expensive to fabricate them from silicone, you know this. We have extinguished our cadmium and copper processing capabilities. The last miner's strike lasted twelve months, unless you've forgotten, and we are struggling to return the mines to capacity now that half the workforce has been wiped out by the sickness. This thing...' The Minister tapped the sigil on the piece of paper, and Hayder noticed sweat beading his upper lip. 'This thing could be our salvation,' he said, leaning in towards her, dwarfing her with his fanaticism.

'And you are going to deliver it,' he continued, staring at her mouth.

No pressure, then, she thought, swallowing hard.

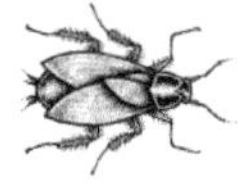

It is obvious, after only a few minutes of walking, that Morgan has not been upon ice before. He has no gloves, and is wearing shorts. His long, thin legs are covered in sore slashes from his crampons. Hayder is surprised that his Sherpa has not told him how to clothe himself properly, or how to walk in crampons: toes out, knees bent, one foot pointing up-slope where possible for extra grip. Morgan hobbles along laboriously, every now and then hissing in pain as he catches the insides of his own legs with his metal spikes. Hayder watches this with a clenched jaw. She flicks her gaze across to Pamuk, who keeps her head down. She is fairly certain she can detect a faint hint of enjoyment around the wizened corners of Pamuk's mouth, and this makes Hayder warm to the old woman, if only a little.

Hayder insists that the pair walk ahead of her. She tries to think of how to rid herself of them. Soon, she will have to make camp. She considers leaving in the night while the pair sleep, but knows she will never be able to pack her tent away quietly enough. This means she will have to try and lose them in the day. She will need a diversion, and a way of putting enough distance between them that she cannot be followed easily. She cannot, for the life of her, think of how to do this. If it was Morgan on his own, she would feel confident.

Pamuk is a different kettle of fish altogether.

Hayder shelves the problem for a while. Sometimes, when answers elude her, she lets them sit for a time. Solutions often present themselves in the most unexpected of ways, if she just leaves things alone. Whatever the answer is, she knows what she knows: that she cannot travel as part of a team.

Hayder hasn't always been like this. Hayder had a partner once, a colleague who doubled as a bedfellow, and Hayder had loved him, very much. They had taken many commissions together on behalf of the Minister, found many treasures. They had taken responsibility for each other. Sometimes, while resting during a gruelling excavation, they would sit crossed legged on the floor, back to back, so that they could lean upon each other, balanced perfectly like keystones in a bridge. They would smoke a cheroot, passing it back and forth until only a tiny, soggy nub remained, and then silently get back to work. There hadn't been much in the way of verbal communication between them, and for Hayder, who hated idle conversation, that was just fine.

Hayder's partner died when a large pillar collapsed during an excavation of the lower layer of a Trujillian temple, five years back. Hayder has recurring nightmares about that moment, and probably always will. A grinding, a shifting of balance. A blur of yellowstone. Her partner, frozen in shock as his fate crashed down towards him. Hayder remembers how a ray of sunlight caught in his hair before her view of him was obliterated. She tries hard, every day, not to think of him beneath the stone, flattened and broken. She tries, and fails. She remembers his right hand, protruding from under the massive column. Blood ran out in rivulets beneath it. She fell to her knees, took the hand gently in hers. She held it until it grew cold, and continued to hold it for two more days and nights, sitting, trance-like, cross-legged, only there was no back to lean against hers, this time. No keystone to support her.

It was the worst pain she has ever endured in her life. More pain than she could have dreamed possible.

She has no intention of ever hurting that much again.

Hayder has been alone ever since. She cannot risk more pain, she cannot allow herself the luxury of responsibility for anyone else. Dependency ruins her chances for survival.

And Hayder must survive.

Because there had been a child, six months after the accident.

A child with hair that also caught the sun when it shone.

A child she had not been in a position to love when it was born, a child she had deposited with a long-distant family member when it was only a few weeks old.

A child she fully intends to send for, once she is rid of the Minister.

But first, she has to find a place to call home, far away from the City, and far away from the reach of the Ministry. And what better place than the unchartered territory beyond the ice field? The Minster couldn't follow her across the glacier, not easily. He most likely would, by now, have a full-scale civil war on his hands. Hayder has no interest in Ore seams. All she cares about is her freedom, and if she can get to the end of this ice field, she can secure it.

She has no intention of letting Morgan or Pamuk get in her way.

The three explorers make camp as the sun is setting. Old Red is in fine form, her peak a vivid, glowing torch against an indigo sky full of slowly emerging stars.

Hayder does not make conversation with Morgan or Pamuk as she sets up her one-man tent and a portable biomass burner. Hayder heats up some oats with a lump of ice she chisels from the glacier, and shovels the resulting gruel into her mouth. It is loaded with synthetic nutrients, everything she needs to keep her body running. Hayder misses real food, though. She misses fruit, herbs, cheese. Fuck, how she misses cheese. She eats swiftly, watching Pamuk as she sets up a tent for Morgan. The tall man stands to one side and pretends to occupy himself with a document while the old woman does this. Then Pamuk prepares a meal, boiling up shreds of dried meat with some herbs and a desiccated root of some sort. The smell is incredible. Hayder's stomach clenches in longing. She displays no outward sign of this envy, but she does raise an eyebrow when Pamuk straightens up suddenly, head turned back the way they have come.

She hears it too, Hayder thinks, because the noise is back. It always comes back when dusk falls on the glacier. The ice bear is getting closer, its peculiar shuffles and clicks only just audible. Hayder again trades glances with Pamuk. An understanding passes between them. *Be careful.*

Something is out there.

Pamuk digs around in the giant bundle she has been carrying, and brings out a tightly coiled spool of razor-thin wire, a bundle of stakes, and a mallet. Wordlessly, she sets up a perimeter around the camp, twisting the two ends of the wire together around a battered looking solar pack. Hayder realises the wire is electrocuted. Pamuk is taking no chances. Hayder approves.

Hayder uses more ice to clean out her pan, and packs everything carefully away, retreating into her tent for the night, pulling her pack and rifle in after her to block the entrance. Morgan watches her do this with a small smile on his lips. Hayder zips her door up, obscuring his smug face, and tries not to think about how flimsy the walls of the tent are.

Once inside, she pulls a box from her pack. She opens the lid, sees a small, rectangular object nestled within on a bed of micro-crystals.

The Vellum.

She presses a finger to the soft rubber power switch embedded into the top of the device, and waits for a second or two. The screen pops into blue, glowing life, and a single word, a word in Old English, materialises on the screen.

Hello, it says.

'Hello,' Hayder whispers back.

It took Hayder four days to reboot the Vellum. Hayder had spent her life studying ancient, obsolete languages and technology. She built her reputation as a young academic not on her prowess as an archaeologist, but her expertise as a forensic antiquities' programmer, someone who managed to get computers that were centuries old to boot despite the limited physical life-times of most electronic hardware. She pieced together degraded computer parts like an anthropologist pieces together the human skeleton. What she couldn't coax into life, she cobbled, using junk from the vaults of the Keep and black-market components stockpiled over the years. Her feats of perseverance caught the attention of the Minister, and this rapidly cemented her status as a favourite pet. Because the Minister had fantasised about discovering and exploiting the Vellum since he had first heard about it as a boy. Hayder's impressive skill set represented his best chance at being able to do so if it was ever found. Sometimes, the Minister felt as if a divine intention had been bestowed upon Hayder, as if she had been created for the sole purpose of helping him fulfil his lifelong dream: restoring the Empire to its glory days.

He might not think that if he knew how virulent her hatred of him was.

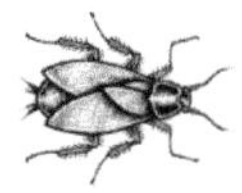

Hayder wakes. She instantly senses that something is wrong. There is a sound coming in through the walls of her tent. It is the sound she has heard on previous nights, only much, much louder.

Ice bear.

Slowly, carefully, Hayder unwraps herself from her sleeping bag, slides her feet into her crampons. She picks up her rifle, loads it. She takes the Vellum out of its case, and slides it down into a pocket between her breasts, one that also carries the worn image of her partner, and their baby. Then, she slowly unzips the tent door, and pokes her head outside.

The glacier is lit by a million stars, stars which have a chance to shine up here in the north, for the skies are clear, and clean, unlike the murky sky that rests oppressively over the City, thick with smog and pyre smoke.

Hayder clambers out of her tent, and stands up. She knows where Morgan is, because she can hear him snoring like a pig, but she cannot see Pamuk anywhere. She slowly pivots, taking in as much of her surroundings as she can, trying to locate the strange, ticking, scrabbling, snuffling noise that has woken her up. She can see the wire perimeter still glinting in the starlight, so nothing has breached the barrier, not yet.

Hayder calls out, softly.

'Pamuk!'

A wizened hand clamps over her mouth from behind. Hayder whirls, and sees Pamuk in the glow of the stars. In her free hand, she holds a long, wickedly sharp machete, unsheathed, the blade serrated near the tip.

Pamuk raises it above Hayder's head.

Too close! Hayder thinks, frantically. *She's too close for me to use my rifle!*

The sound of a thin electric wire snapping rings out into the night air, followed by the strange ticking, clacking, slippery noises, so loud now they are almost deafening.

Pamuk pushes Hayder violently to one side, swinging down with the machete as something vast and dark slides into the exact spot where Hayder was standing only moments before. Hayder crashes into Morgan's tent, collapsing it on him, and rolls off, barely aware of the man now roaring under the torn nylon.

In front of her, lit up by the bold light of the stars, a scene is playing out like nothing she has seen before in her life.

It is not an ice bear.

The thing is massive, the width and height of a man, only twenty times as long. It is a centipede. Hayder sees twin rows of clawed legs undulating as the creature glides across the ice towards Pamuk, and remembers, with a flash, a brown, blurry, many-legged object embedded in the ice wall she climbed. Not dead, but sleeping. *They live in ice burrows, waiting for nightfall.* How many of them are down there now, stirring beneath her feet? How many on this glacier?

And what do they eat?

This one seems to want to eat the Sherpa. Pamuk darts away from it as it bears down, raising her machete again and chopping at the beast's head with the deft violence of a seasoned hunter. Her weapon glances off of the thing's heavy armour. Pamuk springs out of the way again, and just in time: rearing up, the centipede slams itself downwards, chittering and screeching as a vicious pair of mandibles snap at her scaly heels.

Coming to her senses, Hayder realises that her best bet is to get far enough away from the scene that she can use her rifle. She scrambles away from the camp, noticing as she does so that Morgan has wrestled free of his collapsed tent, and is standing, blinking, near-naked despite the cold, watching with wide eyes as Pamuk and the centipede dance.

'Morgan, run!' Hayder cries, following her own advice as best she can in spiked feet.

Morgan does not run. Morgan screams instead, a high-pitched, feminine scream that shreds the night air, and the centipede turns, lightning quick. It glides like silk across the glacier on its thousands of legs, mandibles clicking and clacking, and before Morgan can act, the vast invertebrate is upon him. The snapping, vicious mandibles clamp expertly around Morgan's neck, and with a quick, decisive scissoring motion, Morgan's head is severed from his body with such remarkable efficiency that Hayder stops running for a moment, and stands, stock-still in awe, as the centipede begins to slowly and yet rather delicately stuff the now drooling head of the City's Chief Geologist into its mouth with two of its forelegs.

Fuck, Hayder thinks, and then: *Now's your chance!*

Hayder's trembling hands grip the rifle, and she tries to slow her breathing, so she can get a good aim. She thinks of how Pamuk's machete bounced off the plate armour of the centipede, and refocuses her attention on the thing's eyes, which are large, black, and stuck like blobs of tar to the sides of its ugly head.

She thinks of a baby, who is now a child, growing up somewhere without her.

She thinks of a City, on fire, a place she never wants to return to.

She thinks of a man, leaning warm and solid against her back.

She pulls the trigger.

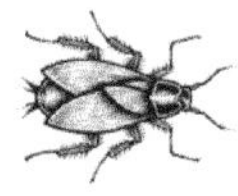

Hayder can now add centipede-slayer to her impressive resume.

It took more than one shot. She missed on the first try, hit a bullseye- or a bug's eye, she supposes- on the second. The centipede is dead, its body twitching on the ice before her. Pamuk is busy hacking its legs off, to keep as mementos, or food, or for some other purpose.

Morgan is also dead, his blood soaking into the glacier, but Hayder has other, more serious things to worry about, at this moment.

Because the Vellum is smashed, beyond repair. It must have flown out of her breast-pocket when she fell into Morgan's tent. The artifact has been trodden underfoot, pierced by the thick spikes of Hayder's crampons. She has trampled upon the empire's most valuable asset, and didn't even notice.

Hayder sinks to her knees.

What do I do now? She thinks. *I cannot go back. I'll be executed if I return empty-handed, without Morgan, and especially without the Vellum.*

And yet, If I go forward, I will get lost upon this hellscape, she reasons, working through her options. *I've been following the Vellum's GPS signal this whole time, to stay on course. Now, it's gone. I could die of exposure out here. There could be more centipedes. I could run out of food.*

Pamuk stops carving up the centipede, and comes to stand next to Hayder, who, for the first time since her partner died, is crying, letting hot tears slide down her cheeks, unchecked.

Pamuk puts out a finger coated with sticky yellow centipede blood, and catches a tear as it drops off of Hayder's chin.

Then, she spots the smashed artifact in her hands.

She stills, and says something in a language Hayder doesn't understand.

'What?' Hayder replies, dully.

Pumuk pulls her clothes to one side. As she does so, the first signs of dawn creep into the sky. Soon, the peaks of Old White and Old Red will be ablaze.

Hayder gasps. The Sherpa has Hecht's sigil tattooed on her right breast.

Hayder holds out a hand, pleading.

'Show me,' she says. 'Please. I don't want to go back there. I can't. I have a child.' *Can she even understand New English?* Hayder thinks, frantically.

Pamuk smiles, and bows her head.

'I will show you,' she says.

THE WOOD ON THE HILL

Clive Barker

Once upon a time in a land far from here, there grew a wood. This wood was dark and very old, for it could remember the times before there were any people on earth, when the sky was always filled with fire, and there lived great birds, more terrible than I have words to tell. It could remember the years when the dragons lived in the valley, until the Great Winter came and they were all driven away by the snow. It was only a small wood then, and a little frightened by the world...

But, by the time I write my story, the wood had grown up, and the people had come to the valley and built cottages where once the dragons had roared and stamped. It was content, watching the slow passing of the years. The warm summers filled with laughter, the ripe autumns, the cold winters, the springs when the snow melted and hope came again into the world. It watched the children who played in its branches grow to be strong men and graceful women, and, in their turn, have children of their own. It watched the brook grow to a stream, and thus to a rushing river. The years passed peacefully, and each day was a joy greater than the last, for the world was still waking.

Now not all that far from the wood stood a large white house with marble pillars, surrounded by tall yew trees and great gardens, all neatly set out with paths of pink gravel and fountains with cupids in the middle. This house belonged to a Duchess who owned all the land around her house, for she was very rich. It said, on a piece of paper which she always kept locked safely away in a box somewhere, that every leaf, every blade of grass, every flower, bird, animal and tree belonged to her. This pleased the Duchess greatly, because I am afraid she was not a very nice person. In fact, at times her manners were absolutely frightful, and she had a very quick temper. When she flew into a rage, which she did quite often, she would scream at the servants (she had thirty-one) until the windows rattled and the china tinkled. And sometimes, if she was particularly vexed, she would kick the furniture or the footman (whichever was nearby at the time). As if that were not bad enough, she was also exceedingly vain. Sometimes she would spend hours sitting in front of the mirror and looking at herself. I must admit that she was indeed very beautiful, but that did not make her vanity any the less dreadful.

Having told you how horrible the Duchess was at times, you might think that she had no friends. But you would be quite wrong. In fact she had lots of friends, all members of the aristocracy (which means they had lots of money and weren't quite sure what to do with it). The Duchess' friends, however, were the most hateful people you could imagine. They were either very fat because they ate too much, or very thin because they would not eat at all, in case they marred their beauty. Beauty! I may truly say that the Duchess' friends were quite the most ugly people in all the world.

Four times a year, at Christmas, on her birthday in April, on Midsummer Night and at Hallowe'en, the Duchess would throw a party, and invite all her friends. Her parties were always wildly successful and were great social occasions. Why they were so successful I cannot possibly imagine, for if you or I were to have gone to one I am sure we would have hated it. All the guests ever did was stand around, talking about the War and the trouble they were having with their servants, and how awful everybody else looked and how boring everybody else's conversation was. I fancy the Duchess knew in her heart how hateful all the guests were, but still she threw her parties, because it was all she had to do.

Now one day, in late September, when the leaves were just beginning to fall in the wood, the Duchess was out riding in the hills. It was a fine, clear afternoon, and she was thinking about what colour she ought to have her new pet dove dyed. You see, she hated it being so white, because she thought it might make her look less beautiful.

The Duchess was so deep in thought, that she rode further from the house than she had ever ridden before, and the servants were just about to pluck up enough courage to tell her, when, quite suddenly, they found themselves at the foot of the hill whereon grew the wood that I told you about. The Duchess had never seen the wood before, and, calling to her servants to help her dismount, she demanded that she be taken to it. At this the servants muttered to each other under their breath, but they feared the Duchess too much to disobey. So Michael, the oldest one, bowing low, said:

"As Your Grace commands," and led the way up the hill.

The other servants followed some way behind, but finding the Duchess too concerned with the wood to notice their tarrying, they halted half-way up and stood, watching in silence.

The evening was drawing on now, and the wood stood quiet and beautiful, a thousand shades of gold and red. When Michael and the Duchess reached the top of the hill, they found that the wind was quite strong, murmuring through the trees and blowing dead leaves about. The Duchess stood for a moment on the edge of the wood, thinking. Then suddenly, she turned to Michael:

"This wood!" she cried, shattering the stillness, "I shall hold my next party here. It will be a Hallowe'en Party, such as none have ever seen before, and I shall invite everybody."

Michael was silent.

"What is it — you miserable old owl?" the Duchess cried. "Is it not a brilliant idea? Everybody else throws their parties in their Grand Halls — oh but not I! No indeed! I shall throw my party here — in the wood on the hill. It will be the greatest celebration the crowd has ever seen."

"But Your Grace –" stammered poor old Michael, suddenly frightened, not by the Duchess, but by something much more terrible, "– you can't!"

"Can't?" cried the Duchess.

"Can't??" screamed the Duchess.

"Can't"???" exploded the Duchess.

"Why can't I?"

"Well…" the old man halted, "well… because…"

"What?"

"It's haunted, ma'am."

"Haunted?" the Duchess said quietly, her anger suddenly gone. "Haunted?" repeated the Duchess slowly, and looked at the wood through her spectacles, as if she were looking for the ghosts.

"Really?" she said after a moment. "Haunted, eh? How quaint!"

(Which was a very silly thing to say, but then again, as I have explained, she was a very silly Duchess.)

"How quaint!" she said again, "Ha! I do… er… so love… er… these peasant superstitions."

Michael shook his head sadly. But the Duchess wasn't looking. She was far too busy talking to herself and making plans.

"It will be the social event of the decade," she said excitedly. "Everybody who is anybody will be there. And it's all so original. Nobody has ever had a ball in the middle of a wood before. I shall be the toast of society for absolutely ages. Oh, why am I so clever? It just isn't fair on the rest of the world!"

She turned to Michael.

"Find the best woodcutters in the country, do you understand?"

"Woodcutters, Your Grace?"

"Yes fool. I want a large clearing cut in the middle of the wood..."

"What?" cried Michael, his eyes wild with anger and fear, "You're planning to chop down part of the wood?"

"Of course," replied the Duchess, "I'm not going to have my guests dangling from the branches like apes!"

"But you can't! You mustn't. The wood isn't yours."

"Isn't mine?" the Duchess laughed. "Of course it's mine. I own all this."

"Yes," said Michael slowly, "You own it all as far as lawyers and pieces of parchment are concerned... But — "

"But what?"

"Oh, Your Grace, the wood isn't — yours. I mean, it is yours legally — but there are others..."

"Who?" snapped the Duchess.

"Just others," the old man replied, avoiding the Duchess' eyes, his hands shaking with fear.

"You're speaking nonsense, you old bat. You're mad."

"Very well then, Your Grace, I am mad. But still –"

"Still nothing. You will do as I say or I'll have you hanged for your silly ramblings."

Michael had no choice but to nod meekly. Well, he thought to himself, what more can I do? It is foolish to meddle with such things, but I can do nothing. What happens now is not my fault.

Then the sun slipped behind the horizon, and darkness fell. Suddenly, the beautiful trees became strangely menacing in the half-light, looming grey and huge above the Duchess and the bowed figure of Michael. The night was upon them, and they were far from home.

"Come –," said the Duchess hurriedly, for she was a little unnerved by this strange transformation. "Let us return."

As they walked down the hill Michael smiled a little to himself. Not a happy smile, you understand, but a resigned smile of one who knows what is about to happen, and who also knows that he may do nothing about it.

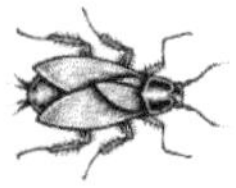

Even if the Duchess was vain, she was certainly no coward, and once she had an idea in her head she flatly refused to let it go. So, although she still had a few lingering doubts about the woods, she was nevertheless resolved to throw her party there. She had long since convinced herself that there was nothing to fear. Well, nothing a bonfire and an orchestra would not cure. Thus, the preparations began.

Invitations were sent to all the neighbouring lands, with:

The Duchess
requests the pleasure of your company
at a Grand Hallowe'en Ball
in the Wood on the Hill
on October 31st
R.S.V.P.

written on them in the finest copperplate.

Meanwhile, in the woods, the clearing was being made, the bonfire piled up, the tables set out, the entertainers rehearsed and a thousand and one other arrangements made. All kinds of people, each with his or her separate task, and each believing that their job was the most important, and that they were working the hardest.

Hallowe'en grew nearer. In the house the Duchess was busy ticking off names on her guest list and ordering wine and food. One morning, about a week before Hallowe'en, the old sorcerer who had been ordered to make the fireworks arrived with his creations, arms full of brightly-coloured squibs and rockets and ripraps and Catherine wheels and Roman candles and dragon-flames and snow-flowers and some that even he had not got a name for, because he didn't know what they would do. When he heard where the Duchess was planning to hold her party, however, he became most upset.

"The woods?" he exclaimed in alarm, dropping the fireworks everywhere, "But that is forbidden!"

"By whom?" the Duchess demanded angrily, "Who forbids it?"

"They do. Those who own it. It is most foolish to hold your party there. It will be a failure!"

At this the Duchess flew into a rage. How dare this tatty old magician suggest one of her parties might be a failure! The arrogance of the fellow!

"Old man!" she screamed, "I suggest you take that remark back. I have but to snap my fingers and you will die."

"Oh," said the sorcerer, undisturbed by the Duchess' tantrums.

"Cower in fear, idiot! I threaten you with a death so horrible that men will talk of it a hundred years hence! I repeat myself — take that remark back!"

"Shan't," said the sorcerer, and yawned.

"Why you — Guards! Guards! Seize him!"

"I think not," the sorcerer said calmly, and disappeared in a puff of smoke. By the time the guards arrived, therefore, the room was empty save for the Duchess, still quivering with anger, and a few dead leaves that the sorcerer had left on the carpet where he had worked. But long after he had gone, the Duchess could hear his soft laughing, and in the end she ordered the room to be locked up and never to be entered again.

Well after that, as you might have guessed, the Duchess began to doubt the cleverness of her plan, and regret her decision. But by that time it was far too late. All the guests had been invited. The wine and the food ordered. The masks and fireworks made. There was nothing she could do.

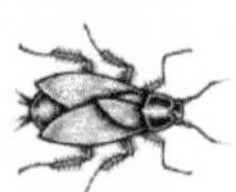

On the morning of October 31st, the Duchess woke — after a terrible nightmare in which she had been chased by something she could not see, through a forest in which the trees were as big as mountains, or else she was the size of a butterfly, one of the two. And in the dream she had met all her friends, the ones I told you about, only they had become monstrously misshapen and horrid. First she had met Lady Boswell-Humphries, who had apparently swapped bodies with a pig because that way, she said, she could eat more. Beside her, sitting on a toadstool, was the Admiral's wife, whose head was slowly turning into a gramophone, her nose becoming the huge black horn. Further along she came upon the Archbishop, dangling from a convolvulus, and trying, so he explained, to fly.

She saw the Marquis' wife too, who had become a spider during the night and was busy drinking the blood of the peasants that had become trapped in her dark web. But worst of all was the General, whom the Duchess discovered in the blackest part of that terrifying forest, trampling on beautiful white flowers and muttering, "tut-tut, terrible waste," to himself as he did so. His head was bowed so the Duchess could not see his face until he looked up at her. But when he did the Duchess collapsed to the cold ground in a dead faint, for she saw with horror that he no longer had a face, but had instead, a grinning skull with no eyes, white in the darkness of that forest.

At that moment, the Duchess had woken from her nightmare, to find that the sun was streaming through her window, and there were birds singing in the yew tree outside. The day could not have been nicer. Dismissing her nasty dream as the result of something that had disagreed with her, and making a mental note to sack the cook, she got dressed and went downstairs.

She was too excited for any breakfast, or lunch, or tea, and spent the morning making a few final adjustments to her hair and then, in the afternoon, having a long, warm bath and getting dressed. She had a beautiful gown, which had been made by a hundred seamstresses especially for the occasion. It was the colour of a silver birch, and was stitched with thread of gold. As evening approached, and the shadows lengthened, she boarded her golden coach and, with her servants riding close behind, was driven to the woods.

By the time she reached the hill the sun had almost set. The wood looked rather as it had that first day, a month ago, when she and Michael had climbed the windy hill. But now, she thought to herself, there was something different about it. It seemed, somehow, darker. She shivered for a moment, though the evening was not cold. Then, putting on her mask, which was a beautiful, intricate design of silver leaves, she made her way between the trees to the clearing, ready to receive her first guests.

Over five hundred guests had been invited to that party, and every single one of them came. Thus, by ten o'clock the clearing was filled with people, all talking or drinking or eating or dancing or laughing or trying to do all those things at the same time. The noise was dreadful. What with the fireworks, the guests and the orchestra playing, the party must have been heard miles away.

Outside the wood, in the white moonlight, the footmen and servants and coach-drivers sat and listened to the muted sounds of laughter and merry-making, and looked up occasionally from their card-games to catch a glimpse of the bonfire or the fireworks between the trees. The horses all seemed strangely uneasy. They shuffled and neighed and some whimpered in the way horses do. But the coach-drivers merely went on playing cards and envying their masters.

About 11:30 p.m. Mrs. Fortesque fainted — "Probably the heat," her escort said — but really because she had drunk too much. She had to be attended to by her friends and then taken home long before the party was due to finish. For long years afterwards Mrs. Fortesque would talk of that night and how divine providence had seen fit to save her alone...

The party continued. The laughter became more hysterical, the music louder and more insistent. Logs were heaped on the bonfire. It crackled and roared. Case after case of champagne was opened and emptied, tray after tray of food prepared and devoured. Beneath their Hallowe'en masks, fat faces dissolved into rolls of hysterics, disdainful faces sneered, military faces looked grim. Each played his or her part better than ever before. And above their heads, unknown to the guests, the trees were whispering to each other softly, whispering in a language as old as the world itself. Whispering of a vengeance planned.

Someone carved his initials in the trunk of an old oak.

"He will die," said the whisperers.

Another man threw a living branch on to the blazing bonfire and smiled as it burned.

"He too," said the whisperers.

And in the midst of her guests, the Duchess laughed beneath her mask of silver leaves, and forgot all that had been told her. And the whisperers hated her the most — for she had begun it all, caused these murders, these desecrations. For her there could be no death too terrible.

The Duchess had arranged that at the stroke of midnight all lights should be extinguished (except for the bonfire of course) and that everybody should take off their masks and reveal who they were (everybody knew really, but it was still fun). So, as midnight grew near, the Duchess told the orchestra to stop playing, which they did. As soon as they stopped, of course, the talking stopped too, and all the guests turned to look at her.

"My Lords, Ladies and Gentlemen," she began (a solitary cheer from the Admiral, who had had a little too much to drink). "It is almost midnight" (another cheer from the Admiral; this time halted abruptly by the Admiral's wife pushing a gooseberry tart into his mouth). "If we are silent," the Duchess continued, "we shall be able to hear the striking of the church in the valley. Then, on the twelfth stroke, let us all make merry until the dawn!"

The clearing was silent except for the bonfire's cracklings. No one moved. The Admiral had fallen asleep, gooseberry tart smeared round his mouth. Then, far, far away, the bell chimed.

One…

Two…

…The Duchess thought something moved in the trees…

Three…

Four…

…Dark forms shifting and gathering…

Five…

Six…

…The sorcerer was right…

Seven…

Eight…

…The woods were alive…

Nine…

Ten…

…And seeking vengeance..!

Eleven…

…Twelve!

On the twelfth stroke, the woods attacked!

From out of the shadows appeared creatures forgotten since the world was young. Black, hideous creatures with eyes of fire and wings of death. Screeching, flapping monstrosities defying description.

The Duchess screamed. A great wind sprang up. The torches were blown out. In the flickering light of the bonfire the guests fled, scattered by huge claws. The wind whistled, colder than ever before, bringing back on its shrieking darknesses the dragons from the north, bringing them back to wreak a terrible vengeance…

The tables were overturned. Screaming people ran everywhere, but there was no escape. The trees were alive! Branches became arms which tightened about men's throats, roots seemed to wrench themselves from the earth to halt the guests' hysterical flight.

For a single, terrible moment, the Duchess caught sight of the General, silhouetted against the blazing fire, crying out:

"No! Don't panic. For goodness sake don't –"

Then a great claw struck him, ripping his mask off. And the Duchess saw that he really did have a skull instead of a face. Then, in madness, she fled from that place of horror. It was almost as if the wood wanted to let her go, for though she feared that at any moment a flapping monstrosity would descend from the trees upon her, none did. Thus, half-weeping and half-laughing in madness, she fled from the wood into the moonlight and ran until the tormented screams were faint on the cold night wind…

The Duchess was never seen again. And when the villagers ventured into the wood they found only the smouldering bonfire, nothing more. No — that's not quite true. They found one other thing. A mask of silver leaves, torn by huge talons, not of our world.

Some say that the Duchess still lives, an old woman now, quite mad since that unholy night. Others say that she ran away to Ireland with an officer in the Hussars, but some people would say that.

But in the valley, the villagers know, for they are free now of their masters and run in the woods as of old, and dance and sing of endless summers to come. They do not fear the woods. For they planted young trees where the old ones were cut down, thus destroying the last remains of that grim celebration, so that none should ever know of it again.

Old Michael still lives to this day, in a cottage built for him on the edge of the woods, and he is the woods' guardian. Only he remembers truly the events of that night, only he knows the fate of his proud mistress, the Duchess. Some say that what he saw turned his mind, and that now he is quite mad. But they are the unbelievers. The villagers know Old Michael is not mad, they know he speaks the truth. The dragons he mutters about are not figments of his imagination, nor are the whisperers in the trees. Old Michael knows the woods, and the woods know him. For Michael talks to the trees, especially with a very beautiful silver birch that appeared, quite inexplicably, in the middle of that dark clearing. A shining silver tree, which Michael tends with great care, even in the deep winter.

And the woods will never be dark again, for each day is a joy greater than the last, and the world is at peace.

By Clive Barker, aged 14, incensed at his parents' removal of a tree in the family's garden

FEAR SUN

Laird Barron

Click.

Wow, this is exciting.

BOO-ooom! *goes the green-black surf against green-black rocks that jut crookedy-wookedy as the teeth of an English grand-uncle of mine.* FAH-whoom! Ba-room! *go the torpedoes bored into the reef like bullets from God's six-shooter (in this case a borrowed nuclear submarine). Then the dockside warehouses on stilt legs fold into the churning drink. Fire, smoke, death. On schedule and more to come in act two of Innsmouth's destruction. Daddy would have a hard-on for this action. Perhaps, in his frigid semi-after life, he does. I bet he does.*

The red light means it's on, lady. Let's hurry this along. All hell is breaking loose as you can see on the monitors. You don't need the gun, I'll speak into the mike. We've never met, but I know who you are and why you've come. I like you, chick, you've got balls. My advice, run. This won't lead anywhere pleasant. The Black Dog is loping closer. Gonna bite you, babe. Smoke on the water hides worse. Okay, okay, ease back on the hammer, girlfriend. I'll satisfy your curiosity even though you'll be sorry.

Speaking of, mind if I have a cigarette? Judging from your expression, it'll be my last.

Okay, let's start with last night and go from there.

Last evening went much the same as most of my nocturnal expeditions among the locals do: Cocktails and appetizers at the *Harpy's Nest.* Bucket of blood on the Innsmouth docks and the closest thing to a lounge within fifty miles. Lobster entrée, ice cream dessert cake. Karaoke night with the locals, oh Jesus. I totally abhor karaoke. I made fat ass Mantooth get up on the dais and sweat his way through "Dang Me." Not bad, not bad. Andi told me that Mantooth graduated from Julliard's drama division before he got into the muscle business. Huh. That goon has opened doors and twisted the arms of my stalkers since I escaped college. Surprising that I never knew.

My dress, a Dior original, cut low as sin. Better believe I danced with a whole bevy of rustic lads. The clodhoppers stood in line. Before the bar closed, my ass was bruised from all those clutching oafs and I got a rash from the beards rubbing my neck and tits.

For an encore, I balled a sailor in a shanty. A grizzled character actor named Zed whom the project team recruited from a St. Francis shelter and planted here in 2003. We shared a smoke and he recited the lore of this hapless burg and its doomed inhabitants.

"That's not the script I gave you." I stroked his dead white chest hair in warning. My nails alternated between red and black.

"It's the truth, missy. The devil's own." His tone made it evident he hadn't a clue with whom he conversed. Not a shocker — I eschew the public eye like nobody's business. It's also possible the drunken fool believed that theater had become life.

Zed's perversion of the project script offended me. Granted, I'd done the equivalent of visiting Disney World, fucking Mickey Mouse and getting offended when the dude in the costume refused to break character. Call me fickle. I whistled and the boys waltzed in and beat him with a pipe. Got bored watching him crawl around like a crab with three legs broken. They pinned his arms while I exorcised a few of my demons with a stiletto heel. The actor gurgled and cussed, but he won't tell. Know why? Because I stuffed a personal check covered in my bloody fingerprints into his shirt pocket. What was on that check? Plenty, although not nearly as much as you'd think.

That's it for last night. Oh, oh, I had a Technicolor dream. Dream may be the wrong word — I seldom do and anyway, I was awake at the time and staring at the motel ceiling, trying to connect the water stain dots and I closed my eyes for a few seconds and had a vision. I got shrunk to three inches or so tall and Dad's head loomed above me with the enormity of a Mount Rushmore bust. Icicles dangled from his ears and his flesh cycled from blinding white, to crimson, to midnight blue as the filament sun downshifted through the color spectrum. Dad said I made him proud and to keep on with the project. *The seas will swallow the earth!* And *All the lights are going out! Beware the ants!* His lips were frozen in place. He boomed his visions telepathically. Reminded me of my childhood.

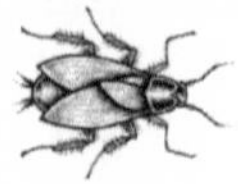

Oh, Daddy.

FEAR SUN

Unless you're a well-connected investor or an FBI special agent, you probably haven't heard of my father. His personal wealth exceeded eighty billion before I got my hooks into it as sole beneficiary. Super!

Most of his projects weren't glamorous, and the sexy radio-ready ones have always operated through charismatic figureheads. Tooms? What etymological pedigree does that connote? We've got relatives all over the place, from East India to Alaska — don't get me started on those North Pole, hillbilly assholes, my idiot cousin Zane especially. Anyway, he's dead. The Mexican Army shot him full of holes and good riddance, says I.

Daddy dwelt in an exalted state that transcended mere wealth; he was supreme. He created worlds: futuristic amusement parks, intercontinental ballistic missile systems, and designer panties. He also destroyed worlds: rival companies and rivals; he hunted tame lions in special preserves for dudes too smart to let it all hang out on safari. He aced a few hookers and possibly his first wife, I am convinced. The earth trembled when he walked. Cancer ate him up. All the money in the world couldn't, etcetera, etcetera. Per his request, the board froze his head and stored it in a vault at a Tooms-owned cryogenics lab — like Ted Williams and Walt Disney! Everybody thinks it's an urban legend. Joke's on them; I've seen that Folger's freeze-dried melon with my own two eyes — the hazel and the brown. What's more, he's merely the ninth severed cranium to adorn the techno ice cave. Every Tooms patriarch has gotten the treatment since the 1890s.

Come Doomsday, Daddy and his cohort will return with a vengeance, heads bolted atop weaponized fifteen-story robot bodies to make the Antichrist wee his pants. For now, he dreams upon a baking rack throne beneath a filament that blazes frozen white light. This private sun blazes cold *and* emits fear. His favorite drug of them all.

Yes, Daddy was a true mogul.

Mother came from Laos. A firebrand. Nobody ever copped to how she hooked up with Daddy. Some say *ambitious courtesan* and those some may be as correct as they are eviscerated and scattered fish food. Not sure if she was one hundred percent Laotian, but I'm a gorgeous puree of whatever plus whatever else. She hated English, hated Daddy, and virulently hated my older brother Increase (the get of the mysteriously late first Mrs. Tooms). She called him Decrease. Doted on yours truly. Taught me how to be an all pro bitch. Love ya, Moms. Mr. Tooms passed when I was sixteen. Mom died in a mysterious limo fire that same winter. Very traumatic for me, although splitting a fortune with my brothers eased the pain.

The family business putters on under the tyrannical thumb of Increase. He knows what's good for him and leaves me to do as I please. No business woman am I.

My talents lie elsewhere. I revel with the merciless ferocity of a blood goddess. I settle for filthy rich, impossibly rich, which means *anything* is possible. Rich enough to buy a tropical island is rich enough to get a hold of a bag of Moon rocks on the black market is rich enough to turn this dying (dead) Massachusetts port town that time forgot into whatever I want. The people: sailors, peasants, moribund gentry, and their slothful cops, alder persons, zoning commissions, and chamber of commerce bureaucrats, mini moguls who measure up to Dad's shoe laces, if I'm generous. I own them too.

Let's step farther back to my vorpal teens.

Time was I aspired to be better than I am. Kinder, if not cleaner. Were I in the mood to justify a career of evil, I'd cite the head games (snicker) Daddy played with me and Increase, and that other one, the one who got away, the one we never speak of. I'd tell you about the Alsatian, Cheops, my best and only friend during adolescence, and how he drowned himself in the swan pond in a fit of despair. Took him three tries. I fished that waterlogged doggy corpse out myself because the gardener got shitfaced and fell asleep in the shed.

Mostly, though, I'm the way I am because I like it, love it, can't get enough of it. Nature versus nurture? Why not some of both? It's impossible to ever truly know the truth. You have to dig extra deep to churn the real muck. You have to afford a person an opportunity to sell her soul. Gods above and below, did I have opportunity to aggrandize an overheated imagination!

The idea for the Innsmouth Project has incubated in my brain since I laid up with pneumonia at age twelve and somebody left a stack of moldy-oldies by the bed. The pinch-lipped ghost of HPL and his genteel madness made a new girl of me.

Great Granddad put ships in bottles. Dad made exquisite dioramas and model cities. Increase enjoyed ant farms. I read Lovecraft and a lot of history. Marie Antoinette's little fake villages captivated me. It all coalesced in my imagination. A vast fortune helped make the dream someone else's nightmare. Frankly, the US government, or a shady subdivision of the government, deserves most of the credit.

Six months after my father passed away I graduated from high school, with honors, and treated myself to a weekend at a Catskill resort that had been a favorite of the Toomses since the Empire State came into existence. No ID required for booze; handsome servants kept the margaritas coming all the livelong day for me and a half-dozen girlfriends I'd flown in for company. Andromeda kept a watch on us. With Daddy out of the picture, there was no telling if Increase or some other wolf might try to erase me from the equation. Ahem, *Andrew.* Andromeda was Andrew then, and not too far removed from his own youth. I read his, *her*, dossier on a whim. She'd majored in paleontology. When I asked why she'd thrown away the chance to unearth dino bones for a security gig, she smiled and told me to mind my business. Most intelligent bodyguard I've ever had, although not necessarily smart.

A guy approached me in the salon and Andi almost broke his arm I signaled. The dude, nondescript in a polo shirt and cargo pants, introduced himself as Rembrandt Tallen. He bought me a drink. I should have known from the ramrod posture and buzz cut that he was military. The next morning, upon coming to in a dungeon, blindfolded, chained to a wall, I also deduced that he was a spook. He removed the blindfold and made me an omelet. Pretty snazzy dungeon — it had a wet bar, plasma television, and the walls and ceiling were covered in crimson leather cushions.

Tallen kept mum regarding his team. The game was for me to assume CIA or NSA, and that's what I figured at first since our family was frenemies with those organizations. Black holes in the ocean was a topic I vaguely recalled. R&D at one of Daddy's lesser known companies looked into this decades before it became kinda-sorta news on a backwater science news site. The military and commercial implications were astounding.

My captor turned on the TV and played a highlight reel of various improbable atrocities that no citizen, plump and secure in his or her suburban nest, had the first inkling.

"Oh, my, goodness," I said as in crystal clear wide-screen glory, a giant hydrocephalic baby jammed a man in a suit into its mouth and chewed. Tiny rifles popped and tinier bullets made scarcely a pinprick on the kid's spongey hide. The action shifted to a satellite image of a village in a jungle. Streams of blackness surrounded the village as its inhabitants huddled at the center or atop the roofs of huts. The camera zoomed in as the flood poured over the village and the figures dispersed in apparent panic. Not that panicking or fleeing helped — the black rivulets pursued everywhere, into huts, onto roofs, up trees, and engulfed them.

"Beetles of an Ur species unknown to our entomologists until 2006. Vicious bastards. Although they refer to themselves as preservationists." Tallen smiled and his ordinary, bland face transfigured in the jittery blue glow. "Bad things are happening out there, Skylark. How would you like to help us make them worse?"

Would I!

The seduction progressed over the course of a couple of years and numerous clandestine rendezvouses. He quizzed me about Majestic 12, MKULTRA, and Project Tallhat. Had I ever met Toshi Ryoko or Howard Campbell? Amanda Bole? No, no, and no, I'd never even heard of any of these persons or things. That pleased Tallen, and seemed to relax him. He confided his secrets.

"It's not important, kiddo. Ryoko and Campbell are flakes. I'd love to see them erased, zero-one, zero-one. They have powerful friends, unfortunately. Forget I mentioned them. Servants of our enemies. Ms. Bole is open to an introduction, assuming you and I reach an accord. We think you're exactly the person to help us with a project."

"You mean my money can help with your project."

"Money, honey. You funnel the cash, we supply the technical know-how and the cannon fodder. You have a vision. We have a vision. It's a can't miss proposition."

Tallen was so smooth and charming. I crushed on him. That corn-fed blandness really grew on me, or the Satan-light dancing in his eyes grew on me, or the fact he believed in elaborate conspiracies excited me (he claimed insects were poised to overrun civilization and that the Apollo explorers found a cairn of bones on the Moon). At any rate, he broke out the maps, diagrams, and the slideshow prospectus. My jaw hit the floor.

His organization (I never did learn its name) had, sometime during the winter of 1975, allegedly established contact with an intelligence residing in a trench off the Atlantic shelf. As in an extraterrestrial intelligence that burrowed into the sediment around the time trilobites were the voting majority.

He laughed when I, unabashed Lovecraft enthusiast, blurted *Dagon! Mother Hydra!* and told me not to be stupid, this verged on Clark Ashton Smith weirdness. His associate in the deep requested some Grand Guignol theater in return for certain considerations that only an immortal terror of unconscionable power can offer.

Tallen, having researched my various childish predilections, proposed that we build and staff a life-model replica of Lovecraft's Innsmouth. Inscrutable alien intelligences enjoy ant farms and aquariums too. Some of them also quite enjoy our trashiest dead white pulp authors. He claimed that this sort of behind the scenes activity was nothing new. In fact, his superiors had been in frequent contact with my father regarding unrelated, yet similar, undertakings.

"Let me consider your proposition," I said. "Who is Bole? Why do I dislike her already?"

His smile thinned. "Mandy is the devil we know. It's tricky, you see. She came to us from across the street, on loan from her people. Her people are overseas, so she's here for the duration." Later , I learned that *across the street* was code for a foreigner who hailed from an extraordinarily far flung location. Off-planet, say, but within a few dozen light years. *Overseas* meant something else that I decided was best left unclear.

I did ask once if Bole bore some familial relationship with the "intelligence." I was high on endorphins and bud.

So was Tallen. That didn't keep him from slapping my mouth. "Are you trying to be funny? That's asinine." He relaxed and kissed away the bits of blood on my lip. "Let's not do that again, eh?"

I smiled, wanting him to believe I liked it, no hard feelings, while I privately reviewed all the ways to kill him slowly.

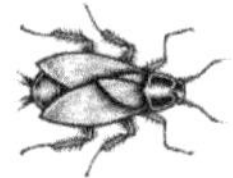

Surviving to majority as a Tooms heiress tempered my enthusiasm with a grain or two of skepticism. I hired world-class detectives — the best of the best. My bloodhounds tracked down scientists and sources within and without the government and from foreign countries. Results from this intelligence gathering dragnet convinced me of Tallen's sincerity. Numerous reports indicated covert activity of unparalleled secrecy off the New England coast. The veracity of his most staggering claim would require personal investigation.

Meanwhile, my detectives and the scores of unfortunate people they contacted, died in mysterious accidents or vanished. I did the math one day. Okay, Mantooth did it on the back of a napkin. Four hundred and sixty-three. That's how many went *poof* because I asked the wrong questions. The number might be bigger; we were in the car on the way to a stockholder meeting.

"You gonna do it?" Only Andi would dare to ask.

Pointless question. She knew my capabilities. She knew I had to do it, because beneath the caviar slurping, bubblegum popping, jet setting façade throbbed a black hole that didn't want to eat the light; it needed to.

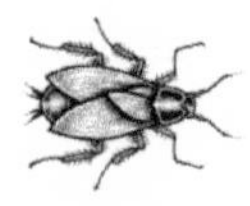

This town had a different name when Protestant fisherman Jedidiah Marshal founded it in 1809. Always off the beaten path, always cloistered and clannish, even by New England standards, afflicted by economic vagaries and the consolidation of the fishing industry into mega corporations, this town proved easy to divide and conquer. I retain an army of lackeys to orchestrate these sorts of stunts. Corporate raiders, lawyers, feds on the take, blackmail specialists and assassins.

First, we drove out the monied and the learned. The peasants were reeducated, or, as Tallen preferred, made to vanish. Gradually more actors were introduced and the infrastructure perfected. Necessary elements within the US government made the paperwork right. All it required was a nudge here and a bribe there from Tallen's operatives. The town was wiped from road signs, maps, from the very record. With the groundwork laid, Innsmouth, my own private economy-sized diorama, raised its curtain.

Assuming you're a casual observer, it's a humdrum routine on the surface.

Children ride the bus to school. Housewives tidy and cook while soap operas numb the pain. Husbands toil in the factories or seek their fortune aboard fishing boats. Come dusk, men in suits, or coveralls or raincoats and galoshes, trudge into the taverns and lounges and slap down a goodly portion of the day's wages on booze. At the lone strip club on the waterfront on the north edge of town, bored college girls and older women from trailer parks dance sluggishly. *The House of the Revived Lord* sees brisk trade Wednesday, Black Mass Friday, and by the numbers kiddie-friendly Sunday. I cherish the reactions of the occasional lost soul who accidentally detours through town: Some bluff day trader or officer worker tooling along Main Street with his uptight wife riding shotgun, her face scrunched in annoyance as she comes to grips with the lies the pocket map has fed her; and two point five kids in the back, overheated and embroiled in child warfare.

Annoyance gives way to confusion, which yields to revulsion at the decrepitude of the architecture and physiognomy of the locals, and ultimately, if the visitors prove sufficiently unwise as to partake of the diner, or gods help them, layover at one of Innsmouth's fine hotels, horror will engulf the remainder of their brief existence.

Even I, maestro and chief benefactor, can see but the tip of this iceberg. Scientists and men in black lurk behind the grimy façades of Victorian row houses — the scientists' purpose is to experiment upon the civilian populace as they might lab rats. Green lights flash through the murky windows, screams drift with the wind off the Atlantic. Ships and submarines come and go in the foggy dark. Andromeda and Mantooth worry about what they can't detect. I don't bother to order them to relax. Worrying is in their job description.

I acquired an estate in the hills. Fifteen minutes leisurely drive from town square. The gates are electrified, the house is locked tight, and guys with automatic weapons pace the grounds.

My first encounter with Miss Bole came when she wandered into my rec room unannounced. I sprawled across a giant beanbag while the news anchor recited his nightly soporific. I knew Bole to the core at first sight — kind of tall, black hair in a bob from the '50s, narrow shoulders, wide hips and thunder thighs. Pale and sickly, yet morbidly robust. Eyebrows too heavy, face too basic, too plastic, yet grotesquely alluring like a Celt fertility goddess cast from lumpen clay. She wore a green smock, yoga pants, and sandals. Sweat dripped from her, although she seemed relaxed.

"Hey there, Skylark Tooms. The Gray Eminence loves your style. I'm Amanda Bole. Call me Mandy." Her voice was androgynous. She gripped my small hand in her large, damp hand and brushed my cheek with cool, overripe lips.

"Gray Eminence. Is that what you call…him?" Pleasure and terror made my heart skip, skip, skip. Sorry, Agent Tallen, but I think I'm in love.

"It, Skylark. *It.* I usually call it G.E. Confuses anybody at the NSA we haven't bought." Her wide smile revealed white, formidable teeth.

I'm usually an ice bitch during introductions. Feels good to keep the opposition on the defensive. Her? I looked into her sparkling frigid eyes and couldn't stop. Nothing in those shiny pebbles but my dopey face in stereoscope. "When will I meet it?"

"Assuming your luck holds? Never, my girl. G.E. has big plans for you."

Mandy pulled me to my feet. We had tea on the front deck by the swimming pool. The deck has a view of the ocean, hazy and smudged in the twilight distance. Lights of town came on in twinkling clusters.

"I think I've seen enough," she said, setting aside her cup.

She stripped and dove into the water. Reflections are funny — she kicked into the deeper end, her odd form elongating as it submerged. Ripples distorted my perspective and made her the length and width of a great white shark, gliding downward and gone as the tiles of the pool dilated to reveal a sinkhole.

Tallen called later. "I'm glad you're all right."

"Any reason I wouldn't be?"

"Ms. Bole told me that she'd decided to terminate your involvement. That would involve being shaken from a fish food can over the Atlantic. It seems she changed her mind."

"Uh, good, then?"

"Convenient! Now we can begin."

Some of what comes next, you already know. The cold death mask of rage, the pistol in your hand, what comes next is why you've returned and looked me up. Here's some context, some behind-the scenes magic:

"Who gets to escape?" Mandy and I were revolving in the sex swing in the rumpus room. Mantooth hadn't seemed completely comfortable installing the equipment. I love that repressed New England prudishness about him.

"The narrator." Mandy's obsidian eyes reflected the light over my shoulder, or trapped it. Her eyes glazed, or shuttered (happened so fast), and reflected nothing from a patina of broken black vessels, a thousand scratches from infinitesimal webbed claws. "Our girl works for an amateur filmmaker. The source material is a trifle staid. Tallen made sure the filmmaker brought a camera crew, per G.E's request. Bubbly blonde, sensible, tough as nails brunette, strapping cinematographer, a weasel tech guy. That way there's a bit of sex and murder to spice up the proceedings. Our heroine, the sensible brunette, will escape by the skin of her teeth. Over the next couple of years, we'll shadow her, dangle the clues, and, ultimately, lure her back in for the explosive finale. Should be fun."

Hard to tell whether Mandy actually relished the impending climax. She remained disinterested regardless the circumstances. I relished it for the two of us.

Earlier, she'd given me a tour of a factory that covered for a subterranean medical complex. Her scientists were busily splicing human and amphibian DNA with genetic material from the Gray Eminence and subjecting that simmering, somatically nucleated mess to electromagnetic waves generated by some kind of Tesla-inspired machine. They'd been at it since the '70s, moving the operation from South Sea lagoons to secret bunkers such as this one. According to the chief researcher, Dr. Shrike, the resultant test tube offspring teemed in the frigid waters along the coast. Allegedly, G.E. found them pleasing. It absorbed more and more fry every spawning cycle. That had to be a positive sign.

A few days later, I received an email. Man, I watched the footage of the pursuit and slaughter of that film crew (all but one) like a jillion times. The only downer, little miss tough as nails brunette stabbed the clerk at the wine shop through the eyeball. Too bad; he was sort of cute, and my god, what exquisite taste.

Point of fact, our heroine stabbed three guys, blew two major buildings to shit (with a few of our drone mercs inside), and steamrolled the Constable as she roared out of town in a wrecker. According to the goon in charge of the affair, at the end his minions weren't even pulling their punches, they were trying to get the hell out of the chick's way.

I was tempted to tell Mandy, sorry, babe, I've got the hots for another woman. Two reasons I kept my mouth shut — one, Mandy scared me oodles and oodles, and two, I suspected she didn't give a damn, which scared me worse.

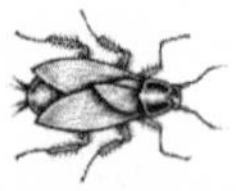

How do we arrive at this junction? The explosions, the chatter of machine guns, screams, and death? Innsmouth crashing into the sea in a ball of fire? All according to the master plan, the Punch and Judy show demanded by the torpid overlord in the deep. This is what happened in the infamous story that HP wrote. I often wonder if he had help, a muse from the hadal zone, maybe.

Who can say where art ends and reality asserts primacy? Mandy's script, our *script, called for you, our dark-haired girl, to return at the van of a fleet of black government SUVs. I hired a mercenary company to dress in federal suits and Army camo and swoop in here and blow the town and the reef to smithereens. Much as you did your first time through, except big enough to warm the heart of a Hollywood exec.*

And here we are, you and I.

Certainly I believed my privilege would shield me, that I could gleefully observe the immolation of Innsmouth from the comfort of my mansion's control room. I figured when the smoke cleared and the cry was over, I'd pack my designer bags and flit off to the Caribbean for a change of scenery. Fun as it has been, nine months of cold salt air a year has murdered my complexion and my mood.

Guess you could say I was surprised when my guards were shot to pieces and an armor-piercing rocket blasted the front door. That's what Mantooth said they hit us with before you waltzed in here and capped him. Through the eyeball, no less. Don't you get it? All this destruction, Mandy and Tallen's betrayal, you glowering down at me, poised to ram a dagger through my black little heart? A mix of prep and improve. Somewhere a dark god is laughing in delight, rapping his knuckles on the aquarium glass to get the fishies spinning.

The question is, do you want to live to see a curtain call. You're the heroine and if we're following the original plot, you have an unpleasant reckoning in your near future. I don't think this version of the tale will see you transforming into a fish-woman and paddling into the sunset. No, this is major league awful. G.E. awaits your pleasure. I doubt even God knows what's going to happen in the monster's lair.

Got to be boring, lying there and emoting telepathically eon after eon. You'll make a pretty dolly, for a while.

Or, you could play it smart. My jet is fueled and idling at a strip just down the road. With my money, we can go damned near anywhere. Take your time and think it over. I'll give you until I finish this cigarette.

BANG! from a gun. A body thuds on the floor off-screen.

GODDAMNIT, *Andi! Why the fuck did you do that to the broad? It was under control. I had her in the palm of my hand. Shit. What do we do now? Mandy is gonna go nuclear. G.E. surely won't be amused. Where do we find a metaphorical virgin sacrifice at this hour? Andi..? Andi!*

You bitch. You almost had me going. No, I'm not sure if anywhere is beyond the reach of our friends. But let's hit the friendly skies and see, huh? Shut that down. I want to watch it later.

Click.

NO STORY IN IT
Ramsey Campbell

"Grandad."

Boswell turned from locking the front door to see Gemima running up the garden path cracked by the late September heat. Her mother April was at the tipsy gate, and April's husband Rod was climbing out of their rusty crimson Nissan. "Oh, dad," April cried, slapping her forehead hard enough to make him wince. "You're off to London. How could we forget it was today, Rod."

Rod pursed thick lips beneath a ginger moustache broader than his otherwise schoolboyish plump face. "We must have had other things on our mind. It looks as if I'm joining you, Jack."

"You'll tell me how," Boswell said as Gemima's small hot five-year-old hand found his grasp.

"We've just learned I'm a cut-back."

"More of a set-back, will it be? I'm sure there's a demand for teachers of your experience."

"I'm afraid you're a bit out of touch with the present."

Boswell saw his daughter willing him not to take the bait. "Can we save the discussion for my return?" he said. "I've a bus and then a train to catch."

"We can run your father to the station, can't we? We want to tell him our proposal." Rod bent the passenger seat forward. "Let's keep the men together," he said.

As Boswell hauled the reluctant belt across himself he glanced up. Usually Gemima reminded him poignantly of her mother at her age — large brown eyes with high startled eyebrows, inquisitive nose, pale prim lips — but in the mirror April's face looked not much less small, just more lined. The car jerked forward, grating its innards, and the radio announced "A renewed threat of war — " before Rod switched it off. Once the car was past the worst of the potholes in the main road Boswell said "So propose."

"We wondered how you were finding life on your own," Rod said. "We thought it mightn't be the ideal situation for someone with your turn of mind."

"Rod. Dad — "

Her husband gave the mirror a look he might have aimed at a child who'd spoken out of turn in class. "Since we've all over-extended ourselves, we think the solution is to pool our resources."

"Which are those?"

"We wondered how the notion of our moving in with you might sound."

"Sounds fun," Gemima cried.

Rod's ability to imagine living with Boswell for any length of time showed how desperate he, if not April, was. "What about your own house?" Boswell said.

"There are plenty of respectable couples eager to rent these days. We'd pay you rent, of course. Surely it makes sense for all of us."

"Can I give you a decision when I'm back from London?" Boswell said, mostly to April's hopeful reflection. "Maybe you won't have to give up your house. Maybe soon I'll be able to offer you financial help."

"Christ," Rod snarled, a sound like a gnashing of teeth.

To start with the noise the car made was hardly harsher. Boswell thought the rear bumper was dragging on the road until tenement blocks jerked up in the mirror as though to seize the vehicle, which ground loudly to a halt. "Out," Rod cried in a tone poised to pounce on nonsense.

"Is this like one of your stories, grandad?" Gemima giggled as she followed Boswell out of the car.

"No," her father said through his teeth and flung the boot open. "This is real."

Boswell responded only by going to look. The suspension had collapsed, thrusting the wheels up through the rusty arches. April took Gemima's hand, Boswell sensed not least to keep her quiet, and murmured "Oh, Rod."

Boswell was staring at the tenements. Those not boarded up were tattooed with graffiti inside and out, and he saw watchers at as many broken as unbroken windows. He thought of the parcel a fan had once given him with instructions not to open it until he was home, the present that had been one of Jean's excuses for divorcing him. "Come with me to the station," he urged, "and you can phone whoever you need to phone."

When the Aireys failed to move immediately he stretched out a hand to them and saw his shadow printed next to theirs on a wall, either half demolished or never completed, in front of the tenements. A small child holding a woman's hand, a man slouching beside them with a fist stuffed in his pocket, a second man gesturing empty-handed at them… The shadows seemed to blacken, the sunlight to brighten like inspiration, but that had taken no form when the approach of a taxi distracted him. His shadow roused itself as he dashed into the rubbly road to flag the taxi down. "I'll pay," he told Rod.

"Here's Jack Boswell, everyone," Quentin Sedgwick shouted. "Here's our star author. Come and meet him."

It was going to be worth it, Boswell thought. Publishing had changed since all his books were in print — indeed, since any were. Sedgwick, a tall thin young but balding man with wiry veins exposed by a singlet and shorts, had met him at Waterloo, pausing barely long enough to deliver an intense handshake before treating him to a headlong ten-minute march and a stream of enthusiasm for his work. The journey ended at a house in the midst of a crush of them resting their fronts on the pavement. At least the polished nameplate of Cassandra Press had to be visible to anyone who passed. Beyond it a hall that smelled of curried vegetables was occupied by a double-parked pair of bicycles and a steep staircase not much wider than their handlebars. "Amazing, isn't it?" Sedgwick declared. "It's like one of your early things, being able to publish from home. Except in a story of yours the computers would take over and tell us what to write."

"I don't remember writing that," Boswell said with some unsureness.

"No, I just made it up. Not bad, was it?" Sedgwick said, running upstairs. "Here's Jack Boswell, everyone…"

A young woman with a small pinched studded face and glistening black hair spiky as an armoured fist emerged from somewhere on the ground floor as Sedgwick threw open doors to reveal two cramped rooms, each featuring a computer terminal, at one of which an even younger woman with blonde hair the length of her filmy flowered blouse was composing an advertisement. "Starts with C, ends with e," Sedgwick said of her, and of the studded woman "Bren, like the gun. Our troubleshooter."

Boswell grinned, feeling someone should. "Just the three of you?"

"Small is sneaky, I keep telling the girls. While the big houses are being dragged down by excess personnel, we move into the market they're too cumbersome to handle. Carole, show him his page."

The publicist saved her work twice before displaying the Cassandra Press catalogue. She scrolled past the colophon, a C with a P hooked on it, and a parade of authors: Ferdy Thorn, ex-marine turned ecological warrior; Germaine Gossett, feminist fantasy writer; Torin Bergman, Scandinavia's leading magic realist… "Forgive my ignorance," Boswell said, "but these are all new to me."

"They're the future." Sedgwick cleared his throat and grabbed Boswell's shoulder to lean him towards the computer. "Here's someone we all know."

BOSWELL'S BACK! the page announced in letters so large they left room only for a shout line from, Boswell remembered, the *Observer* twenty years ago — "Britain's best sf writer since Wyndham and Wells" — and a scattering of titles: *The Future Just Began*, *Tomorrow Was Yesterday*, *Wave Goodbye To Earth*, *Terra Spells Terror*, *Science Lies In Wait*… "It'll look better when we have covers to reproduce," Carole said. "I couldn't write much. I don't know your work."

"That's because I've been devouring it all over again, Jack. You thought you might have copies for my fair helpers, didn't you?"

"So I have," Boswell said, struggling to spring the catches of his aged briefcase.

"See what you think when you've read these. Some for you as well, Bren," Sedgwick said, passing out Boswell's last remaining hardcovers of several of his books. "Here's a Hugo winner, and look, this one got the Prix du Fantastique Écologique. Will you girls excuse us now? I hear the call of lunch."

They were in sight of Waterloo Station again when he seized Boswell's elbow to steer him into the Delphi, a tiny restaurant crammed with deserted tables spread with pink and white checked cloths. "This is what one of our greatest authors looks like, Nikos," Sedgwick announced. "Let's have all we can eat and a litre of your red if that's your style, Jack, to be going on with."

The massive dark-skinned variously hairy proprietor brought them a carafe without a stopper and a brace of glasses Boswell would have expected to hold water. Sedgwick filled them with wine and dealt

Boswell's a vigorous clunk. "Here's to us. Here's to your legendary unpublished books."

"Not for much longer."

"What a scoop for Cassandra. I don't know which I like best, *Don't Make Me Mad* or *Only We Are Left*. Listen to this, Nikos. There are going to be so many mentally ill people they have to be given the vote and everyone's made to have one as a lodger. And a father has to seduce his daughter or the human race dies out."

"Very nice."

"Ignore him, Jack. They couldn't be anyone else but you."

"I'm glad you feel that way. You don't think they're a little too dark even for me."

"Not a shade, and certainly not for Cassandra. Wait till you read our other books."

Here Nikos brought meze, an oval plate splattered with varieties of goo. Sedgwick waited until Boswell had transferred a sample of each to his plate and tested them with a piece of lukewarm bread. "Good?"

"Most authentic," Boswell found it in himself to say.

Sedgwick emptied the carafe into their glasses and called for another. Blackened lamb chops arrived too, and prawns dried up by grilling, withered meatballs, slabs of smoked ham that could have been used to sole shoes... Boswell was working on a token mouthful of viciously spiced sausage when Sedgwick said "Know how you could delight us even more?"

Boswell swallowed and had to salve his mouth with half a glassful of wine. "Tell me," he said tearfully.

"Have you enough unpublished stories for a collection?"

"I'd have to write another to bring it up to length."

"Wait till I let the girls know. Don't think they aren't excited, they were just too overwhelmed by meeting you to show it. Can you call me as soon as you have an idea for the story or the cover?"

"I think I may have both."

"You're an example to us all. Can I hear?"

"Shadows on a ruined wall. A man and woman and her child, and another man reaching out to them, I'd say in warning. Ruined tenements in the background. Everything overgrown. Even if the story isn't called *We Are Tomorrow*, the book can be."

"Shall I give you a bit of advice? Go further than you ever have before. Imagine something you couldn't believe anyone would pay you to write."

Despite the meal, Boswell felt too elated to imagine that just now. His capacity for observation seemed to have shut down too, and only an increase in the frequency of passers-by outside the window roused it. "What time is it?" he wondered, fumbling his watch upward on his thin wrist.

"Not much past five," Sedgwick said, emptying the carafe yet again. "Still lunchtime."

"Good God, if I miss my train I'll have to pay double."

"Next time we'll see about paying for your travel." Sedgwick gulped the last of the wine as he threw a credit card on the table to be collected later. "I wish you'd said you had to leave this early. I'll have Bren send copies of our books to you," he promised as Boswell panted into Waterloo, and called after him down the steps into the Underground "Don't forget, imagine the worst. That's what we're for."

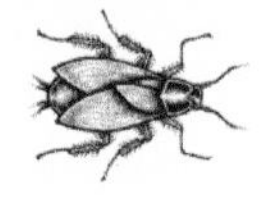

For three hours the worst surrounded Boswell. SIX NATIONS CONTINUE REARMING... CLIMATE CHANGES ACCELERATE, SAY SCIENTISTS... SUPERSTITIOUS FANATICISM ON INCREASE... WOMEN'S GROUPS CHALLENGE ANTI-GUN RULING... RALLY AGAINST COMPUTER CHIPS IN CRIMINALS ENDS IN VIOLENCE: THREE DEAD, MANY INJURED... Far more commuters weren't reading the news than were: many wore headphones that leaked percussion like distant discos in the night, while the sole book to be seen was *Page Turner*, the latest Turner adventure from Midas Paperbacks, bound in either gold or silver depending, Boswell supposed, on the reader's standards. Sometimes drinking helped him create, but just now a bottle of wine from the buffet to stave off a hangover only froze in his mind the image of the present in ruins and overgrown by the future, of the shapes of a family and a figure poised to intervene printed on the remains of a wall by a flare of painful light. He had to move on from thinking of them as the Aireys and himself, or had he? One reason Jean had left him was that she'd found traces of themselves and April in nearly all his work, even where none was intended; she'd become convinced he was wishing the worst for her and her child when he'd only meant a warning, by no means mostly aimed at them. His attempts to invent characters wholly unlike them had never convinced her and hadn't improved his work either. He needn't consider her feelings now, he thought sadly. He had to write whatever felt true — the best story he had in him.

It was remaining stubbornly unformed when the train stammered into the terminus. A minibus strewn with drunks and defiant smokers deposited him at the end of his street. He assumed his house felt empty because of Rod's proposal. Jean had taken much of the furniture they hadn't passed on to April, but Boswell still had seats where he needed to sit and folding canvas chairs for visitors, and nearly all his books. He was in the kitchen, brewing coffee while he tore open the day's belated mail, when the phone rang.

He took the handful of bills and the airmail letter he'd saved for last into his workroom, where he sat on the chair April had loved spinning and picked up the receiver. "Jack Boswell."

"Jack? They're asleep."

Presumably this explained why Rod's voice was low. "Is that an event?" Boswell said.

"It is for April at the moment. She's been out all day looking for work, any work. She didn't want to tell you in case you already had too much on your mind."

"But now you have."

"I was hoping things had gone well for you today."

"I think you can do more than that."

"Believe me, I'm looking as hard as she is."

"No, I mean you can assure her when she wakes that not only do I have a publisher for my two novels and eventually a good chunk of my backlist, but they've asked me to put together a new collection too."

"Do you mind if I ask for her sake how much they're advancing you?"

"No pounds and no shillings or pence."

"You're saying they'll pay you in euros?"

"I'm saying they don't pay an advance to me or any of their authors, but they pay royalties every three months."

"I take it your agent has approved the deal."

"It's a long time since I've had one of those, and now I'll be ten per cent better off. Do remember I've plenty of experience."

"I could say the same. Unfortunately it isn't always enough."

Boswell felt his son-in-law was trying to render him as insignificant as Rod believed science fiction writers ought to be. He tore open the airmail envelope with the little finger of the hand holding the receiver.

"What's that?" Rod demanded.

"No panic. I'm not destroying any of my work," Boswell told him, and smoothed out the letter to read it again. "Well, this is timely. The Saskatchewan Conference on Prophetic Literature is giving me the Wendigo Award for a career devoted to envisioning the future."

"Congratulations. Will it help?"

"It certainly should, and so will the story I'm going to write. Maybe even you will be impressed. Tell April not to let things pull her down," Boswell said as he rang off, and "Such as you" only after he had.

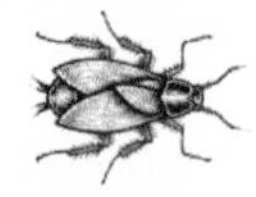

Boswell wakened with a hangover and an uneasy sense of some act left unperformed. The image wakened with him: small child holding woman's hand, man beside them, second man gesturing. He groped for the mug of water by the bed, only to find he'd drained it during the night. He stumbled to the bathroom and emptied himself while the cold tap filled the mug. In time he felt equal to yet another breakfast of the kind his doctor had warned him to be content with. Of course, he thought as the sound of chewed bran filled his skull, he should have called Sedgwick last night about the Wendigo Award. How early could he call? Best to wait until he'd worked on the new story. He tried as he washed up the breakfast things and the rest of the plates and utensils in the sink, but his mind seemed as paralysed as the shadows on the wall it kept showing him. Having sat at his desk for a while in front of the wordless screen, he dialled Cassandra Press.

"Hello? Yes?"

"Is that Carole?" Since that earned him no reply, he tried "Bren?"

"It's Carole. Who is this?"

"Jack Boswell. I just wanted you to know–"

"You'll want to speak to Q. Q, it's your sci-fi man."

Sedgwick came on almost immediately, preceded by a creak of bedsprings. "Jack, you're never going to tell me you've written your story already."

"Indeed I'm not. Best to take time to get it right, don't you think? I'm calling to report they've given me the Wendigo Award."

"About time, and never more deserved. Who is it gives those again? Carole, you'll need to scribble this down. Bren, where's something to scribble with?"

"By the phone," Bren said very close, and the springs creaked.

"Reel it off, Jack."

As Boswell heard Sedgwick relay the information he grasped that he was meant to realise how close the Cassandra Press personnel were to one another. "That's capital, Jack," Sedgwick told him. "Bren will be lumping some books to the mail for you, and I think I can say Carole's going to have good news for you."

"Any clue what kind?"

"Wait and see, Jack, and we'll wait and see what your new story's about."

Boswell spent half an hour trying to write an opening line that would trick him into having started the tale, but had to acknowledge that the technique no longer worked for him. He was near to being blocked by fearing he had lost all ability to write, and so he opened the carton of books the local paper had sent him to review. *Sci-Fi On The Net*, *Create Your Own* Star Wars™ *Character*, *1000 Best Sci-Fi Videos*, *Sci-Fi From Lucas To Spielberg*, *Star Wars™: The Bluffer's Guide*… There wasn't a book he would have taken off a shelf, nor any appropriate to the history of science fiction in which he intended to incorporate a selection from his decades of reviews. Just now writing something other than his story might well be a trap. He donned sandals and shorts and unbuttoned his shirt as he ventured out beneath a sun that looked as fierce as the rim of a total eclipse.

All the seats of a dusty bus were occupied by pensioners, some of whom looked as bewildered as the young woman who spent the journey searching the pockets of the combat outfit she wore beneath a stained fur coat and muttering that everyone needed to be ready for the enemy. Boswell had to push his way off the bus past three grim scrawny youths bare from the waist up, who boarded the vehicle as if they planned to hijack it. He was at the end of the road where the wall had inspired him — but he hadn't reached the wall when he saw Rod's car.

It was identifiable solely by the charred number plate. The car itself was a blackened windowless hulk. He would have stalked away to call the Aireys if the vandalism hadn't made writing the new story more urgent than ever, and so he stared at the incomplete wall with a fierceness designed to revive his mind. When he no longer knew if he was staring at the bricks until the story formed or the shadows did, he turned quickly away. The shadows weren't simply cast on the wall, he thought; they were embedded in it, just as the image was embedded in his head.

He had to walk a mile homeward before the same bus showed up. Trudging the last yards to his house left him parched. He drank several glassfuls of water, and opened the drawer of his desk to gaze for reassurance or perhaps inspiration at his secret present from a fan before he dialled the Aireys' number.

"Hello?"

If it was April, something had driven her voice high. "It's only me," Boswell tentatively said.

"Grandad. Are you coming to see us?"

"Soon, I hope."

"Oh." Having done her best to hide her disappointment, she added "Good."

"What have you been doing today?"

"Reading. Dad says I have to get a head start."

"I'm glad to hear it," Boswell said, though she didn't sound as if she wanted him to be. "Is mummy there?"

"Just dad."

After an interval Boswell tried "Rod?"

"It's just me, right enough."

"I'm sure she didn't mean — I don't know if you've seen your car."

"I'm seeing nothing but. We still have to pay to have it scrapped."

"No other developments?"

"Jobs, are you trying to say? Not unless April's so dumbstruck with good fortune she can't phone. I was meaning to call you, though. I wasn't clear last night what plans you had with regard to us."

Rod sounded so reluctant to risk hoping that Boswell said "There's a good chance I'll have a loan in me."

"I won't ask how much." After a pause presumably calculated to entice an answer Rod added "I don't need to tell you how grateful we are. How's your new story developing?"

This unique display of interest in his work only increased the pressure inside Boswell's uninspired skull. "I'm hard at work on it," he said.

"I'll tell April," Rod promised, and left Boswell with that — with hours before the screen and not a word of a tale, just shadows in searing light: child holding woman's hand, man beside, another gesturing... He fell asleep at his desk and jerked awake in a panic, afraid to know why his inspiration refused to take shape.

He seemed hardly to have slept in his bed when he was roused by a pounding of the front-door knocker and an incessant shrilling of the doorbell. As he staggered downstairs he imagined a raid, the country having turned overnight into a dictatorship that had set the authorities the task of arresting all subversives, not least those who saw no cause for optimism. The man on the doorstep was uniformed and gloomy about his job, but brandished a clipboard and had a carton at his feet. "Consignment for Boswell," he grumbled.

"Books from my publishers."

"Wouldn't know. Just need your autograph."

Boswell scrawled a signature rendered illegible by decades of autographs, then bore the carton to the kitchen table, where he slit its layers of tape to reveal the first Cassandra Press books he'd seen. All the covers were black as coal in a closed pit except for bony white lettering not quite askew enough for the effect to be unquestionably intentional. **GERMAINE GOSSETT,** ***Women Are The Wave.*** **TORIN BERGMAN,** ***Oracles Arise!*** **FERDY THORN,** ***Fight Them Fisheries***... Directly inside each was the title page, and on the back of that the copyright opposite the first page of text. Ecological frugality was fine, but not if it looked unprofessional, even in uncorrected proof copies. Proofreading should take care of the multitude of printer's errors, but what of the prose? Every book, not just Torin Bergman's, read like the work of a single apprentice translator.

He abandoned a paragraph of Ferdy Thorn's blunt chunky style and sprinted to his workroom to answer the phone. "Boswell," he panted.

"Jack. How are you today?"

"I've been worse, Quentin."

"You'll be a lot better before you know. Did the books land?"

"The review copies, you mean."

"We'd be delighted if you reviewed them. That would be wonderful, wouldn't it, if Jack reviewed the books?" When this received no audible answer he said "Only you mustn't be kind just because they're ours, Jack. We're all in the truth business."

"Let me read them and then we'll see what's best. What I meant, though, these aren't finished books."

"They certainly should be. Sneak a glance at the last pages if you don't mind knowing the end."

"Finished in the sense of the state that'll be on sale in the shops."

"Well, yes. They're trade paperbacks. That's the book of the future."

"I know what trade paperbacks are. These–"

"Don't worry, Jack, they're just our first attempts. Wait till you see the covers Carole's done for you. Nothing grabs the eye like naïve art, especially with messages like ours."

"So," Boswell said in some desperation, "have I heard why you called?"

"You don't think we'd interrupt you at work without some real news."

"How real?"

"We've got the figures for the advance orders of your books. All the girls had to do was phone with your name and the new titles till the batteries went flat, and I don't mind telling you you're our top seller."

"What are the figures?" Boswell said, and took a deep breath.

"Nearly three hundred. Congratulations once again."

"Three hundred thousand. It's I who should be congratulating you and your team. I only ever had one book up there before. Shows publishing needs people like yourselves to shake it up." He became aware of speaking fast so that he could tell the Aireys his — no, their — good fortune, but he had to clarify one point before letting euphoria overtake him. "Or is that, don't think for a second I'm complaining if it is, but is that the total for both titles or each?"

"Actually, Jack, can I just slow you down a moment?"

"Sorry. I'm babbling. That's what a happy author sounds like. You understand why."

"I hope I do, but would you mind — I didn't quite catch what you thought I said."

"Three hundred — "

"Can I stop you there? That's the total, or just under. As you say, publishing has changed. I expect a lot of the bigger houses are doing no better with some of their books."

Boswell's innards grew hollow, then his skull. He felt his mouth drag itself into some kind of a grin as he said "Is that three hundred, sorry, nearly three hundred per title?"

"Overall, I'm afraid. We've still a few little independent shops to call, and sometimes they can surprise you."

Boswell doubted he could cope with any more surprises, but heard himself say, unbelievably, hopefully "Did you mention *We Are Tomorrow*?"

"How could we have forgotten it?" Sedgwick's enthusiasm relented at last as he said "I see what you're asking. Yes, the total is for all three of your books. Don't forget we've still the backlist to come, though," he added with renewed vigour.

"Good luck to it." Boswell had no idea how much bitterness was audible in that, nor in "I'd best be getting back to work."

"We all can't wait for the new story, can we?"

Boswell had no more of an answer than he heard from anyone else. Having replaced the receiver as if it had turned to heavy metal, he stared at the uninscribed slab of the computer screen. When he'd had enough of that he trudged to stare into the open rectangular hole of the Cassandra carton. Seized by an inspiration he would have preferred not to experience, he dashed upstairs to drag on yesterday's clothes and marched unshaven out of the house.

Though the library was less than ten minutes' walk away through sunbleached streets whose desert was relieved only by patches of scrub, he'd hardly visited it for the several years he had been too depressed to enter bookshops. The library was almost worse: it lacked not just his books but practically everyone's except for paperbacks with injured spines. Some of the tables in the large white high-windowed room were occupied by newspaper readers. **MIDDLE EAST WAR DEADLINE EXPIRES... ONE IN TWO FAMILIES WILL BE VICTIMS OF VIOLENCE, STUDY SHOWS... FAMINES IMMINENT IN EUROPE... NO MEDICINE FOR FATAL VIRUSES...** Most of the tables held Internet terminals, from one of which a youth whose face was red with more than pimples was being evicted by a librarian for calling up some text that had offended the black woman at the next screen. Boswell paid for an hour at the terminal and began his search.

The only listings of any kind for Torin Bergman were the publication details of the Cassandra Press books, and the same was true of Ferdy Thorn and Germaine Gossett. When the screen told him his time was up and began to flash like lightning to alert the staff, the message and the repeated explosion of light and the headlines around him seemed to merge into a single inspiration he couldn't grasp. Only a hand laid on his shoulder made him jump up and lurch between the reluctantly automatic doors.

The sunlight took up the throbbing of the screen, or his head did. He remembered nothing of his tramp home other than that it tasted like bone. As he fumbled to unlock the front door the light grew audible, or the phone began to shrill. He managed not to snap the key and ran to snatch up the receiver. "What now?"

"It's only me, dad. I didn't mean to bother you."

"You never could," Boswell said, though she just had by sounding close to tears. "How are you, April? How are things?"

"Not too wonderful."

"Things aren't, you mean. I'd never say you weren't."

"Both." Yet more tonelessly she said "I went looking for computer jobs. Didn't want all the time mummy spent showing me how things worked to go to waste. Only I didn't realise how much more there is to them now, and I even forgot what she taught me. So then I thought I'd go on a computer course to catch up."

"I'm sure that's a sound idea."

"It wasn't really. I forgot where I was going. I nearly forgot our number when I had to ring Rod to come and find me when he hasn't even got the car and leave Gemima all on her own."

Boswell was reaching deep into himself for a response when she said "Mummy's dead, isn't she?"

Rage at everything, not least April's state, made his answer harsh. "Shot by the same freedom fighters she'd given the last of her money to in a country I'd never even heard of. She went off telling me one of us had to make a difference to the world."

"Was it years ago?"

"Not long after you were married," Boswell told her, swallowing grief.

"Oh." She seemed to have nothing else to say but "Rod."

Boswell heard him murmuring at length before his voice attacked the phone. "Why is April upset?"

"Don't you know?"

"Forgive me. Were you about to give her some good news?"

"If only."

"You will soon, surely, once your books are selling. You know I'm no admirer of the kind of thing you write, but I'll be happy to hear of your success."

"You don't know what I write, since you've never read any of it." Aloud Boswell said only "You won't."

"I don't think I caught that."

"Yes you did. This publisher prints as many books as there are orders, which turns out to be under three hundred."

"Maybe you should try and write the kind of thing people will pay to read."

Boswell placed the receiver with painfully controlled gentleness on the hook, then lifted it to redial. The distant bell had started to sound more like an alarm to him when it was interrupted. "Quentin Sedgwick."

"And Torin Bergman."

"Jack."

"As one fictioneer to another, are you Ferdy Thorn as well?"

Sedgwick attempted a laugh, but it didn't lighten his tone much. "Germaine Gossett too, if you must know."

"So you're nearly all of Cassandra Press."

"Not any longer."

"How's that?"

"Out," Sedgwick said with gloomy humour. "I am. The girls had all the money, and now they've seen our sales figures they've gone off to set up a gay romance publisher."

"What lets them do that?" Boswell heard himself protest.

"Trust."

Boswell could have made plenty of that, but was able to say merely "So my books…"

"Must be somewhere in the future. Don't be more of a pessimist than you have to be, Jack. If I manage to revive Cassandra you know you'll be the first writer I'm in touch with," Sedgwick said, and had the grace to leave close to a minute's silence unbroken before ringing off.

Boswell had no sense of how much the receiver weighed as he lowered it — no sense of anything except some rearrangement that was aching to occur inside his head. He had to know why the news about Cassandra Press felt like a completion so imminent the throbbing of light all but blinded him.

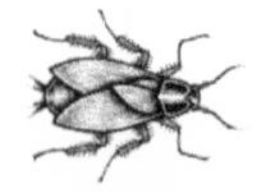

It came to him in the night, slowly. He had been unable to develop the new story because he'd understood instinctively there wasn't one. His sense of the future was sounder than ever: he'd foreseen the collapse of Cassandra Press without admitting it to himself. Ever since his last sight of the Aireys the point had been to save them — he simply hadn't understood how. Living together would only have delayed their fate. He'd needed time to interpret his vision of the shadows on the wall.

He was sure the light in the house was swifter and more intense than dawn used to be. He pushed himself away from the desk and worked aches out of his body before making his way to the bathroom. All the actions he performed there felt like stages of a purifying ritual. In the mid-morning sunlight the phone on his desk looked close to bursting into flame. He winced at the heat of it before, having grown cool in his hand, it ventured to mutter "Hello?"

"Good morning."

"Dad? You sound happier. Are you?"

"As never. Is everyone up? Can we meet?"

"What's the occasion?"

"I want to fix an idea I had last time we met. I'll bring a camera if you can all meet me in the same place in let's say half an hour."

"We could except we haven't got a car."

"Take a cab. I'll reimburse you. It'll be worth it, I promise."

He was on his way almost as soon as he rang off. Tenements reared above his solitary march, but couldn't hinder the sun in its climb towards unbearable brightness. He watched his shadow shrink in front of him like a stain on the dusty littered concrete, and heard footsteps attempting stealth not too far behind him. Someone must have seen the camera slung from his neck. A backward glance as he crossed a deserted potholed junction showed him a youth as thin as a puppet, who halted twitching until Boswell turned away, then came after him.

A taxi sped past Boswell as he reached the street he was bound for. The Aireys were in front of the wall, close to the sooty smudge like a lingering shadow that was the only trace of their car. Gemima clung to her mother's hand while Rod stood a little apart, one fist in his hip pocket. They looked posed and uncertain why. Before anything had time to change, Boswell held up his palm to keep them still and confronted the youth who was swaggering towards him while attempting to seem aimless. Boswell lifted the camera strap over his tingling scalp. "Will you take us?" he said.

The youth faltered barely long enough to conceal an incredulous grin. He hung the camera on himself and snapped the carrying case open as Boswell moved into position, hand outstretched towards the Aireys. "Use the flash," Boswell said, suddenly afraid that otherwise there would be no shadows under the sun at the zenith — that the future might let him down after all. He'd hardly spoken when the flash went off, almost blinding its subjects to the spectacle of the youth fleeing with the camera.

Boswell had predicted this, and even that Gemima would step out a pace from beside her mother. "It's all right," he murmured, unbuttoning his jacket, "there's no film in it," and passed the gun across himself into the hand that had been waiting to be filled. Gemima was first, then April, and Rod took just another second. Boswell's peace deepened threefold as peace came to them. Nevertheless he preferred not to look at their faces as he arranged them against the bricks. He had only seen shadows before, after all.

Though the youth had vanished, they were being watched. Perhaps now the world could see the future Boswell had always seen. He clawed chunks out of the wall until wedging his arm into the gap supported him. He heard sirens beginning to howl, and wondered if the war had started. "The end," he said as best he could for the metal in his mouth. The last thing he saw was an explosion of brightness so intense he was sure it was printing their shadows on the bricks for as long as the wall stood. He even thought he smelled how green it would grow to be.

THE TOWER
Richard Chizmar

This campfire story, for Jimmy Cavanaugh

They found the first body on a Thursday.

A couple of kids on their way home from fishing Hanson Creek stopped at the base of the old water tower to take a leak and almost ended up pissing on the missing girl's Nikes.

In the old days, one of the boys would have stood guard over the body while the other ran into town for help. In these sadly modern times, they did what most other kids would've done: they took out their cell phones, snapped a few pictures to show their friends later, and only then did they call 911 to report their finding.

The police showed up remarkably fast, not even ten minutes later. Three patrol cars almost colliding in a nearby gravel parking lot, before making the short hike to the old water tower. They forgot to bring a roll of police tape — seldom used in a town like Edgewood — so one of the officers had to jog back to his car to retrieve it — which is where he met the girl's hysterical parents.

Some things never change, regardless of the times: news travels fast in a small town.

The officer radioed ahead to warn the others that the girl's parents had arrived and were understandably upset. His Sergeant ordered him to hold them there in the parking lot, but that didn't work out so well, as both Mom and Dad bum-rushed the officer and beat him back to the crime scene by a good forty yards.

Once there, the Dad — a bearded construction foreman of nearly 250 pounds — took one look at his daughter's body sprawled there in the bushes and fainted dead to the ground. The kids whipped out their cell phones, of course, and took more pictures, before they were shooed away by the police, with threats to tell their parents. The boys grabbed their fishing rods and stringer full of crappie and yellow perch and beat it. The entire time, the Mom was down on her knees, eyes closed and praying.

An ambulance arrived a short time later, but the Dad was conscious and back on his feet by then, too distraught to be embarrassed by his fainting. A pair of police officers stood with him by a patrol car, trying to counsel him. The Mom was still off praying in the weeds. It took several more hours for the police to finish their initial investigation and remove the body. In that time, a crowd of townspeople had gathered at the scene. There was incessant whispering and pointing and quite a bit more picture taking. There were also two television reporters and a local newspaperman.

But by dusk, the scene was eerily quiet and practically deserted. A lone officer remained, sitting guard on a folding chair — the kind you might see at a backyard barbecue — reading a magazine by the glow of his flashlight and swatting at mosquitos.

Behind him, lost in the shadows, the old water tower watched over the town.

The dead girl's name was Bethany Hopkins. She was twelve. Tall for her age, nearsighted, and blonde. A straight "A" student, she was also captain of her Swim team and a talented artist. She liked to wear her long hair in braids and was crazy for country music.

Bethany had gone missing the night before. She had eaten pizza for dinner at a friend's house and set out to walk the two blocks home just before eight — but she never made it.

By eight-thirty, her worried parents were combing the neighborhood; her Dad on foot, her Mom behind the wheel of their brand new SUV. By nine-thirty, worry had turned into panic, and they had called in the police. The police did their jobs, and by midnight, every officer in town was on the look-out, a recent school picture of a smiling Bethany Hopkins at their side. Plans were made for a county wide search the next morning, but the two boys discovered Bethany's body before the search could begin. Which explains why the police had been so quick to arrive; they'd all been assembled in the Food Lion parking lot, still going over the details of the upcoming search.

The coroner's report for Bethany Hopkins cited strangulation as the cause of death. There were no signs of sexual abuse or torture. Someone simply choked the life out of the little girl and left here there in the bushes.

The police did their work tirelessly, but there were no leads.

After awhile, people stopped whispering, and life eventually returned to normal.

Until the next body was discovered — and in almost exactly the same spot.

This time by a home-for-the-summer college girl who was jogging along the worn dirt path that snaked through the Hanson Woods and looped past the water tower on its way back toward town.

The old water tower was as much a part of Edgewood as Main Street or the Campus Hills Movie Theater or Tucker's Field, where the annual Summer Carnival and Fall Pumpkin Festival were held. The aging tower stood up there on its hill, overlooking the town, looking all the world like one of H.G. Wells' spindly alien invaders marching over the horizon.

Long ago, when I was a kid, before the trees and thick bramble overtook the slope, we used to sled there on snowy mornings when school was cancelled. I remember playing flashlight tag and kick the can there on countless summer nights, fireflies dancing around our heads, our young, excited voices carrying in the darkness.

Once the woods took over, and the years marched on, the old water tower became known for a different kind of playing.

Instead of sledding, kids snuck up there to party or have bonfires or shoot their father's .22's. Too often, the ground was littered with empty beer cans and broken bottles, left behind and forgotten shoes and shirts and even brassieres. There were stories of drunken fights and carnal abandon and even Satan worshippers in the Summer and Fall of '76.

There were a number of complaints from the older folks who used that stretch of land for daily strolls or bird watching or getting to and from their favorite fishing spots on Hanson Creek, but none of them really made a difference until the local newspaper ran a front page editorial about the issue. That did the trick, though, and soon after, warning signs were posted and the local police added the area to their daily patrol routes.

The bonfires and drinking went away — simply moved somewhere else, of course; kids will be kids — as did most of the litter and trouble. Most, but not all. Things still happened there from time to time. Bad things. People move away, people forget; but I've done neither. I remember…

A local husband, distraught after he discovered his wife was cheating on him with her best friend's husband, jumped to his death from the water tower in 1986.

A decade later, someone climbed the tower in the middle of the night, and spray-painted satanic graffiti all over the damn thing. Goats heads. Pentagrams. Inverted crosses. Pretty much everything except a big red 666. It took three weeks and two budget meetings before the town got its act together and painted over the atrocities.

A few years later, a middle-aged, black woman — a stranger — was found hanging from one of the tower's criss-crossing metal support beams. Neither her identity — nor an explanation — were ever uncovered.

Of course, when a series of dark and mostly unexplainable events occur in the same spot over the course of many years, and most especially when these events occur within the confines of a small town, the spot is inevitably said to be cursed or even haunted — and the old water tower was no exception. Stories spread. Legends grew.

The land around the old water tower was unholy ground; it attracted evil. Ghosts and demons roamed there. It was a backwoods meeting spot for drug runners and gang members traveling on I-95 from New York to Florida. An old witch, her face burned and disfigured, lived somewhere back there in the woods; her cabin hidden amongst the bramble.

A local high school boy even wrote a term paper a number of years ago that spotlighted the area's dark history in great detail. He contended that there was once a slave house that stood on that lonely hill. Long before the water tower ever existed. The slave house was burned to the ground one night by a drunken and enraged master, and everyone inside had perished. Then, during the second world war, while the tower was being built in that very spot, it was reported that a half-dozen workers had either died or been seriously injured during its construction. Workers also reported that dozens of dead animal carcasses were found on the property; a reasonable explanation was never found. As a result, the tower was said to be cursed from the very beginning. Then, there was the story of the newlywed bride who, while on an early morning walk the day after her joyous wedding celebration, was bitten by a mysterious two-headed, red snake while resting in the tower's shadow. The woman died of her wound later that evening, and the snake was never found. There was even a lengthy section discussing the long-rumored worship of devils and demons on the grounds and a handful of witness accounts claiming that the area was haunted by the ghosts of murdered slaves.

There was more, much more — 29 pages in all.

The fact that there were very few truths to be found in this young man's school report did nothing to diminish its impact. The boy received a "B+" on his report (he was said to be a terrible speller) and became a hero of sorts to his fellow students.

And, with the passage of time, as so often is the case, the many stories became truth, the legends became fact.

I would know. Many of the other old-timers moved away or forgot, but not me. No, sir. I've been here since almost the beginning.

My Lord willing, I'll turn eighty-four years old when this chill October rolls around, and I spent just over forty of those years hauling the mail around this town. I've seen it all, and I've heard it all. Trust me, people like to run their mouths and the only person likely to hear more rambling words than a mailman is the bartender down at Loughlin's Pub. But I've learned that drunk people mostly tell lies and folks standing in their sunny front yards holding onto their mail mostly tell the truth — or at least the truth as they believe it.

Lot of folks around this town think I'm just a friendly, old, senile man. They say their polite hellos and offer up their polite waves and keep right on going when they pass me on the sidewalk.

And they might be right, you know it.

But, don't you forget what i said: I have seen things.

The second body was discovered in plain sight. In fact, according to police, the whole thing looked staged.

Our resident home-from-college girl, a bright young lady named Jennifer Ward studying to become a teacher, came jogging around the bend — and stopped dead in her tracks. Her iPod tumbled from her hand down to the ground, yanking her headphones right out of her ears. Justin Timberlake broke the morning silence.

Everyone in town knew Gina Sharretts. She taught math at the local high school and coached the field hockey team.

Gina's limp body lay propped up against one of the water tower's rusting metal legs, her hands folded neatly in her lap. She could have been sleeping if it weren't for her hideously bulging eyes and the dark bruising around her swollen neck.

Jennifer snatched up her iPod and headphones and took off at a sprint. If campus life had taught her one thing, it was that safety was in numbers. Out on the road, she flagged down the first approaching car, and told the driver to call the police.

The patrol cars arrived a short time later, and once again out came the police tape and the picture-takers and the lookie loos, and this time around, it was a distraught brother and sister — Gina was thirty-seven and single on the day of her death — crashing the crime scene.

Once again, in the frantic days that followed, the police did their jobs and did them well — but there were still no leads.

Someone had simply strangled the life out of Gina Sharretts…

…just as someone had strangled the life out of Bethany Hopkins three years earlier.

And left them both there at the base of the water tower.

This clear pattern escaped no one's notice, of course. Most especially that of the police and the press. But even this discovery seemed to lead nowhere. Just one more dead end street in another dead end investigation.

This time it took longer for the town to return to normal.

People were angry and paranoid. Old grudges and suspicions gained new life. Brand new grudges and suspicions were born. There were more drunken fights down at Loughlin's Pub on Friday and Saturday nights. More arguments and mean-spirited gossip between sunburned moms at the community pool.

Interestingly enough, it was the adults responsible for most of the bad behavior. It was summer break, and most of the teenagers chose to hang out together at the quarry or the Dairy Queen or over in Fallston at the new shopping mall. They seemed to feel safer together, and whether they were a fan of Miss Sharrett's math class or not, there was an unspoken agreement that they had lost one of their own.

It was a strange time to live in Edgewood. The constant police presence made it so, as did the daily newspaper headlines and the local television updates. There was no new information, so the news folk simply chewed up the old information to tiny pieces and spit it back out.

Most days were too hot and humid for an old man like me to spend outside, so I usually sat in my glassed-in back porch and drank iced tea and read my paperbacks. Old oaters, mostly, with the occasional spy novel thrown in for good measure. I used to like mysteries and thrillers, but I was a younger and braver man back then.

On mild evenings, I liked to walk down to the park and sit on one of the benches and watch the town wind down for the day. I'd watch the shop owners flip the OPEN signs to CLOSED (or in most cases now, they simply turned off their glowing red electronic signs). I'd watch the lovers stroll down Main Street hand in hand or arm in arm. The mothers and fathers hurrying after their racing children to stand in line at the Dairy Queen. The tired factory workers shuffling into Loughlin's Pub to drink their paychecks as the streetlights blinked on behind them.

To a stranger, it may have appeared to be a Norman Rockwell-ish scene of small town serenity; the kind of golden-tinted picture that makes city slickers wish they could pull up roots and move to a place like Edgewood. But if you stopped and looked closer, *really* looked, you could see the lovers holding onto each other a little tighter than was necessary; the Moms and Dads hurrying after their children, not with relaxed smiles on their faces, but expressions of worry and concern; the workers looking more defeated and angry than tired; and what kind of stores closed up for the night at 7pm, before it was even dark outside? And then there were the patrol cars making their way up and down Main Street with a much higher regularity than anyone would believe necessary for such a small town.

I saw all this — and more — from my park bench. Most evenings I spent in solitude; a silent observer. But some nights folks would do more than just flip me a wave or mutter a hurried "hello." Sometimes, they'd stop and chat for a moment or two, and once in a great while, someone would even sit down next to me on my bench and chew my ear for a time. Usually it was just Mrs. Brown from the library or Frankie from the barbershop, but it was real nice to have company on those nights.

Company kept me from letting my gaze wander...over to the western outskirts of town...where the water tower stood like some kind of dark sentinel.

Company kept me from thinking too much, and remembering...

I used to sled there as a child. I shot my first squirrel in those woods. I used to play kids' games there at night, the air filled with the laughs and screams of happy children. We used to climb the tower's lower beams and dangle from our legs like toy monkeys on a playground. Kids were kids. Knees got scuffed. Bodies got bruised. The occasional bone got broken. But no one died. Not when we were kids. I never even had an inkling that the place was bad.

Until many years later.

I moved away from Edgewood when I was eighteen years old. Six long, miserable years in the Army, and back home I scurried just as fast as my legs could carry me. My Momma was still alive then, and my baby sister, Amelia, too. I settled back into my old bedroom and took a job at the shoe factory, which was a blessing because that's where I met my Beth Anne, God rest her soul. It would be another four years before I started delivering the mail; that didn't happen until sweet old Ralph Jenkins passed in his sleep, leaving the job opening for me to step in and fill.

Anyway, it was probably a month — a happy month, too, believe me — after I came back home from the Army that I found myself standing at the base of that water tower staring up at its expanse. To be honest, and despite seeing the tower outlined in the sky every damn day on my way to and from work, I had mostly forgotten all about the old thing and the times I had spent there.

But that evening I was on my way to Hanson Creek to try my luck for catfish when I stumbled upon it. I stopped and glanced up, and then I slowly turned and looked around me at the woods and the wild bramble — and the tiny hairs on the back of my neck went all tingly. I've read about that kind of thing happening in countless paperbacks, but I never believed it until that night.

I spun in a slow circle, looking all around, suddenly sure that someone — or something *— was hiding there, watching me. I started to hurry away, but then something else stopped me. I stood there, trying to figure it out: was there a smell? was the light somehow different? why was it so quiet all of a sudden? where were the damn birds?*

And then it struck me — there was something wrong with the air. *I know how that sounds, but I swear to you it's true. There was a* thinness *to it, almost like being two places at once, like there was another world underneath this one.*

I stood there and I swear on my Momma's family bible that I could almost see glimpses of movement in the shadows; that I could hear whispered snatches of words in the empty air right beside me.

I thought of the Ray Bradbury stories I loved so much as a young man, tales of faraway worlds and the mysteries that existed right next door to all of us. It could have been a magical experience…

...but this was different.

I realized that I was frightened.

This was a bad place, and I had just had my first real glimpse of it.

I remembered all this sitting there in the park at dusk, but I didn't want to. Lord, no, I didn't.

I have seen things in my lifetime.

And I have done things.

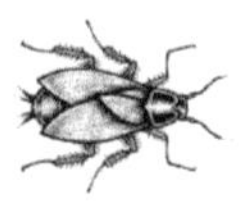

Reverend Parker never made it to the church last night to give Evening Mass. There aren't a lot of secrets in a small town, so most people knew that Reverend Parker was a drinker. He would occasionally be a few minutes late to Mass or Wednesday night bingo, and on rarer occasions you might even catch a whiff of whiskey on his breath when he passed you on the street — but he had never missed Mass before.

Still, most of his parishioners weren't overly concerned. Sure, that old bitty Clara Lotz was put off by his absence and told everyone within earshot exactly that; she had better things to do than wait around for someone who didn't even have the decency to show up to do their job. And poor Hannah Pinborough was visibly worried that she might go to hell without her usual Thursday night worship. But most folks just shrugged their shoulders and went on their merry way.

If it weren't for Sophie Connolly, the church secretary, and a renowned worry-wart, the police probably wouldn't have been notified until long into the next day. Instead, after repeated calls with no answer, Sophie drove to the Reverend's house, used her key to open the front door, and upon finding the house empty, called the police to report the Reverend missing.

She happened to glance at the kitchen clock when she hung up the phone and noticed that the time was 7:13pm.

According to official reports, the police discovered the Reverend's body at 7:29pm.

They had obviously wasted little time before searching the woods surrounding the old water tower — as if they expected to find something there.

And they did.

Reverend Parker was tied spread-eagle to the four foundation posts of the old water tower with four lengths of thick robe. His eyes and mouth were open obscenely wide, a smudge of dried blood crusted his nostrils, and there was severe bruising on his neck. He was still dressed in his preaching clothes, but the gold crucifix he always wore was no where to be found. His bible lay on his chest.

The press had a field day. *Why hadn't the water tower been staked out? Why were there no leads? Was it a serial killer? Why in a place like Edgewood? If the Reverend wasn't safe, who was?*

Stores started closing their doors even earlier. The police and town council were said to be considering a curfew. The Dairy Queen laid off two of the summer help because there weren't enough hours to keep them working. A front page editorial in the newspaper called for the Sheriff's firing.

In the end, the town council called for a Town Meeting on Friday night "to clear the air and inform the townspeople of the appropriate measures which were being taken." Those were the mayor's word, not mine, let me tell you.

Friday night was almost a week away, and most folks weren't buying the "appropriate measures" story. They knew the Sheriff was just trying to buy some time, and who could blame him?

Something very wrong was going on in our town.

Something very bad.

I thought I had a good idea what it was, but there was no one I could tell.

There was no one who would believe me.

I told you before…I've seen and done things.

Things I'm not proud of, nor fully understand.

I thought I'd forgotten most of it; that the passing years and the burning shame and guilt had erased it from my memory, leaving me a simple old man living out the rest of my days in the town that gave birth to me.

I kept to myself all these years, read my books, minded my business, prayed every night. I tried to be a good person and live a good life. I didn't dare pray for redemption, only peace.

I knew I wasn't that man anymore.

That man who had been infected by whatever evil dwelled in that miserable stretch of land beneath that old damn tower.

That man who had been cursed to hear its calling...and proved too weak to ignore it.

That man who had not only heard its calling, but *listened* to it...

Finally luring a stranger there under the pretense of liquid and carnal sins — only to bludgeon her soft skull until it cracked like an egg from my Momma's coop. I buried her that night in the soft, dark soil behind the tower and went home to my own bed.

Only to awaken and complete this horrible act again...and again...and again.

But not without remorse; not without judgment.

I dreamed many nights of killing myself. Or leaving this town and never coming back. I even considered turning myself in to the police. Once, I went so far as to write my own confession, but I burned it to ashes before I could find the courage or conviction.

I realized that I didn't control my own thoughts anymore than I did my own actions.

These thoughts — and my soul — belonged to someone else. *Something* else.

Until my Beth Anne somehow saved me.

I did not — could not — confess my sins to her, but she knew I was struggling; she somehow knew I was in a battle for my soul.

I don't know why my prayers were suddenly answered or why the voices suddenly vanished. I can only believe it was the immense goodness in my wife's heart and her undying faith in her Lord and in me that was responsible. Beth Anne led me back to God and saved me; she saved my very soul. I have no other explanation.

I only know that the things I saw standing there in the *thin* air surrounding that wretched old tower were not of this world; not of any world that contained even a sliver of goodness.

It was an evil, *hungry* place.

In the years that followed, I prayed more than ever before and did my research. I found no record of a slave house or any other building having existed atop that hill. Two men did die during construction of the water tower, and a third worker was killed during an argument with another worker. There were also many credible reports of animal carcasses being found on the property. Not surprisingly, most of the devil worshipping stories turned out to be nothing but rumors and campfire stories; nothing was substantiated.

I believe now it is the ground itself that is *wrong*. It acts as some sort of mysterious conduit, perhaps even a portal or a doorway to another world or dimension. I believe it allows whatever it is that dwells in that other world to control its chosen one in this world. Why it demands blood? I do not know. The tower itself remains another mystery to me. Does it act as a sort of lure to attract people there, so there are higher numbers to choose from? If so, why was I selected? What did it sense inside me?

I don't know these answers — and that is a blessing.

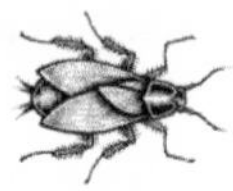

Can you guess now how this story will end?

There will be another body soon, of course.

And they will find it sprawled there beneath that stupid old water tower.

I see the tower silhouetted against the western sky most mornings. I watch the setting sun paint it a golden shade of orange most evenings. But I haven't placed a single foot in its shadow for close to four decades.

Someone else has been chosen; I know that now.

Stranger or friend, I do not know, nor do I wish to.

I pray myself to sleep every night.

I pray for the lost soul of the chosen one.

I pray for the lost soul of this town.

And I pray for the deceased.

But most of all, I pray that I don't wake up one morning and feel the urge to slip on my walking boots and pick up my cane and make the long walk up that hill again.

2055
Republic of Sacramento
Carrier Territories

Nayima's sleep had turned restless as she aged, so the rattling from the chicken coop outside woke her before her hens raised the alarm. The intruder was likely either feline or human, and she hoped it was the former. A cat, no matter how big, wasn't as dangerous as a person.

Nayima ignored the sharp throb in her knee when she jumped from her bed and ran outside with her sawed-off in time to see a hound-sized tabby scurrying away with a young hen pinned in its teeth, a snow globe of downy white feathers trailing behind. The army of night cats scattered in swishing bushes and brittle leaves. The giant thief paused to look back at her, his eyes glowing gold with threat. The cats were getting bigger.

Nayima had been saving that hen for Sunday dinner, but she was too winded to chase the thief. Now both knees throbbed. And her lower back, right on schedule. She fired once into the dark and hoped she'd hit him.

Fucking cats.

The dark was thick to the forsaken east, but to the west she saw the gentle orange glow from the colony in Sacramento, the fortress she would never enter. The town folk had electricity to spare, since their lights never went fully dark anymore. They were building a real-life Emerald City from the ruins, with bright lights and fresh water flowing in the streets — literally, after the levees flooded back in the '20s.

By contrast, her tract, Nayimaland, was two-hundred acres of dead farmland she shared with feral cats made bold because food was scarce — taken by drought, not the Plague. The late State of California had yet more dying to do.

Nayima felt thirsty, but she didn't stop at her sealed barrel to take a scoop. She couldn't guess how long her standing water would have to last. Sacramento owed her water credits, but she would be a fool to trust their promises.

At the rear of the chicken coop, Nayima found the hole the cat had torn in the mesh and lashed loose wires to close it. The hens were unsettled, so she could expect broken eggs. And she couldn't afford to cook one of her reliable laying hens, so she'd have to wait for meat at least another week, until trading day.

By the time Nayima came back to her porch, her two house cats, Tango and Buster, had gathered enough courage to poke their heads up in the window. For an instant, her pets looked like the thief cat, no better.

"It's okay, babies," she said. "One of 'em got a chicken."

Buster, still aloof, raised his tail good night and went to his sofa. But Tango followed her to her bedroom and jumped beside her to sleep. Nayima preferred a bare mattress to the full bed that had been in this room — fewer places for intruders to hide and surprise her. She slept beneath the window, where she could always open her eyes and see the sky. Tango rested his weight against her; precious warmth and a thrumming heartbeat to calm her nerves.

"I can't feed you all," she told Tango. "I'm crazy for taking in just you two."

Tango slowly blinked his endless green eyes at her, his cat language for love. Nayima returned Tango's long, slow blink.

Nayima thought the jangling bells outside soon after dawn meant that a cat had been caught in a cage, but when she went to investigate, she found Raul's mud-painted red pickup slewed across the dirt path to her ranch house. He was cursing in Spanish. His front tire had caught a camouflaged cage, and he was stooping to check the damage. At least a dozen sets of cats' eyes floated like marbles in the dry shrubbery.

"Don't shoot!" Raul called to her. He knew she had her little sawed-off without looking back. "You'll blow off your own culo with that rusty thing one day. ¿Es todo, Nayima?"

Despite the disturbance and his complaining, Nayima was glad to see Raul. He looked grand in morning sunshine. Raul's eyes drooped slightly, giving the impression of drowsiness, but he was handsome, with a fine jaw and silvering hair he wore in two long braids like his Apache forebears. Since reconciliation and the allotment of the Carrier Territories eight years ago, Raul looked younger every time she saw him.

Nayima had turned sixty-one or sixty-two in December — she barely tracked her age anymore — and she and Raul were among the youngest left, so most carriers had died before the territories were allotted. In their human cages.

Captivity had been their repayment for the treatment and vaccine from the antibodies in their blood. They were outcasts, despite zero human transmissions of the virus after Year One. The single new case twenty-five years ago had been a lab accident, and the serum had knocked it out quick.

The Ward B carriers Nayima had barely known still lived communally, or close enough to walk to each other's ranches. But Nayima had chosen seclusion on an airy expanse of unruly farmland that stretched as far as she could see. In containment, she'd never had the luxury of community, except Raul. She had enough human contact on her market trips, where she made transactions through a wall. Or her hour-long ride on her ATV to see Raul, if she wanted conversation. Other people wearied her.

"Sorry — cat problem," she told Raul. "Did it rip?" She had a few worn tires in her shed from the previous owner, but they were at least forty years old.

Raul exhaled, relieved. "No, creo que está bien."

She squatted beside him, close enough to smell the sun on his clothes. She had not seen Raul in at least thirty days. He had begged her to share his house, but she had refused. She needed to talk to him from time to time, but she remembered why she did not want to live with him, and why she had slept with him only once: Raul's persistent recollections about his old neighborhood in Rancho Cucamonga and his grandparents' house in Nogales were unbearable. He always wanted to talk about the days before the Plague.

But after forty years, he was family. He'd been a gangly fifteen-year-old when the lab-coats captured him. Shivering and crying, he had webbed his fingers to reach toward her hand against the sheet of glass.

Nayima missed skin. She felt sorry for the new children, being raised not to touch. She absently ran her fingertips along the dirt-packed ridges in the tire's warm rubber.

"Do you have meat?" she said.

"Five pounds of dried beef," he said. Nayima didn't care much for beef, but meat was meat. "In the back of the truck. And a couple of water barrels."

Water barrels? A gift that large probably wasn't from Raul alone, and she didn't like owing anyone.

"From Sacramento?"

"You're doing a school talk today, I heard. Liaison's office asked me to come out."

Nayima's temper flared. She could swear she'd felt a *ping* at her right temple an hour before, waking her from fractured sleep. The lab-coats denied that they abused her tracking chip, but was it a coincidence she had a school obligation that day? And how dare they send so little water!

Nayima was so angry that her first words came in Spanish, because she wanted Raul's full attention. He had taught her Spanish, just as she had taught him so much else, patient lessons through locked doors. "Que me deben créditos, Raul. They owe a lot more than two barrels."

"You'll get your créditos. This is just…" He waved his hand, summoning the right word. Then he gave up. "Por favor, Nayima. Take them. You earned them." He tested the air pressure in his tire with a pound of his fist. "Gracias a Díos this is okay."

Nayima's shaky faith had been shattered during the Plague, but Raul still held fast to his God. *He told us the Apocalypse was coming in Revelation*, he always said, as if that excused it all. Nayima still believed Sunday dinner should be special, but only to honor the memory of her grandmother's weekly feasts.

Two new orange water barrels stood in the bed of Raul's truck. Large ones. She needed more credits to get her faucets running, but the barrels would last a while. Nayima climbed up, grabbing the bed's door to swing her leg over. She winced at the pain in her knees as she landed. She treasured the freedom to move her body, but movement came with a cost.

"¿Estás bien, querida?" Raul said.

"Just my knees. Stop fussing."

Nayima fumbled with an unmarked plastic crate tied beside the closest barrel.

"Don't open that yet," Raul said.

But she already had. Inside, she found the beef, wrapped in paper and twine. Still not quite dry, judging by the grease spots.

But she forgot the jerky when she saw two dolls, both long-haired girls, one with brown skin, one white. The dolls' hands were painted with blue plastic gloves, but nothing else. They had lost their clothes, lying atop a folded, obscenely pink blanket.

"What the hell's this?" Nayima said.

Raul walked closer as if he carried a heavy sack of across his shoulders. "I wanted to talk to you," he said, voice low. He reached toward her. "Come down. Walk with me."

"Bullshit," she said. "Why is Sacramento sending me dolls?"

"Bejar de la truck," Raul insisted. "Por favor. Let's walk. I have to tell you something."

Nayima was certain Raul had sold her out in some way, she just couldn't guess how. Raul had always been more willing to play political games; he'd been so much younger when he'd been found, raised without knowing any better. So Raul's house had expensive solar panels that kept his water piping hot and other niceties she did not bother to covet. His old pickup truck, which ran on precious ethanol and gasoline, was another of his luxuries for the extra time and blood he was always willing to give the lab-coats.

Nayima climbed out of the truck more carefully than she'd climbed in, refusing Raul's aid. Living in small spaces for most of her life had left her joints irritable and stiff, even with daily exercises to loosen them. If she'd had the energy or balance, she would have shoved Raul down on his ass.

"Start talking," she said. "What have you done?"

"Put the gun down first."

Nayima hadn't realized she was pointing the shotgun at him. She lowered it. "Tell me ahora, Raul. No hay más secretos." Raul's secrets stung more than anyone else's.

"I won a ruling," Raul said.

"About what? Free toys?"

Raul stared out toward the thirsty grasslands. "I have a library portal at my house..." he began.

Of course he did. Toys and gadgets. That was Raul.

Raul went on. "I did some research on...the embryos."

Nayima's cheek flared as if he'd struck her. During Reconciliation, she and Raul had learned that dozens of embryos had been created from her eggs and his sperm, more than they'd known. They had been the cocktail du joir; something about their blood types. Her heart gave a sudden sick tumbling in her chest, as if to drown him out.

"There's a bebé, Nayima," he said, whispering like wind. "One survived."

The world went white. Her eyesight, her thoughts, lost.

"What? When?"

"She just turned four," he said. "She's still in the research compound."

There was a *she* somewhere?

"How long have you known?"

"Six months," he said. "When I got the portal. I saw rumors of the surviving infant, did the research. She's one of ours. They never told us."

Now Nayima's sacrifices seemed fresh: the involuntary harvesting of her eggs, three first-trimester miscarriages after forced insemination, a succession of unviable embryos created in labs, and two premature live births of infants from artificial wombs who had never survived beyond a day. Pieces of her chopped away.

"We can't reproduce," she said.

"But one lived," Raul said. "They don't know why."

"You've known all this time? And you never told me?"

He sighed. "Lo siento, Nayima. I hated hiding it. But I knew it would upset you. Or you might work against me. I didn't want to say anything until I got a ruling. As the biological father, I have rights."

"Carriers don't have rights."

"Parental rights," Raul said. "For the first time — yes, we do."

Nayima despised herself for her volcanic emotions. How could Raul be naïve enough to believe Sacramento's lies? If there was a surviving child — which she did not believe — they would not release their precious property to carriers.

"It's a trick," she said. "To get us to go back there."

Raul shook his head slowly. Impossibly, he smiled. "No, Nayima," he said. "They're sending her to us. To you. She's free under Reconciliation to be with her parents. All you have to do is sign the consent when they come."

Nayima needed to sit, so she ignored her sore joints and sat where she'd been standing, on the caked dirt of her road. The air felt thick and heavy in her lungs.

"No," Nayima said. Saying the word gave her strength. "No no no. We can't. It's a trap. Even if there's a girl…" It was so improbable, Nayima could barely say the words. "And there isn't… But even if there is, why would they offer her except as a weapon against us? To threaten us? To control us? Why do they keep trying so hard to make children from us? She's not from my womb, so she doesn't have the antibodies. Think about it! We're just…reserves for them. A blood supply, if they ever need it. That's the only reason we're still alive."

Raul's eyes dropped. He couldn't deny it.

"She's our child," Raul said. "Ella es nuestra bebé. We can't leave her there."

"You can't — but I can," she said. "Watch me."

Raul's voice cracked. "The ruling says both living parents must consent. I need you with me on this, Nayima."

"I'm an old woman now!" Nayima said. Her throat burned hot.

"And I'm fifty-six," Raul said. "But we had una hija together. The marshals are bringing her here tomorrow."

"You're sending marshals to me?" The last time marshals came to see her in the territories after only nine months, a pack of them had removed her from the house she had chosen and stolen half of her chickens, shooting a dozen dead just for fun. Her earliest taste of freedom had been a false start, victim to a government property dispute.

"Marshals aren't like they were," Raul said. "Things are changing, Nayima." Like he was scolding her.

Raul lowered the truck's bed door and pulled out the plastic crate. He carried it to her porch. Next, he took down the barrels and rolled them to the house one by one. The heavy barrels thundered across the soil.

When he returned, breathing hard, Nayima was on her feet again, with her gun. She jacked a shell into the chamber.

"You could've shot me before I did all that work," Raul said.

"I'm not shooting you yet," she said. "But any marshals that show up here tomorrow are declaring war. They might bring her, but they could take her at any time. We're all property! I won't give them that power over me. She's better off dead. I'm not afraid to die too."

Raul gave her a forlorn look before he walked past her and slammed the bed of his truck shut. "I was hoping for some eggs, pero maybe mañana."

"I swear to your God, Raul, I will kill anyone who comes to this house."

Raul opened his driver's side door and began to climb back inside, but he stopped to look at her over his shoulder. He had left his truck idling. He had never planned to stay long.

"She doesn't have a name," he said.

"What?"

"Nobody bothered to name her. In the records, she's called Specimen 120. Punto. Some of the researchers call her Chubby for a nickname. Like a pet, Nayima. Our hija."

The weight of the shotgun made Nayima's arms tremble.

"Don't bring anyone here," she said. "Please."

Raul got in the truck and slammed the door. He lurched into reverse, turned the truck away, and drove. Nayima fired once into the air, a roar of rage that echoed across the flatlands. The shotgun kicked in her arms like an angry baby.

After the engine's hum was lost in the open air, the only sound was Nayima's wretched sobs.

In her front room, Nayima's comm screen flared white, turning itself on. A minder waited in five-by-five on her wall, as though she'd been invited to breakfast. The light haloing her was bright enough to show old acne stars. Makeup had yet to make a comeback, except the enhanced red lips favored by both men and women. Full of life.

"Hello, Nayima," the minder said. Then she corrected herself: "Ms. Dixon."

Nayima nodded cordially. Nayima's grandmother, born in Alabama, had never stood for being called by her first name, and neither did Nayima — an admittedly old-fashioned trait at a time when numbers mattered more than names.

The minder seemed to notice Nayima's puffed eyes, and her polite veneer dulled. "You remember the guidelines?"

Guideline One and Only: She was not to criticize the lab-coats or make it sound as if she had been treated badly. Blah blah blah and so forth. Questions about the embryo — the *girl* — broiled in Nayima's mind, but she didn't dare bring her up. Maybe the marshals wouldn't come. Maybe she could still get her water credits.

"Yes," Nayima said, testing her thin voice.

"We added younger students this year," the minder said. "Stand by."

Three smaller squares appeared inset beneath the girl's image — classrooms, the children progressively older in each. The far left square held the image of twelve wriggling, worming children ages about three to six sprawled across a floor with a red mat. A few in the front sat transfixed by her image on what seemed to be a looming screen, high above them. Every child wore tiny, powder blue plastic gloves.

Nayima had to look away from the smallest children. She had not seen children so young in forty years, and the sight of them was acid to her eyes.

Hadn't Raul said the girl was four?

Nayima blinked rapidly, her eyes itching with tears.

Crying, she was certain, was against the guidelines.

Nayima willed herself to look at the young, moony faces, braving memories of tiny bodies rotting on sidewalks, in cars, on the roadways, mummified in closets. These were new children — untouched by Plague. Their parents had been the wealthy, the isolated, the truly Chosen — the infinitesimal number of survivors who were not carriers, who did not have the antibodies, but had simply, somehow, survived.

Nayima leaned closer to her screen. "Boo!" she said.

Young eyes widened with terror. Children scooted away.

But when Nayima smiled, the entire mass of them quivered with laughter, a sea of perfect teeth.

Nayima's teeth were not perfect. She had never replaced the lower front tooth she'd lost to a lab-coat she'd smacked across his nose, drawing blood. He'd strapped her to a table, raped her, and extracted her tooth on the spot, without anesthesia.

Nayima had been offered a dental implant during Reconciliation, but a new tooth felt like a lie, so she had refused. In previous classroom visits, she had answered the question *What happened to your tooth?* without bitterness — why should she feel contempt for brutes any more than she would a tree dropping leaves? — until a minder pointed out that the anecdote about her extracted tooth violated the guidelines.

The guidelines left Nayima with very little to say. She chose each word with painful care.

These schoolchildren asked the usual questions: why she had survived (genetic predisposition), how many people she had infected (only one personally, as far as she knew), how many carriers were left (fifteen, since most known carriers were "gone now"). By the fourth question, Nayima had lost her will to look at the children's faces. It was harder all the time.

The girl who spoke up next was not yet eight. Her face held a whisper of brown; a girl who might have been hers. And Raul's.

"Do you have any children?" the girl said.

All of Nayima's work, gone. No composure. No smile. A sharp pain in her belly.

"No, I've never had children," she said. "None that survived."

Nayima shot a pointed gaze at the minder, who did not contradict her. Maybe the minder didn't know about Specimen 120. Maybe a bureaucrat had made up the story to tease Raul.

"Okay," the girl said, shrugging, not yet schooled in the art of condolences. "What do you miss the most about the time before the Plague?"

An easy answer came right away, and it almost wasn't a lie. "Halloween."

When she explained what Halloween had been, the children sat literally open-mouthed. She wondered which part of her story most stupefied them. The ready access to sweets? The trust of strangers? The costumes?

The host looked relieved with the children's enchantment and announced that the visit was over. A flurry of waving blue gloves. Nayima waved back. She even smiled again.

"Don't forget my water credits," Nayima said from behind her happy teeth.

But the minder's image had already flashed away.

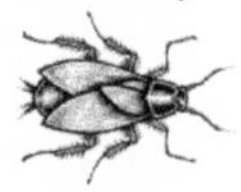

Nayima lined up her contraband on the front table — the sawed-off, a box of shells, an old Colt she'd found in the attic with its full magazine, the baseball bat she kept at her bedside. She'd even found a gas mask she'd bartered for at market. When the marshals came, she would be prepared. In her younger years, she would have boarded up at least her front windows, but her weapons would have to do.

"Raul is the real child," she told Tango and Buster while they watched her work. Buster swatted at a loose shell at the edge of the table, but Nayina caught it before it hit the floor. "He believes every word they say. 'Things are changing,' he says. Believing in miracles. Sending marshals here — to me!"

Tango mewed softly. A question.

"Of course they're not bringing a child here," she said. "A judge's ruling? In favor of carriers? You know the lab-coats would fight to keep her." She shook her head, angry with herself for her weakness. "Besides, there is no child. Babies with carrier genes don't live."

The crate was light enough to lift to the table with only slight pressure in her lower back, gone when she stretched. But she could only roll a barrel slowly, oh-so-slowly, across her threshold. How had Raul managed so easily? She left the second barrel outside. By the time she closed her door again, her lower back pulsed with pain and she felt aged by a decade.

"Lies," Nayima said.

Tango and Buster agreed with frenzied mews.

She would have no Sunday dinner if she died tomorrow, Nayima reminded herself. So she got her cleaver from the kitchen, unwrapped the beef, and began chopping the meat on the table, not caring about dents in the wood. She chopped until she was perspiring and sweat stung her eyes.

Nayima held a chunk with both hands and sank in her teeth. She mostly did not bother with salt in her own cooking, so the taste was overwhelming at first. The cats gnawed at the meat beside her on the table with loud purrs.

"Could there be a child?"

Suppose they'd had a breakthrough, found a way to rewire the genes? But why go through that trouble and expense when other children were being born? The girl must be a failed experiment. A laboratory fluke. Did they need caretakers for a child born with half a brain — was that it? Nayima swore she'd be damned if she'd spend the years she had left tending the lab-coats' mistakes.

"But there is no child," she reminded Tango and Buster. "It's all a lie."

After dark, with her flashlight to guide her, Nayima set her traps for the thief cat with slices of meat and visited the wooden chicken coop Raul had helped her build, as big as her grandmother's backyard shed. She checked the loose wires in the rear, but the hole was still secure. She hadn't collected eggs earlier, so chickens had defecated on some. A few eggs lay entirely crushed, yolks seeping across the straw.

Nayima was exhausted by the time she'd cleaned the nestboxes, scrubbed the surviving eggs, and set them on a bowl on her kitchen for Raul to find later — but she couldn't afford to sleep tonight. The marshals might come at any time.

Nayima fixed herself a cup from of black tea from her new water — so fresh! — and sat vigil by her front window with her shotgun, watching the empty pathway. Sometimes her eyes played tricks, animating the darkness. A far-off cat's cry sounded like a baby's, waking Nayima when she dozed.

Just before dawn, bells jingled near the chicken coop. Heart clambering, Nayima ran outside. The food was gone from the first trap she reached, but the door had not properly sprung. Shit.

More frantic jingling came from the trap twenty yards farther. Nayima raced toward it, her light in one hand and her gun in the other.

A pair of eyes glared out at her from beyond the bars.

The cat scrambled to every corner of the cage, desperate to escape while bells mocked him. This was the one. Nayima recognized the monster tabby's unusual size.

"Buddy, you stole the wrong chicken."

Nayima could not remember the last time she had felt so giddy. She carefully lowered her flashlight to the ground, keeping it trained on the trap. Then she raised her shotgun, aiming. She'd blow a hole in her trap this way, but she had caught the one she was looking for.

The cat mewed — not angry, beseeching. With a clear understanding of his situation.

"You started it, not me," Nayima said. "Don't sit there begging now."

The cat's trapped eyes glowed in her bright beam. Another plaintive mew.

"Shut up, you hear me? This is your fault." But her resolve was flagging.

The cat raised his paw, shaking the cage door. How many times had she done the very same thing? How many locks had she tested, searching for freedom?

Could there really be a child?

Nayima sobbed. Her throat was already raw from crying. Never again, she had said. No more tears. No more.

Nayima went to the trap's door and flipped up the latch. The cat hissed at her and raced away like a jaguar, melting into the dark. She hoped he would run for miles, never looking back.

Is my little girl with those zookeepers without even a name?

"But it's all lies," she whispered at the window, as she stroked Tango in her lap. "Isn't it?"

Dawn came and went with the roosters' crowing. Nayima did not move to collect the morning eggs, or to eat any of the beef she and the cats had left, or to empty her bulging bladder. She watched the sky light up her empty pathway, her open gate.

Why hadn't she closed the gate?

Based on the sun high above, it was nearly noon when Nayima finally stood up.

The metallic glint far down the roadway looked imaginary at first. To be sure, Nayima wiped away dust on her window pane with her shirt, although the spots outside still clouded it. The gleam seemed to vanish, but then it was back, this time with bright cobalt blue lights that looked out of place against the browns and grays of the road. Two sets of blue lights danced in regimented patterns, back and forth.

Nayima's breath fogged her window as she leaned closer, so she wiped it again.

Hoverbikes!

Two large hoverbikes were speeding toward her house, one on each side of the road at a matching pace, blue lights snaking across their underbellies. At least it wasn't an army, unless more were coming. Marshals' hoverbikes were only big enough for two, at most.

"You damn fool, Raul," she whispered again, but she already had forgiven him too.

Nayima was too exhausted to pick up her shotgun. She had failed the test with her cat thief, so what made her think she could fight marshals? Let them take what they wanted. As long as she had Tango and Buster, she could start again. She always did.

As the hoverbikes flew past her gate, Nayima counted one front rider on each bike in the marshals' uniform: black jackets with orange armbands. The second rider on the lead bike was only Raul — his face was hidden behind the black helmet, but she knew his red hickory shirt.

His father had worn one just like it, Raul had told her until she wanted to scream.

"Nayima!" Raul called. He flung his helmet to the ground.

The hoverbike Raul was riding hadn't quite slowed to a stop, floating six inches above the ground, so Raul stumbled when he leaped off in a hurry. The marshal grabbed his arm to help hold him steady while the bike bobbing obediently in place.

"Querida, it's me," Raul said. "Don't worry about the marshals. Please open the door."

Nayima stared as both marshals took off their helmets, almost in unison, and rested them in the crooks of their arms. One was a young man, one a woman, neither older than twenty-five. The man was fair-haired and ruddy. The woman's skin was nearly as dark as her own, her hair also trimmed to fuzz. Had she seen this man during an earlier classroom visit? He looked familiar, and he was smiling. They both were. She had never seen a marshal smile.

The marshals wore no protective suits. No masks. They did not hide their faces or draw weapons. Even ten yards away, through a dirty window, Nayima saw their eyes.

Nayima jumped when Raul banged on her door. "Nayima, ella está aqui!"

"I don't see her." Nayima tried to shout, but her throat nearly strangled her breath.

Raul motioned to the woman marshal, and she dismounted her hoverbike. For the first time, Nayima saw her bike's passenger — not standing, but in a backward facing seat. A child stirred as the woman unstrapped her.

It couldn't be. *Couldn't* be.

Nayima closed her eyes. Had they drugged her meat? Was it a hallucination?

"Do you see, Nayima?" Raul said. "Ven afuera conmigo. Please come."

Raul left her porch to run back to the hoverbike. Freed from her straps, a child reached out for a hand for Raul's help from the seat. Raul made a game of it, lifting the child up high. Curly spirals of dark hair nestled her shoulders. For an instant, the child was silhouetted in the sunlight, larger than life in Raul's sturdy upward grasp.

The girl giggled loudly enough for Nayima to hear her through the window pane. Raul was a good father. Nayima could see it already.

"Now you're going to meet your mamí," Raul said.

Nayima hid behind her faded draperies as Raul took the girl's hand and walked to the porch with her. When she heard the twin footsteps on her wooden planks, Nayima's world swayed. She ventured a peek and saw the girl's inquisitive face turned toward the window — dear Jesus, this angel had Gram's nose and plump, cheerful cheeks. Raul's lips. Buried treasure was etched in her delicate features.

Jesus. Jesus. *Thank you, Dear Lord.*

Nayima opened her door.

THE GUARDIAN

Philip Fracassi

"Welcome to paradise!"

Eva gripped the chrome handrail and stood, bare feet balancing on the boat's laminate floor. Their bronze, shirtless guide eased them into a cove and the small island — which had appeared as nothing more than a thatch of dense palm trees ten minutes ago — took on more dimension and character.

The edges of the cove extended into the ocean like rocky arms sprung with saplings. At the center of its embrace lay a strip of sand that grew as the boat cruised ever closer.

A beach, Eva noted with pleasure.

When they'd decided to give into the local man's sales pitch of taking them to a secluded, uninhabited beach for the afternoon, she had been worried about being ripped off, or worse, but it seemed the guy wasn't pulling their leg after all.

Looks amazing, she thought, and turned excitedly toward Bryce, who now stood beside her. His face showed his own surprise and delight. "Pretty cool, huh?" she said, and he nodded in return. She noticed with a stab of lust how much the vacation agreed with him — his blue eyes bright chips of ice in his tanned face, his russet hair mussed by saltwater wind, his smile white as the frothy wave tips they were cutting through.

Privately, Eva hoped this would be *the* trip, when he'd finally sneak a ring into his pocket to spring on her at the apex of a breathtaking hike, or during an after-dinner stroll along a night-soaked beach.

Now that they'd been here a week, she found it hard to believe she hadn't been initially sold on a vacation in Bora Bora. When Bryce brought the destination up on Google, she'd physically sickened at the idea of being stuck in the middle of a vast ocean on a pinprick of island, hundreds of miles from any major land mass, and that's if you counted New Zealand or Hawaii, both glorified islands themselves.

But when they finally arrived, and she'd seen the row of thatched cabanas along the thin strip of beach that would be their home for the next two weeks, she'd squealed in delight, already eager to dive into the emerald-green, crystal-clear water.

She turned around and looked past their guide to the two couples seated in the rear, roughly shaded by a makeshift canvas canopy. The quartet looked as tanned and eager as Bryce, and she wondered if her own features shared that healthy sheen, that fervent energy.

It had thrown her at first, the other couples. When the fervent young man, who introduced himself as Manu, first pitched she and Bryce on the trip, he'd made it sound exclusive. But when they arrived that morning her stomach sank at the sight of two other couples waiting on the dock. She felt better when one of the men looked at the group and, as if reading her mind, as if reading *all* of their minds, turned up his palms and flashed an easygoing smile. "Hey, we've paid already, right? So let's just hope this is all of us. And look at the bright side," he said, lightly kicking a cheap Styrofoam cooler at his feet, "you can all share the twelve-pack we already have on ice."

They all relaxed then, exchanging names and starting to compare their unique invitations when Manu approached, golden-muscled and smiling, his thick dark hair pulled back in a rough ponytail. He wore nothing but a lime-green sarong around his waist and a split-seashell ornament, that looked to Eva like an arts-and-crafts angel, strung to a choker of brown beads at his throat.

"My friends!" he said, the Polynesian accent warm and rough beneath the words. "Thank you for coming!" He gripped every person's hand between his own while making eye contact, his smile never wavering.

Such a salesman, Eva thought, looking into his hazel eyes. *But a hot salesman, at least.*

After they boarded the boat, and the purring motor had pushed them away from the dock, the six passengers settled in for the 45-minute ride to the mysterious beach that was even more beautiful (allegedly) than the one they'd been basking upon all week.

Manu assured them for the hundredth time, "It's completely virgin. Very exclusive! Only my family can go there. Only *we* have the right. Few people have ever seen it, very few."

Eva didn't care about exclusivity. What she craved was *adventure.* Lying around on a beautiful beach, eating and drinking and screwing and dancing, is all well and good, but after a week of gorging on luxury she felt cagey and in need of some stimulation that involved more than tourist-trap boat tours or lazy hiking trails.

And now, as the boat pulled deep into the harbor — and the strip of beach became more pronounced — she hoped this little trip would be just the trick.

Fifty feet from sand, Manu killed the engine and released an iron-clawed anchor, knotted to a heavy frayed rope, over the side. "From here you must swim," he said. "The beach is beautiful and deep. You can see interesting rock formations, and the water is very good for snorkeling, many turtles and exotic fish.

"One rule, please. Do not go into the trees. There are animals and many snakes. The forest is dense and without proper clothes you could get hurt. Or lost. Remember, there are no homes here. No people. All private."

He smiled widely at this, obviously proud of his access.

"But the beach itself? Very safe. If you happen to see a wild pig, please do not approach it. Let me know and I will take care of it."

"What will you do?" The tight-lipped woman, who had introduced herself on the dock as Karyn ("with a Y", she'd explained, as if it mattered).

In answer, Manu reached into a cutout shelf next to the wheel and pulled out a four-foot wooden spear with an iron tip so whetted that it filled with fire when the sun caught its surface. "Kill it, clean it, and bring it back for a luau!" He laughed, and the passengers chuckled along. "You are all invited," he said, too loudly, and Eva had the sudden urge to get away from Manu and the others.

"Is it okay if we…" she said, sharply enough that every set of eyes locked onto her. She felt a moment of discomfort, but then Bryce took her hand, and she went on. "Can we go?"

Manu opened his arms expansively. "Yes! Please, go! Have fun! Remember what I tell you. Trees off limits. I will stay here, get boat ready for return. You may leave any belongings you wish. I will not leave, I promise."

Eva didn't think any of the group were stupid enough to leave anything valuable behind. She and Bryce only brought the clothes on their backs and a waterproof bag filled with bottled waters, an apple, a couple paperbacks, towels, and a tube of coral-friendly sunscreen. Mike, the handsome fella who settled all their nerves back at the dock, snatched up his Styrofoam cooler. "Remember, you can all share. I have a dozen cans in here, so two for each of us."

There was an assorted chorus of affirmations and then they were bustling — grabbing packs and clothes, snorkel masks and whatever else would make its way landward for an afternoon in the sun.

There was a splash and a whoop, and all heads turned to see Terry, a lawyer from New Jersey, poking his head up through the water. "Warm!" he yelled, as if they'd thought it would be anything but. Karyn, who was Terry the lawyer's wife, tossed him their own waterproof bag, then stepped off the edge of the boat and dropped into the clear aqua sea. Eva and Bryce went next, both jumping off the front like children.

When she hit the water, Eva knew why Terry had exclaimed about the temperature. It was more than warm, it was bathwater. "Lovely!" she gasped when coming up for air. Water splashed the side of her face and she twisted to see Bryce kicking away from her, swimming gracefully, excitedly, for the beach.

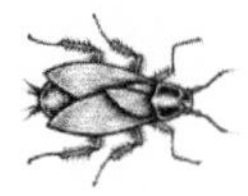

The beach was hot.

The bright sun reflected off the pale sand like new-fallen snow.

The three couples had spread themselves out along the strip of beach, giving each other plenty of room. Bryce had laid down towels side-by-side. Eva, wet and warmed by the quick swim, stripped off her soggy t-shirt, shorts and sandals, revealing a white two-piece bikini and sun-browned skin, before settling down on hers. They'd made camp near the tree line, where the sun was gently broken by the tall palm fronds overhead. There was a light breeze, giving the shadows a relaxing motion on the sand. She stared at the harbor, picturesque with the weathered boat anchored amidst the flat greenish-blue water, the darker blue of the open ocean beyond.

For a moment, she got that creepy feeling again, the same one she'd had when Bryce pulled up the satellite image of Bora Bora. That feeling of being a speck in the middle of an impossible vastness, beyond the reach of society. She imagined it similar to being in outer space, an astronaut floating amidst an impossible void.

Beautiful, yes. But terrifying.

"Sorry to bother," a voice said, and she broke from her thoughts and looked up at Mike, who stood in front of them, shirtless and smiling, holding two cans of beer. "Stacy and I are gonna snorkel, so thought I'd offer the first of your rations while stranded on this horrible island."

Bryce stood quickly and reached for the perspiring cans. "Thanks, man, very kind."

Mike nodded and gave them a wave. "Won't bother you guys again. If you want the other round, just come on over. If we're in the water, feel free to grab 'em out of the cooler."

"Thank you," Eva said.

As Mike walked off Bryce handed her the cold can, which she immediately popped open, taking two large swallows. "Ah!" she said, the alcohol fuzzing her brain and raising goosebumps on her arms and legs. "That's good stuff."

Bryce drank his own, belched, then nodded. "Hell yes. This, my dear, is heaven."

Eva could already feel herself relaxing after the tense morning of the uncertain trip and long boat ride. She'd been more anxious than she realized, and hoped no one else thought her a bitch.

Then she took another long sip, and stopped worrying.

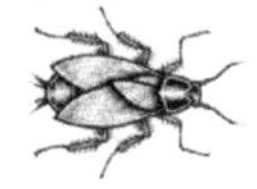

"Ow! Damn it!"

Eva stirred.

She'd been lying on her back, the first beer long gone, dozing gently on the towel, frond shadows playing across her body, the sun bright on her unshaded, but sunscreen-coated, legs.

She sat up on her elbows, noticed that Bryce was already sitting up, staring down the length of the beach where the other couples were staggered.

Karyn and Terry were in the middle, close to the water. Mike and Stacy at the far end. It appeared they were done snorkeling and now walked along a rocky outcrop pushing up from the sand like the ridges of a dinosaur's back. Their eyes were down, probably studying the famous tidepools Manu had recommended.

Thinking of their guide, she looked to the boat, but saw no one on board.

He's likely taking a nap, she thought. *Or spear hunting a wild boar.* She smiled at the image of Manu emerging from the trees, bloody spear held high, dragging a slayed black pig behind him, smile bright as the sun, hair loose and wild…

Eva felt herself getting turned on, suddenly wanting nothing more than to get back in the boat and across the water to their thatched cabana, and their bed. She reached for Bryce's hand and squeezed lightly.

"Everything okay?"

Bryce turned to look at her, and she was surprised at his expression. She thought he'd be offering her that lazy smile of his, but it wasn't a smile at all. His brow was furrowed, his eyes worried.

She sat up. "What?"

He shook his head, looked down the beach again. "Something's wrong with Karyn. She's acting weird."

Eva leaned forward, tented a hand over her eyes.

The couple were standing near the water. Terry, in a knee-length blue suit, had his hands out to his sides, as if unsure what to do with them. Karyn, wearing a black bikini and a floppy straw hat, was bent over and — from what Eva could gather — staring at her legs.

Karyn lifted one foot, then hooked it across the opposite knee while she and Terry studied the bottom of it.

"What are they…"

Eva was interrupted when Karyn screamed — not just *kind of* screamed, as if startled or stung by an insect — but screamed as if someone had broken into her house and was stabbing her in the chest with a butcher knife. *That* kind of scream.

Hearing it chilled Eva's blood.

"What the fuck?" Bryce said, and stood up. Eva did, as well. She noticed that Mike and Stacy, small in the distance on the rocky formation, were also staring.

"Should we go over there?"

Bryce looked at her, unsure. "I don't know. What can we do?"

"Yeah, we don't even know what's wrong with her," Eva agreed. "Maybe she's crazy."

"I'll go," Bryce said, and Eva saw that Mike had been struck with the same testosterone-fueled idea. *GIRL TROUBLE, ME FIX!* Eva thought, then felt a wave of shame, and gratitude. She sure as hell didn't want to go near the crazy screaming lady.

"Bryce, I…"

And then things got weird.

Because that's when Terry began to scream, as well.

Bryce took a step but Eva, reacting to a long-dormant survival instinct, grabbed his elbow firmly. "Wait."

He turned, a mixture of confusion and annoyance on his face. "Eva…"

"Just wait. Look! That Mike guy is going over there."

And he was, albeit slowly.

Cautiously?

What's he afraid of?

Karyn, still screaming, ran for the water.

Eva couldn't be sure, but she thought there were large dark splotches covering Karyn's body. Her feet, calves, thighs.

Maybe shadows?

Terry was on his ass, rubbing at his ankles and feet, as if feverishly brushing something off his skin.

He made horrible sounds as he did so. Guttural, gut-wrenching, inhuman shrieks.

Eva's eyes moved from Terry to Mike, who was yelling something back toward Stacy, still perched atop the rocks crumbling upward from amidst the fat river of sand.

"Jesus, what the hell's going on?" Bryce said, thankfully staying put.

"I don't know. What's Mike saying?"

Mike was backing away from Terry and Karyn, toward the rocks. His hands were cupped around his mouth and he was yelling something toward Bryce and Eva.

But with all the screaming, Eva could only make out every other word.

"…shoes! …away! …sand!"

"I can't…" Bryce stammered.

Then Mike turned and *ran* across the beach, back to Stacy and the rocks.

"What do we do? Oh God!" Eva watched in horror as Karyn, sputtering in the shallow water like she was drowning, let out a final, gurgling wail of despair so deep it dug into Eva's core and hollowed it.

Her body, so recently warmed by the bright sun, went ice-cold. "Bryce?"

"I don't know…" he started, but stopped, dumbfounded.

Karyn was *crawling* back onto the beach, leaving the water like an early stage of evolution, as if she were the first of their species to try for dry land. Her elbows dug into the wet sand as she army-crawled toward Terry, who lied flat on his back, twitching convulsively.

Karyn's legs, in full view as they pulled free of the surf, were black and… *shriveled.*

Lifeless.

Eva could hear her loud, wet sobbing. By the time she made it to Terry's body, his convulsions had stopped, and he lay very still.

Yeah, Eva thought, *but his skin is still moving.*

Karyn rested her body over Terry's, and now Eva could easily see the large black splotches covering her back, her arms.

The woman's legs were charcoal-colored, and appeared to be diminishing. Evaporating.

As if being eaten.

Eva spun away and vomited into the sand. Bryce put a hand on her back. "It's okay… It'll be okay…"

When she was finished, she wiped her mouth and looked back toward the couple. Both bodies had turned bumpy and black. Motionless.

The screaming, for now, had stopped.

"You guys!"

Bryce and Eva looked beyond the corpses to Mike, perched atop the line of stones a hundred feet away. Hearing him now was effortless.

"Stay off the beach!" he yelled, slowly articulating each word. "Swim to us over here! To the rocks! Put on your sandals!"

Stacy said something to him then and he turned to reply. She shook her head and he continued. "It's in the sand! You hear me? They're in the sand!"

Eva looked down at her feet. She was on the towel, but sand was blown across the fabric. *I walked here barefoot. I slept on the towel… but my hand, my hair. Were they in the sand?*

She looked at her hands, her legs. Looking for… what? She didn't know. Everything seemed fine, but she brushed her skin clean anyway, tried to ignore the paranoid, phantom sensation of something crawling along her scalp like lice.

Bryce was doing the same, but Eva noticed that, unlike her, he was standing in the sand already, the bottoms of his feet buried in it.

"What's he talking about?" Bryce said, his voice small and afraid.

"I don't know, but get on the towel, babe. Where are the sandals?"

"By the bag."

Which, Eva noticed, was buried in a bright patch of beach a few feet away. She leaned out, trying to keep her balance without having to put a hand down, and snagged the bag. She lifted it carefully, looking for signs of anything strange, keeping it at arms-length. She brought it closer and reached inside.

Unzipped... great. Whatever's in the sand could have crawled inside.

She debated dumping the contents onto the towels but decided against it. If the bag was safe, she didn't want all their things... contaminated... with whatever had blackened — *eaten* — the skin of Terry and Karyn.

She pulled the sandals free one-by-one, inspecting each as she did. She handed Bryce his, and he quickly slipped them onto his feet.

"Can't imagine this is much protection," he said, staring at the thin flip-flops. "But if it gets us to the water."

"I don't even know what the fuck we're supposed to be avoiding." Eva was surprised to feel tears run down her cheeks. "I mean... what's going on? How are we going to stay off the sand... on a fucking beach?"

Her voice was raised but Bryce looked at her calmly, nodding along. "I know, it's weird," he said, his composed tone soothing. She felt a surge of love for him and put a hand on his shoulder.

"Sorry..." she said, but he shook his head.

"Don't be. I'm fucking terrified. Now..." He took a deep breath, let it out. "Should we do this? Are we walking or running?"

She looked to the edge of the water waiting beyond a thirty-foot stretch of beach. "I think we walk. Focus on keeping the sandals between us and... whatever. If we run, we'll kick it all over ourselves."

"Okay," he said. "Ready?"

She clenched the sack tightly in one hand, gripped his elbow with the other. For a second, she wondered about bringing the towels.

Fuck that, she thought, and took a step into the sand.

Twenty steps later, they'd made it to the water without incident, both of them pushing into the sea until they the bottom dropped away and they were forced to swim.

"Wonder what happened to Manu?" Bryce said, studying the boat anchored in the harbor. "You think we should go there instead? Might be safer."

Eva eyed the boat, but shook her head. "Let's see what Mike has to say. I want to know what's going on."

"Okay," Bryce agreed, and began swimming parallel to the beach.

When they were halfway, they both stopped, treading water, staring at the corpses — *because there is no doubt about it, folks, those are CORPSES* — from the supposed, relative safety of the water.

"Holy shit," Bryce said, the first tendrils of panic slipping into his voice. "They look fucking burned!"

"Let's keep going," Eva said, already swimming ahead, feeling a recurrence of nausea twist in her belly.

When they reached the far end, Mike and Stacy were waiting.

The other couple stood on the rocks, which Eva noticed was an archipelago of sorts, a series of rocks surrounded by sand on all sides, the closest about a dozen feet between the waterline. The gaps between the humped brown stones varied from a few feet to a few inches, the jagged line random as a roll of dice.

Eva called out across the water. "Is there room for us?"

"Plenty," Mike said, smiling weakly. But Eva noticed Stacy wore a frown, one that was leaning toward a scowl, as if the idea of sharing was not something she'd agreed upon.

"What happened?" Bryce asked. They'd moved closer, but not close enough to where they'd be standing on the sand, even underwater.

"Not sure," Mike said, turning to look at what remained of Terry and Karyn. "I got within a few feet, and I don't know man, it looked like the sand… hell… it looked like the sand was *alive*."

Bryce looked at Eva. "You have your sandals?

"Holding them," she said with a gasp, a mouthful of saltwater slipping into her mouth. She coughed and spit it out, ignored Bryce's concerned look. She was feeling the burn in her muscles from ten straight minutes of swimming and treading water.

"You wanna do this?"

"Well," she said, her lungs also beginning to strain. "It's either that or sink. I doubt I could swim to the boat now."

"I could help you…"

"Bryce, fuck it, come on."

She began to swim toward shore, done having languid chats while her muscles cried for mercy. When she was shallow enough, she slipped both sandals on beneath the water, and dropped her legs into the mucky seafloor.

Oh, sweet relief, she thought, but her good vibes were cut short as her feet sank into the wet sand. Bryce came up next to her, and they both stepped cautiously forward, aiming for the rocks.

"Try to keep your feet off the sand. Your skin, I mean."

Eva was disheartened to see that Mike wasn't watching them as much as he was watching the sand between the lapping waves and the rocks. *Looking for movement, for the things that had laid waste to good old Terry from Jersey and Karyn with a "Y".*

As Bryce and Eva emerged, dripping, from the sea, they both took a moment to study the stretch between them and the stones. Eva didn't notice any movement, saw nothing strange crawling around or on top of the bright sand.

"You guys will be fine, but I wouldn't dawdle too much," Mike said.

Eva agreed, and they walked across the beach, hand-in-hand, until they stepped gratefully onto the rocks.

Once atop one of the large rounded stones, Eva looked down at her feet, her legs, and saw nothing untoward. There was a fine mist of sand on her toes, her heel, but nothing moved, nothing turned her skin black or made her want to scream out in agony.

Not yet.

She saw Bryce doing his own inspection before looking at her and nodding.

"Well, this sucks," Eva said, and appreciated Mike chuckling at her shitty attempt at levity.

"It does at that."

Then, as one, they all turned to study the blackened corpses, this time with a more studious disposition.

"So, you think something… what? Bit them?"

"Infested them. Some strain of sand fleas, sand lice, whatever they're called," Mike said, shrugging. "It isn't that uncommon and, well, I've heard horror stories. I mean, me and Stacy do a lot of traveling, sometimes to some pretty remote places."

"Maybe," Bryce said. "But come on… *look* at them."

"I know, I know. This is totally fucked. I have no idea what…"

"HELLO!"

A booming voice interrupted Mike's thought, and they all turned to see Manu standing at the bow of his boat, having seemingly appeared from nowhere.

Was he hiding? Eva thought, trying not to get carried away, overly paranoid. *Sleeping, more likely.*

Mike waved back, but dropped his arm when he saw the big smile on Manu's face, the expression blatant even from seventy-five feet away.

"I see you've discovered my friends!" he yelled across the water, and then laughed as if it was a hilarious prank, a joke they'd all be laughing at later, perhaps while eating charred boar off a spit at the infamous Manu Luau to which, Eva recalled, they'd all been invited.

A chill went up her spine at Manu's choice of words, and her defensive, sardonic inner-wit scurried away, leaving a void of empty fear behind. *My friends?*

"What the hell…" Bryce said softly.

"Please, come pick us up!" Mike yelled.

"I don't think so!" Manu called back. "The blood gets them stirred up, you know. Can you see?" He pointed in the direction of the couple, and their eyes followed.

And yes.

Yes, now… they *could* see.

"Oh God," Eva groaned.

The sand *was* moving. It seemed okay close to the rocks, but there was a wide swath of beach extending outward from the dead bodies that was definitely, without a doubt… *teeming.*

"Sand mites?" Bryce looked at Mike. "Is that what you think?"

"Shit man, I don't know. Whatever they are, they're quick and deadly as piranha."

Stacy, who Eva had all but forgotten about, suddenly joined the discussion. "You think he did this on purpose?" she said, her voice high-pitched and cracking. "You think he brought us here to *die?*"

"Take it easy, hon," Mike said softly.

"There's not much left of them now," Bryce said, and it was true. The bodies were still lumped on top of one another, but the flesh had been eaten away, leaving bloody tissue and flashes of wet gristle, like raw hamburger beneath a charred shell. A red stain of blood surrounded them.

Their flesh seemed to boil.

"You can stay on the rocks. Most people do," Manu called cheerfully. "But sooner or later…" he shrugged, giving them his best *what are you gonna do* expression. "To help you avoid temptation, I will leave now. I hope you are still alive when I come back, because that would be much more interesting!"

Manu pulled up the anchor and started the boat, gave them all a cheerful wave as he turned it around and motored slowly out of the harbor.

"Son of a bitch," Bryce said, his tone heated. "Why is he doing this?"

"Don't know," Mike said.

Eva turned around, studied the shadowed tree line. "What about the trees? He made a big deal about us staying out of there, so maybe there's help there. Safety."

Mike nodded. "Good point. Still, there's a lot of sand between here and there."

"We could also try swimming to the edges of the harbor," Bryce added, "climbing those rocks and seeing what lies beyond. He claimed this island was uninhabited but, to Eva's point, he was probably lying, wanting to keep us on the sand."

Stacy groaned and they all looked at her. She was looking down, one palm on her chest, pressed against her heart. "Oh no…" she said.

Mike studied the area Stacy was fixated on.

"He's right," he said with a sour grimace. "Blood does get them stirred up."

Hesitantly, Eva looked back toward the beach between the rocks and the water, the imbedded footprints of her and Bryce's path still evident.

The sand was crawling.

All of it.

Mike cursed and leapt to a far rock, nonchalantly skipping over three feet of sand without hesitation. He picked up a black nylon belt that had been thrown into a pile along with the couples' snorkeling gear. There was a *rip* of Velcro and Mike dropped the belt, but held onto a black-handled knife sprouting a four-inch serrated blade.

"What are you gonna do with that?" Bryce asked. His voice was level, but Eva could hear a note of caution running beneath it.

"For one, use it to gut that bastard if I can get close enough. Two, I'm gonna want it as protection when I make it to those trees. He may have been lying about the wild pigs in there, or God knows what else, but I'm gonna stay on the side of caution."

"Mike, no!" Stacy said, clamping a hand to her mouth.

"How will you get there?" Eva asked. "It's gotta be thirty feet of sand. Did you see the beach? Whatever it is… it's *everywhere.*"

"I know, but look." He lifted a foot casually, showing off a dark green rubber scuba slipper. "These will keep those things off my feet, better than sandals anyway. Once I get to the trees and the hard ground, I should be okay. I'll search for help. Worst case, I'll find something we can use to get you three to safety."

Eva turned to Bryce, to ask him what he thought of the idea, but Bryce was no longer paying attention to them.

He was studying his feet.

Eva followed his gaze, down the tanned legs, past the bumps of his ankles… "Bryce?"

He looked at her, his eyes wide and crystal blue.

And wild with fear.

"I think," he said, then abruptly slid one foot free of the sandal, bent his knee and turned his foot so the bottom shown upward.

A black, blistered swirl stretched from his heel to his big toe.

Eva could see the bugs under the skin, crawling, infesting.

Eating.

"Jesus, Bryce!" she yelled, reflexively taking half a step backward, nearly pitching herself ass-backward off the rock.

"I'd felt it a few minutes ago. I guess I hoped… boy, it's bad, I mean… oh! Oh God!"

Bryce sat down on the rock butted against the one he stood on. Its slightly higher elevation allowed him to sit, one ankle over the other knee, to more closely study his foot.

"It really hurts!" he said, hysteria creeping into his voice.

"Eva, move!" Mike ordered, already skipping back toward them. "Don't get them on you!"

"I…" Eva felt like she was in shock. "What do we do?"

Bryce tapped her waist gently with one hand. "Do it, Eva. Move away, please."

Eva stepped to a stone a few feet closer to the tree line, let Mike slip past her on his way to Bryce. Stacy hadn't moved, but watched it all from nearby, a dispassionate observer.

Are they on me, too?

Eva pulled one foot from her sandal, inspected it.

Nothing.

She repeated it with the other foot, felt a rush of guilt-laced relief to see it was also clear.

Bryce, meanwhile, was beginning to panic.

"Help me!" he yelled at Mike, and Eva could see whatever had been eating at the bottom of his foot had moved *upward* — streaking black lines ran over the top of the foot, the ankle, along the side of one calf. "It really hurts, man. I can *feel* them eating me… Fuck, I can feel them crawling underneath."

The bottom of Bryce's foot was completely black and bubbling, frantic with the invading creatures. The skin looked like burnt paper, and the dark lines continued to move steadily up his leg.

"Here," Mike said, and handed Bryce the knife, handle-first. "See if you can, shit man, see if you can scrape them off or something. Don't let them get higher."

"Bryce!" Eva cried, his name coming out like a sob as she watched his eyes turned wide and terrified, his lips quiver. He looked up at her, face red and wild, tears streaming down his face. Then he grabbed the handle of the extended knife, and began cutting.

He began by scraping the bottom of his foot, using the flat of the blade as a straightedge, heel-to-toe.

Black, bug-infested flakes fell from his foot to the stones. Mike took a giant step back, isolating Bryce and whatever was being peeled off him.

Rivulets of blood began to run off the foot where the flesh had come away. "I think I'm getting them!" he yelled. "It hurts, though. Really fucking hurts." He scraped again, revealing more red flesh, more of the dead, blackened skin falling in wet, leaf-sized patches.

One black tendril needling up his thigh had now traveled beneath the opening of his suit. Bryce jerked the fabric back toward his crotch. He stuck the tip of the knife into the top of the festering line as it crossed to his inner thigh, teeth gritted, sweat and tears dripping off his face.

"I don't know how…"

"Try…" Mike started, then swallowed. More softly, he continued. "I don't know, brother. Try cutting them out I guess."

Bryce, blood now flowing freely from his foot, began cutting along one of the black lines. More blood sprang through the cuts, but the tiny creatures didn't fall away, they *multiplied,* as if the fresh blood only energized their frenzied feasting.

From one heartbeat to the next, the stripe on his leg widened, darted up past his crotch and emerged from the waistband of his suit, crisscrossing over his stomach.

"Aah!" he screamed, throwing his head back. "Oh God no please!"

He began stabbing at his leg with abandon.

"No! Bryce, stop!" Eva yelled, and then suddenly there were arms around her, turning her around and holding her tight. The skin was soft, fragrant. Female.

Not Mike then, but Stacy. She of the perpetual frown, the seeming distaste, was now keeping Eva's face tucked into her shoulder, her voice soft and urgent in her ear.

"Don't look, Eva. Whatever you do, don't look."

Bryce continued to scream as they all stood nearby, helpless.

"I have to!" Eva said into Stacy's shoulder. "I have to see him!"

She struggled free of the woman's grasp and twisted around.

And screamed.

Bryce was covered in them. His chest, arms, shoulders… all boiling with black, swarming infestation. His jaw opened and closed soundlessly, his eyes bloodshot and vacant. The knife, Eva noticed, was stuck deep into one shriveling thigh.

"Get back, Mike," Stacy said through her own tears. "For God's sake, get away from him."

"The knife…" Mike said lamely.

"Fuck the knife!" Stacy screamed, and Mike nodded and stepped another rock away from where Bryce was sitting, the creatures running through him like water, devouring his flesh so fast that he appeared shrink before their eyes.

Eva put her face into her hands and sobbed. She couldn't look at him anymore. Part of her — a part that was likely dead forever — wondered if he'd had an engagement ring in the pocket of that swimsuit, tucked into the pocket on the inside of the waistband that you used for keys when you couldn't leave them safely on shore. Maybe she could check, later, after the rest of him was gone — *had been eaten* — maybe then she could check for a ring.

They wouldn't eat the suit, would they? It was such a stupid question, she thought. *I must be in shock, because otherwise I'd still be screaming. Screaming because my boyfriend, the man I share my bed with, is turning black and crispy just a few feet away, being eaten alive, in fact. How very odd it all is. Yes… I'd surely be screaming.*

But she *was* screaming. And Stacy clutched her as best she could, grabbed her and held her while she wailed and wept and baked beneath the hot, careless sun.

Hours later, Manu's boat came puttering back into the harbor.

Eva, Mike and Stacy were perched on the highest rocks they could safely get to.

What was left of Bryce had fallen over into the sand, where the remaining flesh had been quickly covered. He'd been reduced to nothing but black dust on a brown stone, a blue swimsuit, and a blackened, skeleton-thin husk of the man he'd once been.

His teeth are still white, Eva noticed. But his blue eyes were gone. And his hair looked brittle and dark, the luscious, blonde-streaked russet color somehow sucked dry.

Eva remained free of the creatures in the sand. She was badly sunburned, but couldn't bring herself to care.

Mike and Stacy had spoken softly with one another — too softly for Eva to overhear — over the last few hours, and she figured Mike was making his case for a run to the trees.

For help.

But after seeing what happened to Bryce, seeing what those things did *close-up*, Eva thought Mike seemed less enthusiastic about stepping off the rocks, rubber booties or no.

As the boat neared the beach, all three survivors stood to watch.

Manu didn't wave this time, and Eva could make out an uncharacteristic frown on his handsome face.

"Think we disappointed him," Mike said.

"Good," Stacy replied, without enthusiasm.

Eva looked at the other two. "He thought we'd be dead."

Mike nodded. "He certainly doesn't seem as exuberant as he was earlier."

They all continued watching as Manu parked the boat thirty feet off their position, cut the engine, and lowered the anchor once more.

"I wonder," Mike said.

"What?" Eva asked, seeing that Stacy was eyeing him hotly.

"Well, if I could get to that boat before he pulled in the anchor..."

"Across the sand," Stacy snapped. "And don't forget he has that stupid spear."

"True," Mike said, but Eva didn't think he sounded worried. Mike looked to be in better-than-average shape. Lean and rippling with muscle. She wondered if he had some sort of combat experience. He seemed comfortable enough with that knife, anyway.

"Hello again!" Manu addressed them once more from the bow of the gently rocking boat.

He's trying to put on a good face, but I don't think he's happy at all, Eva thought.

"You guys are hard to kill!" he said, and then he did flash a smile. "That's okay! Like I said, more interesting for me!"

"This might be our only chance," Mike said quietly, head bent toward Stacy. "The scuba shoes will protect my feet. I can make it to that boat in three minutes flat. There's no way he could get the anchor up and the engine started before I reach him."

"And a spear in the eye for your trouble!" she retorted, and Eva winced at how loudly she'd said it. She didn't want Manu hearing Mike's idea.

Personally, she was all for it. Mike was right, he *would* be protected with those rubber booties. And if he could overpower Manu, then they could all get out of here. They could take turns with the shoes, maybe. There *had* to be a way!

"Eva, stand aside, would you?"

"Mike, please don't..."

"It's this or we die. Right here. All of us. It could be our only chance."

Eva stepped carefully to another rock, her eyes lowering to the spot where Bryce had crumpled. She saw the glimmer of the knife, fallen free of Bryce's thigh, which now looked more like beef jerky than flesh.

"Mike," she said, pointing.

He followed her finger to the knife. "Can you grab it?"

It seemed a small risk compared to what Mike was willing to do. It was stuck between two rocks, so Manu couldn't see it. She slowly bent her knees, minding her balance while watching the sand for movement.

There was some subtle activity near Bryce's corpse, but the handle was *above* the sand. Only the blade was buried. She lowered her hand, slowly, gripped the handle, and pulled the blade free. She waggled the knife a little to throw off any loose sand still clinging to it.

"Looks okay," he said, wiping his mouth. "I don't think they care about stuff that's not, you know, organic." Mike spoke the words softly, and Eva hoped he was right.

She straightened, keeping her body between the knife and Manu, who was likely watching from the water. Mike pinched the metal blade between two fingers and gave it another little shake. Finally, he gripped the handle in one fist.

They all held their breath.

A bead of nervous sweat dripped off his chin. "Think it's okay." He exhaled with obvious relief, then deftly turned the knife in his hand so that the metal was hidden by his forearm.

This guy is definitely military, Eva thought. *Either that or he's a helluva boy scout.*

"Good luck," she said.

Mike held her eyes for a moment, and she noticed they were a lovely shade of green, with dark blue specks throughout. Then they shifted over her shoulder, to their target. He took a deep breath, exhaled and, without another word, leapt from the rocks.

Eva and Stacy watched Mike sprint across the sand, diving before he reached the lapping surf, slicing into light green shallows.

Manu disappeared from the bow. First he ran to the anchor, but Mike was coming fast, so he slipped away, hidden from their view. When Mike reached the side of the boat, Manu reappeared with the spear, jabbing downward as if trying to stab a pike from a creek.

Mike yelled once, as if injured, then grabbed the shaft of the spear on Manu's next strike and jerked it downward, out of the islander's hands.

"I'm going," Stacy said, and jumped off the rocks.

Eva studied the woman's feet as she ran away, saw she wore similar rubber booties as Mike, but that they didn't cover the tops of her feet as well as Mike's had.

Before Eva could yell out for her — a warning, a shout of encouragement — Stacy was diving headfirst into the water, cutting through the low waves toward Mike, who had somehow managed to get onto the boat, he and Manu now grappling like cage fighters. Mike got the larger man into a choke hold, and Manu kicked wildly, throwing blind backward punches.

Eva waited on the stones. She watched as Manu broke free and Mike raised the knife, thrusting it at the other man, backing him up until Manu had no choice but to leap from the boat. As he treaded water on the far side, Mike lifted Stacy, clutching the fallen spear, up the other. Once aboard, Stacy threatened Manu with the spear's sharp point every time he swam near, shrieking like a madwoman. Mike, meanwhile, brought up the anchor, hand-over-hand, until it clambered over the side and dropped into the boat.

He started the engine.

"Hey!" Eva cried, waving both arms like a castaway who'd spotted a plane buzzing overhead, or a distant steamer plowing through the mist, hazy as a ghost.

Mike raised a hand in return as the engines grew louder. Stacy approached him and they argued, the words lost amidst the air-splitting buzzsaw of the engine.

Manu, meanwhile, had swum toward the beach, stopping a few feet short of the sand. He stood in the shallows, the water lapping at the top of his sarong, his back to Eva, his eyes on the boat.

Mike yelled something, hand cupped around his mouth, but it was near-impossible to hear over the engine. To Eva's horror, it sounded like: "We'll get help!"

So she watched, helpless, as the boat backed away from the beach, slowly rotating until the bow faced the ocean, away from Eva, from the island. If not for the presence of Manu standing in the water, she might have made a mad run for it, risking death for a chance of rescue.

"No!" she screamed. "Mike, please! Don't leave!"

Minutes later, the boat was pushing out of the harbor, long past earshot of Eva's protests. It banked left, accelerated and, after a few moments, disappeared from view.

Eva sobbed as the boat vanished. She sat down hard on the warm stones, feeling the heat of the late afternoon sun on her head, back and shoulders. She dared not look at the licorice-limbed corpse of her boyfriend, or the similar corpses of Terry and Karyn that littered the beach a dozen yards away.

"No no no…" she whimpered, drained of strength, of hope.

Long after the sound of the boat's engine had vanished, she lifted her eyes. Manu, still standing in the shallows, watched her.

"Why did you do this?" She knew that she would die here, in this virgin paradise, with no one but a strange man at her side, a man who wanted to kill her.

"If we wait until dark, they will retreat," Manu said, his tone implausibly casual as he studied the sky, as if contemplating the remaining daylight. "When night falls, it will be safe, Eva. They don't like the cold."

"I don't believe you!" she screamed, nearly slipping off the rock in her anger. "You tried to fucking kill me! Why did you bring us here!"

But Manu said nothing, only continued to watch the sky.

Hours passed, and the boat did not return.

No rescue boat appeared.

Ravenous despite everything, Eva found her scuba bag, pulled out the apple she'd brought as a snack, back when this was going to be a quick trip of a few hours. She ate it angrily, staring daggers at Manu, who stood silent in the shallows, not venturing closer, but not swimming away.

"Almost time now," he said.

Eva looked at the darkening sky — a gorgeous royal blue so clear that she could perceive a smattering of stars sprinkled like diamond dust beyond the earth's atmosphere, as if she were glimpsing another dimension.

The sun was a red boil on the horizon, split in two by the great ocean, lowering slowly into its depths.

The day was ending.

Later, when it was full dark, and the canopy of night was bursting with glittering stars and the shimmering powder of galaxies, and the day had split from the night, Manu walked out of the water and onto the beach.

He hesitated a moment, then smiled, his teeth bright in the moonlight.

"It's okay," he said. "You can come down."

"No fucking way," Eva said, wishing she had a weapon. A knife, a gun, a spear… but she had nothing. No clothes, no possessions.

Just fear.

"I won't hurt you, Eva," Manu said. "And if you come with me, I'll show you things you've never seen. Things you've never imagined."

He walked boldly up to the stones, magnificent in the moonlight, bare-chested and native as the island itself. Unblemished.

She looked at his exposed feet in the sand.

Nothing attacked him.

"Come with me, Eva. Let me show you." He held out a hand. "I swear on my father, you will be safe."

Eva looked toward the black ocean, the diamond-crusted waves, the onyx abyss of its massive, infinite body. She regarded the night sky and saw the mirror image of the waters, as if the entirety of reality beyond the island was nothing but endless void.

Exhausted beyond reason, she reached out and took his hand. It was warm and dry, and it tugged at her to follow.

She dropped off the rocks, onto the sand.

Together, they walked across the beach, unharmed, toward the line of dark trees.

"Promise," she said, as they stepped off the shoreline and into the fertile ground of the untouched garden. "Promise you won't hurt me."

Manu looked down at her, his shadowed face a dark chasm of infinite night.

LOW HANGING CLOUDS

T.E. Grau

Rain was coming, but it never rained here. Not anymore. Not since the Clippers snagged four crowns in a row back in the 20s. But this morning, it definitely felt like rain was on the way. Odd...

From what Nick could remember of the wetter days, this had all the makings of a real downpour. Dawn exposed a charcoal sky stretching from hilltop to horizon, poised to unleash a holy baptismal on this parched city teetering at the edge of the undrinkable sea.

Untamed water was a childhood dream. Swimming pools, Raging Waters, even the oscillating fountains at The Grove. Everything was green, flecked by streaks and blobs of bright blue. But now, the landscape was a pantomime of how it once was. A mockery. Lawns were an exercise in green paint. Flowers, a forgotten song. These were the Dry Times, with plumbing kept to a rationed trickle, fed by far away river water hijacked three states upstream.

Nick knew this. It was drilled into his bones, passed down by the elders, who wept when they spoke of the rain, stepping in for God by leaving drops of wet, salty guilt on the pavement. Every generation ate away at the future of their progeny. This was the way of man.

But today, people were placing pots and buckets and anything else capable of collecting volume on their porches and stoops. Today, it was bound to rain. It had to. The land couldn't wait any longer.

Nick left for work as early as he could once he glanced out the window. Traffic, with the added shock of an historic rain, would be murder today.

The house that he shared with his wife was situated up on the eastern hills overlooking the city, and the clouds seemed to bear down on this high vantage point like a moist, fuzzy blanket. Nick wanted to stay home, wake his girl, and marvel at this breathtaking anomaly, but he had to make his 9:15 client meeting with some asshole comedian from Tel-Aviv. Comedians always turn out to be assholes. Being from Tel-Aviv was just a bonus. And Nick was jockeying for a raise, so being late was out of the question.

With one eye cocked above, Nick dashed out of the house while his wife still slumbered under the stout wooden beams that ribbed their high ceiling. Like being in the bowels of a Viking longship. She slept better in the morning. During the night, when she was alone with the dark, she heard screams coming from the hills above. Could be coyotes. Could be worse. The whispering city never gave clues.

As Nick wound down from the hills and into the chattering teeth of Sunset Boulevard, he noticed that the traffic was unusually light, even for a Monday. As if everyone decided to declare a holiday and stare up at the weirdness in the sky. Groups of excited people gathered on street corners, oohing and aahing and snapping photos. Nick craned his neck out the car window, looking at the dazzling cloud cover topping the high peaks above his neighborhood. It was extraordinary. Clouds. Actual fucking clouds. Descending on Los Angeles, threatening renewal. Relief. An overdue scrubbing.

Nick just stared, and contemplated pulling over and joining the underemployed gawkers. But it was Monday, and a surly Israeli comedian was heading toward his office, probably from a better neighborhood. Couldn't be late. Not even today.

Nick drove down the mostly deserted streets, heading toward Century City, which had the dubious distinction of being the highest concentration of lawyers in the country west of New York City. The East still got rain. Sometimes. And more lawyers. Yet they still came to L.A. to complain. Where was everyone?

Heading west up Olympic, Nick looked up toward his destination, as he did every morning, gauging the minutes he'd be late by the distance from his twenty-story office building that always waited just a few more miles ahead.

But today his building was cut off at its midsection. Obscured from view by a swath of low hanging clouds.

A creamy frosting of pure white rimmed Century City under a black sky. It was beautiful, the contrast. Cars were stopping in the middle of the street now, and people got out to see this miracle forming above them. They needed to see it without glass between them. Nick swerved around people and cars. 9:09. Six minutes to go.

About a mile out from work, Century City loomed larger now, and Nick saw things falling from the buildings. From *his* building. Did someone toss something out the window? But the windows didn't open. Anywhere.

He was just blocks away when he noticed - in a detached way, as if watching it all on television - that the tops of the buildings had been sheared off at the lowest lip of the cloud.

Now it *was* raining. Raining sparks and dust and floating paper ... body parts and shrieks. Just like the old footage of that day called "9/11" Nick saw in grade school social studies.

Nick crushed his brakes. Tires screeched, panic seized him. He looked around, and noticed the layer of pure, impenetrable white covering everything above a hundred yards as far as he could see. Buildings, phone towers, the topless mountains in the distance.

Nick choked, spun his car around with jerky, frantic movements, and gunned his engine, heading back the way he came. The stunted buildings grew small behind him.

He dialed his phone with a quivering thumb, trying to reach his wife. He had to reach home... Reach her, sleeping inside the Viking longship. Had to...

Nothing. No service. The clouds took it away.

He sped on like a madman, slaloming through stopped cars, screaming people. Howls. Reach her...

Nick turned a corner and made a straight shot for home.

Looking up into the foothills he saw his neighborhood, or the beginning of his neighborhood.

His house, further up the hillside, was obscured by clouds.

DEAD-WOOD

Joe Hill

It has been argued even trees may appear as ghosts. Reports of such manifestations are common in the literature of para-psychology. There is the famous white pine of West Belfry, Maine. It was chopped down in 1842, a towering fir with a white smooth bark like none anyone had ever seen, and with pine needles the color of brushed steel. A tea house and inn was built on the hill where it had stood. A cold spot existed in a corner of the yellow dining room, a zone of penetrating chill, the exact diameter of the white pine's trunk. Directly above the dining room was a small bedroom, but no guest would stay the night there. Those who tried said their sleep was disturbed by the keening rush of a phantom wind, the low soft roar of air in high branches; the gusts blew papers around the room and pulled curtains down. In March, the walls bled sap.

An entire phantom wood appeared in Canaanville, Pennsylvania, for a period of twenty minutes one day, in 1959. There are photographs. It was in a new development, a neighborhood of winding roads and small, modern bungalows. Residents woke on a Sunday morning and found themselves sleeping in stands of birch that seemed to grow right from the floor of their bedrooms. Underwater hemlocks swayed and drifted in backyard swimming pools. The phenomenon extended to a nearby shopping mall. The ground floor of Sears was filled with brambles, half-price skirts hanging from the branches of Norway maples, a flock of sparrows settled on the jewelry counter, picking at pearls and gold chains.

Somehow it's easier to imagine the ghost of a tree than it is the ghost of a man. Just think how a tree will stand for a hundred years, gorging itself on sunlight and pulling moisture from the earth, tirelessly hauling its life up out of the soil, like someone hauling a bucket up from a bottomless well. The roots of a shattered tree still drink for months after death, so used to the habit of life they can't give it up. Something that doesn't know it's alive obviously can't be expected to know when it's dead.

After you left — not right away, but after a summer had passed — I took down the alder we used to read under, sitting together on your mother's picnic blanket; the alder we fell asleep under that time, listening to the hum of the bees. It was old, and rotten, it had bugs in it, although new shoots still appeared on its boughs in the spring. I told myself I didn't want it to blow down and fall into the house, even though it wasn't leaning toward the house. But now, sometimes when I'm out there, in the wide-open of the yard, the wind will rise and shriek, tearing at my clothes. What else shrieks with it, I wonder?

JUDE CONFRONTS GLOBAL WARMING

Joe Hill

Georgia was in the music library, knitting little silver skulls on a shawl, and listening to the radio, when Jude wandered into the room.

"...3,000 scientists signed the strongest statement yet on the subject of global warming," said the newsman. "The letter paints a dark picture of the earth's future, warning that melting ice caps, super hurricanes, and coastal flooding are inevitable if the global community doesn't act decisively to address climate change. Concerned consumers are advised to consider lowering their energy consumption, and to look at alternative energy cars..."

Jude flipped the radio over to FUM. They were playing Soundgarden, *Black Hole Sun.* Jude turned it up.

"What the fuck you do that for?" Georgia said, and chucked a sewing needle at the back of his head. It bounced off his shoulders. Jude ignored it. "I was listening to that, asshole."

"Now you're listening to this," Jude said.

"You're such a dick."

"Oh hell," he said, turning back toward her. "They were wetting themselves over global *cooling,* twenty years ago. Remember that? No, probably not. Big Bird didn't talk much environmental science."

She threw the other sewing needle at him. He ducked, stuck an arm up to protect his face. The needle glanced off his wrist. By the time he looked up over his arm, she had huffed out.

Jude followed her into the kitchen. She bent into the fridge, to paw out a bottle of that cranberry red stuff she drank now, one of her wine coolers. To Jude, it tasted like Kool-Aid, as prepared by the Rev. Jim Jones.

"It's a crock," Jude said. "Nobody knows."

"*Everybody* knows," she said. "There's data that shows the earth's temperature has been rising every year for the last fifty years. No one argues that."

He had to clamp down on a laugh. It was always funny to him, when Georgia used words like *data.* He was maybe not entirely successful at disguising his amusement, because she threw the cap of her wine cooler at him.

"Will you stop throwing shit at me?" he said.

She turned away on her heel, glared back into the open fridge for something to munch on. Her lips were moving, as she whispered angrily to herself. He caught just a word here and there: *fuck; Jude; ignoramus.*

He eased around the chopping block, slipped up behind her, and put his arms around her waist, clasping her body to his. At the same time he peered over her shoulder into the refrigerator. Nothing to drink except those fucking wine coolers.

"C'mon. I hate when we fight about stupid shit," he said, and slid his hands up to give her melons a squeeze.

"It isn't stupid shit," she said, elbowing him off her, and wheeling around, her eyes giving him the old death ray. "Take a look at your cars. Why you got to drive everywhere in those shitty gas guzzling old cars of yours? Just because they make you feel like a badass? First it was the Mustang, then it was the Charger. They both get about three miles to the gallon, and when people are stuck behind us in traffic, you can see 'em turning black in the face from breathing your exhaust. You ever thought about taking yourself out and buying a nice responsible hybrid — one of those superlow emissions vehicles that get such great mileage?"

"I was thinking about taking myself out to get some beer," he said, and burped in her face. "Oops, sorry — runaway emissions."

She punched him in the chest, gave him the finger, and told him to eat shit, roughly all at the same time. He turned away, laughing, grabbed his black duster off the back of a chair.

"The people who drive hybrids look like weenies," he said. "I wouldn't be caught dead."

He left her in the kitchen, and cut through Danny's old office, headed for the driveway. Jude opened the side door, shaking his head, and stepped out into the Atlantic Ocean.

He hadn't expected it to be there — the ocean hadn't been waiting outside the front door yesterday — and he sank straight down, his motorcycle boots filling with icy seawater.

"Blub," he said. A jellyfish moved past him in pulses. He turned to go back inside, but the currents already had him, and he was rolled away through dark water. The hubcap of his Dodge Charger sailed by. *Shit,* he thought, *the Charger.* It had to be underwater too. The engine, the leather upholstery, the custom radio system…the whole thing was probably fucked.

Then Jude drowned.

SUMMER THUNDER

Stephen King

For Kurt Sutter and Richard Chizmar

Robinson was okay as long as Gandalf was. Not okay in the sense of everything is fine, but in the sense of getting along from one day to the next. He still woke up in the night, often with tears on his face from vivid dreams where Diana and Ellen were alive, but when he picked Gandalf up from the blanket in the corner where he slept and put him on the bed, he could more often than not go back to sleep again. As for Gandalf, he didn't care where he slept, and if Robinson pulled him close, that was okay, too. It was warm, dry, and safe. He had been rescued. That was all Gandalf cared about.

With another living being to take care of, things were better. Robinson drove to the country store five miles up Route 19 (Gandalf sitting in the pickup's passenger seat, ears cocked, eyes bright) and got dog food. The store was abandoned, and of course it had been looted, but no one had taken the Eukanuba. After June Sixth, pets had been the last thing on people's minds. So Robinson deduced.

Otherwise, the two of them stayed by the lake. There was plenty of food in the pantry, and boxes of stuff downstairs. He had often joked about how Diana expected the apocalypse, but the joke turned out to be on him. Both of them, actually, because Diana had surely never imagined that when the apocalypse finally arrived, she would be in Boston with their daughter, investigating the academic possibilities of Emerson College. Eating for one, the food would last longer than he did. Robinson had no doubt of that. Timlin said they were doomed.

He never would have expected doom to be so lovely. The weather was warm and cloudless. In the old days, Lake Pocomtuck would have buzzed with powerboats and Jet Skis (which were killing the fish, the old-timers grumbled), but this summer it was silent except for the loons...only there seemed to be fewer of them crying each night. At first Robinson thought this was just his imagination, which was as infected with grief as the rest of his thinking apparatus, but Timlin assured him it wasn't.

"Haven't you noticed that most of the woodland birds are already gone? No chickadee concerts in the morning, no crow music at noon. By September, the loons will be as gone as the loons who did this. The fish will live a little longer, but eventually they'll be gone, too. Like the deer, the rabbits, and the chipmunks."

About such wildlife there could be no argument. Robinson had seen almost a dozen dead deer beside the lake road and more beside Route 19, on that one trip he and Gandalf had made to the Carson Corners General Store, where the sign out front—BUY YOUR VERMONT CHEESE & SYRUP HERE!—now lay facedown next to the dry gas pumps. But the greatest part of the animal holocaust was in the woods. When the wind was from the east, toward the lake rather than off it, the reek was tremendous. The warm days didn't help, and Robinson wanted to know what had happened to nuclear winter.

"Oh, it'll come," said Timlin, sitting in his rocker and looking off into the dappled sunshine under the trees. "Earth is still absorbing the blow. Besides, we know from the last reports that the Southern Hemisphere—not to mention most of Asia—is socked in beneath what may turn out to be eternal cloud cover. Enjoy the sunshine while we've got it, Peter."

As if he could enjoy anything. He and Diana had been talking about a trip to England—their first extended vacation since the honeymoon—once Ellen was settled in school.

Ellen, he thought. Who had just been recovering from the breakup with her first real boyfriend and was beginning to smile again.

On each of these fine late-summer postapocalypse days, Robinson clipped a leash to Gandalf's collar (he had no idea what the dog's name had been before June Sixth; the mutt had come with a collar from which only a State of Massachusetts vaccination tag hung), and they walked the two miles to the pricey enclave of which Howard Timlin was now the only resident.

Diana had once called that walk snapshot heaven. Much of it overlooked sheer drops to the lake and forty-mile views into New York. At one point, where the road buttonhooked sharply, a sign that read MIND YOUR DRIVING! had been posted. The summer kids of course called this hairpin Dead Man's Curve.

Woodland Acres—private as well as pricey before the world ended— was a mile farther on. The centerpiece was a fieldstone lodge that had featured a restaurant with a marvelous view, a five-star chef, and a "beer pantry" stocked with a thousand brands. ("Many undrinkable," Timlin said. "Take it from me.") Scattered around the main lodge, in various bosky dells, were two dozen picturesque "cottages," some owned by major corporations before June Sixth put an end to corporations. Most of the cottages had still been empty on June Sixth, and in the crazy ten days that followed, the few people who were in residence fled for Canada, which was rumored to be radiation-free. That was when there was still enough gasoline to make flight possible.

The owners of Woodland Acres, George and Ellen Benson, had stayed. So had Timlin, who was divorced, had no children to mourn, and knew the Canada story was surely a fable. Then, in early July, the Bensons had swallowed pills and taken to their bed while listening to Beethoven on a battery-powered phonograph. Now it was just Timlin. "All that you see is mine," he had told Robinson, waving his arm grandly. "And someday, son, it will be yours."

On these daily walks down to the Acres, Robinson's grief and sense of dislocation eased; sunshine was seductive. Gandalf sniffed at the bushes and tried to pee on every one. He barked bravely when he heard something in the woods, but always moved closer to Robinson. The leash was necessary only because of the dead squirrels and chipmunks. Gandalf didn't want to pee on those; he wanted to roll in what was left of them.

Woodland Acres Lane split off from the camp road where Robinson now lived the single life. Once the lane had been gated to keep lookieloos and wage-slave rabble such as himself out, but now the gate stood permanently open. The lane meandered for half a mile through forest where the slanting, dusty light seemed almost as old as the towering spruces and pines that filtered it, passed four tennis courts, skirted a putting green, and looped behind a barn where the trail horses now lay dead in their stalls. Timlin's cottage was on the far side of the lodge— a modest dwelling with four bedrooms, four bathrooms, a hot tub, and its own sauna.

"Why did you need four bedrooms, if it's just you?" Robinson asked him once.

"I don't now and never did," Timlin said, "but they *all* have four bedrooms. Except for Foxglove, Yarrow, and Lavender. They have five.

Lavender also has an attached bowling alley. All mod cons. But when I came here as a kid with my family, we peed in a privy. True thing."

Robinson and Gandalf usually found Timlin sitting in one of the rockers on the wide front porch of his cottage (Veronica), reading a book or listening to his battery-powered CD player. Robinson would unclip the leash from Gandalf's collar and the dog—just a mutt, no real recognizable brand except for the spaniel ears—raced up the steps to be made a fuss of. After a few strokes, Timlin would gently pull at the dog's gray-white fur in various places, and when it remained rooted, he would always say the same thing: "Remarkable."

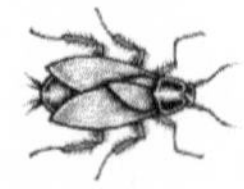

On this fine day in mid-August, Gandalf only made a brief visit to Timlin's rocker, sniffing at the man's bare ankles before trotting back down the steps and into the woods. Timlin raised his hand to Robinson in the How gesture of an old-time movie Indian.

Robinson returned the compliment.

"Want a beer?" Timlin asked. "They're cool. I just dragged them out of the lake."

"Would today's tipple be Old Shitty or Green Mountain Dew?" "Neither. There was a case of Budweiser in the storeroom. The King of Beers, as you may remember. I liberated it." "In that case, I'll be happy to join you."

Timlin got up with a grunt and went inside, rocking slightly from side to side. Arthritis had mounted a sneak attack on his hips two years ago, he had told Robinson, and, not content with that, had decided to lay claim to his ankles. Robinson had never asked, but judged Timlin to be in his mid-seventies. His slim body suggested a life of fitness, but fitness was now beginning to fail. Robinson himself had never felt physically better in his life, which was ironic considering how little he now had to live for. Timlin certainly didn't need him, although the old guy was congenial enough. As this preternaturally beautiful summer wound down, only Gandalf actually needed him. Which was okay, because for now, Gandalf was enough.

Just a boy and his dog, he thought.

Said dog had emerged from the woods in mid-June, thin and bedraggled, his coat snarled with burdock stickers and with a deep scratch across his snout. Robinson had been lying in the guest bedroom (he could not bear to sleep in the bed he had shared with Diana), sleepless with grief and depression, aware that he was edging closer and closer to just giving up and pulling the pin. He would have called such an action cowardly only weeks before, but had since come to recognize several undeniable facts. The pain would not stop. The grief would not stop. And, of course, his life was not apt to be a long one in any case. You only had to smell the decaying animals in the woods to know what lay ahead. He'd heard rattling sounds, and at first thought it might be a human being. Or a surviving bear that had smelled his food. But the gennie was still running then, and in the glare of the motion lights that illuminated the driveway he had seen a little gray dog, alternately scratching at the door and then huddling on the porch. When Robinson opened the door, the dog at first backed away, ears back and tail tucked.

"I guess you better come in," Robinson had said, and without much further hesitation, the dog did.

Robinson gave him a bowl of water, which he lapped furiously, and then a can of Prudence corned beef hash, which he ate in five or six snaffling bites. When the dog finished, Robinson stroked him, hoping he wouldn't be bitten. Instead of biting, the dog licked his hand.

"You're Gandalf," Robinson had said. "Gandalf the Grey." And then burst into tears. He tried to tell himself he was being ridiculous, but he wasn't. He was no longer alone in the house.

"What news about that motorhuckle of yours?" Timlin asked.

They had progressed to their second beers. When Robinson finished his, he and Gandalf would make the two-mile walk back to the house. He didn't want to wait too long; the mosquitoes got thicker when twilight came.

If Timlin's right, he thought, the bloodsuckers will inherit the earth instead of the meek. If they can find any blood to suck, that is.

"The battery's dead," he told Timlin. Then: "My wife made me promise to sell the bike when I was fifty. She said after fifty, a man's reflexes are too slow to be safe."

"And you're fifty when?"

"Next year," Robinson said. And laughed at the absurdity of it.

"I lost a tooth this morning," Timlin said. "Might mean nothing at my age, but…"

"Seeing any blood in the toilet bowl?"

Timlin had told him that was one of the first signs of advanced radiation poisoning, and he knew a lot more about it than Robinson did. What Robinson knew was that his wife and daughter had been in Boston when the frantic Geneva peace talks had gone up in a nuclear flash on the fifth of June, and they were still in Boston the next day, when the world killed itself. The eastern seaboard of America, from Hartford to Miami, was now mostly slag.

"I'm going to take the Fifth Amendment on that," Timlin said. "Here comes your dog. Better check his paws—he's limping a bit. Looks like the rear left."

But they could find no thorn in any of Gandalf's paws, and this time when Timlin pulled gently at his fur, a patch on his hindquarters came out. Gandalf seemed not to feel it. The two men looked at each other.

"Could be the mange," Robinson said at last. "Or stress. Dogs do lose fur when they're stressed, you know."

"Maybe." Timlin was looking west, across the lake. "It's going to be a beautiful sunset. Of course, they're all beautiful now. Like when Krakatoa blew its stack in eighteen eighty-three. Only this was ten thousand Krakatoas." He bent and stroked Gandalf's head.

"India and Pakistan," Robinson said.

Timlin straightened up again. "Well, yes. But then everyone else just had to get into the act, didn't they? Even the Chechens had a few, which they delivered to Moscow in pickup trucks. It's as though the world willfully forgot how many countries—and groups, fucking *groups*!— had those things."

"Or what those things were capable of," Robinson said.

Timlin nodded. "That too. We were too worried about the debt ceiling, and our friends across the pond were concentrating on stopping child beauty pageants and propping up the euro."

"You're sure Canada's just as dirty as the lower forty-eight?"

"It's a matter of degree, I suppose. Vermont's not as dirty as New York, and Canada's probably not as dirty as Vermont. But it will be. Plus, most of the people headed up there are already sick. Sick unto death, if I may misquote Kierkegaard. Want another beer?"

"I'd better get back." Robinson stood. "Come on, Gandalf. Time to burn some calories."

"Will I see you tomorrow?"

"Maybe in the late afternoon. I've got an errand to run in the morning." "May I ask where?"

"Bennington, while there's still enough gas in my truck to get there and back."

Timlin raised his eyebrows.

"Want to see if I can find a motorcycle battery."

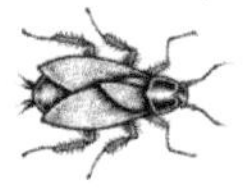

Gandalf made it as far as Dead Man's Curve under his own power, although his limp grew steadily worse. When they got there, he simply sat down, as if to watch the boiling sunset reflected in the lake. It was a fuming orange shot through with arteries of deepest red. The dog whined and licked at his back left leg. Robinson sat beside him for a little while, but when the first mosquito scouts called for reinforcements, he picked Gandalf up and started walking again. By the time they got back to the house, Robinson's arms were trembling and his shoulders were aching. If Gandalf had weighed another ten pounds, maybe even another five, he would have had to leave the mutt and go get the truck. His head also ached, perhaps from the heat, or the second beer, or both.

The tree-lined driveway sloping down to the house was a pool of shadows, and the house itself was dark. The gennie had given up the ghost weeks ago. Sunset had subsided to a dull purple bruise. He plodded onto the porch and put Gandalf down to open the door. "Go on, boy," he said. Gandalf struggled to rise, then subsided.

Just as Robinson was bending to pick him up again, Gandalf made another effort. This time he lunged over the doorsill and collapsed on his side in the entryway, panting. On the wall above the dog were at least two dozen photographs featuring people Robinson loved, all now deceased. He could no longer even dial Diana's and Ellen's phones and listen to their recorded voices. His own phone had died shortly after the generator, but even before that, all cell service had ceased.

He got a bottle of Poland Spring water from the pantry, filled Gandalf's bowl, then put down a scoop of kibble. Gandalf drank some water but wouldn't eat. When Robinson squatted to scratch the dog's belly, fur came out in bundles.

It's happening so fast, he thought. This morning he was fine.

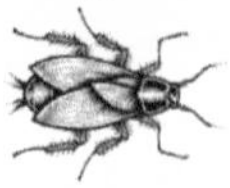

Robinson went out to the lean-to behind the house with a flashlight. On the lake, a loon cried—just one. The motorcycle was under a tarp. He pulled the canvas off and shone the beam along the bike's gleaming body. It was a 2014 Fat Bob, several years old now, but low mileage; his days of riding four and five thousand miles between May and October were behind him. Yet the Bob was still his dream ride, even though his dreams were mostly where he'd ridden it over the last couple of years. Air-cooled. Twin cam. Six-speed. Almost seventeen hundred ccs. And the sound it made! Only Harleys had that sound, like summer thunder. When you came up next to a Chevy at a stoplight, the cager inside was apt to lock his doors.

Robinson skidded a palm along the handlebars, then hoisted his leg over and sat in the saddle with his feet on the pegs. Diana had become increasingly insistent that he sell it, and when he did ride, she reminded him again and again that Vermont had a helmet law for a reason...unlike the idiots in New Hampshire and Maine. Now he could ride it without a helmet if he wanted to. There was no Diana to nag him, and no County Mounties to pull him over. He could ride it buckass naked, if he wanted to.

"Although I'd have to mind the tailpipes when I got off," he said, and laughed. He went inside without putting the tarp back on the Harley. Gandalf was lying on the bed of blankets Robinson had made for him, nose on one of his front paws. His kibble was untouched.

"Better eat up," Robinson said, giving Gandalf's head a stroke. "You'll feel better."

The next morning there was a red stain on the blankets around Gandalf's hindquarters, and although he tried, he couldn't make it to his feet. After he gave up the second time, Robinson carried him outside, where

Gandalf first lay on the grass, then managed to get up enough to squat. What came out of him was a gush of bloody stool. Gandalf crawled away from it as if ashamed, then lay down, looking at Robinson mournfully. This time when Robinson picked him up, Gandalf cried out in pain.

He bared his teeth but did not bite. Robinson carried him into the house and put him down on his blanket bed. He looked at his hands when he straightened up and saw they were coated with fur. When he dusted his palms together, the fur floated away like milkweed.

"You'll be okay," he told Gandalf. "Just a little upset stomach. Must have gotten one of those goddam chipmunks when I wasn't looking. Stay there and rest up. I'm sure you'll be feeling more like yourself by the time I get back."

There was still half a tank of gas in the Silverado, more than enough for a sixty-mile roundtrip to Bennington. Robinson decided to go down to Woodland Acres first and see if Timlin wanted anything.

His last neighbor was sitting on the porch of Veronica in his rocker. He was extremely pale, and there were purple pouches under his eyes. When Robinson told him about Gandalf, Timlin nodded. "I was up most of the night, running to the toilet. We must have caught the same bug." He smiled to show it was a joke, although not a very funny one. No, he said, there was nothing he wanted in Bennington, but perhaps Robinson would stop by on his way back. "I've got something *you* might want," he said.

The drive to Bennington was slower than Robinson expected, because the highway was littered with abandoned cars. It was close to noon by the time he pulled into the front lot of Kingdom Harley-Davidson. The show windows had been broken and all the display models were gone, but there were plenty of bikes out back. These had been rendered theftproof with steel cables sheathed in plastic and sturdy bike locks.

That was fine with Robinson; he only wanted to steal a battery. The Fat Bob he settled on was a year or two newer than his, but the battery looked the same. He fetched his toolbox from the bed of his pickup and checked the battery with his Impact (the tester had been a gift from his daughter two birthdays back), and got a green light. He removed the battery, went into the showroom, and found a selection of maps. Using the most detailed one to suss out the back roads, he made it back to the lake by three o'clock.

He saw a great many dead animals, including an extremely large moose lying beside the cement block steps of someone's trailer home. On the trailer's crabgrassy lawn, a hand-painted sign had been posted, only two words: HEAVEN SOON.

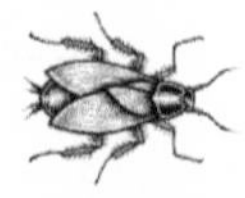

The porch of Veronica was deserted, but when Robinson knocked on the door, Timlin called for him to come in. He was sitting in the ostentatiously rustic living room, paler than ever. In one hand he held an oversize linen napkin. It was spotted with blood. On the coffee table in front of him were three items: a picture book titled *The Beauty of Vermont*, a hypodermic needle filled with yellow fluid, and a revolver.

"I'm glad you came," Timlin said. "I didn't want to leave without telling you goodbye."

Robinson recognized the absurdity of the first response that came to mind—Let's not be hasty—and stayed silent.

"I've lost half a dozen teeth," Timlin said, "but that's not the major problem. In the last twelve hours or so, I seem to have expelled most of my intestines. The eerie thing is how little it hurts. The hemorrhoids I was afflicted with in my fifties were worse. The pain will come—I've read enough to know that—but I don't intend to stick around long enough to experience it in full flower. Did you get the battery you wanted?"

"Yes," Robinson said, and sat down heavily. "Jesus, Howard, I'm so fucking sorry."

"Much appreciated. And you? How do you feel?"

"Physically? Fine." Although this was no longer completely true. Several red patches that didn't look like sunburn were blooming on his forearms, and there was another on his chest, above the right nipple. They itched. Also…his breakfast was staying down, but his stomach seemed far from happy with it.

Timlin leaned forward and tapped the hypo. "Demerol. I was going to inject myself, then look at pictures of Vermont until…until. But I've changed my mind. The gun will be fine, I think. You take the hypo."

"I'm not quite ready."

"Not for you, for the dog. He doesn't deserve to suffer. It wasn't dogs that built the bombs, after all."

"I think maybe he just ate a chipmunk," Robinson said feebly.

"We both know that's not it. Even if it was, the dead animals are so full of radiation it might as well have been a cobalt capsule. It's a wonder he's survived as long as he has. Be grateful for the time you've had with him. A little bit of grace. That's what a good dog is, you know. A little bit of grace."

Timlin studied him closely.

"Don't you cry on me. If you do, I will too, so man up. There's one more six-pack of Bud in the fridge. I don't know why I bothered to put it in there, but old habits die hard. Why don't you bring us each one? Warm beer is better than no beer; I believe Woodrow Wilson said that. We'll toast Gandalf. Also your new motorcycle battery. Meanwhile, I need to spend a penny. Or, who knows, this one might cost a little more."

Robinson got the beer. When he came back Timlin was gone, and remained gone for almost five minutes. He came back slowly, holding onto things. He had removed his pants and cinched a bath sheet around his midsection. He sat down with a little cry of pain, but took the can of beer Robinson held out to him. They toasted Gandalf and drank. The Bud was warm, all right, but not that bad. It was, after all, the King of Beers.

Timlin picked up the gun. "Mine will be the classic Victorian suicide," he said, sounding pleased at the prospect. "Gun to temple. Free hand over the eyes. Goodbye, cruel world."

"I'm off to join the circus," Robinson said without thinking. Timlin laughed heartily, lips peeling back to reveal his few remaining teeth. "It would be nice, but I doubt it. Did I ever tell you that I was hit by a truck when I was a boy? The kind our British cousins call a milk float?"

Robinson shook his head.

"Nineteen fifty-seven, this was. I was fifteen, walking down a country road in Michigan, headed for Highway Twenty-two, where I hoped to hook a ride into Traverse City and attend a double-feature movie show. I was daydreaming about a girl in my homeroom—such long, lovely legs and such high breasts—and wandered away from the relative safety of the shoulder. The milk float came over the top of a hill—the driver was going much too fast—and hit me square on. If it had been fully loaded, I surely would have been killed, but because it was empty it was much lighter, thus allowing me to live to the age of seventy-five, and experience what it's like to shit one's bowels into a toilet that will no longer flush."

There seemed to be no adequate response to this.

"There was a flash of sun on the float's windshield as it came over the top of the hill, and then…nothing. I believe I will experience roughly the same thing when the bullet goes into my brain and lays waste to all I've ever thought or experienced." He raised a professorly finger. "Only this time, nothing will not give way to something. Just a flash, like sun on the windshield of a milk float, followed by nothing. I find the idea simultaneously awesome and terribly depressing."

"Maybe you ought to hold off for awhile," Robinson said. "You might…"

Timlin waited politely, eyebrows raised.

"Fuck, I don't know," Robinson said. And then, surprising himself, he shouted, "*What did they do? What did those motherfuckers do?*"

"You know perfectly well what they did," Timlin said. "And now we live with the consequences. I know you love that dog, Peter. It's displaced love—what the psychiatrists call hysterical conversion—but we take what we can get, and if we've got half a brain, we're grateful. So don't hesitate. Stick him in the neck, and stick him hard. Grab his collar in case he flinches."

Robinson put his beer down. He didn't want it anymore. "He was in pretty bad shape when I left. Maybe he's dead already."

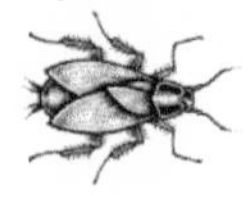

But Gandalf wasn't.

He looked up when Robinson came into the bedroom and thumped his tail twice on his bloody pad of blankets. Robinson sat down next to him. He stroked Gandalf's head and thought about the dooms of love, which were really so simple when you peered directly into them. Gandalf put his head on Robinson's knee and looked up at him. Robinson took the hypo out of his shirt pocket and removed the protective cap from the needle.

"You're a good guy," he said, and took hold of Gandalf's collar, as Timlin had instructed.

While he was nerving himself to go through with it, he heard a gunshot. The sound was faint at this distance, but with the lake so still, there was no mistaking it for anything else. It rolled across the hot summer air, diminished, tried to echo, failed. Gandalf cocked his ears, and an idea came to Robinson, as comforting as it was absurd. Maybe Timlin was wrong about the nothing. It was possible. In a world where you could look up and see an eternal hallway of stars, he reckoned anything was. Maybe—

Maybe.

Gandalf was still looking at him as he slid the needle home. For a moment the dog's eyes remained bright and aware, and in the endless moment before the brightness left, Robinson would have taken it back if he could.

He sat there on the floor for a long time, hoping that last loon might sound off one more time, but it didn't. After awhile, he went out to the lean-to, found a spade, and dug a hole in his wife's flower garden. There was no need to go deep; no animal was going to come along and dig Gandalf up.

When he woke up the next morning, Robinson's mouth tasted coppery. When he lifted his head, his cheek peeled away from the pillow. Both his nose and his gums had bled in the night.

It was another beautiful day, and although it was still summer, the first color had begun to steal into the trees. Robinson wheeled his Fat Bob out of the lean-to and replaced the dead battery, working slowly and carefully in the deep silence.

When he finished, he turned the switch. The green neutral light came on, but stuttered a little. He shut the switch off, tightened the connections, then tried again. This time the light stayed steady. He hit the ignition and that sound—summer thunder—shattered the quiet. It seemed sacrilegious, but—this was strange—in a good way.

Robinson wasn't surprised to find himself thinking of his first and only trip to attend the annual Sturgis motorcycle rally in South Dakota, 1998 that had been, the year before he met Diana. He remembered rolling slowly down Junction Avenue on his Honda GB 500, one more sled in a parade of two thousand, the combined roar of all those bikes so loud it seemed a physical thing. Later that night there had been a bonfire, and an endless stream of Stones and AC/DC and Metallica roaring from Stonehenge stacks of Marshall amps. Tattooed girls danced topless in the firelight; bearded men drank beer from bizarre helmets; children decorated with decal tattoos of their own ran everywhere, waving sparklers. It had been terrifying and amazing and wonderful, everything that was right and wrong with the world in the same place and in perfect focus. Overhead, that hallway of stars.

Robinson gunned the Fat Boy, then let off the throttle. Gunned and let off. Gunned and let off. The rich smell of freshly burned gasoline filled the driveway. The world was a dying hulk but the silence had been banished, at least for the time being, and that was good. That was fine. Fuck you, silence, he thought. Fuck you and the horse you rode in on. This is my horse, my iron horse, and how do you like it?

He squeezed the clutch and toed the gearshift down into first. He rolled up the driveway, banked right, and toed up this time, into second and then third. The road was dirt, and rutted in places, but the bike took the ruts easily, floating Robinson up and down on the seat. His nose was spouting again; the blood streamed up his cheeks and flew off behind him in fat droplets. He took the first curve and then the second, banking harder now, hitting fourth gear as he came onto a brief straight stretch. The Fat Bob was eager to go. It had been in that goddam lean- to too long, gathering dust. On Robinson's right, he could see Lake Pocomtuck from the corner of his eye, still as a mirror, the sun beating a yellow-gold track across the blue. Robinson let out a yell and shook one fist at the sky—at the universe—before returning it to the hand- grip. Ahead was the buttonhook, with the MIND YOUR DRIVING! sign that marked Dead Man's Curve.

Robinson aimed for the sign and twisted the throttle all the way. He just had time to hit fifth gear.

THE MAID FROM THE ASH: A LIFE IN PICTURES

Gwendolyn Kiste

The Maid from the Ash: A Life in Pictures
Museum of Postmodern Art
Limited Engagement

Thank you for joining us at the opening of *The Maid from the Ash: A Life in Pictures*. This program will guide you through each of our eighteen exhibits. For the sake of other visitors in the museum as well as for your own safety, we caution against any use of photography, flash or otherwise. During the installation of this collection, we learned too well that some of the photographs prefer if you don't stare too long. So please keep this in mind and do be courteous during your stay with us.

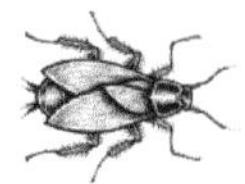

Exhibit 1: "The Maid from the Ash" (Polaroid Instant, Forensic photographer)

This is the first known image of the Maid from the Ash, taken the day she was discovered at a ramshackle abode in rural Pennsylvania. In the picture, two uniformed men escort her away after a fire, but she drags her feet and stares back at the place she called home. Due to the widespread commotion of the police and fire trucks, nearly everything in the picture is blurred. Only her eyes, eternally gazing heavenward, are in sharp focus.

It started with a 911 call. A hiker reported smoke coming from an area of the forest believed to be uninhabited. Emergency services arrived at the scene of a two-story shack surrounded in a ring of flames. Not until they extinguished the blaze, a feat that took nearly an hour, did they find the girl sitting on the front porch, her dark eyes the color of dusk. While the grass and surrounding property were scorched to the salt, she and the house were untouched except for the ash.

"She wasn't scared," said the sheriff, retired by the time we interviewed him. "She wasn't anything at all. Just stone-still and serene, like a body preserved in a morgue."

In a melee that appeared to annoy the girl, the paramedics checked her vitals (heart rate 80, blood pressure 90/60) as officials all agreed the house had no business in that location, that no one had applied for the requisite building permits, that nobody — not even a park ranger — frequented that area, which was inaccessible besides a dirt path that flooded six months of the year.

When they asked the girl why she was there, she shrugged and said, "It's my home."

But it wasn't much to speak of. The forensics team described it as "a lopsided sepulcher."

The house — if you could call it that — was spackled together with lark feathers and sinewy thatch and ancient birch faded to a silvery gray. Not one nail or proper board on the whole property, wrote one of the Philadelphia-based investigators called in after the fire. *Certainly not a place fit for a young girl.*

The team's initial tests uncovered higher-than-normal calcium deposits in the walls, leading to early rumors that the house was constructed of human bones, but further examination all but proved the structure was banal in origin.

(The fire itself was later determined to be the result of heat lightning, which dovetailed with the girl's own crude description of "a great fire from the sky.")

This photograph, circulated by the police in hopes of uncovering the girl's identity, appeared in the local newspaper and quickly went viral, eventually gracing numerous national magazine covers with the headline, *Who is this Maid from the Ash?* Issues that featured the photograph performed unexpectedly well, thanks to eager readers determined to solve the mystery themselves.

Still, even with the assistance of enthusiastic housewives and sleuthing college students, they never found her parents or learned anything else about the girl. According to all extant records (the sheriff's office suffered an inexplicable basement fire six months before the debut of this exhibition, so files are limited), no official search was ever conducted to locate her family members. Likewise, she never asked for them or mentioned their names.

"It was as if," the sheriff said, "she was born from those flames."

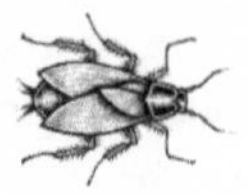

Exhibit 2: "Day in Court" (Cell phone snapshot, posted on the *Gabby Gossipmonger* website)

In this blurry image taken on a 2009-model flip phone, the girl is seen exiting the courthouse after the judge's ruling on her emancipation status. Despite the image's pixilated quality and the crowd of hundreds surrounding her with cameras, she is easy to spot, off to the left side of the frame, her hair a mussed curtain across her eyes.

No certificate of live birth could be located for the girl, so after the fire, the police took her to a local physician who determined she was no more than sixteen. This prompted juvenile services to enter an official case file under the name of Jane Doe. (The aforementioned doctor would not respond to requests on precisely how he made that determination of age, nor would he release any of her medical records for this installation.)

At her hearing, the judge had to demand order six times to quiet the packed courtroom. By this point, the public couldn't get enough of the Maid from the Ash. A crowdfunding page was set up in her honor (donations peaked at $415,674, though whether or not those monies were ultimately sent to the girl is unclear), and in a recent online search, we located more than two-hundred fan pages on Facebook, Twitter, and other social media set up in her honor, most of which have long since been abandoned.

The hearing, which permitted bystanders direct access to the girl for the first time, proved irresistible. Dozens camped out at every motel, spare room, and rest stop in the Central Valley.

"It's not every day you have a chance to make a difference like this," said one Missouri housewife who had towed her three children to the courtroom that day. "We need to help this poor, young creature."

At the girl's request, the court was ruling that day on whether or not she was fit to take care of herself. But the judge had apparently made his ruling long in advance.

"Why in the world at the age of sixteen should we allow you to live on your own?" he asked, glowering at her over the edges of his little square glasses.

"Because I want to be on my own," she said. "I can cook and clean and forage. I survived just fine by myself."

"Until the fire. You nearly died."

The girl shook her head. "The house wouldn't let anything hurt me."

"Houses can't help you, dear," the judge said, and the crowd chortled in agreement. "We have to give you somewhere to belong."

"What if I don't belong with you?" she said, but her words were lost among the crashing of a gavel and the screech-owl cries of a crowd certain they'd done the right thing.

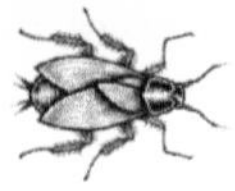

Exhibit 3: "The Maid from the Ash: One Year Later" (Print article, *The Observer News Gazette*)

A human-interest piece documenting the girl's progress, released on the anniversary of the fire. Accompanying the article are three black-and-white photographs of her sitting with her latest family, the Whitcombs. Her new mother and father are all dazzling smiles, but the girl has no expression at all. She simply sits at the far edge of the room on a three-legged ottoman, her lips twisted to one side and her eyes set on the ceiling, studying something that isn't there.

By now, the girl was on her third family. She had fled the previous two placements in Pennsylvania, and during one escape, she'd made it as far as the county line near her former home before the police caught her. When they demanded to know why she ran, all she said was she had somewhere to be.

In an attempt to curb further flights, juvenile services moved her to upstate New York, several day's walk from her property. At the time of this article's release, she had a new hometown of Ogdensburg and a new name: 'Flannery.'

"It was important to call her something," her latest mom Jeanette is quoted as saying. "She needed to feel like a whole person, a *real* person."

The reporter asked the girl if she liked her new moniker, but Flannery only shrugged.

"It's as good as any other," she said.

Her new parents blathered on about school supplies and school clothes and Flannery's new private school, all while repeating that the public had not forgotten the Maid from the Ash.

"Not a week goes by that someone doesn't come up to the door, sometimes whole families, eager for a photograph with her," said her father, who the reporter described with words like *loquacious* and *beaming*. (However, we found him to be neither — he refused to participate in this exhibit in any way, having relocated to Utah following his divorce from Jeanette last year).

"And she photographs so well," Jeanette said, smiling *incandescently* (again, the reporter's word of choice). "Everybody tells us how beautiful she is."

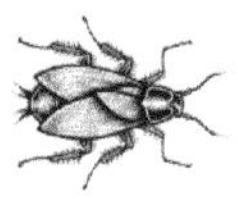

Exhibit 4: "A New Beginning" (Webcam image from the Whitcombs' computer)

Flannery stands against a blank wall in an unfurnished bedroom, her hands clasped in front of her, her eyes lined in liquid green. This was her debut post to social media, and by the end of her first week online, she boasted over 50,000 followers, a number that at the height of her popularity would top out at 10 million.

This image appeared two weeks after the previous article hit newsstands, and curiosity about the Maid from the Ash surged once again. Given her previous reticence, the precise reason why Flannery became interested in an online presence is unknown, and debate exists on whether she wanted this image taken or if the Whitcombs cajoled her into it.

In our interview, Jeanette insisted the idea was all Flannery's. "She wanted to meet other people. I think she hoped that one day, she might find someone like her."

And though it probably wasn't who she intended, she did find plenty of people. In her first month online, Flannery uploaded twenty-five more photos (all of which were eventually deleted along with this one, printed here as a screencap). After every new post, the comments and likes poured in.

"Everybody just adored our little girl," Jeanette said brightly.

In those early weeks, fans reached out repeatedly to Flannery, and while she was never gushing, she did respond to many of their questions. An example of such an exchange — this time during an Ask-Me-Anything chat — is archived below.

ashfan4E: hi, flannery! so great to meet you! i've been following you since the beginning! super glad you've got a family now. and a name! WOOT! do you like your new home?

flimflan: I guess it's okay, but I liked my old house better. I can't wait to turn eighteen so I can go back there.

teamflannery: OMG SO AMAZIN TO TALK WITH U, FLANNERY! I'M UR BIGGEST FAN!!! SO I'VE GOT A QUESTION FOR U! IF U COULD HAVE ONE THING IN THE WORLD, WHAT WOULD BE UR WISH???

flimflan: To return home.

teamflannery: BUT THERES NO POWER OR COMPUTER THERE, RIGHT?!?!?!?! HOW WOULD U TALK WITH US?

ashfan4E: yeah, we totally cant live without you! so… what's your second greatest wish? ;)

flimflan: That people would stop carving off pieces of my house. It makes my chest ache every time they do.

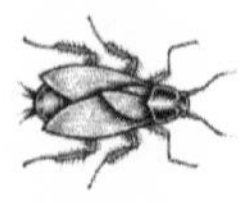

"She would invent the strangest tales," Jeanette said when we asked about the last comment. "Carving off pieces of the house? We never told her that, and she hadn't been back there since they rescued her. Why would she say such a thing?"

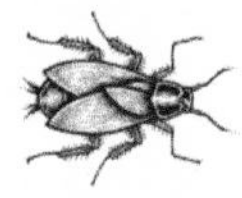

Exhibit 5: "The House that Flannery Built" (Digital photograph for a college student's senior project, taken approximately the same timeframe as Flannery's Ask-Me-Anything chat)

The colorless house stands sullenly in the shadows of dusk. In the thirteen months since the fire, the property remained more or less the same (the scorched grounds never grew back), but the ring around the house seemingly protected it from decay. However, if you examine the image closely — we've provided a magnifying glass — you might notice what look like small notches on the corners of the house where it appears as if fingers dug out bits of the feather and birch.

In the year after the fire, police chased away scores of fans who made their macabre pilgrimages to the property. After he noticed trails of shredded wood along the foundation, the sheriff questioned one of the girls he caught there.

"This is a holy place for us," she said to him, fumbling with her oversized bag. "But we would never take anything as a souvenir. *Never.*"

"There wasn't much we could do to stop them," the sheriff told us. "The house legally belonged to nobody. It would be like telling a kid not to carve their initials into a tree trunk. You can try, but it's almost impossible to enforce."

The most intrepid fans would stay on site overnight. No one, however, ever made it the whole evening inside the house. Instead, they would turn up at the sheriff's office at three in the morning to report a distant weeping in the walls. When we inquired about the wails, the sheriff waved us off. He claimed he investigated multiple times and could attribute it only to the wind.

"The woods are a haunted place at night," he said. "People think they can hear God himself speaking."

Exhibit 6: "Test Shots" (Twenty-five slide photos of Flannery, the best images marked with red grease pencil)

In her first semiprofessional photographs, Flannery wears a carnation pink dress that is too loose around the waist and too tight around the shoulders, giving the illusion that her body is convex, the inverse of an hourglass. She doesn't smile in the images, and her eyes are obscured by a blur the photographer could never explain.

(Special Note: Please ignore the significant charring around the edges of the slides. This damage was due to a projector overheating when we were reviewing the images prior to this installation.)

After the success of her social media posts, a fashion photographer in Albany contacted the Whitcombs about submitting pictures of Flannery to major modeling agencies in New York.

Little is known about this particular shoot, and even the photographer, who has since given up his camera and is now an accountant in Florida, had almost no insight.

She didn't say much, he recently recalled via email. *But she didn't have time to talk. Her parents were always hovering on set and offering "helpful" suggestions. Once, when they were out of the room for a smoke break, she did mention to me how she was counting the days until she turned eighteen and could escape.*

"Modeling was a great way for her to meet people," Jeanette said. "And remember: that's what she wanted. It was always her choice."

Within two weeks of the shoot, Ionize Modeling Agency contacted the Whitcombs and signed Flannery that day. She started work within the month.

I felt bad for the kid, the former photographer wrote in closing. *She'd been through enough, and I've always wondered if my photographs only made it worse. But I was trying to help, you know? I thought it would make her happy. How was I supposed to know it would turn out this way?*

Exhibit 7: "Haute" (Tear sheet from *Fashion Heir Magazine*, taken by photographer Ray Hendrickson)

A stone-faced Flannery glides down the runway in a floor-length dress constructed of peacock feathers. (Our apologies about the condition of this exhibit; we believe the heavy wrinkling is from water or possibly heat damage.)

Following a series of promotional jobs — including an all-night appearance at Times Square that sent twenty-seven of her overzealous, dehydrated fans to the hospital — Flannery made her runway debut at Fashion Week. This was perhaps her happiest since the fire, not because of the job, but because of the date. The next week, she was turning eighteen — or what the court had ruled was her eighteenth birthday.

"This is my first fashion show," she said to the reporters before the event, "and it will be my last too. So enjoy it now!"

She was unaware of the Whitcombs' recent (and unusually private) conversations with the court.

"Unfortunately, she wasn't making enough progress," Jeanette told us. "She was still such a restless girl. And withdrawn too. At night, she would murmur in her sleep that the wolves were at the door. How could we abandon her in that condition?" Jeanette shook her head. "I couldn't fail her like that."

To ensure Flannery's safety, the court ruled that the Whitcombs could continue their conservatorship of her for an indefinite period.

"Or until she was better," Jeanette repeated three times in our interview with her. "We only wanted her to get better."

Just before the show, the press heard a single scream backstage, presumed to be Flannery learning of her parents' subterfuge, though this was never confirmed.

After the event, no one saw her leave, but the following morning, during a lightning storm, she crawled out her second-story bedroom window. It was too far for her to reach the wilds of Pennsylvania, but that didn't matter. She ran. For a hundred miles, through thickets and along back roads, she ran. They found her two days later tangled in briars, unconscious and barefoot and hypothermic. Her recovery took almost six weeks.

During her convalescence, one fan asked how she was doing. Flannery was very clear on her intentions:

flimflan: I don't care what they do to me. I won't ever stop trying to get home.

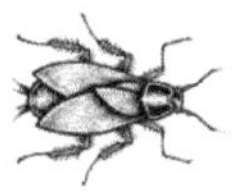

Exhibit 8: "Everything to Dust" (Blurry Smartphone Image, Anonymous fan)

Flannery's property at dusk. The house is gone, and in its wake, all that's left is a pile of rubble.

The fans knew what they needed to do.

"It was in her best interest," said the individual who submitted this picture. "As long as that house was standing, it would always torture her. We had no choice. We had to set her free."

At first, the flash mob tried to burn it, but their matches flitted out, leaving behind only a lonesome stench of sulfur. So they opted instead for their old standby: they disassembled the house, piece by consecrated piece. With over one hundred people gathered there, it took less than an hour.

Exhibit 9: "The Cover" (Film Stock, *Fashion Heir Magazine*)

An extreme close-up of Flannery's face. Her cheeks smolder with a preternatural rosiness, and black tears from her dark eye makeup drip down to the curve of her jaw.

That same afternoon, Flannery was on set in New York for a cover shoot, working with Ray Hendrickson, the same photographer who had taken her picture at the fashion show (he had specifically requested to work with her again). At the moment her house was turned to sawdust (approximately 1:57 p.m. Eastern Standard Time), Flannery let out a banshee-wail and collapsed in her locked dressing room. When they broke down the door, they found her curled in the corner, covered in angry red scratch marks, and repeating one word over and over: *wolves*. Her injuries were later attributed to the sharp edges of her acrylic nails that the makeup artist applied earlier in the day, although the depth and shape were not consistent.

Jeanette begged them to curtail the shoot ("Under those circumstances, no normal person would have made her continue"), but Ray insisted on taking just a few images.

"He claimed her pain was too beautiful to waste," Jeanette said.

So they swathed Flannery's skin in pancake foundation to conceal her wounds, and they shoved her beneath the blaring lights.

And without a word, she posed for them, her figure almost liquid, almost unreal against the flimsy paper backdrop. She moved with purpose, with a clarity all the previous photos lacked. Like an angel, some said at the time. Like a demon, some say now.

Although we don't recommend it, if you look closely, they say you can see a ring of flames in her eyes, but Jeanette assured us that it was only a trick of the light.

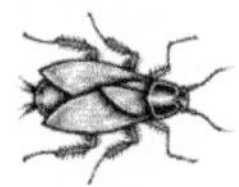

Exhibit 10: "Real Me" (B&W self-portrait, posted to social media)

Flannery stands alone in a field, dressed in a tight sheathe. Her eyes are not turned upward, and she's not edging bashfully to one side. Instead, she's in the center of the frame, and she's staring straight into the camera. Into you.

Following the destruction of her house, Flannery vanished from public view for almost six months. The Whitcombs said she needed time to recuperate ("She didn't stop crying for weeks," Jeanette confided), but other reports suggested Flannery was perhaps not such a delicate hothouse flower. Among conspiracy theorists is the claim that she spent her sabbatical in deep meditation, not leaving her bedroom for weeks at a time, sleeping and eating and living in the dark.

When at last she reemerged, it was with this picture captioned, "Real Me" (hence the title of this exhibit). Nobody knew where the photograph was taken or with what camera, but overnight, it became her most liked image — and perhaps her most controversial.

"Everybody was so glad to have her back," the sheriff said, "that we didn't want to bring it up."

What they chose not to discuss at the time was the effect of this particular picture. In the weeks after the image materialized, thousands of fans reported a rash of headaches, nausea, and blurred vision as well as complaints about the inexplicable scents of campfire and earth in their homes. If you examine this exhibit too long even now, the room might suddenly smell of flames and sorrow and childhoods lost long ago.

So perhaps it's best to move along.

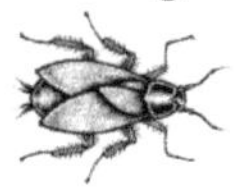

Exhibit 11: "The Stew of My Blood, Bone, and Heart" (Twelve self-portraits, first appeared in *Conway's Haute Style*)

In a dim room, Flannery poses in a black dress and a flowing black veil. In the first picture, she stands against the far wall, no more than a tiny inkblot. But as the images progress, she creeps closer to the camera until in the final picture, her face fills up the whole frame, and all you can discern is a single eye, draped in gauzy chiffon, watching you.

This strange photo collection appeared in the offices of *Conway's Haute Style* one morning, bearing no address of any sort. The envelope was inscribed with a simple note: *For Your Consideration.*

Upon the pictures' release, critics vacillated wildly in their critiques, with some calling the series "overwrought" and "childish" while others gleefully christened Flannery "the Cindy Sherman of the macabre." Even *Conway's* was initially skeptical.

"We weren't in the habit of publishing such crude selfies," the senior editor told us, as she sipped *chocolat chaud* as thick as mud at a mostly abandoned Madison Avenue cafe. "But something made us change our minds. *She* made us change our minds."

Of course, now it's easy to understand the appeal.

(WARNING: We would prefer if you proceeded now to the next exhibit. Even among those with no preexisting conditions, these pictures bring considerable risk; for example, several otherwise healthy college interns became light-headed during this installation and could not continue with us despite their best intentions.)

We know you're still here. We wish you weren't.

Fine.

For the strong-stomached, please inhale once, and a perfume of wintergreen will make your eyes heavy and your skin buzz. The room might spin for an instant, and your head might loll like a useless ragdoll.

Inhale twice, and every sinew in your body will hang heavy on your bones, as the air twists with the scent of rotten thorn apple. You might not have realized you knew what thorn apple smelled like, but now you'll never forget it again.

We don't recommend inhaling a third time. Instead, please move on to the video room located to your right.

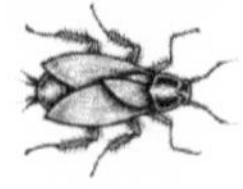

Exhibit 12: "A Maid Looks Back" (Footage on loan from the Smithsonian)

A never-before-screened documentary featuring Flannery. The interviewer is Ray Hendrickson, who had been desperate to work with her again after their cover shoot. This documentary was his brainchild, since it provided him an intimate opportunity to speak with her.

The running time is a full hour, and we understand that given the recent harsh weather, you might want to be home before dark, so we've included the transcript of our favorite scene below.

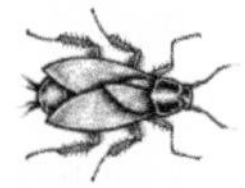

Flannery: Rather rude, don't you think? Destroying a person's home? I can't fathom anything so devilish as that.

Ray (*from behind the camera*): I guess. But you were about to tell me about that day the police found you.

Flannery (*smiles to herself*): Yes, I was, wasn't I? (*She twists her lips to one side.*) I wasn't ready for them. What happened with the fire proved that. I was young, and the young are always such fools. If I'd been ready enough, I would have hidden.

Ray: And how would you have done that?

Flannery: Maybe I would have disguised myself as a great elm or been as invisible as the wind. (*She hesitates.*) But I wasn't strong then. I was trying to be strong, but I failed.

Ray: And now? Are you stronger now?

(Flannery says nothing. She merely shifts her eyes upward and smiles to herself again, as the camera dissolves to black.)

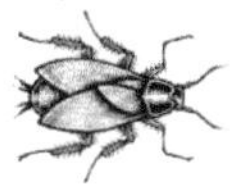

Exhibit 13: "From the Char-Black Ash" (Smartphone picture, Courtesy of the sheriff)

An image of the grounds where the house once stood, one year after its destruction. While the police received no reports of vandalism on the property, and Flannery was nowhere near the area, the house is no longer a heap of shredded rubble. Instead, there is a vague outline of a mud foundation, and pale tree limbs pile in the place where the porch once stood. The grass remains scorched in a ring, and when compared to the previous images of the property, you will notice that the decomposing land casts a wider girth, spreading beyond the initial border of the fire to the edges of the frame and beyond. This blight, however, does not touch the renewed framework of the house.

In the weeks after this photograph was taken, the rubble grew several feet higher.

No longer were there sporadic reports of an unknown individual weeping. Instead, police fielded at least a dozen calls a week from hikers in the nearby forest who claimed to hear a gentle thrum rising from the ground, as though a sleeping child was singing or murmuring to herself.

"We could never locate the source," the sheriff said. "We wanted to believe it was just the wind spooking city folk who didn't know what to expect out there."

It is also worth noting that this was the first season the crops in surrounding areas withered on the vine or refused to ripen altogether. As you now know, it was not the last.

Exhibit 14: "From Tears to True Love: Ash Maid Meets Her Match!" (Photocopy of two-page tabloid spread)

An article about Flannery's love life, accompanied by four full-color photographs. In each one, she's smiling next to Ray.

After the documentary, Ray repeatedly contacted the Whitcombs until they agreed to allow him to take Flannery to dinner.

"He was such a huge fan of hers," Jeanette said, smiling. "He had all her press clippings."

(Perhaps in an attempt at diplomacy, Jeanette never used the words that some of Flannery's fans chose to describe him, which included *obsessed*, *creepy*, and *stalker-ish*.)

At first, Flannery wasn't too keen on dating, but Jeanette said she eventually thawed to the idea.

"When she learned he was from Pennsylvania too, that gave them something to talk about, especially with everything happening there at the time," she said in reference to the dying crops in Clinton, Tioga, and Potter counties.

As one date gave way to dozens, it's impossible to know how Flannery felt about this relationship — unless you think she's speaking to you now. Take a moment to lean closer to this exhibit, and you might notice how her gaze slides slowly away from her beau, as she stares to the sky, her eyes as cold as the ancient dead. Then she'll smile to herself, a specter of a grin, and you might think you've gone crazy.

(But don't worry. You aren't the only one who sees it.)

In all these photographs, the Whitcombs are in the background, chaperoning the young couple. At this point, despite having reached the age of twenty-one, Flannery remained under conservatorship. Technically, even now, she's still under conservatorship. These days, though, there's not much left to conserve.

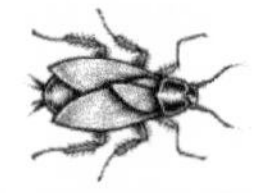

Exhibit 15: "Something Borrowed" (Tear sheet from *White Weddings Magazine;* please note the sidebar titled "What to Do if Your Wedding Spot is in the New Dust Bowl")

An aerial shot taken during Flannery's wedding reception. She lingers alone in the center of the crowd, arrayed in her embroidered satin gown and a lace train that stalks a full ten-feet behind her, like a shackle or a leash. Beneath the incandescent glow of the white string lights, she could be a ghost hiding in plain sight.

After six months of dating, Flannery and Ray were married at a private estate in upstate New York. This is the sole photograph from the wedding that we could locate. At Flannery's request, no cell phones or personal cameras were permitted at the ceremony, and her husband refused to release any images from his own collection.

"Those pictures are ours," he said when we contacted him for this exhibition. "They're not for prying eyes."

Despite repeated phone calls and emails (and even one painfully thwarted house visit), that was the only quote we could glean from him. Since the wedding and the failed excursion that followed it, he quit the fashion industry and relocated to the hills of Oregon where even the trees are different enough not to remind him of her.

Exhibit 16: "Moon of Honey" (Image recovered from the memory card on Ray's camera, donated to us by a magazine assistant who prefers to remain anonymous for fear of litigation)

Flannery stands among the Ringing Rocks of Pennsylvania, wearing a white cotton dress, and flashing a smile so bright it's nearly blinding.

This is the last confirmed photograph of her.

Following the wedding, Flannery insisted on doing another photo shoot with her groom.

"She was ready to get back to work," Jeanette confirmed.

For their first editorial together as husband and wife, Flannery requested to visit the area near her groom's birthplace. It was the first time she'd returned to her home state since joining the Whitcombs in New York. The Pennsylvania Tourism Bureau, desperate for any and all attention since the farmland plight had overtaken a twenty-county radius, welcomed her with open arms. After all, the return of the Maid from the Ash — one of the state's greatest exports — was a welcome occasion.

When we asked if they worried about Flannery being near her former property, Jeanette bloomed a hundred shades of red.

"Why should we have been concerned? There were thirty people on the set. Everyone was watching her, especially her husband. She had a new life. She was *happy.*"

"Besides," Jeanette added, red splotches lingering on her cheeks, "the location was a four-hour drive away from where they found her. How could she possibly make it home on foot?"

Of the six assistants we interviewed who were on set, everyone agrees the day started out humdrum enough: Ray conducted a couple quick light tests before they commenced the photos. And that's when it all goes gossamer.

Though nobody can remember quite what happened next, they all agree on this: with Flannery's every smile, every tilt of her head, every toss of her hair, their vision blurred, and they found themselves fading out. They leaned against one another to catch their breath. Then the aromas of campfire and wintergreen and regret filled them like empty hourglasses, and they wilted, the same as the fallen wheat of Pennsylvania. Together, they curled in the laps of trees, and slept a sleep so deep and dreamless that it might as well have been the slumber of the long interred.

"She knew what she was doing," said the assistant who donated this photograph. "She probably had it planned out from the first time she heard Ray was from Pennsylvania."

Though the memory was filmy, the last thing anyone can remember seeing was Flannery with a grin on her face, her feet quivering off the ground.

"What a sacrilegious lie," Jeanette said. "My girl wasn't a witch."

Perhaps she wasn't, but what we do know is that by the time the crew stirred awake, their heads stuffed with gauze, dusk had ushered in a lightning storm, and Flannery was gone.

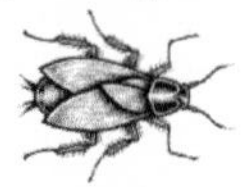

Exhibit 17: "Going Home" (Film Stock, Anonymous Photographer)

This is the only image in the collection that we cannot substantiate as Flannery. However, it was taken at sundown on the day of the failed photo shoot, and the figure in the image is wearing the same white cotton dress. Her back is turned to us, which makes her identity forever a mystery.

Though sharp at the edges, the center of the image is blurred, so that her dress and the slant of the fading afternoon light create the illusion that she is becoming one with the house.

A male hiker, who preferred not to be named, was photographing the wilting wildlife when Flannery materialized among a patch of weeds.

"Like she dropped straight from the sky," he said with a laugh.

Over a ten-minute phone call with us, he explained how he didn't recognize her.

"I don't read magazines," he said from his home in California. "That tabloid junk is the undoing of the world."

Other than her entrance, nothing about their interaction was inexplicable.

"She just smiled at me," he said. "Then she walked toward the house. The sight was so pretty and peaceful that I couldn't help but take a photo of her to capture that moment."

The property has been subsequently closed off due to the blight that's overtaken all of Pennsylvania and spread due north into New York and beyond. But that day, the man said the forest was as beautiful as she was.

"No rot, at least nothing that could detract from her."

He left before she came out again. "Something told me she would be okay, that she would be safe there."

He hesitated on the phone, a wave of lonesome static crackling between us.

"She belonged there," he said before abruptly ending the call.

Exhibit 18: "Epilogue" (Digital Photography, Original for this installation)

A recent image of the house. The Army Corps of Engineers has cordoned off the area with electric fencing, so the closest we were permitted was a quarter mile away. Even with a high caliber telephoto lens, the house remains obscured in shadows and strange angles. From this distance, it looks like a tower of thorns.

Flannery — or whatever name she prefers now — has not been spotted in over two years.

"We're terrified she died in there," Jeanette said to us, but her voice snapped apart as though she was more terrified her once-daughter didn't die at all. (We recently attempted a follow-up interview with Jeanette, but her phone had been disconnected without notice.)

Unfortunately, with no sighting of Flannery and no access to her house, we couldn't report much from the property. But one thing we noticed: the ground there no longer weeps or murmurs. Now it laughs without reservation, laughs with the echo of a voice you might recognize, a voice we wish we could forget.

In the sheriff's last conversation with us (like many others in the region, he has since moved West with his family to escape the ever-growing decay), he shook his head when asked for any parting wisdom.

"Maybe I was wrong before," he said. "Maybe she didn't come from those flames. Maybe it was always the other way around."

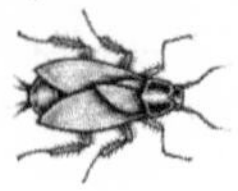

Thank you again for attending *The Maid from the Ash: A Life in Pictures.* On your way home, please take care in your travels. Given the unseasonably warm temperatures, meteorologists predict the recent heat lightning will continue throughout the evening, possibly bleeding into next week or even next month.

Or perhaps there will always be lightning now.

INUNDATION

John Langan

For Fiona

There is water coming into the basement.

It's an old basement, fieldstones stacked and mortared together, a dirt floor. Water bubbles up from the dirt, arcs from gaps in the mortar. A trench runs along the periphery of the basement, intended to channel the annual spring seepage to the room's northwest corner, where a sump pump in a round hole waits to push the water through a black plastic pipe out the front of the house, where it will run down the short, step front yard to the street with its deep gutters. But the pump is designed for modest floods, an inch or two at most, not the briny two and a half feet that has accumulated already and shows no signs of diminishing. The pump continues disgorging water outside, but since there is water springing from the front yard, fountaining out of long cracks in the street, transforming the asphalt into a muddy stream, it's fair to say it isn't helping the larger issue. Water pours over the other side of the street, downhill to the house built there, striking its foundation with a dull hiss, churning up its front door. Did the neighbors get out? Their Subaru is parked beside the house, submerged to the bottom of its doors in swirling water. This does not augur well for Lena and Mike and their daughter, Jo. On the other hand, they had a boat, didn't they? a canoe they secured to the roof of the car for weekend excursions, so maybe the three of them piled into that and paddled for higher ground.

Should the waters swallow the neighbors' house, which looks ever more likely, that is the plan for Mick and his husband, Vin, and their son, Edward: use the boat they've improvised outside the garage to float to safety. Already, Edward is on the vessel, surrounded by a barrier of suitcases, knapsacks, and duffel bags, each filled to bursting with as much of the house as they could squeeze into it. Vin continues his last minute inspection of and adjustments to the boat, checking the cords that lash the heavy plastic barrels to the platform, the seal on the boards of the top deck, the plastic sheeting sandwiched between it and the lower deck. He wanted to add gunnels to it, if only lengths of plywood nailed upright, but there hadn't been time. He settled for a three foot post at each corner of the platform, clothesline wound around them to form a rope perimeter. Water foams around his shins, sliding in a long sheet down the ridge behind their house. Mick feels a twinge of anxiety that it might lift the boat and sweep Edward away from them, but Vin has employed a pair of thick chains to anchor the vessel to their Jeep on one side and the garage on the other.

From his spot at the side door to the house, Mick can look left to Vin and Edward, right to their neighbors' house (around which the water has risen, finding an entrance to the structure in a window that has collapsed under its pressure), and straight ahead along Main Street — Main Stream, more like. The local radio station's last broadcast included a report of something sighted in that direction, a gray, leathery hump the size of a barn, rising in the vicinity of what had been Sturgeon Pool and then sinking again. For the last three days, similar stories have come from points up and down the eastern US, as the water has erupted. Before they lost wi-fi and cable, there were images, photographs and videos, the majority of them blurred, difficult to distinguish, full of immense shapes and shadows, a few frighteningly clear, a grey fin rising behind a sailboat, something like a hand grabbing the bridge of a trawler. Anecdotal evidence indicates creatures larger still, capsizing Coast Guard vessels, shouldering aside supertankers. Mick finds the prospect of animals of such dimensions terrifying. He remembers a whale watch he and Vin took out of Provincetown, early in their relationship, and the queasy sensation that squeezed his stomach once they found a trio of humpbacks, and he gazed down at them and realized each whale was the length of their ship, and more, the whales were in their native element, whereas he and Vin and the other passengers were intruding. (At the same time, a secret part of him, which continues to delight in old movies about giant monsters wreaking stop-motion mayhem upon major cities, is made giddy by the thought of these things, come alive.)

Vin gives him a thumbs-up, shouts, "Come on!" He hates leaving things to the last minute, while Mick is chronically late. Opposites attract, and all that. Given the situation, it's probably best they do things Vin's way. He turns for a final look into the house, at the area beside the side door that's served as his home office, whose bookcases still have too many volumes on their shelves, and at the long room beyond it, for which they never found a suitable purpose. Edward used it as a play space, carrying his wooden Thomas trains and tracks down from his room and filling the vast carpeted floor with rail lines. How often did Mick put aside whatever article he was supposed to be writing to assist him? It's something his son has always loved to do, gather his toys and arrange them into elaborate scenes, frequently with an accompanying narrative. He's used the back room, the kitchen, the staircase, the upstairs bathroom, his bedroom. His toys have congregated on the stoop outside the side door, in the back seat of the Jeep, in the side yard. What Edward christened his set-ups have occupied him in all manner of weather, from humid summer to frost-bitten winter. Lately, he's been obsessed with water, enlisting Mick and sometimes Vin's help in digging shallow trenches and holes in the yard, at one end of which he tipped a jug full of water, creating a miniature river that swept those toys unfortunate enough to find themselves in its path aside, filled the first hole to overflowing, raced through the channel to the next hole, carrying more hapless toys with it. All the while, Edward voiced the toys' distress, saying, "Oh no!" and, "Aaaah!" and, "Help!" When everything started happening with the water everywhere, Vin asked Mick if he thought Edward's play might have been connected to it, if their son wasn't plugged into it in some way, you know, psychically. Mick told him not to be ridiculous.

The Fracture: that's the name the cable news channels settled on to describe what's continued to happen. A break in the barrier separating their world from another occupying almost the same space. It's a watery place, teeming with all manner of strange fauna. A couple of pundits referred to the other world as Atlantis, but given the steady rise of the waters here, Mick thinks this word might have a better claim to it. No one is certain how long the catastrophe is going to last, how high the waters are going to rise. The last broadcast to come across the transistor radio advised those who could to head for the Catskills, to higher ground, so that's their plan. If the Catskills go under, then Mick guesses they'll try for the Adirondacks, a considerably further destination. Beyond that, he doesn't want to contemplate.

"Come on!" Vin waves him toward the boat, which shudders as the water begins to lift the barrels. He's right. Mick closes the door on this, the first house they bought, purchased with the help of the first-time-home-owner's tax credit, back when the crash of the housing market was the definition of calamity. He steps from the stoop into the roiling water.

Something slides under his foot, a piece of debris jammed against the base of the stoop by the current. For a moment, Mick is confident he can maintain his balance, and then he's going over, splashing into water that is deeper than he realized, that is already carrying him down the side yard toward the street. He twists onto his belly, grabbing at the ground for purchase it refuses to offer. Salt water slaps his face. The house rises high above him as he drops to the street, under the water streaming there, cracking his chin on the asphalt. Stars flare before his eyes. He pushes to his hands and knees, back into the air, grateful for the road's roughness, giving him a way to brace himself against the flood threatening to continue his journey across the street and down his neighbor's front lawn. The current is frighteningly strong. He isn't sure how long he can maintain his position. He's on the verge of panic when he sees Vin descending the yard toward him. Due to the rope tied around his waist, and looped over one of the boat's corner posts, he's much steadier on his feet. In short order, he's standing beside Mick, one hand under Mick's right arm, shouting to him to grab hold of the rope, use it to get to the boat, he'll be right behind him.

Relief surges through Mick's chest, tightens his throat. He turns to say, "I love you," to his husband, and catches sight of a figure standing in the middle of the street, maybe a hundred feet from them. It's shaped like a man, albeit, one seven and a half feet tall, heavy with muscle. The skin of its arms and legs is ghost white, the hue of things used to living far from sunlight. Rough bronze armor wraps its torso. A bronze helmet like a cage, like the jaws of some nightmare fish, conceals most of its head, but Mick can pick out great white eyes staring at him and Vin. What could be a sword, four feet of jagged bone and metal braided together, hangs from the figure's right hand. It pays no heed to the water churning at its knees.

I, for one, welcome our Atlantean overlords. The paraphrase of a line from an old episode of *The Simpsons* occurs to Mick without warning, almost causes him to laugh. There's no guarantee the figure is hostile, right? The armor, the weapon, could be for its protection, scouting an unknown location. Right?

In the middle distance beyond the (*Atlantean*), something large splashes through the water, moving closer. Hand over hand, Mick begins to pull himself up the hillside, towards the boat where his son waits for him. Because what else is there for him to do?

LOVE PERVERTS

Sarah Langan

**On Display at the Amerasian Museum of Ancient Humanity, 14201*

The Following is a primary source document from a member of America's Colony 14 before Asteroid impact, dated January 14, 2031.

I'm checking my Red Cross crank phone when Jules walks up. We're the last American colony not to get implants, which places us pretty firmly in the technological third world. My pipeline town in Pigment, Michigan might as well be a flood plain in Bangladesh.

"Ringing mommy dearest?" Jules asks.

"The Crawfords remain indisposed," I tell her.

"Sucker," Jules says, not in a mean way, though she's capable of that. She's got Schlitz-sticky hair down to her hips and her cheeks are covered in glitter from last night's rave. Colony Fourteen's heat and electricity got shut off last week, so her nips push through the spandex cat-suit she's wearing, hard as million year-old fossils. We're all about energy conservation here at the dawn of apocalypse.

"I'm just curious," I say. "I mean, did they even make it to Nebraska?."

Jules hip-checks my locker so it rattles. She's got this rage she doesn't know she's carrying — it's made her heavy-footed and graceless. "Here's what you do," she pretend-cranks a gear at her temple. "You just delete. Done! They're dead."

"Yeah. Okay," I say. Like that's possible. They've been my parents for seventeen years. Not to mention my baby sister Cathy, who they totally don't deserve. And by the way, I know it's whom. I'm just not an asshole, like you.

"Chillax! You think too much. I did the same thing with my ex until I figured it out. Then I just pretended he died and it was his robot clone I had to sit next to in Mrs. Viotes' art. Delete!"

"Colby Mudd?" I ask.

"Don't even say his name. Can you believe he's still here? I mean, half the town is dead, but he's still gnoshing turkey jerky? Jeeze! My God! What does he see in that spoiled princess? You're bringing me down. Point is, fuck your family! I'm your family!"

"Sure. I'll just change my last name or some nonsense. How was the rest of last night?"

Jules blushes, giggles. Glitter abraids the whites of her eyes, making them red.

"That good?"

I left around midnight. Home brew drugs are for hicks, case in point: as soon as Avery Ryan from the bowling team broke out the meth, everybody went native. They dragged this black-light-painted hunk of granite to the middle of the factory floor and prayed to it like it was weeping Jesus on the cross. For the big finale, a mirror-clad priestess offered herself up. She shattered her mirrors against it, cutting herself bloody. Then everybody started screwing. Clothes off in negative-ten degree weather, spilled corn whisky turned black ice on the floor. Kids, grown-ups, pipeline scabs and militia, all partying together like some prediction straight out of Revelations.

I mean, what the hell?

Growing up, my dad's job in resource excavation took us all over, and every place was the same: falling apart. It got a lot worse two years ago, when an astronomer played with some numbers and reconfigured Aporia's trajectory. He predicted a direct hit somewhere near Chicago. We'd all known a big one was due, give or take a billion years. But nobody could agree on what to do about it. Since the Great Resources Grab of the 20s, the colonies weren't talking to each other. Asia was all messed up. And you know the French. I mean, they see a problem and they step over it and blame the dog.

Anyway, some private multinationals got together, which goes to show you they're not all bad. They tried redirecting Aporia by attaching rockets. They tried spattering its far-side with black paint, so the sun's rays altered its trajectory. They tried opening a black hole, which wound-up swallowing most of Long Island before it collapsed.

Then President Brett Brickerson, the former child actor from "Nobody Loves an Albatross," got on the Freenet last month and announced that we had one last hope: shooting an atomic bomb-rocket at it, head on. He laid down Martial Law in all of America's sixteen colonies. Pipeline towns like Pigment saw the heaviest military occupation. It's supposed to be our job to siphon every last drop for the rocket. But pretty soon after that, the union guys striked over working conditions shady operations by management. The scabs poured in, lured by a governmental guarantee of double their normal salary, paid in gold. Like the militia, they did whatever they wanted, to anybody they wanted, for the simple reason that there was no one around to stop them.

The locals started leaving for Antarctica and Australia. The ones stuck here once the law clamped down got hysterical, suicidal, and shot. "What's the point of going on like this?" I overheard my mom asking my dad, which I found pretty insulting. I mean, I'm the point, right? Me and Cathy. We're the whole Goddamned point.

The stores sold out of supplies and the school's cafeteria served just jerky and canned corn, a donation from the heartland. You can't be seen on the streets or the militia messes with you for vagrancy. Non-compliants hide in their shelters at the old Chevy Factory. It's quiet during the day, while everybody sleeps off their rave.

Last night's theme was cosmic mirrors, hence the shattered priestess. I didn't bother with that nonsense. I just wore my uniform: jeans and an ironic Dead Man's Plaid t-shirt, plus two denim jackets since some burnout stole the winter coat out of my locker. Jules wrapped herself in tin foil and glitter, teeth chattering the whole walk there. Some of the really popular kids showed up in fancy stolen cars they'd made the underclassmen push. Total *Mad Max*.

Used to be, only the locals knew about the raves. But then the militia and scabs started showing up. They're bad people. I read my Faulkner and I know what you're thinking: nobody's absolutely good or absolutely bad. But ask yourself this: what kind of sociopaths occupy America's fourteenth colony, imprisoning its citizens inside ground zero, under the pretense of "maintaining order for urgent oil extraction?"

Let me explain something to you, because I'm taking basic physics this year, so I know. Aporia is one mile-wide and more dense than iron. Nukes will crack her, but at this point, she'll hit earth no matter what. Only, if she breaks into pieces, she'll be more democratic about impact. She'll slide into the President's bunker in Omaha, or the shelters in Rio, or the Sino-Canadian stockpiles under the glaciers. So what do you think? Do you think that's the plan?

Or do you think President Brickerson and all the other world leaders are lying, and there is no nuke rocket? Do you think the governments and corporations joined forces, and built escape shelters? Do you think the pipelines are heading straight for those shelters, for use after the apocalypse, for the lucky survivors with tickets to the show?

Thanks, Mr. President.

Thank you, too, dear reader.

No, wait. Scratch that. Fuck you, dear reader. Seriously, Fuck you.

So, yeah, back to the militia and pipeline scabs. What kind of morons suck the oil from a dying civilization's veins for a few worthless pounds of gold? They show up at high school parties and screw girls thirty years younger. Screw guys like me, too, when they can get me loaded enough. How many prisons did they crack open to staff this operation? How many New Jersey pedophile colonies did they raid? You think I'm kidding, but seriously, who else do you think they could get?

So yeah, I read my Faulkner. But did that dude ever live in Pigment three days before human annihilation?

I used to be so into the zombie apocalypse. I figured I'd be this hero in a society risen from ashes. Me, the phoenix of the new world order. But the real thing sucks. Because I'm going to die, and I can't figure out which is more cowardly; resigning to that fate, or fighting it.

At my locker, glittering Jules grins. It's eerie. Why's she happy? She lifts her middle finger at me, holds it. Then her index and thumb rise as she mouths: *one, two, three.*

"What?" I ask, but I already know. Jules is such a wreck.

"A three-way," she says. "One of 'em stuck a rifle up my cooter!"

"I guess you can scratch that off your bucket list."

"Right on the dance floor. Everybody was clapping. Don't give me that *concerned dad* look, Crawford, he shot it empty first…"

"Discharge."

"Vocab king!" She winces, lowers her voice. "I think Colby was there… Like, clapping."

"He's not worth you."

"Jeaaa — lous?" Jules grinds me in her gauze-thin cat suit.

"Don't," I say. She grinds even freakier, which means she's pissed off. Because a machine gun up your hole probably sounds okay when you're high, but not the next morning, when your female parts and what-have-you probably hurt. But there's no point talking about it. Aporia's hitting in less than three days, so who wants to spend the time crying over rape by blunt object?

I realize I'm mad, too. At myself, for leaving her alone with those scabs. At her, for being so stupid. At colony fourteen, for buckling so easily. At everybody. Especially the people on the other side of my crank-phone, who won't tell me where they are, or how I can find them, or even if my baby sister, who's stuffed bunny they forgot, survived the trip.

"Faggot," Jules sneers. She's gone completely radioactive. It's about the machine gun. It's about the asteroid. It's about her denial-blind mom and sister, who think Aporia's a hoax. Mostly, it's about me. Because I love her in every way but the way she wants.

"Don't be mean to me," I tell her. "You're my only friend."

"I'm not mean; I'm honest! You're a faggot orphan and once your family got their tickets they threw you away," she shouts with veiny-necked rage.

"You're trash. Your sister's a stripper. You're dumb as toast!" I shout back. This last part isn't true. She's one of the sharpest people I know.

Nobody's listening, not even the militia or my old gym teacher or Colby Mudd, who trifled with Jules to make another girl jealous, and she'll never see that, because she uses men like spikes to stab herself against.

"They're *not* trash. One of 'em said he'd marry me!" Jules flashes her hand. She's wearing a small, yellow-gold engagement ring. It had to have come from a dead body. Some salt-of-the-earth old lady, a suicide pact with her true love after fifty good years.

"God, Jules."

The homeroom bell rings. The halls clear like mopped-up jimmy sprinkles. Front and back door militia in desert fatigues bang the butts of their guns against cinderblock. They're like orangutans at mealtime.

"It's jewelry from a man," Jules says, and I can tell she hates it, and the hand that wears it, and herself.

"Throw it away, Jules. It's garbage!" I tell her. And like's been happening lately, I'm so upset that the bad thing happens. I imagine cutting her up. Peeling her skin off and poking out her eyes.

Jules squeezes out a pair of tears. "You're just mad because someone loves me, and nobody loves you."

And the guns are banging, and my homeroom teacher is waving for me to come in. Only it's my gym teacher, because my real homeroom teacher is gone. Faces keep dropping away. No one knows what happened to them. It's like a visual representation of Alzheimers. "That's an awful thing to say," I tell her.

Jules starts laughing.

I'm walking away. The sound of her gets louder as it echoes.

"Hospital tonight?" she calls.

I hate her.

"Sorry, Tom Crawford," she calls. "I suck, literally. I'm a spooge-whore-bitch."

I keep walking with these iron-heavy feet, imagining the whole world of fire. I am the asteroid. Dense and without feeling. I am the destroyer of all in my path.

She flings the ring so it skates past me down the hall. I turn back and there's Jules. She fluffs her hand out in pretend-pompousness as she bows, then blows me a kiss. "I'm your dumb-as-toast best friend."

I pretend-twist a gear along my temple. "Forgotten. Forgiven. Everybody but you is dead, you big skank."

Mr. Nuygen is the only real teacher left and he's taking it seriously. He passes out a physics quiz, which he's written by hand because there aren't any crank printers. We're supposed to convert joules and calculate work. There's only four other students here, and none of us have pens.

I crank, then send a text on my phone: *Where are you? Is Cathy OK? If you only have two tickets and she's not allowed in, I'll come get her. Does she need Baby Bunny?*

Nuygen hands me five ball point Bics and gestures for me to pass the rest around. The guy's relentless. He wears dirty polyester button-downs and his parents were refugees from Vietnam. Last plane out and all that. He probably wishes he was still there.

"Focus," he says. But I can't. My paper's black letters on white. They could scramble and rearrange, and then what would they be?

Nuygen perches on the edge of his desk. He's got three small kids at home. His wife is fat. Not like Orca. Happy, well-fed Hobbit fat. "Young ladies and gentlemen," he says. "What if it's not the end of the world, and you're still accountable for your actions? Did you think of that? Take your test."

In my mind, everybody in this room goes bloody. They're just meat, and I'm wondering: Where's the stunt camera? I mean, really. Death by asteroid? I thought I was more important than this.

The loudspeaker clicks on. Everybody twitches. Maybe it's a militia-led public execution. They happen often enough that I'm starting to look forward to them. The routine comforts me. Which is fucked up, obviously. I know that, so don't take notes or underline this or whatever.

The assistant principal or vice-secretary or some jackass's voice pipes through. "This can't be right," she says.

Just read it! Some guy demands.

"Darlins, I got some bad news," she says. I realize it's Miss Ross, a native Colony Eight who teaches auto shop. She gave me a -C, which I hated her for but deserved. "Aporia's gonna interrupt satellite communication pretty soon, so don't be surprised if your phones stop working. Also, new research tells us that impact is thirty-six hours away; not three days. Angle's closer to 70 percent. They're saying Detroit — what's that, about a century and a half from here? — Can that be right?"

Keep reading, the other voice tells her through a muffle of static.

"Dang it! I heard you the first time!" she says. "President Brickerson sent out a last communication just before. Since most of your crank phones don't have get Freenet, the militia wants me to pass this along... Brickerson says not to worry. The rocket will ...eviscerate? Sure, okay, that's a word. It'll eviscerate Aporia before impact. Until then, we gotta stay put. So there's no looting, transgressors between colonies'll be shot. Anyone caught stealing fuel'll be shot... Anyone messing .... Ah, forget it. Run, darlins'. Just run. Get as far away as — "

Nuygen clicks off the loudspeaker. It doesn't spare us. We still hear the gunshot. I go hard, which doesn't mean I enjoy it. I dream about drowned puppies at night, and I kind of like puppies.

Nuygen lets the reverb settle, then takes the quiz from my desk and crinkles it into a ball. Tosses it like a hoop-shot but misses the garbage. "Who wants a lesson in falling bodies?"

Twenty minutes later, he's got it all written out. Seventy degrees, density = 8000kn/m3, speed at impact: 30km/s. Force = a trillion megatons. He's not smiling or pretending brave. He touches the word *megatons* on the blackboard, totally freaked out.

"Meg-A-Tons..." he says. The guy's a Tesla nerd — he figured out how to turn garbage into gasoline and there's rumors he siphoned the plant generators to power his house. "Would you ladies and gentlemen find it comforting to have me describe impact to you?"

I'm not ready to be comforted. There's still tricks in this pony. But everybody else seems relieved, like, Thank God. They can finally all surrender to the awful truth.

Nuygen squints, picturing it. "If it collides with Detroit, we'll see the blaze in under a minute. Brighter than the sun. The whole sky will be red. Don't worry. It won't hurt. Our nerves will go before our minds… It's like the distance between thunder and lightning during a storm. It should be quite beautiful."

I'm thinking about how, if you cut somebody's head off fast enough, then turn it around, they can see their own detached body. This does not sound especially beautiful to me. "What about people in Omaha? Offutt? My family's there," I say.

He slaps his khakis with his wooden pointer, then winces in pain. It's a weird thing to do, all things considered. "All three of them left without you?"

I nod. "Yeah. I know it's supposed to be whole families, but I guess the president cut down on tickets. So I told them to go ahead without me." I'm lying, obviously. If I had my way, my parents would have stayed behind like grown-ups, and it would be me and Cathy in that shelter.

"You didn't get a ticket?" Nuygen asks.

I nod. Nuygen looks at me for an uncomfortably long time. Slaps his leg again with the pointer. It's weird. I can't be the only loser if his life who got anti-raptured. "Okay!" he claps. "Good question! Will! Offutt! Survive!?"

"It all depends on how deep underground they are — what their ventilation apparatus looks like. They'll survive the heat and seismic turmoil, but no one knows about the ejecta. Who can describe ejecta for me?"

Carole Fergussin raises her hand. "It's the rocks and stuff the asteroid kicks up."

"Right!" Nuygen says. "Ejecta! There's evidence that the asteroid that killed the dinosaurs sprayed ejecta as high as the moon before it rained back down into our atmosphere. Our guess is that the rocks will be about the same temperature as volcanic lava, and about the size of aerosol particles. So, our friends in the shelters might survive underground, but we've got no idea for how long. It depends on the quality and pervasity of the ejecta and the apparatus they constructed in its anticipation."

"Couldn't we have done something before now, Mr. Nuygen?" Anais Bignault asks. She's crazy skinny, like she stopped eating a week ago but her skeleton insists on taking the rest of her out for strolls.

"Call me Fred," he says, and Jesus, I don't want to call him that.

"What if we all get together, everybody in Pigment. In the whole Colony? We dig a shelter?" Carole Fergussin asks. She's wiping the tears from her big, brown eyes. I feel like Carole and Anais ought to get an award for best sad puppy impressions on the eve of apocalypse.

Then I picture drowning them.

Nuygen shrugs. "I wish they'd selected me to engineer something like that. I really do But with impact 36 hours away, can we build something that we can survive inside for ten years? Twenty? Ten thousand?"

"Can we?" I ask.

Nuygen points out the window at the refinery. It smokes above metal spires three miles away. "We'd need a lot of fuel. And a small population."

"Like Offutt," Carole says.

Nuygen nods.

I'm picturing Cathy in a dark, underground city. Picturing her safe and loved. Picturing the evolution of the survivors, people like my parents, over a thousand generations. I'm trying real hard to find the bright spot, here, but the future looks pretty monstrous.

"Did I ever tell you my parents' story?" Nuygen asks, then answers himself in a lower voice: "Of course I didn't. Why would I do that?"

"Tell us," Carole says through her sniffles. I consider throwing my desk and announcing that this is not group therapy. During my last hours on earth, I do not want to hear anyone's crappy life story. I just want to hold my baby sister. Oh, yeah. And not die.

"It really was the last plane," Nuygen says. "My father bribed a town official for the spot. And here I am today. I never wondered about those other people left behind. Survivors don't do that kind of thing. But now I wonder. That's because we're not the survivors anymore. But we're still the heroes of our own stories. You understand?"

I don't. I want him dead. I imagine that I am Aporia, colliding. I am bigger than this whole planet, and my wrath is infinite.

"What I'm saying is, I always thought I'd be famous and my children would be rich. Why else would I be so lucky, born in America? But does dying make me less? I'm still Fred Nuygen, aren't I?"

He looks at me, "Some of you, your parents abandoned you. Some people sold their own children's tickets. That makes them villains, you understand? But you can still be heroes."

The kid in the back row who used to be Harvard bait spits a wad of chewed-up quiz. "Liar!" he says. "Human consciousness was a bad mutation. Aporia is earth's self-correct. There's nothing after this."

Nuygen throws a piece of chalk at him and we're all totally shocked. "I'm not talking about God! Who cares about that idiot! I'm talking about the devil. You don't have to let him out. Scramble for some false promise of salvation; climb over your own neighbors for crumbs. I won't leave my family to live in some hole! I'm going to die with dignity!"

The bell rings.

We all kind of sit there. What the hell? Is he having a nervous breakdown? At least he picked a good day for it. Then I figure it out — clear as the open gates of heaven: Mr. Nuygen has a ticket.

Jules and I eat jerky in my shelter after school. I'm fantasizing about stealing Mr. Nuygen's ticket and saving Cathy from our idiot parents. I'll show up at their barracks, baby bunny in hand, and for time since the five days they've been gone, Cathy will stop crying and smile. Then I'll glare at my mom and dad until the guilt drops them dead. They'll resurrect again after Aporia, turning them into decent people instead of assholes. We'll live a few years down there, until I figure out the environmental cure for ejecta that makes earth's surface habitable. Then everybody will elect me king and they'll all say how awesome it is to be gay.

We'll wear as much goddamned pink as we want.

It's the first happy fantasy I've had in a long time and I wish I could keep it going. But the shelter's cold, and Jules is smacking her lips. We've got the crank-CB tuned to the scabs. They were worked-up about a missing rig a little while ago. Somebody broke through a checkpoint with it during the night. Then the call we've been waiting for comes in. A catalytic reformer went smash.

"Check it out?" Jules asks. She's been kissing me and I've been letting her. Once, we tried to go all the way. The experience was miserable, which she tells me is normal.

I start climbing the wooden ladder out. I built this shelter with my dad. We dug for more than a week, then realized that under any seismic stress, the whole thing would collapse. *Son*, my dad had said, looking down the twenty-foot hole. *Buried alive's an unaccountable way to go.*

When I was twelve, my dad found my Freenet porn. Nothing crazy — just guys on guys. He called me a perversion. It made me feel like I was covered in herpes or something, and I'm starting to think it's why they left me behind. And you know, maybe with all these dead-puppy-skinned-meat-people fantasies I've been having, he was onto something. Then again, maybe calling somebody a perversion makes them act like one. Or maybe everybody's having these thoughts, because the apocalypse sucks.

The truth is, my parents are the real perverts. They're love perverts. You're supposed to care more about your children than about yourself, and they messed it up. The whole fucking world of adults messed it up.

Jules and I get on our bikes and ride through Sacket Street. The grocery is dark. So's the pharmacy. It's blue-dick cold. We're over the tracks, racing just ahead of the supply train headed for Omaha. It's a thrill. The kind that makes you feel like Superman.

"Arm or leg?" Jules asks as we race, out of breath and too cold to cry.

"Arm?"

"Okay. Arm, your turn. Leg, I get to be the doctor," Jules says.

"Game on."

We drop our bikes on the grass and head for the crowd. Grass is long in spots, dead from spills in others. I want to take off my shoes and feel the cold, frozen earth. Squeeze it between my toes and tell it to remember me.

We push through. The top steel beams of the reformer have collapsed. Some rent-a-cops retract a jaws of life and pull a guy out. They amputate his leg, thigh down. Then they give it to him. He's holding the thing, high on morphine. Jules and I clench hands. I wonder if this turns me on, touching her. Or if it's the suffering that has my erection going.

The generators start cranking again. Smoke spouts. Jules and I book after the ambulance.

There's nobody in admission or reception at Pigment Hospital, just this janitor mopping floors. He picks at this stuck-on bit of grime with his fingernail.

I'm Jules' bitch today, so I take the nurse coat, and she doctors up. We head to the ER, where they always take the scabs.

Some doctor is just closing the curtain behind her. She's one of the last in this skeleton crew. I wonder why she comes at all, but then again, why not?

Jules walks with purpose. I've got my clipboard and Nuygen's Bic pen. I'm thinking about Cathy, who got born here. She smelled like milk and I loved her. I love her still.

"How are you this morning?" Jules asks.

The guy kind of blinks. He's pale from blood loss.

"Not so good?" she asks.

I'm completely serious when I tell you that Jules would have made a great doctor. She's not squeamish.

She peeks inside his bandage. He bites his lower lip to keep from crying, but that doesn't help; he cries anyway. He's one of the rave guys. I can tell because he's got glitter on his cheeks.

"I've seen worse. Don't' worry," Jules says with this big smile.

The guy calms down. "Do I know you?"

"We're gonna take great care of you, mister. That's what we do in here in Pigment," she says with this made-up hick accent and I grin because it's funny, this whole thing. It really is.

"Can it be saved?" he asks. He's talking about his stump, which he's holding like a baby.

"We'll try real hard," she says. Then she turns to me. She's smiling that angry smile from this morning. I'm a little scared of her, and a little turned on. What's wrong with me?

"You'll need to change his bandages every few hours," she says.

I scribble *Bandages x2hrs* because I'm a terrible liar, so it's important to make this as real as possible. When I play the doctor I just stare while Jules does the talking.

"And you'll need morphine every six hours. Three-em-gees per."

I jot that down, too.

"Dwight here's from Kansas," she says, nodding at me. "Where you from, sweetness?"

The guy's sweating from the pain — morphine comedown. "Jersey," he says. "But really no place. Bopped around the rigs in Saudi a while… You sure I don't know you?

"I'm sure," she says. "Any family? Because there's some experimental treatment for your predicament, but it's a hella lotta dinero."

The guy looks at her funny, shakes his head. "No family. I got six gold bricks, another coming tomorrow."

I'm waiting for the punch line, because Jules usually makes this game fun. We even help a little, make the guys feel better. Listen to them talk about their ex-wives and good times. *You'll be saved*, we reassure them. *We'll all be saved by the giant nukes in the sky*!

"Aw," she says. "Then I guess you'll just have to pray the fuckin' thing gets all spontaneous regeneration, you fucking cripple."

She's running out through the curtain and I'm just standing there, so it's me he grabs. He's sweating even more, and I'm wondering if he's shotgun-up-the-cooter-guy. I wish I was the type to ask, but I'm not.

"Let go of me!" I'm crying, even though this guy can't stand up. His detached leg rests in his lap. I swivel, leaving him with just the jacket.

Jules is waiting for me in admission, white coat gone, like it never happened.

"You ever think about killing a guy?" she asks.

"Yeah," I say. "All the time."

We're at Jules' house for dinner. It's some carrots her big sister dug up from their yard. Everybody munches. I used to pretend that I could trade these guys for my real family. But it doesn't work that that. My parents yanked me across every pipeline on six continents. I know French and Hindi. When I'm introduced to someone, I shake firm, look people in the eye, and repeat their name back at them. I've got three million dollars in a trust fund I'm not allowed to open until I'm twenty-one. Jules' family is dirt poor. They're mean and they laugh out loud when you make a mistake. They give their boyfriends free rein, which is one of the reasons Jules is so mad all the time. Every time she puts a lock on her door they take it right down. If she had an ounce of self-awareness, she'd probably understand that it's also why she only falls for men like me, that she can't have. "I can't wait to get out of this town," she told me the first time we met.

Jules' mom and sister want to play Gin Rummy after dinner. They're starting to realize that Aporia's real, which is making them pretend all the more desperately that it's not. "Did you see that crank-operated device sales went up 2000%?" her mom asks. "It's a conspiracy, this whole asteroid business. Mark my words!"

"I have to shove off," I tell them as I stand. Then I look at all three of them, and realize they've all got Jules' dull marble eyes. "Take care of yourselves," I say. Then I'm out the door.

"The asteroid's a hoax!" Jules' sister shouts behind me. But it's right outside, big as the moon and in the opposite direction. It glows, making the night doubly bright.

I'm on my bike, headed I don't know where. Well, actually, yes. I do know. I've been thinking about it all day.

"Hey!" Jules calls after me, and she's riding, too.

It's biting cold. We're wrapped in Hefty garbage bags to keep warm. "You go ahead. I don't wanna rave," I tell her.

"Where else is there?"

"Omaha," I say.

She doesn't chew me out for a half-brained plan, like riding our bikes six hundred miles in below-freezing weather. She just pedals right along with me, fast as she can, like the whole world behind her is on fire.

We stop at this arts and crafts house in the middle of town. It looks like gingerbread.

Jules doesn't even ask whose house we're at.

I ring the bell. I'm so nervous I'm panting.

"Don't leave me," Jules whispers. She's sniffling. "You're my family."

But she's not.

A Hobbit opens the door. Mrs. Nuygen, I presume.

"I'm looking for Fred," I say.

Twin baby girls and a toddler boy crowd the mom's legs. Warm air gushes out. It's been so long since I felt radiator heat that I almost mistake it for magic.

Mrs. Nuygen brings us to a plastic-covered couch. The kids surround us, drooling. Out of habit, I pick one up and squeeze her thigh until she laughs. I'm going to murder Mr. Nuygen if I have to. This doesn't change that.

Mrs. Nuygen brings us blankets and steaming hot cocoa with little marshmallows. Where did they get all this stuff? The sugar is so sweet that my mouth dries on contact, then waters all over again.

"Jesus God this is good," Jules says.

Mrs. Nuygen grins. "Don't tell the Militia about our heat!"

We fake smile back.

"Mr. Tom Crawford, Ms. Juliet Olsen," Mr. Nuygen says as he walks in. He's still in khakis and a dirty shirt. He seems pleased we've come.

"I want your ticket," I say. "I know you have one."

Jules squeezes my knee.

Mr. Nuygen sits on the arm of a Lazy-Boy. The kids squirm and roll like seals. Mrs. Nuygen brings out hot brie and crackers.

"I love food," Jules says as she scarves. "I'm so happy about food!"

"Are you staying for dinner?" Mrs. Nuygen asks.

"I want a ticket," I say. "My sister needs me. She can't be raised by those people."

"You know your parents got four tickets, don't you?" Mr. Nuygen asks.

I'm holding a dull cheese knife, which should be funny, but isn't. I'm also crying. Everybody looks horrified. Mr. Nuygen is standing between me and his kids. Mrs. Nuygen is holding the twins. Even crazier, Jules has the little boy.

"Give me your ticket!" I'm shouting, waving the damn cheese knife.

Mr. Nuygen opens his wallet. He pulls out this credit card-looking-thing and hands it to me slowly and I want to yell, *Seriously? You think I'm going to cheese knife your stupid family?*

The ticket is clear with engraved writing:

Offutt Refugee Center, First Class
Thomas J. Crawford
109-83-9921

I'm holding both the card and the cheese knife, and for just a second, I'm happy. Fred Nuygen is a magician.

Jules leans over, babe in arms. "Why do you have his ticket? Did you steal it?"

"His parents traded it for fuel to Nebraska," Mrs. Nuygen shout-apologizes. "Now, dear, may I have that knife?"

I'm looking at Mrs. Nuygen, who's holding these sweet baby girls who just happen to be the same age as Cathy. And I'm wondering if it would break her heart if I stabbed them.

"What are you, the sultan of petroleum?" Jules asks.

"My husband prepared a year ago. They should have chosen us. We deserve to live," Mrs. Nuygen says.

"Take the children," Mr. Nuygen says, and Mrs. Nuygen starts to reach for the boy in Jules' arms but I stop her.

"My parents stole my ticket?"

Nuygen nods. "I meant to give it back to you. I'd been hoping to get more, for the rest of my family," he opens his arms to signify his wife and kids. "The clock ran out."

"As long as you're giving them away, you got another ticket for me?" Jules asks.

"Please put the knife down, Thomas," Mr. Nuygen says.

I'm looking at Jules and the boy in her arms. She kisses his cheek, because it's human nature to love children. For most people. All I'm thinking about is murder. Then she turns to me. "Put the stupid knife down, you psycho! You're freaking me out."

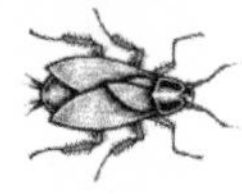

We leave with eight gallons of gasoline and my ticket. It's more than enough to get me to Offutt. Jules helps me carry it to the back seat of Nuygen's Kia. They've also packed a lunch for us, white bread peanut butter and jelly. Because Jules is a mess, she's already forgiven them. She hugs Mr. Nuygen, his wife, and his kids good-bye.

"Should I drop you off with your family?" I ask once we're on the road.

"I don't want to die with them. I'll go with you as long as this goes," she tells me. Which won't be long. There are four checkpoints between here and Offutt and you need a ticket to get through every one.

Through static on the AM dial, a scientist is talking about how we're all slightly lighter from the gravitational pull of the asteroid. My crank-phone has stopped getting reception. We've got twenty hours and six hundred miles to go.

I stop at the hospital first.

"Wait in the car," I tell Jules.

"What's your plan, Sherlock?"

"I need to finish something." I shut the door and leave her in the warmth, then jog to the entrance. I grab a scalpel. That legless guy is in the same bed. There aren't any doctors around. Just that same janitor, scrubbing those same floors.

"You hurt my friend," I say to him.

The guy smirks. He's still got glitter on his cheeks. His stump rots in the corner. He was scared yesterday, but now it's funny. He's one of those.

I want to cut him up. Take my revenge on Jules' behalf. That way I'll have done right by her. I won't feel bad about leaving her to die in this town that she hates.

"You think you're so special," I say. "But that doesn't excuse you."

I'm not getting through. The smirk is horrendous. I squeeze the bandaged stump until the scab breaks open along with the stitches. Blood oozes. He writhes. Now is the time to slit his throat. Now is the time to be what I was always meant to be. Important.

But I'm not thinking about puppies and skinned people or all the bad things anybody's ever done to me. I'm trying to let the devil out, and I realize Nuygen wasn't a genius after all, because there's no devil in there. There's just fucked up me, and I'm just nauseous.

I let go and I'm walking backward. "It's coming," I say. "And no one loves you."

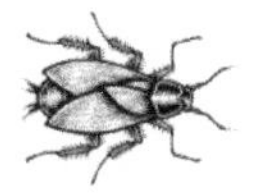

We make it to Offutt. The checkpoints were abandoned by the time we passed through. It's a wonder my ticket didn't get stolen all over again. Makes me almost believe in God. A storm is brewing — everything seems especially light.

We reach the final checkpoint — Offut. Here, there's lots of soldiers. I get an idea. Maybe it'll work.

They don't necessarily believe my story, but they pass it up the chain. We get to the final line. I can see the elevator to salvation about 500 feet ahead. It's iron, with linked chain pulleys. It goes down three miles, where there's enough self-generating fuel to last 10,000 years. There are 200,000 people and 50 miles of tunnels down there. These are the facts we've learned from the crowd along the way.

"This is my sister, Alison Crawford," I tell the manager. He looks like he hasn't slept since 2010. "My father stole her ticket and gave it to his girlfriend. That's why we're so late. We were looking for it. He's inside."

The manager starts talking on his CB. He tells us to wait in a holding tank with a few thousand other people. Some of them are crying, some sleeping. Most too nervous to stand still.

You'd think they'd riot, but in the end, we're all lambs.

I work on my letter, this one right here that you're holding.

The asteroid in the sky is bigger than the sun.

It's minutes to impact.

A guard comes back. I can't believe he's still doing his job. They all are. "Your parents are real beauts," he says. "They sold their baby's ticket for better sleeping quarters."

"Cathy? Where is she?" I don't know how I missed her. But I see her in an old woman's arms. And then I'm holding her, giving her baby bunny.

I'm crying. Cathy is squeezing my face. I love her so much.

"Let us in," I beg.

"One ticket. One person," the manager says. "I'd do it. But then I'd get shot and the elevator would lock. The last men down are the guards. I gotta take care of my own skin."

Jules is crying and trying not to. She's still in that stupid cat suit. I hate her, I really do. I give her my ticket.

"Naw," she says.

"Take it." It's funny. I finally feel like a hero.

"I love you," she says.

"I know," I say, like Han Solo. "Sorry about the toast thing."

The manager puts his arm around Jules and takes her to the elevator. The elevator won't go. They walk back to us, and I'm kissing Cathy so my lips warm her forehead.

"They changed the code," the manager says. "Dealing with overflow. It has to be the person whose name is on the ticket."

"I'll take care of Cathy. You go," Jules says. Her eyes are those same dull marbles. Like her whole life has been a disappointment.

I break the ticket. It's just plastic.

On his last trip down, I give the manager my finished letter. Cathy's sleeping in my arms. Jules is leaning into me. For once, she's not trying to kiss me. She's calm. And I think: this is my family. So I look to the sky, for the most beautiful night in three billion years.

And you, dear reader, are my witness. The survivor-hero of this story. In ten thousand years, your dirt-blind, rodent species of monsters will study this document, and wonder what the fuss was, about love.

IN THE COLD, DARK TIME

Joe R. Lansdale

For Neal Barrett

It was the time of the Icing, and the snow and razor winds blew across the lands and before and behind them came the war and the war went across the lands worse than the ice, like a plague, and there were those who took in the plague and died by it, or were wounded deeply by it, and I was one of the wounded, and at first I wished I was one of the dead.

I lay in bed hour on hour in the poorly heated hospital and watched the night come, then the day, then the night, then the day, and no time of night or day seemed lost to me, for I could not sleep, but could only cough out wads of blood-tainted phlegm and saliva that rose from my injured lungs like blobby bubbly monsters to remind me of my rendering flesh. I lay there and prayed for death, for I knew all my life had been lost to me, and that my job in the war was no longer mine, and when the war was over, if it was ever over, I would never return to civilized life to continue the same necessary job I had pursued during wartime. The job with the children. The poor children. Millions of them. Parentless, homeless, forever being pushed onward by the ice and the war. It was a horror to see them. Little, frost-bitten waifs without food or shelter or good coats and there was no food or shelter or good coats to give them. Nothing to offer them but the war and a cold, slow death.

There were more children than adults now, and the adults were about war and there were only a few like myself there to help them. One of the few that could be spared for the Army's Children Corp. And now I could help no one, not even myself.

In the bed beside me in the crumbling, bomb-shook hospital, was an old man with his arm blown off at the elbow and his face splotched with the familiar frost-bite of a front-line man. He lay turned toward me, staring, but not speaking. And in the night, I would turn, and there would be his eyes, lit up by the night-lamp or by the moonlight, and that glow of theirs would strike me and I would imagine they contained the sparks of incendiary bombs for melting ice, or the red-hot destruction of rockets and bullets. In the daylight the sunlight toured the perimeters of his eyes like a firefight, but the night was the worst, for then they were the brightest and the strangest.

I thought I should say something to him, but could never bring myself to utter a word because I was too lost in my misery and waiting for the change of day to night, night to day, and I was thinking of the children. Or I tell myself that now. My thoughts were mostly on me and how sad it was that a man like me had been born into a time of war and that none of what was good in me and great about me could be given to the world.

The children crossed my mind, but I must admit I saw them less as my mission in life than as crosses I had borne on my back while climbing Christlike toward the front lines. Heavy crosses that had caused me to fall hard to the ground, driving the pain into my lungs, putting me here where I would die in inches far from home.

"Why do you fret for yourself," the old man said one morning. I turned and looked at him and his eyes were as animal bright as ever and there was no expression on his crunched, little face.

"I fret for the children."

"Ah," he said. "The children. Your job in the Corp."

I said nothing in reply and he said not another word until the middle of the night when I drifted into sleep momentarily, for all my sleep was momentary, and opened my eyes to the lamp light and the cold hospital air.

I pulled a Kleenex from the box beside my bed and coughed blood into it.

"You are getting better," he said.

"I'm dying," I said.

"No. You are getting better. You hardly cough at all. Your sleep is longer. You used to cough all night."

"You're a doctor, I suppose?"

"No, but I am a soldier. Or was. Now I am a useless old man with no arm."

"In the old days a man your age would have been retired or put behind a desk. Not out on the front lines."

"I suppose you're right. But this is not the old days. This is now, and I'm finished anyway because of the arm."

"And I'm finished because of my wound."

"The lungs heal faster than anything. You are only finished if you are too bitter to heal. To be old and bitter is all right. It greases the path to the other side. To be young and bitter is foolish."

"How do you know so much about me?"

"I listen to the nurses and I listen to you and I observe."

"Have you nothing else to do but meddle in my affairs?"

"No."

"Leave me be."

"I would if I could, but I'm an old man and will not live long anyway, wounded or not I have the pains of old age and no family and nothing I would be able to do if I leave here. All I know is the life of a soldier. But you will recover if you believe you will recover. It is up to you now."

"So you are a doctor?"

"An old soldier has seen wounds and sickness, and he knows a man that can get well if he chooses to get well. A coward will die. Which are you?"

I didn't answer and he didn't repeat the question. I turned my back to him and went to sleep and later in the night I heard him calling. "Young man."

I lay there and listened but did not move.

"I think you can hear me and this may be the last I have to say on the matter. You are getting better. You sleep better. You cough less. The wound is healing. It may not matter what your attitude is now, you may heal anyway, but let me tell you this, if you heal, you must heal with your soul intact. You must not lose your love for the children, no matter what you've seen. It isn't your wound that aches you, makes you want to die, it's the war. There are few who are willing to do your job, to care for the children. They need you. They run in hungry, naked packs, and all that is between them and suffering is the Children's Corp and people like you. The love of children, the need not to see them hungry and in pain, is a necessary human trait if we are to survive as a people. When, if, this war is over, it must not be a war that has poisoned our hopes for the future. Get well. Do your duty."

I lay there when he was finished and thought about all I had done for the children and thought about the war and all that had to be done afterwards, knew then that my love for the children, their needs, were the obsessions of my life. They were my reason to live, more than just living to exist I knew then that I had to let their cause stay with me, had to let my hatred of the world and the war go, because there were the children.

The next day they came and took the old man away. He had pulled the bandage off of the nub of his arm during the night and chewed the cauterized wound open with the viciousness of a tiger and had bled to death. His sheets were the color of gun-metal rust when they came for him and pulled the stained sheet over his head and rolled him away.

They brought in a young, wounded pilot then, and his eyes were cold and hard and the color of grave dirt. I spoke to him and he wouldn't speak back, but I kept at it, and finally he yelled at me, and said he didn't want to live, that he had seen too much terror to want to go on, but I kept talking to him, and soon he was chattering like a machine gun and we had long conversations into the night about women and chess and the kind of beers we were missing back home. And he told me his hopes for after the war, and I told him mine. Told him how I would get out of my bed and go back to the frontlines to help the refugee children, and after the war I would help those who remained.

A month later they let me out of the bed to wander.

I think often of the old man now, especially when the guns boom about the camp and I'm helping the children, and sometimes I think of the young man and that I may have helped do for him with a few well-placed words what the old man did for me, but mostly I think of the old one and what he said to me the night before he finished his life. It's a contradiction in a way, him giving me life and taking his own, but he knew that my life was important to the children. I wish I had turned and spoken to him, but that opportunity is long gone.

Each time they bring the sad little children in to me, one at a time, and I feed them and hold them, I pray the war will end and there will be money for food and shelter instead of the care of soldiers and the making of bullets, but wishes are wishes, and what is, is.

And when I put the scarf around the children's necks and tighten it until I have eased their pain, I am overcome with an even simpler wish for spare bullets or drugs to make it quicker, and I have to mentally close my ears to the drumming of their little feet and shut my nose to the smell of their defecation, but I know that this is the best way, a warm meal, a moment of hope, a quick, dark surrender, the only mercy available to them, and when I take the scarf from their sad, little necks and lay them aside, I think again of the old man and the life he gave me back and the mercy he gives the children through me.

THE EVOLUTIONARY

Tim Lebbon

The man should never have been there.

Daniel knew the woods well. He was familiar with the sounds and sights that prevailed when he was here on his own, and they were ever-present today. There was no one else to disturb his wandering and wondering, no one to spy on him or hide away, slinking between trees like a shadow looking for a home. He was alone. The man should never have been there. And yet, there he was.

He stood beside the old tree that Daniel had named Sparrow Oak. It was where Daniel had seen his first dead bird. That had been the previous year when he was ten, when his parents had at last allowed him to leave their garden and venture into the woods beyond. The sparrow's corpse had come as a shock. Though his garden was alive with birds, Daniel had never seen one of them dead. He had never even thought about it until the sparrow, and then the reasons began to plague him; they rarely died, they lived to a hundred, they were immortal.

Or perhaps they came here to pass away in secret.

The man was a flicker at first, a haze in the woods that Daniel had to second-glance to see properly. And then when he did see him, Daniel knew that he had not been there before, not like this, not solid, the definite shape of a man standing in the shadow of a tree. A second before he had been only maybe, perhaps, possibly, an echo still considering being.

In his hands he held a dead bird.

"Hello, Daniel," the man said.

Daniel was not afraid. Surprised and startled, but not afraid. His parents had always warned him to stay away from strangers, and one rainy night when they were out his older sister Josie had told him what strangers did to small boys, smiling as she stoked his terror. But this man was not a stranger. Daniel had never seen him before now, but there was no doubt in the boy's mind that he was a friend.

"Hello," Daniel said. He left the path worn through the woods and approached the tree, pressing between a spray of ferns to the left and a wood ants' nest of pine needles to the right. The nest came up to his waist, and its surface was a constant blur of motion. At any other time he would have looked for a caterpillar or beetle to throw in, watch the ants swarm across it and pull it down into the darkness. But not now. The man had said hello, and in his voice there was a calling.

"Is that a sparrow?" Daniel asked.

The man smiled sadly, and though he was sad, the smile lit his face with something approaching joy. It was a strange blurring of expressions, and Daniel was confused.

"Alas, the common sparrow has its problems," the man said. "Its food sources destroyed by deforestation, its habitat ever-changing. But today isn't the sparrow's day. No, this is a siskin. See?" He lowered his hand to show Daniel.

The bird was splayed across the man's grimy palm, its wings spread, yellow streak on its head level with the man's thumb, its claws raised and clasping at the air. One side of its head had been flattened by an impact.

"What happened to it?"

"It flew into the tree," the man said. "Its eyesight isn't what it should be. Its nest is on the far side of these woods, in an old sycamore tree that grows right at the edge of the farmer's fields. That sycamore is dead. Its pores have sucked up so many pesticides and chemicals from the field that it gave up on life a decade ago. Yet little fellows like this still choose to nest there, giving the dead tree a semblance of life. And sometimes, those chemicals bleed through. This bird isn't quite blind, but will be in a few more months. Unless I fix it."

Daniel felt sadness at the bird's death, and confusion at the man's comments, talking as though the bird were still alive. It's head was flattened, skull crushed, brain turned to mush.

One of its wings twitched.

Daniel stepped back. "I thought it was dead!"

"Well, yes," the man said. "But this is a very special bird. An exceptional siskin. It has a future, and it should never have died. I'm here to see what I can do."

There was something not quite right about the man and his words, not quite here, as if he were acting in a film instead of standing in the woods with Daniel. "Can I watch?" Daniel asked.

The man smiled. "I was hoping you would. Now, sit down here at the base of the tree — "

"Sparrow Oak."

"Is that what you call it? I suppose you would. All birds die, Daniel. That was just the first dead one you saw."

Daniel wondered how the man knew his name and why he had named this tree. But only briefly. The bird and the man had grasped his interest, and such matters seemed unimportant.

They both sat at the foot of the tree — Daniel conscious that wood ants could be swarming over him in seconds, the man calm and quiet, holding the dead siskin before him — and the woods seemed to pause. Birds and animals and the breeze in the canopy waited to see what would happen next.

"A few days ago, this little siskin uncovered seed buried under the carpet of dead leaves on the forest floor. It used its claws. Small birds like this usually use their beaks to do something like that. This one found the seed whilst keeping its head up to watch for any dangers."

Daniel frowned. The dead bird twitched again. Perhaps it was the man moving his hand.

"It will teach its young how to do that," the man said.

He fell silent, and seconds later he started to touch the bird with the fingers of his free hand. Its claws first, then its small feathered body, and then its head, crushed and bent out of shape from where it had flown into the oak's trunk. His fingertips smoothed across the bird's body, pausing here and there and pressing down, shifting its feathers, changing the way light fell upon them and subtly altering their colour. Daniel knelt up so that he could see better, leaned in until his head cast a shadow over the bird. The man did not seem to mind.

"But it's dead," Daniel said, as if in anticipation of what he was about to see.

The man did not reply. Instead, his fingers slipped inside the dead bird's skull.

Daniel felt the world tilt around him, dizziness threatening to spill him to the forest floor where the wood ants would overwhelm him. It felt as though reality had stumbled. But the man glanced up, and one look from him restored Daniel's balance.

"Watch," the man said. His fingers delved and twisted. He worked quickly and confidently, remoulding the brain, going deeper, fixing links and connections that had been torn away, mending thoughts and restoring instincts destroyed by death. Somehow Daniel knew exactly what he was doing, as if the man's efforts were charted in a book or on a TV programme. The brain reconfigured, the skull knitted together by a delicate touch, skin and feathers folded back into place, the bird rolled and sat on its clawed feet, stroked, whispered to in a language and tone that Daniel could never understand.

The siskin blinked.

A breeze gasped through the trees overhead, astounded.

"That bird was dead," Daniel said.

"That's why I'm here," the man said. "I have to look after the future."

The siskin sat on the man's hand and looked around, its head jerking this way and that, amazed at everything it saw. *And it should be*, Daniel thought. *It should be amazed. It's seen death, and now there's life in front of it again. What can that be like?*

"I don't understand," said Daniel.

The man stared off between trees. "None of you do." He threw the bird into the air and, having little choice, it flew away into the tree canopy, singing its surprise.

"Time for you to go home," the man said, smiling at the young boy.

"But I came here to play," Daniel said, thinking of everything he had wanted to do today; dam the stream, explore the basement of the demolished house in the woods, climb trees.

"You've come here to learn."

"What's your name?"

The man's smile slipped from his face. He averted his eyes, searching as though he would find a name pinned to a tree. "I had one once," he said, "but now it's long gone."

"But what do I call you?"

"You don't need to call me anything." And the nameless man stood and walked away without saying another word.

Daniel thought to follow, but suddenly his sister's gleeful description of what strangers did to little boys kicked home. So he sat there and watched the man pass away between the trees, listened as he pushed through the undergrowth, and finally he was seeing and hearing nothing but the woods. Birds sang, and maybe the siskin was one of them. *It's head was crushed*, Daniel thought. *It was* dead*!*

Suddenly the forest sights and sounds felt less friendly.

Daniel ran home, and every step brought the woods pressing in around him. The bird song sounded louder, trees felt closer together, leaves and mud stuck to his trainers to slow him down, and when a startled bird took flight past his ear he lashed out, striking himself instead of the bird, his ear burning red as if the man in the woods was talking about him somewhere else.

He leapt the stream, vaulted a fence, and then he was running across a field toward the village, his house already in sight.

His parents were in the garden, trimming bushes and cutting the grass.

"There was a bird in the woods!" Daniel gushed as his dad halted the lawnmower, "and it was dead and its head was crushed and it was a siskin, but it flapped its wings and then took off again 'cos it used its claws to find food not its beak, and it'll teach that to its young!" He gasped for breath, and his smiling father ruffled his hair.

"Calm down, Dan. Catch your breath. Have you been looking for dead birds again?"

"No, Dad, I wasn't. I was just walking and then I saw the man and — "

"Man?" his mother asked sharply. She held her secateurs open, ready to take the next snip. "What man?"

"There was a man in the woods, and he couldn't tell me his name. And he picked up the bird — "

"I've told you to never talk to strangers!" she scolded. "Daniel, what did he say to you?"

"Nothing, Mum. Just that the bird was dead but it was special, so he brought it back to life."

His parents glanced at each other, and his father sat on the stone steps. "Listen Dan, what was the man like? Did he ask you to go anywhere with him? Did you know him?"

"Dad!" Daniel said. "You know I wouldn't have gone anywhere. I'd have kicked him in the bollocks like you told me."

Daniel's mother uttered a short bark; a laugh or a gasp, Daniel could not tell. "Did your father really tell you that?"

His father smiled sheepishly. "Well, yeah. But that was supposed to be man's talk, wasn't it?" He reached out and grabbed his son.

Daniel laughed, trying to tear away from his father. The familiar smell of him was a comfort; the tang of aftershave, the staleness of coffee on his breath. Daniel was home, and he was glad.

"I don't want you going in those woods again for a while," his mother said.

"Aww, Mum!"

"I mean it! Unless you recognised this man from the village, we don't know where he's come from."

"I don't think he does either," Daniel said, realising the truth as he spoke it. *He's lost*, he thought. But he decided that would not sound good in front of Mum and Dad.

"So you and he had a good chat?"

"Well, I watched him fix the bird, then it flew away, then he left."

"And he didn't ask you anything? Didn't invite you anywhere?"

"No, Mum. I know all about pervs and stuff."

"Okay, Dan. Go in and wash, we're going to the pub for dinner."

"Yay!" Daniel ran inside, cleaned up, changed, read a comic book, watched some TV while his parents got ready, and as they walked to the local pub the memory of the man and the siskin was as clear in his mind as ever.

Daniel's summer break from school was filled with new things, and he welcomed them all. He and his mother went bowling, his father took him to an archery range, and the four of them spent a weekend in Cornwall hunting through rock-pools for crabs, eating fudge and pasties, and trying to prevent sea gulls from stealing their chips on the sea front. Dan recalled the man in the woods less and less, though there were a few occasions when he came to mind. Once, they found a dead crab washed up on the beach, a huge specimen almost as big as his head. Its shell had been holed and some of its insides eaten, and Dan thought, *I wonder if he could fix that?* The man's memory followed him across the beach for a few moments but was gradually eroded by the waves. Another time, when they were driving through the narrow Cornish lanes, Daniel heard a crunch beneath the car. His parents exchanged a brief glance and his mum muttered, "Gross!" *That was a rabbit*, Daniel thought, *squashed by the wheel.* Beyond hope. Beyond even him. They arrived at the outdoor water park, and with every slip down a slide the man's shadow was diluted more and more.

By the time Daniel returned to school the man was gone from his day, haunting only the occasional dream. And these were dreams where there was much more going on. "I wonder about diseases," he said to his mother one day, "and why we just can't take them out bit by bit."

"I'm sure the doctors have thought of that," his mother said, still reading her book in the back garden.

"But they try to stop it or kill it with drugs, instead of just taking it out and throwing it away."

She put down her book and sighed. "Well, sometimes they do. If you have a disease growing in you, they cut it out and burn it."

"Euch," Daniel said, thinking, *Well maybe they should teach people to take out every disease like that, whether its growing in you or not.* But he said no more, because his mother was reading again.

That night he dreamed of pulling a disease from his head and drowning it in the garden water tank. The disease was black and greasy, and it screamed.

It only took a few weeks for Daniel's mother to forget about his forest ban. He guessed his talk of a stranger had receded in her list of Important Things — adults seemed to be preoccupied all the time with new things that seemed to matter so much — and he chose the right moment to ask.

"Be back at five for dinner," she said, without even looking up from her newspaper.

Daniel ran before she could change her mind.

Approaching the edge of the forest was strange. It had grown up. He was not really afraid, but as memories of that time with the stranger and the dead siskin resurfaced, the trees and undergrowth seemed to take on a whole new sheen. A fir tree waved, beckoning him in. Brambles at the edge of the wood rustled secretively, though there was little breeze. The darkness in there stared right back at him. It could have contained a million eyes.

He was not scared. But he was aware.

Passing between the trees seemed to draw the memories out and lighten them. The bird had not really been dead. The man without a name had meant no harm, he had simply been playing a joke on Daniel. But every bird Daniel saw could have been the resurrected siskin, and he scanned the forest floor for shapes uncovering seed with their claws.

He explored far that day, arriving home half an hour late, though his parents seemed not to mind. They ate dinner together, chatted, but nothing he said seemed to make sense to them. He and his sister bickered as usual, and his mum and dad had their own grown-up thoughts to contend with. After dinner, he returned to the woods.

He found a sick squirrel close to the stream. It was lying on its side, breathing fast, its eyes wild and terrified. He picked up a long stick and prodded at the rodent. It hissed but barely moved. Its front paws clawed at the air.

"What's wrong with you, then?" Daniel asked, looking around for the man. But he did not appear. Perhaps this was not a special squirrel.

Over the space of a few minutes Daniel crawled closer and closer to the creature, nudging it with the stick, frustrated by its lack of movement. It seemed to be dying before his eyes and he wondered about illness, what was killing it, and why now. Finally he flipped the squirrel over. There was no sign of any injury. It still panted, foaming slightly at the mouth now, its back legs shoving at the ground and kicking up a pile of dead leaves.

Why can't I just take it out? Daniel thought. *Open it up — just like that man — and take out its illness, and make it better? Why should it die just because it's here on its own? It's not fair.* He thought about sickness and things going awry. He thought about death and why it could not be prevented. It seemed so wrong that someone could catch a disease and die, so pointless, and buried deep within those concerns were forbidden images of his parents fading away in a hospital bed. His darkest nightmares, surfacing now because of this squirrel.

"That's not right!" he said. Nature should be perfect. Why allow its imperfections?

He took out his pocket knife, opened the largest blade, held the squirrel with his left hand and cut it open to see what had gone wrong.

Daniel gasped as the creature's blood pulsed over his skin. His idea of delving inside for the sickness suddenly seemed mad, a young child's bloody fascination, and he fell back onto his rump, crying. He wiped his hand on his shirt. The dying animal's blood was sticky and warm.

It hissed as it faded away.

And then he saw the man standing on the other side of the stream.

"Have you come to save the squirrel?" Daniel asked tearfully.

The man shook his head. "Why? It's just a dead squirrel. Death is essential for moving on."

"But the bird … you saved the bird!" Daniel was shaking now, shocked at what he had done. It had been dying anyway, but he had quickened its death.

"The bird was special and should not have died. I told you that."

"This squirrel isn't?"

"Not in the same way. It wasn't fit, so it didn't survive."

"That's not fair!" Daniel shouted.

"'Fair' is something for people," the man said, "and they're the least fair of all."

Daniel cried some more, taking some strange comfort in the tears. Perhaps because they prevented him from seeing the small grey corpse.

"I travel," the man said, and his voice was so filled with a child-like wonder that Daniel stopped crying instantly and looked up. The man held out his hand and smiled. "Will you travel with me?"

Don't go with strangers, his parents said.

They touch you, Josie said.

"Travel where?"

"Everywhere!"

Daniel held the man's hand, and in his grip there was only goodness.

They walked together, strange man and confused boy, and slowly they faded away from the forest. Daniel saw the familiar path changing, the geography of his memory struggling to keep up, and the man took them left into an area of evergreens, finding a path that had never been there before. They were remote from the forest. It existed around them but there was little interaction; no spider webs breaking across Daniel's face, no smell of freshly fallen pine needles, no spongy give underfoot. As they moved, time seemed to shift. It lapped against the shores of his consciousness, making itself felt and yet showing little. He had a staggering sense of time passing in huge waves; ten, a hundred, a thousand years with each breath. The trees remained the same, but with every step other aspects seemed to alter. He felt the forest flexing around him, shrugging time from its shoulders just out of sight. The man's hand clasped his own as if afraid to let him go. Daniel wondered what would happen if he did. He wriggled his fingers and the man squeezed even harder, glanced at him in alarm, shook his head.

"You'd be lost," he whispered, and it seemed so loud.

The forest settled down, and the man and boy became real again. Daniel's feet sank into the carpet of pine needles, the sun slanted through the tree canopy and speckled his skin, and birds chattered in a startled symphony at their sudden presence.

"Where are we?" Daniel asked. He knew every inch of the forest behind his house. He did not know this place.

"The forest," the man said. "Just not when you think."

"Then when?" Daniel asked.

Something was coming at them through the trees. A grey shadow, slinking from trunk to trunk, feigning covertness and yet destroying its effort with a long, low whine.

"A long time ago," the man said, "I came here to fix something. I'll do it again now, and you can see what it is I do. It's important you see this. Watch, Daniel. Take note."

"Do you want me to do it?" Daniel asked. *Is that what he wants?* he thought. *Is he teaching me? Is he —*

And then he saw the wolf. It emerged from behind a fallen tree, glanced at them and tried to slink away. But it was injured. Something had cut it from behind its head, around its shoulder and down across its front left leg. The wound was open and raw. Blood soaked its pelt, black and dry, red and wet. Its eyes held a dozy sheen, like pain-induced cataracts.

"This one shouldn't die," the man said. "A human slashed at it with a sharpened stick, caught it with a lucky blow, and now it's looking for its own death in these woods. It will die, rot into the ground, add its essence to the trees and bushes and ferns, and it will be forgotten. Its cubs will be abandoned by its pack, and they will be picked off by eagles and bears. But one of them will find out how to catch fish. Not soon, but later in its life. If this wolf dies now, that will never happen."

"But you can't change time," Daniel said. Every film he had ever seen, every science fiction book he had read, assured him of that fact. You can't change time, because …

The man looked down and touched Daniel on the back of the head. "Daniel, it's already been changed. I've just come back again to show you."

He knelt and held out his hand to the wolf. The injured animal lay down on its stomach, whining as the movement opened its wound some more. Daniel saw that the cut went deep; the white of bones, the dark purple of something inside that should never be seen. It growled as the man approached, but it seemed to have no energy to wrinkle its lips. By the time the man held his hand beneath its nose, the wolf was almost dead.

"It smells me," he said. "It knows I'm not here to do it harm." Daniel saw the beast's nose twitch slightly. *Dry nose*, he thought, *must be really bad.*

"Come and watch."

Daniel moved closer and knelt beside the man.

He touched the wolf's head first, stroking the fur to calm the animal. It had started shaking, as if cold. Its eyes shimmered.

The man's hand went in deeper than the cut. The tendons in his wrist flexed, muscles danced, and as he drew his hand out the slash melded together, skin fused, fur closed over the wound. He put his hand in again, further down its neck toward its shoulder, and pulled down as if zipping up the injured animal. The blood was still there on the wolf's fur, incongruous now that the wound was gone.

When the man's hand plunged into the wolf's wounded shoulder it opened its eyes and howled.

Daniel fell back, terrified and exhilarated at the same time. *There's a wolf howling in the woods behind my house!* he thought. When he got home he would listen for its echo every night.

The man worked quickly, using his other hand to press the wolf's body on the outside. His fingers massaged the grey pelt in ways that could not have been random. He frowned in concentration. Sweat ran into his eyes and he shook his head to clear them, his hands and fingers never halting for an instant. His mouth twisted into a grimace and he cursed, a word Daniel had never heard, a language that seemed impossible from the man's mouth. It was as if he were talking animal.

The wolf growled and grumbled deep in its throat, then stood and pulled away. The man's hand left its body, fingers clawed like a dead spider, and its pelt fell closed. The animal staggered sideways for a few steps. It leaned against a tree and looked around, as if amazed that it was still here. The blood on its pelt was almost all dry now, and the wolf sat like a dog and began to clean itself.

Daniel realised that the animal was beautiful. In his astonishment at seeing a wolf he had failed to appreciate its grace, its grandeur. And now, fixed and better, it stared at him with eyes yellowed by sunlight refracting through the tree canopy.

"That's it," the man said, sighing and sinking back onto his haunches. He seemed to be lessened somehow, and Daniel reached out to touch his arm.

"What's wrong?" he said, and he thought, *How will I get home if anything happens to him? Where is home? Where am I, really?*

"Tired," the man said, "I'm just tired. I'll sleep for a while, and then we need to travel again." He lay down on his side, asleep before his head touched the ground.

Daniel sat alone and watched the wolf disappear between the trees.

They travelled.

They remained in the forest but faded in and out of existence, passing through the years and settling here and there, places where the man had performed his work in the past. He had been here already, he told Daniel, but it was important for Daniel to see what he had done, and to understand. *Why?* Daniel asked. *It will all become clear*, the man replied.

Near a rocky outcropping that Daniel had never seen, where the stream burst from the ground as if forced by some pressure from below, they found a dying frog.

"Someone stepped on it," the man said, and when Daniel asked who, he shook his head, smiled. "We're a long time ago, and you'd barely recognise the people who live here right now. But even in its earliest days, humankind was interfering with nature."

Daniel was confused, but as he watched the man go to work again, fascination smothered his bewilderment. Fingers moved across the frog, searching for the injuries, finding them inside even though its skin was unbroken, forming no hole yet going inside the frog to touch its organs, meld its flesh, restart its heart and set it down again. With a slight nudge the frog launched itself into the stream and disappeared.

They travelled again, and this time Daniel saw signs of humanity. At first he thought there were fallen trees, but as he and the man hid behind a screen of ferns he realised that he was looking at an ancient settlement in the woods. Trees had been felled to form the backbones of several shelters, constructed from heavy branches covered with moss, mud and sheets of bracken. They blended so perfectly into the forest that they were all but invisible, but the people wandering around gave them away.

Daniel could hardly believe what he saw. These people wore animal furs, had long black hair, dark skin, stumpy limbs, and only one or two of them stood any taller than him. A woman sat with a baby suckling at each breast while she gutted a rabbit; a man squatted by the fire and worked at other animal corpses, spearing and resting them high above the flames on timber spits; two children tumbled and rolled across the carpet of pine needles, naked yet hardy, one of them growling as if pretending to be a bear.

"This is like prehistoric times!" Daniel said.

The man smiled. "Not as long ago as you think, Daniel. No dinosaurs here. But yes, pre-history, in a time when humanity was thought to be at one with nature. But there has always been that destructive spark." Daniel looked up at the man and saw a glimmer of anger in his eyes, reflected from the fire.

"What are you?" Daniel asked. The questions surprised him, and seemed to jolt the man as well.

"That's a big question for a little boy," he said. "Come on. We have work to do over here." He pulled Daniel away and retreated into the forest, still hunkered down low to keep out of sight.

We have work, he had said. Daniel followed, and that question echoed through his mind: *What are you?* Though the man seemed to have no harm in him, its potential answers were terrifying.

Half an hour later they found the black bear. It was not as huge as Daniel had always imagined a bear to be, but it was twice as vicious. Its leg seemed to be buried in the ground and it lashed out as they approached, lethal-looking claws whistling at the air. It growled, dribbling bloody spittle, its whole fleshy body shaking with each lunge.

"Trapped," the man said.

"Where's its leg?"

"There, in the ground. They dig a small hole, set sharpened sticks in its base and catch anything from a rabbit to a bear. A rabbit would fall in and impale itself, the bear just gets its foot trapped."

"Will they eat the bear?"

"That's their intent. And its pelt will be highly prized. But not this one, not this time. This bear is special."

Daniel had already been expecting this. "So what can it do?"

"Nothing unusual," the man said, "but its fit and healthy, larger than normal, and now is not its time to die. Its bloodline is needed in the future. It's young, and has yet to mate."

"But there are no bears in England now," Daniel said.

The man nodded and knelt next to Daniel, so that they could talk face to face. "Knowing the future doesn't change the many presents," he said. "If I disregarded this bear's predicament just because of what I know of its species' future, everything could change."

"What do you mean?"

The man shook his head. "Sometimes even I don't understand."

They travelled further, back and forth through the forest and through time. At one point during that walk Daniel thought, *This is it, this is where my house is at some time later than now.* There seemed to be no pattern to their journey. One time they arrived during a terrible storm, another time it was daylight and parts of the forest were aflame from a clumsy human's fire. Of all the animals dying from fire and smoke inhalation, the man chose a small butterfly to pick up from the ground, mend its scorched wings, slip into its minute head to reassemble shattered connections, carry it away from the fire and set it free. The butterfly fluttered into the sky and merged with the clouds of ash drifting through the trees.

"A butterfly flaps its wings …" the man said, and he smiled down at Daniel. "Every second of this journey, you've seen me making the future into what it should be."

Later, back in the forest that Daniel knew, he wondered what influence he himself had made on this time he called his own.

Though he had travelled far, he arrived home just an hour after leaving. His mother was dishing up dinner, chatting with his sister as she laid the table, and his father arrived home from work just as Daniel ran downstairs from getting changed.

The excitement of where he had been and what he had seen carried Daniel through the usual argumentative meal, and afterwards he ran upstairs to his bedroom. Sitting at the window, staring out over the fields to the forest, he wondered where the man was now, and what he was saving from death. Special, he had called all the creatures he saved. *Who's to say?* Daniel thought. *Might there be special people, too?*

A butterfly fluttered past his window, hanging in the air outside for a few seconds like a memory demanding recollection. Daniel stared, amazed. It was different from the butterfly the man had rescued — larger, its wings a deeper orange — and yet the boy saw it as a sign. Of what he was not yet sure, but he was plenty old enough to see the relevance in such coincidences. He opened his window and reached out to touch the butterfly. It danced further away, dipping and rising like ash on the breeze, and Daniel stretched some more. His arm burned with the effort of holding the windowsill, his feet lifted from the floor, and for a few seconds he was balanced on his stomach and hand, swaying there fifteen feet above the ground. His heart jumped and stuttered, and he was certain that the only factor affecting his fate — tumble back into his bedroom, or fall to the hard patio below — was whether or not the butterfly landed on his outstretched hand.

It fluttered closer to him, flew beneath his hand, and he tilted back into the room.

He slammed the window closed and gasped. *Was he here then? Did I actually fall in another now, and he came and changed it and now I'm back here again?*

Daniel was a boy who fought with problems until he had a solution, real or not. He was tenacious. He went to bed that night dwelling on what had happened. And when he woke up he knew how he could find out how special he really was.

On his way to school next morning Daniel saw a snail squashed into the pavement. He paused and let his friend walk on, kneeling beside the glistening remains, leaning in close enough to smell it.

"Dan?" his friend said. "What you doing?"

"Dead snail," Dan said. He had almost forgotten that Billy was there. Someone must have stepped on the snail recently, because its insides were still oozing out under their own pressure, catching the sun in bubbles of goo. He reached out and touched the remains. They were cool, wet, and he closed his eyes, waiting for the rush of whatever power he may feel at that moment, wishing it in and yet fearing it as well. *What will it be like?* he thought. *Will I know what I'm doing. Does* he *really know?*

"Gross!" Billy said. He stepped back from Dan, uttering various expressions of disgust. "Dan, what the fuck you doing?" Fuck was a word the boys knew and used on occasion, and usually its shock brought them out of whatever they were up to. But Dan did not move. He barely even heard Billy.

"Come on," he whispered, prodding, poking, working his finger in beneath the crushed mass and trying to find the centre of things. "Come on snail, maybe you shouldn't die yet, maybe you'll go on to grow wings or something." But the snail remained crushed, his finger dripping with its innards. After a few more seconds he sat back, looked at his finger and gagged.

"Your head's messed up!" Billy said. "You going to taste it now?" He sounded appalled and fascinated.

Dan looked at his friend and shook his head. "Just thought I saw something," he said.

"What?"

Dan shrugged. "Pearl. Or something."

"That's oysters, you turd!"

"Well they have shells as well. Maybe …" Dan trailed off. He could not talk to Billy about what he had been trying to do. All the way to school his friend quizzed and mocked him, and eventually grew angry. But Dan remained silent on the subject. By the time their first break arrived Billy had forgotten the incident.

Not Dan, though. As he ran around playing, he was wondering what he should try next. *That snail just wasn't special. But eventually something will be.*

But nothing ever was.

Over the next few weeks Dan realised how many dead things were lying around, if only you went looking for them. One Friday evening he found a mouse in his back garden behind a flower pot. It was still breathing, even though it had been holed by something; perhaps thrown there by his father when he had cut the grass. Its little grey sides shifted with its rapid breathing, its eyes were shiny and black, and when Dan picked it up by its tail a slick of something grey and wet exited the wound in its body.

He held it in one palm and stroked it with a finger, slipping his fingertip across the wound, trying to press inside, all the while thinking, *Get better, get better.* But the mouse did not get better. As he forced at the wound it stiffened, then died. It suddenly seemed heavier. The mouse was not special.

A week later Billy told him about a cat that had been run over on the other side of the village. It lay in a ditch, stiff and dead. Dan slipped away later that day and found the cat. He probed its cold, hard body, scraping aside blood-dried fur, but he found no way in. The cat remained dead, not special.

A blackbird, shot with an air rifle, already crawling with maggots. A woodlouse, poisoned by his mother's rose spray and curled into a ball. A spider, light and dry in a saucepan beneath the sink. He even found a rabbit hauling itself into a field, back legs crushed by a car.

None of them were special. Daniel tried, but all he received for his efforts were fingers both bloody and cold. He would nurse the dead or dying things and project his thoughts, *Get well, get well.* He would search for the power he thought he must have, the same power as the man in the woods, and even though he found nothing he was convinced that there was something about him, something special that set him aside from his sister and Billy and his other friends. He believed this so deeply that eventually he began to feel it as well. It was deep down inside him, past dark places that he had never seen, and sometimes it itched. He began scratching at his stomach and back, and he closed his eyes and imagined the man's fingers and hands slipping inside the siskin, the wolf, the bear.

Daniel spent that Christmas holiday hearing about Jesus and how special He was, and he cried himself to sleep one night, wondering whether the man had watched Jesus' crucifixion with a tingle in his fingers that could never be answered.

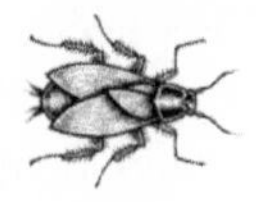

I could try to kill myself. The man will come. He'll save me. He'll have to, and he'll let me know what I can do. He'll let me know what the itch is inside me and help me scratch it. I know there's something there, I can feel it, I can taste it when I sit still long enough and don't eat or drink anything else. Mum and Dad don't even notice. Billy hasn't called me for days, he says I'm going weird. I don't want to lose the itch. I never *want to lose it. All I want is for it to grow bigger and clearer.*

I could try to kill myself.

He'll come …

I could try …

Daniel had seen films and read books where people killed themselves. Shotguns to the face, pills, jumping in front of cars, leaping from clifftops, lying across train tracks, slitting wrists in the bath … each image haunted and disturbed him, leaving a deep-felt sense of wrongness that he could not shake. He felt as if he had witnessed something not only sinful, but not of nature. The suicides shifted themselves out of reality. It was not only death, but the manner of death that mattered. The more he thought about it, the more Daniel believed that nothing the man could do — no touch, no muttered invocations — could ever save a suicide.

Still, the thought lingered for a while.

But as time ran and fate frolicked, choice was taken from him.

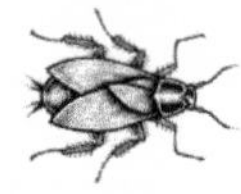

The following spring, he and his family spent a weekend in a caravan on the Cornish coast. Daniel had shaken loose any ideas of trying to do himself harm, moving on and leaving that troubled boy behind. He was glad. Christmas had seemed to act as a point of change, and successive weeks and months had blurred the memory of the man, diluted the impact of those strange journeys. By the time buds appeared on trees and flowers pushed their way up out of cold soil, the man had become a dream. Sometimes Daniel could remember him, sometimes not. He thought of a wolf and a frog and a butterfly, but he could not see them in his mind, could not picture whatever wounds should have killed them.

Sometimes a dream can edge into reality, but more often the opposite happens. Part of Daniel's life became a dream, and he was happy to sleep the sleep of the innocent and let it play itself out.

On their trip to Cornwall the family did a lot of walking, tracking the coastal path as far east as the little village of Polperro. It was lunchtime when they arrived, and the cafes and pubs were filled with tourists eager to stake their claim on table-space. Daniel and his family bought fish and chips and sat in the harbour, relishing the strong afternoon sun on their flushed cheeks. Seagulls buzzed them, darting in to snap up any scraps that fell to the stone breakwater. His sister smiled at him. His mother and father held hands and sat close together. It was the sort of day that goes by in a pleasant haze but lives in your memory as one of the best. And Daniel knew that. He was more than aware of growing up, and he knew that times like this would not happen for very much longer. He would soon be a teenager, and much as he looked forward to discovering his own place in the world, he was still young enough to mourn what would be lost. His mother kissed his forehead. His father took him down onto the beach and followed him into the narrow cave, and they both jumped back in shocked fright when they found a dead seagull with flies buzzing its open stomach. Daniel even held his sister's hand as they walked up through the town, heading for the bus stop to catch a bus back to their caravan site.

The bus did not stop. It ploughed straight into Daniel and his family, throwing his father and sister across the road into the front of a building, and his mother into the stream. Daniel was caught beneath the front wheels and scoured across the road, flesh and bone tearing and splintering, living long enough to feel the bus grind to a halt against a stone wall.

Why do you think you met me?

The voice came from far away, so quiet that it may have been a memory.

You always knew I'd be here if you needed me.

Pain, in rhythm with the voice, as if controlled by its shifting cadences.

And here I am, and here you are, and there's not long left until you know.

Daniel tried to open his eyes, but he was not sure that they were his anymore. None of his body felt like his. He could feel something happening — agony here, there, erupting at random points, flaring and then subsiding again — but feeling it did not mean that he belonged.

He had come back from a place where he had known nothing, *been* nothing, and now he was trying to accept something again. He did not know what that something was, but it felt important. It felt like life. Behind him the gravity of emptiness struggled to haul him back. He felt its endless weight, always there and always known, and it seemed to snatch away his thoughts as soon as they happened. He could recall nothing, and nothing fresh arrived. Back there, in the heavy void, lay everything he sought.

But there was a problem.

You can't go back, the voice said. Daniel felt pain blossoming, and he heard a sound. His soul was touched and slapped, as if to wake it up. That sound again, a croak, and he recognised it. His voice, crying out in pain.

"Lie still," the other voice said, and Daniel heard rather than sensed it. "Time doesn't matter to you right now."

When Daniel opened his eyes, the pull of the emptiness suddenly faded and let him go.

A shape knelt by his side. The man from his dreams. He looked no different, although his face was washed of humour by the splashes of blood speckling his skin. His eyes shifted and met Daniel's, and he smiled.

"Trust me," the man said. "There's so much to do." He leaned forward, and Daniel felt something happening in his chest. At last, his itch was being scratched.

Other voices rose up, filled with shock and concern and something that could have been disgust. *What are you doing? Look at that. Is that his hand? Lucky to be alive, all of them … except the poor boy … no way he'll live … That man, is he a doctor? Ambulance on its way.*

Daniel opened his mouth, emptied himself of the scream that had been building, and then said, "Am I going to be left behind?"

"You'll never be on your own," the man said.

"Mum, Dad, Josie?"

"They're alive."

Daniel tried turning his head but the man held it there somehow, pressing down inside so that it could not be moved, and Daniel felt another galaxy of pain fade away.

Good, he thought. *I can't live without them.*

"I've been waiting for this," the man said. "You're the special one now." That phrase again, as if it was a reason, an excuse, an answer, all rolled into one.

Daniel tried to shake his head to deny the truth, but he could not move. Perhaps the man had yet to reach his spine. "Why?" he asked instead, verbalising the endless question. So many people ask it, so few ever hear a reply. He suddenly realised that perhaps he would be one of the few.

"If I told you that," the man said, "it could never be."

And suddenly he was gone.

Faces appeared above Daniel, professional concern failing to hide the shock, and then his mother with blood in her eye and cuts on her cheek. Her tears speckled his face and he was glad to feel them.

A mask shut him off from the world, but only for a while. Daniel knew that he would be given back very soon. And then he would grow into a future that would be, in every way, extraordinary.

TEENAGE GRAVEYARD WATCHMAN

Josh Malerman

Behold…a burial…

…wet maple leaves trampled, footprints in the mud, a mist more than a rain and yet a lot of it, like how a whisper can sound angry…black cloaks for the pallbearers; not friends of the deceased, the disgusting mailman had no friends, had two sisters still in Ohio — as if having decided long ago to get as far from their brother as possible…the mailman caught with lips in his trunk; leaves and laundry and lips…no plastic bags, no cooler, just the mouths of nine people and none of the mouthless here, at his burial and yet…silence…perhaps the silence he'd wished for (the mailman never explained himself, never gave Samhattan the manifesto the city expected; *I just wanted them to all shut up, I couldn't stand the sound of them*; nothing given, nothing like that)…the mailman in the box, can't call it a casket, can't call it a coffin, can't call it a crypt, the mailman in the *box* and the wood damp from the mist, could grow weak, could get soft enough to bust-up, to break apart, to release him if he had the life and strength in him to want it…strength…a black frock; Father Stockard doesn't want to be here either, doesn't care for these types of ceremonies; not that they test his faith, nothing tests his faith, but he'd rather be reading rather be sitting in a silent home staring at a fire that births calm than standing here in the rain, protecting the good book, yodeling for the soul of a thin balding mail carrier who must have known who would be home when and when home alone…the creaking of the box from the uneven passage from the cemetery building to the cemetery plot, from the rigid grip of the pallbearers, all of them having read the *Samhattan News* through the whole horrid affair, saw the photos of Officers Bobby and Bloomberg standing by the trunk of Randy Scotts's car (he, the mailman), outside Duncle's Bar, Scotts inside sipping gin, thin and balding, meek and wild-eyed, gin to his lips, his own lips, still attached to his face, still able to smile, still able to sip…the pallbearers saw the newspaper photo too of Bobby and Bloomberg on either side of Scotts, escorting him into the Samhattan Courthouse, time for trial, time to face the big bad Judge Walker who had a daughter of her own, a daughter with lips, and who delivered the death-sentence through her mouth, still had a mouth, could sympathize with those who suddenly had theirs taken away...*Guilty*...behold...guilt and a burial but not the burying of guilt; the burying of a dead monster, he who brought mail, delivered bills and notices of love, too, nodded and said you're welcome while eyeing the smiles of the homeowners on his route, no doubt finding this mouth more attractive than that, these lips more desirable than those, until he had them for himself, taken them, then forgot them like used kid toys in the trunk to loll about over the bumps and humps in the road on his way to the next set, the next pair, the next lips he had to have...

...behold...

...a photo, taken at the burial...Scotts in the box...Don Miller from the *Samhattan News*, the lone reporter though more of a photographer...even the *News* had finally agreed with greater Samhattan about what the Scotts case had become; nothing to talk about...nothing more to report...the collective sigh of the community when he was captured...the second, lesser relief, felt with Walker's sentence...all of it echoing into oblivion...into nothing to talk about...nothing at all, save the thoughts and fears of those at home; bad dreams about the mailman out in the hall, a creaking of a board, a weakling with a pair of scissors...

...thunder...above...though still a mist...still the noncommittal storm...like Scotts in the box...uneven images...incongruent man...on his back now...hung by Walker for the crimes of removing nine mouths...none of the nine died...and none here...at the burial...but you know who they are in town, easy to spot...the mummies...the invisible men and women with gauze wrapped around the lower half of their faces...at the grocery store...at the bank...at the post office, too...

FLASH!

...not lightning...a photo; Miller from the *Samhattan News*, a solitary shot of the pallbearers lowering the box to the canvas, to be lowered by Michael Donner on the lever, the big creaking wheel...Michael the young impressionable night watchman as well...Father Stockard speaking now to nobody, reciting rote verses; nothing really applies, no passage in the book says *just bury him and forget him, move on* — his voice like a man trying not to lie, feigning respect for life; Stockard has no respect for Scotts, nobody does...the college kid Donner turning the crank and Stockard nodding to him yes yes, get this over with can you roll any faster, kid?...the box lowering, going down...the mist dampening the wood, making mud of the hole…even the pallbearers turning their backs on the grave, discussing other things; sports, beer; not interested in the mailman descending; the mailman is where he should be now and all of Samhattan knows this; nothing to talk about, nothing more to photograph so Miller doesn't step to the grave's edge, doesn't ask questions, doesn't take a photo of Stockard priesting as Father Stockard has asked not to be associated with this one, doesn't want to be tied to the hideous man in the box, the thing nobody saw coming…so just Michael actually engaged, Michael of all people, hungover from a night out, last night, rotating the wheel, rounding the lever, lowering the box 'til it stops…it stops…Father Stockard midway through a passage stops as well and takes hold of a shovel, helps the bearers dump the dirt, figures one more set of hands will make it all go away faster, will get him home quicker…and the job *is* a fast one, nobody to console, nobody to talk to; silence between the bearers and Stockard and Michael, too, Michael with no shovel but on his knees in the mud, shoving dirt into the hole, helping any way he can, to get this over with…

FLASH!

…lightning this time, not Miller the photographer; Miller's camera is already put away, he's already halfway to the cemetery gate; Scotts is buried but nobody cares any more about the meek man with the scissors who took mouths and grew bored of them and tossed them into the trunk (and what did he *do* with the lips…did he kiss them?…did he set them on the opposite side of the kitchen table and talk to them over dinner?)

…buried now…night…Michael all alone…Michael in the cemetery office where he watches television…the plots marked by the Givens Sensor Board behind him, along the back wall…each cemetery plot marked by a dead light, none of them blinking, none of them had ever blinked, thank God, the Givens Sensors Board installed five years ago, installed in every cemetery in America…gone were the days of formaldehyde…what if people don't really die? the Givens family had asked, what if people didn't quite die the way we thought they died and here we've been filling their veins with formaldehyde and burying them alive, see? burying everybody on Earth alive, but we don't have to, see? we can bury 'em like we used to, only put a sensor in there, a Givens Sensor, a *button* a buried man can press to alert whoever's in the office…a beeper and a button and buzzing to let the staff know they better call an ambulance, better go get a shovel themselves…and the world laughed at the Givens Sensor until one cemetery agreed and one blinking light came to life and one woman was discovered buried alive and she lived to tell, to talk about it on television, to write a book, and dammit if the Givens Sensors didn't become law less than a year later; every cemetery in America; a mortuary revolution and the Givens family got rich, so rich, so many appearances on television; in the half decade since the law was passed, six more blinking lights, six people we all thought were dead, six people dug up, gasping for air, ready to write memoirs of their own…

FLASH!

…not a photo, the photographer long gone, but lightning, again, erupting in the Samhattan sky, skinny fingers across the black; deep nighttime now; Michael Donner alone in the office…eating chips…watching a movie, a comedy about dogs and cats…reading a book, a thriller about a blind man…the storm outside growing, getting meaner, just the kind of night Michael enjoyed at the cemetery, half the reason he'd applied in the first place, *imagine me in the office at night, thunder and lightning outside!*; a *cool* gig, the coolest he'd ever heard of; a man with a paperback and a bunch of dead bodies, if that doesn't thrill you nothing will…FLASH!. . . another thunder-crack and Michael smiles, shakes his head, this is cool, this is amazing, sitting here in the office as the black sky cries, as the dogs of Samhattan lose their minds, all bark at once…Michael thinks of Father Stockard 'cause Father Stockard has a dog, a famous one here in Samhattan, a wolfhound, one of those huge gray dogs; is Stockard quieting the thing now?, telling him be quiet dog, I had a dark day, dog, that man stole mouths, dog, or was Stockard already asleep (perhaps) having showered the eulogy off himself…Michael doesn't know, doesn't really care either, just cares about this movie and these chips and that book and the girl Pamela from school who said she'd like to come visit him one night on the job, liked scary things, fancied herself macabre…Michael cares about her, very much so, cares about calling her up and inviting her tonight, right now, and so he does, call her up, says come eat chips with me in the dark, wants to say come let's have sex in the cemetery office at night if you're so into the macabre, if you're so dark as the black nail polish you wear, come on by tonight, Pamela…a FLASH!…CRACK-*BOOM!*…lightning again and the girl says yes, she'll come, but give her a minute, and Michael takes that minute to turn up the volume of the funny movie and chomp another chip…gets up to use the bathroom, passing the Givens Sensor Board like one of those Light-O-Rama things or maybe more like the information map at a state park, HERE is where you might see owls, HERE is where you might see moose; Michael likes it, the board, never lit, just sitting there like so much potential, so freaky, something to thrill Pamela with, the board and the ledger and the stone cottage/office and the creaking chair that he sits in to watch movies, watch over the cemetery, make sure no kids sneak inside (except for the ones he sneaks inside), and of course the lone window in the free-standing office ("the cemetery tollbooth," Michael likes to call it), the small square overlooking all those *graves*…graves and gravestones and broken limbs fallen from the trees and black leaves in the mud, footprints, many of those Michael's own…it is as cool a view as Michael could offer a lover of the macabre and if Pamela doesn't like it, who cares, the movie is good, the book is good, the pizza he has in a box (box) upon the black filing cabinet is good, too…no worries on the job, nothing to get upset about, getting paid to sit in a stone cottage, do whatever he likes to do, take a piss when he needs to–

FLASH!

…lightning only heard, Michael in the pisser, sitting down in the dark, rising when he's done; back through the little hall, back to the desk with the small television, the papers, the chips, and his phone…his phone letting him know someone wrote him, someone said they're here, I'M HERE, Pamela already?, and Michael sticks his head out the little window and sees (yes) Pamela standing at the gate, alone, anxious, no doubt, by the way she sways…

FLASH!

…Michael out of the office, the green wooden door slamming shut behind him, racing to greet Pamela, nodding to her through the bars; follow me, he's saying, this way…

…behold…

…Michael letting Pamela in through a small door in the brush, Pamela remarking on it, saying how cool, a fucking door into a graveyard at night…Michael nodding yeah but come on it's raining pretty bad now and the office is dry, come on, you're gonna like this…and they run through the rain and she's laughing and Michael doesn't care if she makes too much noise, doesn't care if he does either, let someone notice, let him get fired, there are other cool gigs like the night watchman at a hospital, the night watchman at a train station…

FLASH!

…in through the green door, damp wood, and into the office and she looks so wonderful drenched like this and Michael notices for the first time she's carrying two beers on the end of a six pack plastic thingie and he says,

"ah man I probably shouldn't drink here"

and she says

"just one, each"

and he shrugs and shows her around the office; shows her the letterhead SAMHATTAN CEMETERY, shows her the file cabinet with all the dead records and the little radio and the television and realizes he's run out of things to show her then remembers the Givens Sensor Board, and turns around and shows her that, too…

"if one of these lit up…"

FLASH!

…they're kissing, not the way he had planned but so what; she's not straddling him in the office chair, but their lips are together, two sets, warm and wet, he's the one against the wall and she's the one making this all happen — and with his eyes closed he hears one of the beer cans open and she's handing it to him and now they're drinking beers and kissing and dogs and cats are making a bunch of noise on the television and Michael is in young man's heaven…

FLASH!

CRACK!

…they're watching the movie together, eating pizza; Pamela uses the bathroom and Michael likes that, feels for a second like they live here together in this really cool place…they take turns looking out the one window; Pamela says the rain and tombstones look like the Old West together and Michael shrugs and then they're laughing at her jokes, Pamela's funny, Michael really likes her, likes that they only kissed and nothing else is going to happen; he isn't sure what he would do, isn't sure how to do things like that; glad enough for the kiss and receives a second flurry of kisses when it's time for her to leave, here in the office, their lips together, so good, then a goodbye at the door in the brush and Michael scurrying across the grass, then pavement, back into the office where the movie has ended and it's an hour past midnight and he already has a message on his phone that says THAT WAS FUN and Michael howls with delight and pumps a fist in the air and gets up on the chair and changes the channel…new movie…how about a black and whiter?…an old one…a funny one?…Michael shrugs; the movie isn't funny, isn't supposed to be, but it's good…black and white…except every now and then he sees a flash of yellow on the screen, some sort of mistake on the channel's part; or maybe the movie is so old that it's hard to show it the right way, maybe it's like a yellow stain, appearing, pulsing, rhythmically—a commercial comes and Michael hops down off the chair and crosses the office and sits down in the bathroom…he's thinking of Pamela sitting here; it's too gross to get too excited but still…when he's done he leaves the bathroom and on the walk back to the chair sees the yellow light is still pulsing on the television screen and something very dark swirls in Michael's belly; pizza, beer, love, lust, he isn't sure, then thinks oh no, I might know what might be making that light, that pulsing, and he turns around to face the Givens Sensor Board for the first time ever with a mind to see if it's come to life…

…a flashing…

…it has…

…it's come to life…

…Michael's mouth is hanging open and he's burning up with fear, not sure what to *do*, this isn't supposed to happen this has never happened before…and he's an inch from the board now, his fingertip at the blinking light, trying to determine which plot it is, who is sending him a signal, is this really happening?, PLOT 22, he's checking the ledger, who is where?, but does it matter who it is? PLOT 22 is blinking, holy Christ, someone is alive out there…

FLASH!

…Michael runs to the window and looks out at the greater cemetery as if the person using the sensor might be standing upon their grave, calling for a stewardess…then he's back at the board and knows who it is, knows of course who it is because there's only one body in Samhattan Cemetery that could be breathing still, only one body buried today…

FLASH!

…lightning, and the mailman's sensor, too…

FLASHing

…Michael on the phone, immediately, talking to the police, telling them Randy Scotts's sensor is going off, yes, the Givens Sensor, first time

Michael's ever seen one blink, PLOT 22, yes, what am I supposed to do?, should I start digging?, do I wait for you guys to get here?, do I —

FLASH!

...and the brief flat response from the officer on the phone...

"Leave him."

...two words followed by something else, a barb at the dead man, but *leave him* is all Michael hears...

...Michael on the phone with an ambulance now, worried that the police will arrest him somehow for disobeying (*leave him*), but what else to do, calling, frantic, getting someone on the line, someone in charge, someone to help, and that someone pauses and with no knowledge about how the police reacted, no way of knowing they were echoing the sentiments of Samhattan's police, they repeat,

"Leave him."

...Michael off the phone now, staring at the blinking Givens Sensor Board, shaking his head no, there's a man out there, begging for help, isn't dead, I can see his tombstone through the window, oh GOD HOW MUCH AIR IS IN A BOX THAT SIZE?!?!...Michael turning to face the black and white movie but he can't watch a movie now, can't eat a thing, has to get out of this office, has to get...

FLASH!

...on the phone with the Cemetery President...Bailey Smith...Bailey will tell him what to do...that he should already be doing it...but Bailey *isn't* saying that, Bailey is talking about how some people deserve things, some people make their own beds, leave him, Michael, leave him in the box...

CRACK–*BOOM!*

...Michael alone, more alone than before...feels the weight of the graveyard pressing in, like it's crawling in through the little window, all that decay, and Michael shaking his head no, come on, no, I'm gonna have to do this alone...

...out the office door, the wood crashing against the stone behind him...he's running to the shed, gets there faster than he plans, breathing hard, he's opening the shed, grabbing a shovel, still wet and muddy from this afternoon...

FLASH!

...lightning yes but the Givens Sensor Board blinking in his memory, too...with a shovel Michael runs along the pavement, his sneakers slick on the ground, crosses over wet grass, wet stones, giving earth, weak from the storm…

…PLOT 15, 16, 17…

…Michael is thinking about Pamela, maybe he should call her, his phone is back in the office, maybe he should call Pamela, tell her he needs help, needs another hand, there's no way he's going to dig this guy up in time, how much time does he have?, do you know, Pamela? do you?…

…PLOT 18, 19, 20…

…rain pools at his brow and pours down his cheeks, his nose, falling to his lips…

…PLOT 21…

…he's thinking about Pamela, about her kissing him, their lips together in the office, how good it felt…how good it felt to talk to her, to laugh with her, to kiss her…

…PLOT 22…

…Michael jams the shovelhead into the dirt, still soft, so soft, just buried today, so easy to get him out of there, hardly any work at all, but there's a sound, a cracking, not lightning, not a photo, but a footstep, behind him, behind Michael, from the shadows of the trees at the graveyard's edge, and a form, too, a big body in black, as if he's wearing the same shadows he emerges from…

"What are you doing. Michael?"

Father Stockard, standing so close now, close enough to reach for the shovel if he wanted to.

"The Givens Sensor Board," Michael starts to explain.

"Leave him."

Stockard's voice as level as his eulogies.

"Father?"

"Think of the girl's lips," Stockard says. "Think of the lips on the girl."

Rain falling. A grave at their feet. A light no doubt still blinking in the office.

"How did you know?"

It's only a half-question. And at the same time, it's two:

How did you know about the girl?

How did you know to be in the woods?

But both answers are obvious.

Father Stockard raises a hand, the palm flat toward the grave.

"Leave him."

Michael thinks about Pamela's lips.

Leave him, they said. They all said.

Michael backs up from the fresh plot, from the man who presses the button within.

Leave him, they said. They all said.

He's thinking of Pamela's lips. As Stockard recedes back into the shadows, Michael thinks of those lips against his own.

He's thinking of a whole town, too, agreeing to bury a man alive.

He turns and, as if just now realizing he's wet, huddles up into his shirt and crosses the cemetery again, carrying the shovel like it's just something to be put away, property of Samhattan, part of his job.

At the office he doesn't turn around, doesn't look back to PLOT 22 or any of the others.

He's thinking of Pamela, kissing him.

Thinking of her lips.

He leans the shovel against the stone wall and enters the office. Inside, he hops onto the chair and moves the television, trying so that it doesn't reflect the Givens Sensor Board behind him.

But it blinks. Whether he looks at it or not, it blinks.

It blinks to the rhythm of a whole town saying *leave him, leave him* — and it blinks, too, to the beat of Michael thinking of Pamela's lips and the wonders in there, in kissing a woman, as her nails dig into your back a little, your arms, not like fingernails on wood at all, not because she has done something wrong and needs to break free, but needs to break free all the same.

CALL THE NAME

Adam L.G. Nevill

Upon sand the colour of rust and beneath a sulphur sky, a great shape is stretched across a long, flat beach. Embedded haphazardly about the vast bulk, scores of milky eyes stare at nothing. Black salt water slaps the grey mass of lifeless flesh and cloaks the corpse with foam. In the far distance, unto the reddish headlands at either end of the shore, the body remains shiny where unbroken, and pulpy where deterioration has ulcerated the smooth flanks. The only mercy here is that in dreams there is no sense of smell. In yolky light falling through thickening, stationary clouds, a long beak is visible, open and lined with small killer-whale teeth that suggest a smile. What might have been a great fin or flipper is as ragged as a mainsail hit by grapeshot but still points to the heavens.

In other places, on a shoreline that might have bordered an empty lake on Mars, long pellucid protrusions of jelly streak the sand, as if the wall of flesh was disembowelled during a battle between Leviathans in the lightless depths of the black ocean.

Cleo cannot tell. No birds fall upon the beached giant.

Her appalled study of the corpse occurs upon a shore she now recognises as the old Esplanade of Paignton. What remains of the Shoreline restaurant becomes visible. Its supporting steel posts have fallen; the building must have been smashed onto its face and been taken away by the sea. A shore as much transformed as the atmosphere and ocean. Changes that her mind aches to comprehend, until Cleo realises she is no longer alone on the beach.

Behind an outcrop of red rubble, a few hundred feet from where she stands gaping, two whiskered heads appear. The heads are black and as sleek as seals. But those aren't seal faces that grin upon the necks of these creatures. Nor do seals have muscular shoulders and arms.

Looking over her shoulder at the rocks, Cleo moves away as fast as one can move on loose sand in a dream, which is neither fast nor far.

The smooth heads disappear only to reappear closer to her position, beside a cement wall washed as smooth as a pearl. The black things raise their snouts in the manner of expectant dogs amidst the fragrance of food.

Somewhere behind the long headland of rubble and rock at the rear of the beach, a great shriek rends the air. A terrible whimpering follows the roar. This piteous cry issues from a second party. The sound of distress breaks a shard from Cleo's heart.

Beyond the shore, the dull thump of a heavy body being thrown to the ground registers as a tremor as much as sound. What resembles the breaking of a tree's thick limb is augmented by a series of excited shrieks. Something large is being put to death by something bigger and fiercer than itself.

In her haste to flee, the thing that Cleo runs over is crispy beneath her bare feet and recoils into itself as she treads the form deeper into the sand. She peers down at what she has crushed.

A face, once human, looks up at her. The long bleaching body beneath the face is that of a seahorse. A spiny tail flicks hopelessly. The beast's expression conjures a sense of a living thing reaching the end of deep suffering. An all too human mouth gulps at the air. Pink gills flutter in an increasingly translucent neck.

Cleo sobs and wishes to obliterate the delicate head with a rock to end its misery. But her own pursuers now lean over their rocky perches. They hiss as her panic and weariness increase.

Ahead, the way is barred by a mottled trunk, white-spotted with disease. The vast, inert bulk at the shoreline must have flung this appendage up the beach in its death throes.

Cleo's belief that her attempt to escape in any direction will be futile is matched, horribly, by the instinctive certainty that her end in the sand will not come easy. Among the corpses on the beach, and amidst the audible splinterings of bone behind the seawall of rubble, she understands that this is the way of things here, in this time. This revelation is the worst thing of all.

Cleo shivers awake. Her face is wet. She's been talking in her sleep, or crying out.

Her throat is sore.

She nearly weeps with relief as her familiarity with the living room's interior slowly returns. Some parts of the room remain strange and are not part of her home; at least not part of the home that she can recall. Maybe tomorrow these alien features and objects will be recognisable and bring comfort instead of anxiety.

Another twenty-degree night.

Cleo drinks water from the teat of a closed cup that sits upon the tray attached to her easy chair. Once she's calmed herself with two anti-anxiety tablets, she turns on the media service and watches the world fall apart on a screen.

Fifth refugee ship intercepted by Italian Navy in three days. Thousands confirmed dead. No survivors.

Night-vision footage in a live broadcast, beamed from the Mediterranean.

The metal walls inside the drifting vessel are the tragic grey that Cleo associates with war at sea or maritime disaster. Pipes traverse a low ceiling studded with rivets. Paint bubbles with rust. Dust glitters and drifts through darkness like plankton in a sunken wreck. As the moving camera pans the greenish air a moth's frantic capering is lit up.

Immobile forms haphazardly cover the lower deck. They create a lumpen procession reaching out of sight: blankets, exposed limbs, discarded sandals, disparate piles of baggage, and the pale soles of feet that have walked so many miles to reach the ship but will never walk again. The far end of the wide space is a void.

A figure moves into view. Bulky, too upright, it emerges slowly like an astronaut in zero gravity; a CDC or military scientist encased in a protective biosuit, carrying an equipment bag. Another two men appear, identically dressed in unventilated suits attached to hoses. Waddling cautiously through the jade umbra, their faces remain undefined behind the tinted lenses of their masks. They also carry plastic crates. All are being filmed by a fourth figure with a camera attached to a helmet.

There are close-ups of swollen faces, eyes open and bloodshot, the mouths slices through which ochre-filmed teeth grimace. Long-necked, his expression a rictus chiselled from agony, one man opens his jaws wide as if his last act was to scream at death itself. Beside him, a mother clutches a motionless child in a papoose. The small head of the child is turned away as if afraid of the camera. Most of the dead face the floor, suggesting the life they have departed was too unbearable to look back upon, even once.

The footage cuts to the exterior of a large, antique merchant freighter, bloodied with tributaries of corrosion. The bridge is lightless; a vessel adrift. Flares colour the water red. PT boats and a frigate circle at a distance while white searchlights fix the vessel as if it were a specimen on the black surface of the sea. Rubber dinghies rise and fall with the swell alongside the hull. Marine commandoes huddle within the smaller craft, but peer up with their weapons trained upon the railings above.

The fore and aft decks of the merchant vessel are similarly littered with the unmoving lumps of a discarded humanity. The oily sea laps with the usual indifference about another ancient vessel that never made it across.

The children.

So far away, in the relative comfort and safety of her apartment in Devon, England, Cleo closes her eyes and her mind swims in a ruddy, private darkness. She wants these sights to remain poignant, but to see too much horror is to normalise it and stop caring.

But even this new disease and the never-ending refugee crisis are trifles in the scheme of things.

When she opens her eyes, politicians and civic authorities, military personnel and scientists are announced by subtitles that she lacks the energy to read. Each speaks in separate portions of the broadcast.

The ship sailed from Libya, its cargo entirely human, more of the desperate from east, west, central and north Africa.

A new recording occupies the report within seconds.

Amidst a panorama of dark green foliage, enshrouded by mist, a scattering of black shapes can be glimpsed amidst long grass. A subtitle and map indicates a forest in Gabon. Recent footage too, because Cleo has never seen these pictures on any of the twelve news channels that she flicks between whilst remaining motionless in the infernal heat.

Though her academic discipline and background are in marine life in British coastal waters, as a retired conservationist she is unable to resist any news story about the desecration of the natural world. Like a masochist, she watches the Sixth Great Extinction unfold in detail and at its own inexorable, determined pace in this short Anthropocene Period. Guiltily, she feels no more compassion for her kind than for the fates of the other species with whom humanity shared the world, and which it subsequently annihilated. Sixty per cent of the world's wildlife is now extinct because the planet has to accommodate so many people: nine billion and rising. Cleo wishes she'd never lived to see this.

She alters the setting and the room fills with sound. The recordings originate from one of the last stretches of trees in Equatorial Africa. This is believed to be a record of the very end of the wild gorilla. She had no idea that any were still alive. It appears that a final 237 gorillas have clawed out an existence deep inside one of the last private forests. They now lie with their silver bellies up, or are hunched, heavily furred, stiff with death and wreathed by flies.

The news service confirms that the seventh outbreak of Gabon River Fever is responsible for this extinction event; the same pandemic that swept away the remaining wild primates from the Central African Republic, Democratic Republic of the Congo, Cameroon, Republic of the Congo, and Uganda. The gorilla had become officially extinct, along with the entire complement of refugees on board another freighter carrying the same virus.

The only question she asks herself is the same one she asked over forty years earlier, in 2015: *what did we think would happen once food aid and food exports eventually ceased?* How could the countries of Equatorial and then North Africa not collapse? As with the viruses that have scattered across the planet in their multitudes over the last three decades, Cleo knows that Gabon River Fever is zoonotic, spread from animals to humans. Those people still hanging on in Equatorial Africa have little to eat but game. In desperation they have eaten the dead flesh of the last apes, fed upon the bush-meat carcasses and so contracted and then spread a deadly virus from its origins in bats; another species driven from its habitat and thus panicked into unleashing a pandemic that was benign in the reservoir host.

Invaded ecologies always seem to call us out eventually and fight back. But Cleo is convinced that it is not only the virus in the bats that had its survival in mind.

'In mind': was that even the right phrase for what was stirring beneath the world? Could something so vast and enduring be considered to have a mind that we would understand? Or was it an independent living cosmos in which our feeble shreds of consciousness make feeble comparisons between ourselves and *it*?

On screen, an academic commentator from Rome comments upon the irony of another species of our closest ancestors ceasing to exist, reaching its end in the very place where our own precursors emerged. He likens the burden of man upon the Earth to that of a flu infecting an eighty-year-old woman. The comparison is, at least, sixty years old. Not much use recycling it now. Metaphors only reshape horror, they don't prevent it.

The heatwave, the forest fires in Europe, the Chinese famine and the escalation between India and Pakistan have been greedy and monopolised any news she's seen in months. At least the fate of the last apes is given a late-night spotlight. Though even that is soon swept away by additional reports of another lethal virus; this outbreak reported from Hong Kong and not yet named.

Breaking news, reporting its endless cycles of catastrophe, continues to flicker and flash through the humid innards of Cleo's living room as she stares at the window, a black rectangle of hot darkness. She can smell the warm, foamy brine of high tide. The distant sighs of the wind in the bay fail to move the curtains. Those as elderly as Cleo are told to stay indoors and be still, even at night. They cannot cool down after the sweltering days. Right across Europe, for three months, heatstroke has cut another swathe through the aged. A perennial event for the continent and its islands.

But what Cleo discovered within a few miles of her own home is of far greater significance than anything that is reported on the news.

The women of her family, distinguished scientists and environmentalists, whose pictures line her sideboard and whose framed specimens decorate her home, all believed that the desecration of the planet by mankind's thoughtless extensions disturbed something greater than we could ever amount to.

The very rapacity of her own species has functioned as the worst wake-up call since the Cretaceous-Tertiary mass extinction, 65 million years before. Life can never be still or silent; the cries of infants for succour will always be heard by predators.

Cleo knows the world will no longer continue as it is. Not while the great fields of permafrost in Alaska, Siberia and Canada so hurriedly release their terrible, long-withheld breath into the air — enough methane and carbon dioxide to nullify and exceed all revised greenhouse gas emission targets.

The forests and oceans are absorbing far less carbon dioxide now too. The feedback loops are a tourniquet around mankind's throat.

The average global temperature is three degrees higher than it was in 1990. The higher latitudes are five degrees warmer. Nine billion pairs of fingers are clutching at the wire strung about their throats, some more frantically than others. Sometimes, in her daydreams, Cleo believes that she can sense nine billion pairs of feet kicking up the dust as the chokehold tightens.

The subtropics and mid-latitudes have all but lost their rain. The great collision of the polar cold and the heat from the equator, up there in the sky above the vast, heaving, warm bodies of water, now retreats like another refugee upon the exhausted Earth. Tired, spreading out and meandering to higher latitudes and distant poles, the great writhing cables of wind that once reeled so fast and so high, those great definers of air masses, are taking their precious cool air and delicious rain away with them. The winds are removing all that they can carry out of the heat. The fresh water and the nourishing blankets of gentle, golden warmth are vanishing, along with those near-forgotten climates that allowed so many to exist.

Her own precious oceans are becoming deserts. Canadian salmon are all but gone. North Sea cod is as extinct as the pliosaur. The shell food upon the rocks is dissolving to debris. Great coral reefs from Australia to Asia, the Caribbean, the Virgin Islands and Antilles are a cemetery of exhumed white bones, patchily buried beneath six feet of seaweed.

One in three of all the creatures in the oceans is dying. Corpses blanket the ocean floor in the way that dust and ash sand-dune the crematoria. If any human foot could walk where there were once great vivid cities of coral antlers and waving banners, the ruins would crumble like sandcastles bleached by the sun's relentless heat and aridity.

Vapours and gases have carbonated and acidified the monumental depths and vast glittering surfaces of the seas. Great masses of life, the megatons of phytoplankton that were responsible for producing half of the biosphere, have slowed their engines — vast green factories poisoned by man, the blundering chemist.

The colossal leafy lungs in the Amazon produce the other half of the atmosphere. But the trees burn while the sea bleaches.

Momentarily paralysed by the range of her thoughts, Cleo imagines the epochal destruction man brought to the fetid shores around *it*, where *it* lay stinking.

The old trespasser. He created us a long time ago, accidentally, unthinkingly, beneath the grey and furious waves. The great visitor has always existed beneath the surfaces of the world, never upon them.

As her mother taught her, as her mother was taught by her mother, and so on, and as Cleo reported to all of the scientific journals that no longer even replied to her submissions: all life evolved from the tiny organic scraps of an impact against the planet.

Something once tunnelled through space, 535 million years gone.

As a subspecies of it, we have grown into a multitude of treacherous usurpers.

She has no doubt now that *it* will finish the destruction initiated by the burning of coal on an industrial scale. Mankind has obliviously, yet fastidiously, spent its last two hundred years waking an angry parent.

Cleo long ago decided to see out the end while close to her beloved coves: near the shoreline where her family had been finding the signs for generations, and where she too found her own first signifier. Portents that the world should have been studying, signs obscured by the incremental collapse of civilisation.

New voices now sang through the wind, rain and relentless tides, and in dreams that required a lifetime of interpretation. But every shriek in her nightmares foretells far greater horrors, yet to be endured.

Who has listened to a 75-year-old woman, fighting her own last stand against dementia, the local eccentric whose mother committed suicide in an asylum? As Cleo ambled round supermarkets and the seaside attractions of this insignificant little bay in the southwest of England, she has told the few who will listen that something too terrible for anyone to fully comprehend, let alone believe in, exists. She has told them that *it* has been stirring for many years in local waters.

Out there, under the world, but also within life as we know it.

Eventually Cleo finds the strength to break from her inertia, a blank listlessness often interspersed with racing thoughts. She turns off the media service.

The darkness of the room intensifies. The heat about her chair thickens.

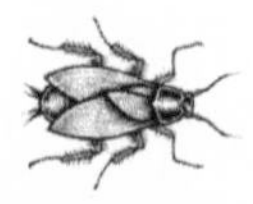

That night Cleo dreams of polyps, tens of thousands of blue gelid forms rising from the seabed, growing and trailing their translucent rags until the water of the bay resembles a pond dimpled and thickened by frogspawn.

Among them many elderly men and women stand upright, submerged to their chests. They raise their withered arms to a night sky unlike any Cleo has seen before. A canopy of impenetrable darkness wreathed by distant whitish vapour trails that appear wet, or webbed, and glisten like dew-drenched spider webs.

The old people wear hospital gowns, tied at the neck. They laugh or cry with happiness as if witnessing a miracle. One or two call out for help. Among those, she recognises her dead mother.

When the surface of the water is a vast, rubbery carpet reaching unto the distant horizon, that rises and slops nauseously in the swell, the thousands of grey and white heads call out a name in unison.

Issuing the scream of a frightened child, Cleo breaks from sleep.

In the early morning it is cooler. Cleo begins the short walk to Broadsands Beach, intending to walk over the headland to Elberry Cove. She inspected and protected the seagrass in that cove during forty years of marine conservation work for the Environment Agency. Too old to dive now, she still visits the cove, as often as she is able, to monitor the progression of another matter.

Cleo isn't supposed to leave her home unsupervised. Yolanda, the nurse and carer who visits her home three times each day, isn't due for another two hours. By then it will be too hot to venture outside.

Before someone sees her in the street and calls an ambulance, Cleo shuffles home; she's left the house without dressing properly. Halfway down Broadsands Road, as she passed beneath Brunel's abandoned viaducts, those stone Leviathans that still bestrode each dawn, she realised she was wearing nothing besides a nightshirt and underwear.

By the coatrack in the hall she looks at the notice she can't remember writing or tacking to the wall, reminding her to take her medication as soon as she awakes each morning.

Finally dressed and medicated, she stands upon the sea wall on Broadsands.

Five a.m. and the sun is rising, turning the bay a withering blue. The sky is polished a piercing silver that will broil brains in a few hours.

Cleo watches an unusual formation of black-necked grebes. So strange again are their number and positioning on the sand below. She fumbles for the camera about her neck and finds it missing. She has forgotten to bring it, and not for the first time.

Until this last year, she has never seen more than three grebes fishing together at this spot. She spots twenty today. A white debris of gulls litters the sand. They gather in their hundreds. They watch the sea disconsolately. None take flight or call out.

Where the beach huts once stood, a viewing platform has been erected by the council for the coming solar eclipse. That too is festooned with seabirds engaged in an uneasy silence and a motionless peering at the horizon.

As with each recent summer, a great green skirt of *Himanthalia elongata*, or thongweed, coats the beach like wet wool and is piled at the water's edge. It floats, entirely concealing the surface of the sea for a good fifty metres offshore. Within the broad blanket of immobile weed that appears to have suffocated the very tide, she sees a vast barrel jellyfish, stranded.

Other large, pale discs of barrel and moon jellyfish become visible along the shore. They resemble unsightly blisters poking through the diseased pelt on a large animal's back. Beneath the weed she imagines their great white tendrils coiled about the impenetrable green fronds of the weed.

Once, the waters of the bay resembled those of the Mediterranean. The officers in Nelson's navy settled the area because it had reminded them of Gibraltar.

Cleo ponders the hundreds of thousands of spectators who will soon flock to Torbay to watch the cosmic event. She believes they are destined to see a sight that the subdued birds, who are too afraid to fish, already anticipate.

Her progress is interrupted by frequent stops to catch her breath as she walks the coastal path, and crosses the common, to reach Elberry Cove. She has less than two hours before the heat becomes unbearable. Power shortages have rationed the air conditioning so her apartment won't be much cooler, but her thoughts are convoluted and troubling enough without the sun's heat lighting a fire under them.

As she walks along the cliffs, the defunct fishing port of Brixham visible ahead, a familiar hot wind picks up from the sea and rustles the trees circling the common. Cleo struggles with her balance and wayward hair. She believes she just heard those trees call a *name*.

From the beach behind her, as the wind strikes the shore, the gulls break their unnerving silence and cry out in alarm. They take flight. Cleo watches a great squadron of dry wings beating a passage inland, away from the bay where they once felt safe.

About her on the coastal path, the gnarled trunks of pine, sweet beech and larch bow away from the sea. Their posture suggests they are striving to uproot and flee the moorings that anchor them perilously close to the water. Across the last decade, from Dorset to Cornwall, the leafy heads of the remaining trees on the cliffs and open shores have taken on an aspect of fearful supplication. Or perhaps their decrepit tilt is a despairing acknowledgement of the danger restlessly building out there, deep down, that nothing will evade.

Few notice how these trees lean, or they attribute the slant to the wind. Most people have lost the ability to understand what the natural world whispers. But not all. Ever restless in winter, or motionless and sullen in summer heat, the trees of the bay know only a tense expectation of what nears the shore, something felt but unseen. *Right here*, she is sure, is clear evidence of a peculiar apprehension that shudders through the natural world.

Long ago, Cleo learned to identify the Earth's signs, just as her great-great-grandmother, great-grandmother, grandmother and mother had done before her. She knows the trees will soon thrash their last in the coming storms. They will crash beneath great carapaces of turbulent seawater as the oceans rise even higher than the levels reached in the last three decades.

At the end, as the creator rises, the trees will shriek out *that name*, in a deafening chorus of panic before they all fall silent for ever. *As we must too*. She has seen and lived through the *coming* when she sleeps; has visualised what comes after. Sometimes, now, the portents flicker into chaotic life within her open eyes.

The name: the younger trees sheltered in Marriage Wood call it now too. She can hear them responding to the unnatural wind in the distance. Older members of that ancient woodland hush them.

And as she rounds the headland and descends to Elberry Cove, Cleo hears the name arise from the very water. Not for the first time either. In the retreating pull of the surf across a myriad pebbles, all rolling together, she often hears *that name*. In the slap and hiss of the sluggish waves upon the baked shoreline exists that dreadful signifier.

No one has seen the face of God and it remains ineffable, but Cleo believes she knows *its* name, in the many languages of the trees, the birds, the sea, and also from the strange languages of her dreams. Her mother once told her that it was only a matter of time before she would hear that name everywhere and in all living things. That she would become *a receiver.*

When Cleo first heard the calling of the name her doctors were certain that the voices were the beginnings of the family taint, the early onset of the bedlam in her bloodline, a hereditary taint of dementia that remained strong after three generations of daughters were all declared insane. Mercifully, Cleo is childless and the curse will end with her; she would never willingly inflict what she knows upon a child.

Most days, she struggles to recall her dead husband's face, or even when he died. Yet Cleo refuses to believe a hereditary illness is transmitting this *name* into her thoughts. She believes the disease that slowly shrivels her brain creates a susceptibility to the natural transmissions from the Earth. Messages that only a disordered sixth sense can detect.

She takes the pills, or some of them, and never utters her family's theories to her doctors.

Her ancestors all claimed *the name* was first heard in fossils in this bay. Her own experiences began in this cove too, though not in fossils, but at the edge of the seagrass pasture.

In the woodland dividing the cove from the drought-resistant maize that grows on the old golf course, Cleo scratches about the paths and undergrowth until she finds the tracks she seeks.

The 'ambulances' have made recent deliveries at high tide; tyre tracks, the thinner tracks of barrows, and the parallel furrows of the gurney wheels carve the pebbles apart.

The grooves lead Cleo to disturbances upon the red clay in the wood behind the cove. More evidence of a commotion — a procession, no less, of those who try to adapt to the future world they have dreamed. Some local people wish to undergo a great transformation for a creator whom they have worshipped in secret for generations. A few of their number have already sunk beneath the waves and not returned.

Cleo wonders if some of *them* survived in the colder water, beyond the seagrass, or if their drowned, contorted carcasses were washed ashore to be buried amongst the bent and mournful trees of the woods.

The sea quickly grows deep in the cove. A bank of pebbles drops to smooth red sand. Thirty metres out, at a depth of six metres, eighty hectares of seagrass still thrive. One of the largest surviving meadows in the British Isles. Until she was too old to dive, Cleo spent hundreds of hours in the pasture. Down there she would scour the marine flora with torch and camera, watching the thick, lustrous grass moving in the currents. She took a thousand samples across three decades and discovered nothing untoward amongst those fronds. But she still asks herself now, from where did that stone come? A dolmen that stands sixty metres offshore, hidden on the sea floor where the sun's light barely reaches.

During one of her last dives, before she was *retired*, she caught sight of a large, black silhouette at a distance, at the end of her torch's reach. Where the currents caused by the slipway and the reef made it unsafe to swim, *something* had been deposited. She found the effigy five years ago and believes that it remains in place.

Once her fear and panic crashed, Cleo realised that the object was stationary: a rock formation. Drifting out another ten metres –a risky business as the tide was turning and she was not at her fittest when pushing seventy in the spring of 2050 — she had been able to see more of the rock that reared from the underwater gloom like a saurian head. To her enduring astonishment, Cleo found herself approaching what suggested the presence of a large black chess piece — a knight, no less — upon the sea floor. Emerging from preserved grasslands was an installation, clearly manmade, though crudely, and casting an onyx gaze around itself over the seabed.

The object suggested a monument or underwater marker; even an idol. At first she believed it must have been pitched over the side of a boat. Eventually she found evidence of its congregation, and one that needed no illumination by a marine biologist's lamp; because those responsible for the sculpture existed on land, in the village of Churston Ferrers.

The memory prompts her to make another visit to the Kudas, who live in the village. And soon, when she regains the stamina to walk that far, because she wants to determine whether the Kudas have made their final leap beneath the waves. They seemed due the last time she looked in on them.

It is getting late and will soon be too hot to move around. Cleo takes a pained look at the water and marvels again at what has lain hidden here for so long. More evidence of the creator's slow waking. According to the women of her bloodline the visitor relocated to this bay from south of the Equator, 235 million years ago, to slumber as the Earth reshaped its surface.

Time was running out; that was all that mattered. The eclipse was mere weeks away. The sun had turned up its infernal heat. There would be no autumn.

Cleo sits alone and perfectly still inside her living room. The blinds are drawn across the balcony doors. The media service is silent and blank. A familiar agitation spreads through her body as the anti-psychotic medication nears the end of its cycle. A palsy quivers in her hands and feet.

Yolanda medicates Cleo until she has calmed, stroking her hair until she settles. Yolanda is a former refugee from Portugal who works as a carer for a few of the multitude of dementia sufferers in the bay. She arrived minutes after Cleo returned from the cove.

Reclining on the sofa, while Yolanda busies herself preparing a midday meal, Cleo's attention drifts to the portraits of her forebears: Mary Anning, Amelia Kirkham, Olive Harvey and her mother, Judith Oldway. She wipes at the tears that immediately film her eyes.

As you were, so am I.

Around their pictures are the polished madrepores that her mother had passed down. Upon the walls, pressed seaweeds hang, mounted and framed by Amelia Kirkham; Cleo's great-grandmother.

After making significant contributions to marine botany and Earth science, Cleo's forebears all died raving. Once Cleo began to hear the natural world issuing *that name*, five years ago, and building to a veritable din inside her own head, she took measures to prevent a repetition of her ancestors' fates. To dampen the shrieks and the visions, she swallows the psychotropic salves that her earliest forebears had lacked.

Her mother Judith chose to eschew anti-psychotic medication. As a result of what her mind struggled to contain and process, Judith was one day shy of her sixtieth birthday when she took her own life.

Looking at the family portraits never fails to make Cleo ponder the futility of her conservation work in a world that could not reach consensus. A world incapable of saving itself. And a species that could not conceive its insignificance upon the Earth, let alone the Earth's insignificance in the cosmos. The women of her family all endured their own Damascene moments, haplessly. They had changed none of the minds around them, but had deranged their own.

'The women of your family were beautiful,' Yolanda says, as she fastens the tray on the armrests of Cleo's chair. She follows her patient's gaze to the photographs on the sideboard.

'And clever too. Thank you, dear,' Cleo says, her interest briefly moving to the neatly cut sandwiches. 'My great-grandmother was none other than Amelia Kirkham. You won't have heard of her, Yolanda. Her aunt was the world famous Mary Anning.'

Cleo isn't sure if she has told Yolanda this before. But evidence of *the visitor*, the creator, was first discovered by Mary Anning, and then passed on to her niece, Amelia Kirkham, who pursued these curious traces of evidence with vigour. The knowledge she recovered, the very sense of it, had driven her mad.

'Mary Anning was an amateur palaeontologist. A near-unique woman in her time. This was the early nineteenth century, dear. Careers in science were forbidden to women. But she, my dear, was a true pioneer. Much of what we know of prehistoric life and the Earth's history is owed to her.'

'You too, I think, will live so long.'

Cleo tries to smile but lacks the strength.

After winter landslides on the Blue Lias cliffs, it was Mary who found and correctly identified the first ichthyosaur. She also uncovered a plesiosaur from the same rubble, and the first pterosaur beyond the borders of Germany, as well as many other fish fossils whose uncanny influence contributed to the decline of one branch of her family: Cleo's.

'Your lunch, ma'am. You need to eat.'

'Yes. It was those damn belemnites, Yolanda. Mary Anning showed them to her clever niece. And they began my great-grandmother's obsession. Amelia then made an astonishing leap of faith. Few scientists will even acknowledge this. Though in secret, oh, how they whisper now.'

'Of course.'

Cleo's great-grandmother, Amelia Kirkham, eventually died, raving aloud her belemnite dreams to the very end in Churston Hospital.

'That's Amelia, next to Mary Anning. A brilliant woman. But the great love of Amelia's life was seaweed, Yolanda. Not fossils. Her first two books are still in print. The first editions are on display at the Royal Albert Memorial Museum. That's in Exeter. I've seen them.'

'Yes, ma'am.'

Amelia's first two volumes of *Algae Devonienses* (Seaweeds of Devon) were relative bestsellers. Much of *Phycologia Britannica*, which catalogues and illustrates all known British marine algae, was dependent upon Amelia's lifetime of study. But any talk of Amelia's books inevitably led Cleo to thoughts of Amelia's third and final volume, though Cleo does not share this information with Yolanda. That third and final book was mostly destroyed by embarrassed members of the family. A single copy was passed down to Cleo by her mother, just before she too was put away to scream *that name.*

Cleo speaks between the mouthfuls of bread and ham that she slowly chews. 'My great-grandmother, Amelia, collected fossils and seaweeds all the way from Cornwall to North Devon, and along the East and South Devonshire Coasts. You know, one large weed was even named after her.

'The leading botanists of her day were her close friends, dear. With them she shared her finds, and *some* of her theories…' She also shared ideas augmenting her own late aunt's more radical theories about the southwestern coastline. But why trouble Yolanda with that? She couldn't possibly understand. And Amelia's end was neither illustrious nor happy.

It was Amelia Kirkham's third volume, *A Dark, Slowly Flowing Flood*, that caused such grave damage to her reputation; the work was a surrealist dream narrative. Amelia was a scientist who attempted to encapsulate great spans of time and the ever-changing position, shape and environment of the local coastline, but through the media of poetry, water colours, pen and ink.

The book never enjoyed anything but a brief, meagre print run from a local publisher, part-funded by Amelia. But the lurid contents of

Amelia's only non-scientific work remain the sole evidence of what beset and preoccupied her for ten years prior to her incarceration in an asylum.

When Amelia took up with an unorthodox spiritualist group, The Fellows of the Broken Night, towards the end of her liberty, she was already binding her eyes with scarves, and threatening to claw them out from the root should her blinds be removed. But layers of linen strips did nothing to stop the sights unfolding behind her eyes. And these sights formed the ghastlier revelations recorded in *A Dark, Slowly Flowing Flood*. The visions that she was stricken with informed her notorious ravings upon the seafront and piers, where she stood upon a wooden crate, her face bound save for her mouth, to address the ladies and gentlemen of Torquay.

A Dark, Slowly Flowing Flood was filled with drawings of the fossilised marine life that Amelia Kirkham had uncovered and scraped clean. Even more detailed impressions of what she derived from the partial fossil forms were fleshed out in Amelia's imagination, a creative faculty informed by her visions. It was those images that resembled the *creator*, this destroyer and re-maker of worlds. A visitor to the Earth that Cleo's lineage had long dreamed of, but recreated and expressed in ways only communicable through the medium of insanity.

Cleo didn't need to open Amelia Kirkham's book to see again the gelid grotesques that drifted through the last, harrowing, tormented years of her great-grandmother's turbulent consciousness. Merely imagining those things had driven her witless. When these forms had opened their flabby mouths to sing the *name* in her dreams, Amelia had been lost to the world for ever.

Amelia had always believed that she was dreaming of an alien species, adrift amidst the deepest oceans of space and time in the cosmos. Forms that had been creating life out of themselves, and then extinguishing that very life, for eight billion years: the lifespan of the universe.

The following week, on Friday, at dawn, Cleo attempts to see through the dimpled glass panel set beside the Kudas' front door. She is confronted by a greenish light that ripples like water reflected upon the wall of a swimming pool. During her first hurried scrutiny of this reception, four years before, she realised that the entire lower floor of the Kudas' home was sunk beneath the level of the ground and tiled aquamarine like a swimming pool.

Cleo opens the letter box and stares into one of 24 houses in Churston Ferrers with their ground floors permanently converted to the storage of liquid. Could she have subsequently suffered the same hallucination so many times in the same place? Her dementia is better controlled than that.

Despite three restraining orders, and two cryptic threats upon her life, she still comes here.

The death threats, she believes, originated from a local faith group, either The Latest Testament or One Eye Opening. Her age and mental instability were the only factors sparing her the punitive sentences of the magistrate's court.

She moves to the rear of the Kudas' property and experiences a familiar delinquent glee at her daring trespass.

Like always, the windows at the rear are shuttered, as are those of the Kudas' similarly affected neighbours. The garden is ordinary and typical of the neighbourhood: palm trees, the *Trachycarpus wagnerianus*, pink stone paths, tall fences, immaculate lawns and flower beds and a honeysuckle-covered pergola.

The only remarkable feature of the orderly rear gardens is the variety of stone lawn ornaments, all of which, inside the Kudas' yard, depict black seahorses, perched upon what are either castles or reefs — Cleo has never been able to decide. She knows the Kudas' sculptures were created by an artist who worked with living models, stark realism his aim.

Cleo intuits an ugly provocation in the bestial eyes of the four Hippocampus pieces on the lawn.

Her suspicions about this village were first aroused when she followed tracks from Elberry Cove, through Marriage Wood, and linked them to the activity of the private ambulances in the surrounding lanes of Churston Ferrers at night. This at a time when one of the newer 'scientific' religions burned through the area with an intensity of devotion not seen since the Black Death cursed Devon, 700 years before.

The arrival of new faith groups preceded her discovery of the statue beneath the sea in Elberry Cove by a few years, though she believes the churches were active for a long time, albeit disguised in plain sight as something else.

The ambulances belong to one of the age-care charities created by the new churches, who have bought the Church of England buildings of Paignton, Brixham and Torquay, and then set about changing all of their windows into a single curious design. Few local antiquarians have seemed bothered, or they have been silenced. Cleo doesn't know. But attendances, she's heard, are way up now. The congregations are almost entirely elderly.

Cleo has resisted their repeated attempts to entice her into their faith-based care programmes, along with their extensive leisure activities within the community. Her neighbours used to regale her with stories about the wonderful entertainments and events, until she told them to shut up.

The mayor and council are happy because the church groups are relieving the beleaguered local health services of much of their burden. Seventy per cent of the population of the bay is now over sixty. The corporate charity wing of the church, One Eye Opening, has purchased over half of the region's care homes within the last five years. The quality of the care is unsurpassed.

But Cleo will never consider an association with any faith that reshapes church windows into that eye. One great eye. Big, luminous but somehow idiotically blank and unsympathetic, and always in a green, yellow and black stained glass that she considers reptilian.

The design suggests the church windows are engaged in a penetrating scrutiny of those who pass below. Surreptitiously, building by building, and even in the listed buildings, she has noted the removal of the cross.

These days, the garden ornaments of Churston Ferrers are no longer odd to her, because the actual interiors of that settlement, upon which she has spied so diligently, have proved far more interesting.

Much of the rear patio closest to the Kudas' house has been taken over by an apparatus consisting of white plastic tubes or hoses attached to a generator that produces enough heat to warm her entire body when standing a few feet away. The air near the machines contains an oily electric odour. The two largest tubes pass through the rear wall of the affected houses. Vibrations can be felt through the hoses. If she moves her face close enough she can hear water bubbling through the PVC piping.

The apparatus is some kind of pump. Above the machine, an extractor fan expels tepid air with a not unpleasant odour of salt water. Each of the church's ambulances that visit the village has been similarly fitted with a mechanism for filtering seawater.

Standing on tiptoe, Cleo peers through the mesh screen before the whirring plastic blades of the fan. Until the balls of her feet burn, and her old spine cramps, she remains fixed in position and stares with wonder and revulsion at the Kudas' wide living room.

The lens of a light fitted into the front of a limestone rock illumines the watery space. There is no conventional furniture, only several large boulders arranged around the edges of the room and all containing embedded lights. Upon the floor, a gentle swaying motion is produced by a pasture of submerged *Alismatales*, or seagrass.

In the dim, greenish illumination she sees Mrs Kuda first, crouched upon her rocky perch. And above this bizarre grotto, the naked lady of the house observes an activity out of her sight, in another region of the room.

Until she found this pair, Cleo had never before seen a human being covered in such unsightly skin below the neck. Not only has Mrs Kuda been cursed with a hunched back, or a great mane of flesh spiked by the vertebrae beneath, but her skin is mottled by large plates of pink-orange psoriasis. Cleo's initial suspicion was that this indicated the presence of a rare disease in which an amphibian environment offered comfort to the sufferer. But this is no medicinal pond. Judging by the rock-effect walls and lifelike encrustations — shells, molluscs and several kinds of hermit crab — the Kudas' living room is fashioned into a facsimile of a rock pool.

That morning, at least five minutes pass before Cleo catches her first glimpse of the man of the house — if his condition justifies the title. What Cleo sees of Mr Kuda is often obscured; he mostly remains submerged and facedown. Only when his gleaming body passes through the beams of the three rock-mounted lights can she make a fuller assessment of his disability.

His skin condition matches his wife's, while his chest, arms, shoulders, head and neck are those of an adult man, albeit one aged, hunched and stooped. But Cleo has become convinced that Mr Kuda has no legs. Or perhaps only one leg. And that morning, whatever it is that extends from his lumpy abdominal region curls around a clump of grass in the manner of a tentacle. Using the long, wavering weed for grip, he then wheels his large body around in the water while his head remains hidden. Cleo has never yet observed him rise to take a breath.

Agilely, Mr Kuda now swishes himself through the water. Ripples from his silent, circular activity spread out and lap the rock upon which his wife sits. At the foot of her outcrop, he stops wheeling and, like a child, gently raises his face to just beneath the water's surface. Carefully, unsteadily, his scaly wife shuffles off the stone seat and sits beside him in the water. Facing each other, they engage in something approximating a kiss.

What troubles Cleo about this intimate activity is the gap between their faces, and the way in which Mrs Kuda rolls her eyes upwards and so whitely within her lined face. What remains of her withered bosom also palpitates, suggesting a pumping action or rapid respiration.

When Mr Kuda eventually detaches himself from the ghastly contact, Cleo sees a thin, dark object, resembling a long tongue, dart back inside her wide-open mouth.

Evidently Mr Kuda has been dancing, down in those verdant seagrasses, to woo his partner. That hideous wheeling in the paddling shallows is some kind of mating display, one that Cleo has repeatedly observed in the Hippocampus of the local coves.

Since her first sighting of this pair, and the other less well-formed couples in the village, she finds that the sound of the Kudas' generator and fan will follow her home, locked inside her skull. When she closes her eyes to sleep, she is sure that the white ceiling of her bedroom ripples like the ceiling of a cave into which the sea flows at high tide. What also abide in her mind, in unwelcome fashion, like an incorrect slide inserted into a projector, are her unpleasant observations of Mr Kuda's belly, and of the bellies of the other retired men in the neighbourhood. After they break from the kisses with their wives, and glide out of sight across the watery floors of their living rooms, their gently distended bellies often move, as if from the squirming of a multitude within.

In the warm, shallow seawater of their village dens, Cleo has observed so many who are infirm on land but have managed a miraculous transformation, or second life, in water. These aged people now frolic and glide through the swaying seagrasses with which they have sown the sunken floors of their living rooms.

If she tells anyone, she will be thought mad and delusional. She will be accused of hallucinating, and although she does plenty of that, the same was also said of her mother, her grandmother, her great-grandmother and her great-great-grandmother. But the burden of what she knows, she is sure, will soon bear the most unappealing fruit in the local waters of this cursed bay.

That night Cleo dreams of small islands with faces formed from black shadows cast by the great sun that rose behind them, near blinding her sight and turning the seawater the colour of polished steel.

She stood upon a cliff edge she didn't recognise and looked across a panorama of new red cliffs. Great fresh gouges of scarlet rock were exposed along the coastline. Vast slopes of rust-coloured rubble had tumbled into the shining water below, as if a great storm had caused centuries of erosion in a matter of days.

From what she could see of the distant hills, she might have been near Goodrington. But if she was, the coastline of South Devon was undergoing rapid reformation.

Whatever bobbed in the sea beneath her position tried to attract her attention. Large, black lumpen forms, but slippery and shining as they turned and wallowed, dived and surfaced, barking out sounds that seemed similar to human voices if she listened closely enough. The distant faces bore doglike suggestions of whiskered snouts and flattened ears. The eyes and teeth were human.

Cleo awakes in her living room. The first thing she sees is Yolanda rising from her chair. The nurse approaches on soft feet, her face one big smile, her lovely eyes wide and glittering with an excitement that Cleo assumes has little to do with her patient waking up.

The nurse must have let herself in as Cleo slept; it has gone nine. She slept badly for the first half of the night, and then tried to stay awake on account of the dreams that her anti-psychotic medication was failing to suppress. Cleo has been in a bad way in the week following her visit to the Kudas.

On the far side of the room the media screen flickers with the sound muted. Her carer was watching the news and leafing through the journal Cleo writes to keep track of each day, the sudden emergence of memories, the effects of medication cycles. Perhaps Yolanda has been amusing herself with Cleo's recollections. Cleo doesn't think her journal offers any comic value, but then she can't recall much of what she's written in it. Her prescriptions will never preserve her mind, but they have slowed the deterioration and moderated her mania successfully — providing Yolanda visits three times each day to make sure that Cleo takes what has been prescribed.

Cleo reaches for her glass of water, drinks through a straw. It has become tepid in the languid heat of night. She notices her hands are trembling and hastily swallows the three pills that Yolanda has already placed upon the side table.

Yolanda attempts to block the screen with her body. 'This news is not so good. Let me turn it off.'

'Is it ever good? But let me see. What have I missed?'

The world. She certainly hasn't missed that while she's slept. A narrowing space in her mind is often fatigued by a weakening attempt to understand how people have allowed things to get so bad. And in the last few days the seemingly endless war between Turkey, Iraq and Syria has escalated to new levels over control of the headwaters of the Euphrates and Tigris. The Indians still have their rain, but the Pakistanis have none; they are also going to war again over water.

Even with the sound lowered, Cleo no longer cares to watch the great dust clouds of the continual air and drone strikes, the detritus of devastated vehicles, the moonscape of obliterated cement blocks that is now much of the Middle East, Kashmir and North Africa. Cleo assumes Yolanda has been following updates on the various escalations.

'Something terrible has happened *here*,' Yolanda says, her face stiff with shock.

'Here?' It is local news on the screen. 'Turn it up! Quickly.'

There have been several arresting events of late, portents and signs on her doorstep, but they rarely make the local news. But this was national news on the screen broadcasting from Berry Head, not two miles from where she lives.

Cleo can see footage of the nature reserve's unmistakable shape, shot from the air. A limestone headland, and the vestiges of what was once a great tropical coral reef, 375 million years before. The women of her family, whose portraits stood on the sideboard, had even considered Berry Head to be one half of a very old doorway.

As Cleo watches the report, augmented by Yolanda's excited narration, she can see that a great many people recently tried to step through that *doorway*.

'Dear God,' Cleo says. 'Those people are from local care homes.'

'It is terrible. I do not think you should watch.'

'Nonsense. You think I am surprised by this? *They'll* do anything to get them into the water.'

'What do you mean?'

'Open Heart, Open…never mind.'

How those poor creatures flap and flail after they step from the edge and plummet to the sea. At least seventy people from two local care homes. The infirm and the demented, all shrieking as they plummet through two hundred feet of empty air.

There are only two films of the incident that took place during early morning as Cleo slept: footage from the lighthouse security camera, and a shaky film taken by a carer who is now in police custody. Yolanda says the films have been on repeat every thirty minutes since she arrived at eight. Despite all that is happening in the world, Torbay is making international news; the elderly people from two retirement homes have all leaped from the edge of a cliff, together.

The police are looking for the staff who drove these confused people to the precipice. Speculation is rife. The carers helped the victims on and off the buses, before guiding and wheeling them by torchlight to the terrible precipice that Cleo had never liked standing near.

In the recordings, the din of the seabirds is excessive: guillemots, razorbills, black-legged kittiwakes, the gulls. They are always noisy in their cliff-side nests, but as that tired and stooped parade of the thin and infirm hobbles and shuffles off and into the abyss, and down to the terrible black rocks and the churning, bitter sea below, the noise of the birds becomes a cacophony rising to a crescendo of panic. Those birds should have been sleeping. But in that riotous avian climax, Cleo hears *the name* screamed with abandon and with the ecstasy that precedes tribute. Because that is what she is watching: *sacrifice*. Those were sacrifices at Berry Head; not the victims of mass suicide, or mass murder, as the press are claiming. This is human sacrifice at the doorway, at the very threshold of what is waking.

Those poor fools who were taken to the cliffs by their carers, nurses, doctors, porters and orderlies of the Esplanade and Galmpton Green nursing homes all shrieked *the name*, raising their frail but impassioned voices to join the din of the birds. They dropped out of sight individually or as couples holding hands, and even in one disoriented clump, down into the waves and the rocks where they must have come apart like kindling. None was pushed; all walked, calling *the name*.

The residents of those care homes were promised they would see out their final days in as much comfort as anyone could hope for in such desperate times in the country. But Cleo knows that long preparations had facilitated this mass evacuation from life.

The news moves to breaking reports about a dozen similarly affected retirement homes in Plymouth and North Cornwall. There, many elderly residents have been discovered making their way, slowly, on walking frames and in wheelchairs, in the early hours of the morning, toward Whitsand Bay and other beaches. Perhaps with the intention of throwing themselves into the sea too. It is unclear how many were not prevented from achieving their goal.

Cleo always thought it strange, and perplexing, and unnerving, how local fossils have been shaped into the exterior walls of the Esplanade Care Home in Roundham Gardens in Paignton, as if to create some decorative feature using local materials. This alteration occurred once the property came into the possession of One Eye Opening.

Cleo has written to the council to explain the hidden activity within these very stones, but never received a reply. The same innovation has been replicated in the churchyard walls in Paignton after the crucifixes were taken down. Cleo guesses those fossils were embedded in the mortar to influence the end-of-life decision made by so many last night.

She can only assume that the dimming and deranged minds of the aged provided the best material for such manipulation. They were the best receivers of transmissions from down beneath the waves of the bay; such transmitters, the fossils, were deliberately placed in proximity to these poor, confused minds.

Each of the affected care homes in the morning news is owned by One Eye Opening, a wealthy nonconformist religion, or so it is being described on the news, for want of a better definition, which Cleo has ready: a *cult*. A cult that made its disingenuous inroads into the religious community, and end-of-life care, in a county overrun by an elderly population.

It seems unfair, and horribly Darwinian, that some are being transformed while others were sacrificed to the sea in this manner. Though the residents of Churston Ferrers, like the Kudas, are wealthy; perhaps the selection of who swims and who leaps to their death depends upon nothing more sophisticated than money.

Cleo is shocked but not surprised. During the last five years she's noticed many other local curiosities. The great ructions on the seabed reported by both the Royal Navy and the marine biology unit at Plymouth University. Fishermen using sonar have also claimed that new topographies are emerging upon the seafloor. Sailors, from what was left of the South Hams fishing fleet, have long been fetching unusual catches from local waters.

With her scepticism in suspension, Cleo never debunked the stories she found online about what was tugged out of the fishermen's nets and quickly confiscated by the Environment Agency. Some of the catches were still being examined in the Plymouth University labs. The two marine biologists in Brixham, Harry and Phillip, with whom Cleo retains a vague and hardly reciprocal association since her retirement, are desperate to eschew any classifications or rumours of a Fortean nature that Cleo immediately attaches to them. Harry and Phillip know why Cleo was retired, but won't admit that they have personally examined five specimens of *Eledone cirrhosa*, the curled octopus — creatures generously exceeding all previously recorded sizes and weights. They were caught in waters off the South Hams coast during the previous year.

Cleo's contacts have also confirmed that the rumours of a giant squid spotted in local waters are not entirely fictional either. They have yet to refute claims that an impossibly sized *Haliphron atlanticus* octopus, with only six legs but of lengths stretching to ten metres, has been caught and killed by a Royal Navy PT boat near the mouth of the Dart Estuary. There were reports that the creature had menaced a ferry, and made several attempts to drag at least one passenger overboard. Her contacts claim that what was found in the thing's belly, partially digested, link to the rumours of the fate of three missing canoeists, who were last seen in the channel below Greenway and heading towards Totnes the previous year.

Has Plymouth's harbour not been deluged with *Octopus vulgaris*, not three years ago in 2052? A species not seen in British waters since the early sixties of the previous century.

And it didn't stop there for anyone predisposed to seek synthesis amongst the freakish incidents and recent curiosities found in the county's waters. Stone plinths, carved with designs the Celts had imitated and Iron Age man replicated in stone throughout Cornwall, were found off Salcombe by engineers tasked with building a wind farm. Great undersea basalt circles, arranged like teeth in the untidy mouths of what resemble eyeless faces, have been discovered close to Start Point, South Devon, during the laying of new cables to transport British nuclear power to the drought-stricken parts of Southern France. Two discoveries that revived local folklore about the possibility of the ruins of Atlantis existing off the coast of Devon and Cornwall. Something is down there for sure, though Cleo doubts it is Atlantis.

The newly managed care homes of Torbay have fossils in their walls, and the windows of the churches have been altered to represent an eye. A geriatric cult has willingly extinguished itself at the cliffs of Berry Head the night before the solar eclipse. Have they not been hearing *the name* and receiving its imagery inside their failing minds? Cleo wonders if she should cuff her own ankle to the bedstead and swallow the key, during what time remains before the cosmic event, lest she join Torbay's flightless snow birds who seem so intent on leaping to their deaths.

Yolanda returns at 4 p.m. that day, thirty minutes late, and wakes Cleo from a short doze.

Yolanda claims the news from Berry Head is upsetting for her, and asks Cleo if she can change the television channel. 'I cannot see it again. But it is all they show today. They are bringing in some bodies. I would rather watch the wars.'

Cleo acquiesces as Yolanda will only be around for an hour. The nurse's visit was delayed by the traffic congestion that has built ahead of the eclipse. Thoughts of the cosmic event are making Cleo feel sick.

'Why not tell me about your family?' Yolanda asks as she carries Cleo's tea into the room on a tray. 'I know these women are so important to you. Maybe they can take our minds from this terrible day.'

I doubt that, Cleo thinks, but she looks at the pictures of her grandmother Olive Harvey, who continued her own mother's work, with the weeds and rock pools. Olive was a conservationist and artist, selling shells, polished madrepores and pressed weeds to tourists.

As she eats, Cleo tells Yolanda how Olive spent most of her life outdoors and on the Paignton Coast, south of Goodrington Sands, dipping into the rock pools of Saltern Cove and Waterside Cove. A woman who fastidiously continued the family trade, photographing and collecting the intertidal flora and fauna: the flat wracks, knotted wracks, red seaweed, snakelocks anemones and spotted gobies, and, most importantly, *Galathea strigosa*, the squat lobster. Olive's mother, the brilliant but tragic Amelia Kirkham, had both dreamed and then screamed about what that thing had originally dispersed from.

Olive spent decades scraping and digging her way into the cliffs, and in places where fluvial breccia from the Permian Age amassed about the slates and sandstones from the Devonian Period. The locations of the best fossils were suggested to Olive by the work of her predecessor. With the promise, or warning, that future generations of scientists would uncover even greater marvels and terrors from those cliffs, her forebear led Olive to the shore at low tide.

After decades of coastal erosion since her ancestors first collected and processed their evidence, the shore of Goodrington revealed a submerged forest bed, the very tree stumps emerging after the last ice age. That was Olive's own find. The discovery made her name in the circles that cared about such things. It was Olive Harvey who also discovered the breccia burrows and then quickly reburied them.

In those preserved burrows were the restless relics of animals that had lived in the deserts of the Permian Age, 248 million years before. One extinct occupant issued the grave songs that initiated the destruction of Olive's mind; the song wailed from a burrow left by a giant *Arthropleura* myriapod, a millipede at least four metres long.

In her journal, Olive recorded how she'd once sat in the fossil bed to rest and lost two days and nights. Her mind, in her own words, 'unravelled through its substance and memories' and entered a psychosis that Cleo most commonly associated with a bad experience on LSD.

What Olive had rubbed against, and become irradiated by at a deep subconscious level, was nothing more than a near-microscopic fragment of a substance that had originally dripped from the writhing and shedding of some monumental form. This occurred 248 million years previously, when this part of the British Isles was a desert, near the Equator. But so began another member of the family's inexorable decline into socially unacceptable enlightenment.

Cleo continues with her story and tells the captivated Yolanda about her own mother, the tormented and twice-divorced environmentalist Judith Oldway. Judith put an end to her own severe and unmanageable cerebral rout at 59. Judith succumbed to what was thought to be early onset dementia and took an overdose. Despite the great blanks in her memory, Cleo had never forgotten that day.

When she'd been alive, Judith often reminded Cleo of what Amelia and Olive had each explored, discovered and subsequently *believed.* She told Cleo all about what her own mother, Olive, had passed down to her: the knowledge that our planet was but one tiny krill floating amongst billions of fragments in a cold, hostile ocean of gas and debris. And that our infinitesimal fragment was transformed by a *visitor* 535 million years before. A world subsequently destroyed and remade so many times over as a consequence of the visitor's dreadful whims and rages as it stirred. Her forebears all shared the same dreams; the fossils they exposed were the equivalent of a few smudged fingerprints on the walls of a vast crime scene, as big as a planet.

Cleo's mother would flavour her own interpretation with her background in Earth science. Judith passionately claimed that had we crept across this Earth in smaller numbers, and not congregated in such carbon-rich cultures, while flashing our arrogant, thoughtless presence into the stars, and had we not made toxic and eroded the soils, bled our faecal wastes and effluents into the black deeps, crisscrossed the ocean floors and mountain ranges with cables to broadcast our infernal jabber, exhausted the fresh water and melted the glaciers, changed the wind and rainfall, heated the Earth's belly and melted the ice caps, exhausted the great populations of fish and mammals...*if*...we had not grown to nine billion minds and created such an intensification of teeming consciousness on one small planet, whose neural activity transmitted so far outwards...*if* none of this had happened then *it*, *the visitor*, might never have half-opened that one eye, *down there*, where it slumbered.

In the preface to Amelia Kirkham's *A Dark, Slowly Flowing Flood*, the author wrote: 'Just as every God has slept through our Godless endeavours, any God can yet awaken.'

Amelia's final words to the priest who administered the last rites were also alleged to have been: 'What have we done? Oh, God, what did we call out to? Is that thing God?' Not 'a god', but 'God', *the* God: the ultimate creator.

Judith used to wonder aloud to Cleo, and ask why, as a species, we'd not had more sense than to create the requisite conditions in which that name could be called out by the exhausted, dying planet, and by what expired upon it. The Earth now heralded an awakening; Judith had told her that before she was ten.

Near the end of her life, Judith even begged Cleo to bear no children. 'For God's sake,' she'd cried from the bed in which she was often restrained, 'don't continue this!'

Cleo had assumed 'this' was the hereditary taint of insanity, but had subsequently realised that Judith referred to us. To all of us, the species. Judith had wanted to end our burden upon the outer skins of this little planet in our solar system, in which resided a far older occupant, one that had dreamed such foulness as the great lizards, the food chain, viral life, decomposition and mortality, and *us* too, around its eternal *self*, and across so many billions of years that our understanding of age bore no relation to its own. Cleo had obeyed her mother and remained childless.

And Judith always made sure that Cleo wrote down her dreams.

When Cleo has finished speaking, she remains unsure for how long she has been talking, or whether much of what she's said, has been said only to herself. The medication is strong.

Yolanda is already putting on her sunhat. 'On Friday, we watch the eclipse together, from here, yes? On the balcony. I will come early.'

'I'd rather you spent that day with your family, my dear.'

'Oh, Cleo! You still think the world will end during the eclipse?' Yolanda laughs.

No, Cleo doesn't think that. Not exactly. 'The end of us will be the end of us, my dear, but not the end of *everything*.'

She does often wonder, though, if the coming eclipse will herald an extinction-level event. How can she not after all of those dreams? And will it be a cataclysm heralded in true biblical fashion by the transformation of the firmament?

Cleo is not entirely convinced by the idea, or by her predecessors' thoughts in this area, or by proclamations made by the new churches, who are far too dependent on *A Dark, Slowly Flowing Flood*, among the other, older texts that they favour from Providence, New England.

'I believe our end will be near total, Yolanda, but with a partial evolutionary transformation of whatever survives. I can't give you any timescale, or date, but it will be relatively swift in Earth-life terms. And miserably incremental like the consequences of climate change, surrounded by diebacks we've not seen since the bubonic plague in Europe and Asia. So, I'm giving us, at least, another two centuries amidst the rubble of our civilisation. But those will be times like nothing we've had to cope with so far. I mean, how many of us can breathe underwater? It may really be that simple, in most places on the Earth.'

'Oh, Cleo! You make me smile.'

'The world has been changing rapidly and bewilderingly towards a critical mass, Yolanda. Surely you have noticed? And I believe dear old Torbay has a specific role to play in this epochal event.'

Yolanda laughs as she swings her bag over her shoulder. 'Whatever you say, Cleo! There is so much going on in your head. But you are making great progress. You must take the relaxants if your mind races. The doctor says so.'

'And you may ask –' Cleo was not to be stopped, even as Yolanda was halfway through the door '– why don't I flee to higher ground? But if you consider what the women of my family discovered, who would want to survive what is coming?'

[Excerpt from the diary of Cleo Harvey]

July 18th, 2055

My dearest Yolanda,

I may not remember to tell you this. I may become distracted, or sleep through your next visit. But as I am enjoying a good period of clarity this afternoon, I feel I owe you some explanation so that you can better make sense of the disparate stories that I have been telling you over the last two years; stories about my family and our work here in this bay.

My great-grandmother, Amelia Kirkham, whom I may have mentioned to you during our association, was certain that what she called the Old One, *or* Great Old One, *as she was wont, arrived on our planet in the Ediacaran Period, 535 million years ago, and during the last gasps of the Pre-Cambrian ages.*

Her methods for deducing this timeline were complex, and involved as much science as imagination; or where the two enmeshed in her dream life. Even with her eyes closed, and while she was away in other places and times as she slept, she still had an eye for the landscapes that she saw, and for the forms of those things that left the imprints she found in the cliffs.

Amelia surmised that the arrival *occurred during the time of the great soft-bodied inhabitants. Those that had existed for hundreds of millions of years, ever consuming each other and recycling their drifting forms. These indigenous denizens of the young Earth left almost nothing for fossil hunters to find, because they had no bones, shells or teeth. But she learned that vast creatures had burrowed through the Earth during Ediacaran times, and trawled the oceans too; great tunnels and gouges were found here in Torbay and in Australia, though nothing of what left the creases in the stones.*

Amelia, however, caught sight of them, the vast iridescent jellies and the great drillers of the planet, as if she was floating among them, or scurrying through the debris of their excavations. And in her waking life what Amelia recalled both fascinated and traumatised her. These tremors of shock loosened her rickety mental foundations. But the monstrous shapes, the diaphanous swellings of the poisonous skirts, the viscous trailings through the hot green deeps and the blind squirmings that she tried to describe and paint, were nothing compared to that which blasted through the atmosphere and then dispersed itself into incalculably new forms. The visitor.

The Cambrian Period, as we know, is renowned for the creativity of its seas. Nothing lived on what little land existed. That far back, the maelstrom of creation was still in the deeps, and what wallowed in the watery expanses became varied and all too abundant. But it was our visitor *who made these new ways of life possible. What it stimulated into being about its landing site crept and leaped, crawled, swam and burrowed to escape parental predation. There were shells, encasing such young life, at least in these Cambrian times, carapaces made in the image of the old visitor's armour. What was still soft and boneless was mostly swept away, or simply reinvented.*

But the visitor, the Great Old One, was not satisfied, or so my forebears all muttered in their bloodless and traumatised states in a local hospital that is now long gone (luxury apartments, would you believe?).

Great ructions and upheavals were emitted as the slowly rusticating visitor remade and remade again the environment that flooded past its often slumbering form beneath the waves. One such mighty cataclysm was the Ordovician-Silurian mass extinction. The trilobites, brachiopods and graptolites were mostly rendered obsolete because of decisions that we can only guess at, if 'decision' is the right word. Human terms are imprecise, for although we share a minute fragment of the Old One's vast consciousness within our own sentience, we are not like it.

This slaughter or genocide of what had either been created or adapted from the insensate drifters of the fathoms occurred 443 million years ago, in two stages divided by hundreds of thousands of years in which the monarch of our watery rock rested between its annihilations.

My poor forebears all cited the alien deity's sensitivity to temperature and climate, and claimed that it drew great ice sheets over itself and its resting places following the Ordovician-Silurian mass extinction. It also used a new armour of ice to drastically alter the chemistry of the oceans and the atmosphere above the waters. But the ruler continued to vandalise its own newly created habitat, repeatedly, across the next 380 million years, whenever its meditations became fitful or disturbed. The planet was plunged into apocalypse and collapse in the Devonian, Permian, Triassic, Jurassic and Cretaceous Periods. There were smaller mass extinctions too, and in each of these eruptions of the roused tyrant's rage, half of the species that it had formed or evolved were destroyed again.

Varied evolving parts of itself were discovered upon our shores by my fossil-hunting family. Most of the clues to what came before mankind were from the Devonian and Permian Periods, and because the slaughtered littered their corpses in the bare cliffs of our beautiful, sheltered Torbay, my forebears dug them up. Do you see?

The Devonian was the Age of Fishes. The sea levels were so very high and the temperature of the water too hot for some, like our ruler, at thirty degrees in the tropics. So a great wrath from below was invoked by this heat. Now this is important, if you consider the temperature of our own world now. But three quarters of all the species on this planet were made extinct across a slow, deliberate and sadistic cull lasting for several million years. At one point, you could say chemical weapons were employed by the Great Old One. The oxygen was removed from the waters, as the creator noted such a chronic dependence upon that gas amongst its myriad subjects. The wiping of the slate was also embellished by the Old One's wilful alterations in sea level, by changes in the climate and by disruptions in soil fecundity.

Even great rocks, passing through the heavens, were pulled down by its rage on the seabed; a rage that our own baboonish antics today inadequately mimic. The fury *that destroyed what had been created must have been incendiary, incandescent, and so cruel. My relatives only found fragments of the war-torn carcasses. They had been buried in rubble for 359 million years, but they were still smoking with a psychic trauma at a bacterial and subatomic level.*

The visitor *covered the world with ice again. It banished the Earth from its sight and slept in the ruins. The survivors struggled on. The land welded together its wreckage into the Pangaea supercontinent, in which every bleeding and shell-shocked continent came together to shiver in the ice. This diaspora began 290 million years ago. But what life and activity there was heated the planet all over again and melted the ice.*

Such was the savagery and merciless genocide of the visitor *upon awakening this time that all previous mass extinctions were rendered irrelevant. You could say that the Great Old One came out swinging with both eyes open, and The Great Dying began. The fish, and even the insects, were smashed and cast aside. He called down a rain of stones from that canopy of debris that flowed through the solar system. He opened his bellows and poisoned the Earth with methane, rid the air of oxygen and suffocated his multitude of abandoned children. Up rose the tyrant's seas and down they crashed upon what we call life. The annihilation was near total. All but four per cent of the species of the Earth were put to death. My mother told me that his indifference alone had allowed the four per cent to survive. All of what is left alive today began life in the four per cent that survived The Great Dying.*

Two hundred million years ago, and then 65 million years ago, he laid waste again and again to what swam, flew and crawled anew around his throne. And again, he used the climate as his weapon.

Sixty-five million years after that final massacre, our species heated this Earth again, and we have become noisome, noisy and populous. Only the flora, water and the animal kingdom can sense the destruction and extinctions of the past ages, and they have begun to scream that name *in alarm and terror again. They know that one of our creator's eyes has opened. Bleary with slumber maybe, but red with a demented rage that is as hot as a star.*

As I watch the news on the screen in my home, and as I reel through the data from every kind of scientific observation and analysis that overloads our poor and troubled minds, in all of this chaos, I believe that we have fatally roused the Great Old One with our careless tenancy. We have begun to wake him with the heat we created. The visitor is the sole creator, and always has been, but we have dared to ape a deity's excesses. So this time his wrath will explode with a creativity that not even the cruellest god or devil in any of our mythologies could imagine to inflict upon its subjects.

This is why I think it best that you spend the day of the eclipse with your loved ones.

I sincerely wish that I, and my mother, and her mother, and her mother, really were nothing but insane, deranged and delusional old women.

Your fond friend,

Cleo

At the end of sleep, Cleo dreams of the bay. The same dream she's suffered for months. Or has it been months? It feels familiar, but how will she really know? But from Hope's Nose to Berry Head, she dreams of the great body of water turning as black as oil before roiling like a weir as wide as an ocean.

The thin outline of the sun's silhouette diminishes, then vanishes.

Stars she recognises, and many that she does not recognise, and many other shining objects, crisscross the vast canopy of sky, leaving silvery trails like snails upon patio stones.

And when the sun begins to reappear the people who gather on the shore all call out a name. Their myriad, faraway voices sound like a small wave washing upon sand before dying into silence.

The horizon changes its shape.

Soon, it is as if all the water in the world is rushing forward from out there, in the form of a long black wall. Behind the great wave, she thinks she sees something, vast and lumpen in shape, that could be a new mountain emerging from the Earth's crust, rising to conceal the sun again.

Cleo awakes to the sound of screams. Tens of thousands of them. Screams on the shore one mile away combining in unison with the screams on the television screen that flickers beside the balcony doors of the living room. The whole world seems to be shrieking at the same time.

Yolanda is on the balcony. She is naked.

In her waking delirium, for some reason that Cleo cannot understand, her nurse has entered her home that morning and removed all of her clothes.

'Yolanda!' Cleo calls out with a throat so dry the word sounds like a croak.

Even in the din below the balcony that now resembles a crowd in a football stadium, or a hundred school playgrounds filled with terror, Yolanda hears Cleo. The nurse turns around, smiling.

As Yolanda steps into the room the first thing Cleo notices is the eye tattooed upon her flat brown stomach. An eye that she recognises. She's seen it around and the tattoo is a good likeness.

The wind that hits the building turns the curtains vertical and Yolanda staggers, but never stops smiling. Her face is wet with the tears of an intense, private joy.

The ground shakes and everything in the apartment rattles. Amelia, Olive and Judith's pictures fall upon the sideboard, as do the preserved and pressed weeds that hang upon the walls.

The din outside might have been caused by a plane crashing in a thunderstorm; or the roar might have been the very Earth being twisted and broken within a pair of great hands. The sea doesn't sound like the sea any more. It becomes a bestial roar. Cleo believes most of the air in the room has been sucked out through the balcony doors.

No more than a few feet before Cleo's seat, Yolanda opens her mouth, but Cleo has no chance of hearing what comes out of it. From the movement of the nurse's lips she can still be certain that a name has been called.

Yolanda helps Cleo out of her chair and begins moving her towards the balcony, either to see what is happening or to make her a part of the commotion. Cleo winces and whimpers when she sees the long, livid gills where Yolanda's ribs should be.

BLACK QUEEN

Nuzo Onoh

Grandfather told us that the River Omambalu was a woman, unfathomable and unpredictable like most women are. And, just like every scorned woman, her grudge was deep and her spite, deadly. He had a name for the river; he called her Black Queen. Grandfather said that despite all our sacrifices to her, it was impossible to tell when her mood would change and her tumultuous rage, turn on all of us. Grandfather said we must therefore, always treat Black Queen with respect, with greater respect than we accorded him, which was a riverful of respect, seeing as he was the most respected of elders in our small riverine village, nestled behind the thick forest of towering trees that formed a living barrier, one-mile-long, between us and Black Queen. There were Iroko, Cedar, Gum, and Melina trees thriving inside the great rainforest that housed the mischievous Monkeys and moody Chimpanzees, the graceful Antelopes and crying Bushbabies, as well as birds, fowls, insects, and reptiles in every size, shape, and colour.

'What will happen if we don't respect Black Queen?' Ifedi, my little sister asked, her wide eyes bright with the seeking light that had earned her the nickname of *"Onye-ajuju"*, meaning, "The Questioner".

'Then she'll open her mighty jaws like a great monster and swallow us up inside her black bowels,' Grandfather said.

'Even you, too?' Ifedi asked, her eyes wide with disbelief.

'Even me too,' Grandfather confirmed, nodding his grey head.

We all looked at ourselves with wonder, my siblings, half-siblings, cousins, and the rest of the clans-children gathered under the great Mango tree in our large hamlet to listen to my Grandfather's nightly tales of mystery and lore. It was impossible to us that anything, even Black Queen herself, could defeat our great hero. You see, Grandfather was the strongest and wisest man in our village. He was the only person to have survived the African Rock Python's squeeze and even more incredibly, succeeded in destroying that ancient reptile in their deadly combat inside the great forest. Prior to Grandfather's feat, uncountable villagers had forfeited their souls to the mortal squeeze of that fearsome reptile, who struck with uncanny intelligence and cunning malignancy, creating widows and widowers, orphans and ruined clans in both our village and the other small villages that bordered the thick forest that led to the Omambalu river. Grandfather's right arm had been his salvation, together with the African porcupine trapped inside his hunting bag. He had been able to stick out his right arm, and with *Amadioha*-might, shoved the spiky rodent into the Python's jaw as it leaned in for the kill. The spikes pierced the reptile's throat, forcing it to untangle its lethal coil on Grandfather's body in a frenzy of pain and confusion. Grandfather had been able to stab it multiple times with his hunting spear till he finally defeated that forest terror.

Every child, woman, and adult in the village and beyond, knew the story of Grandfather's duel with the great reptile monster. It had long gone down in the annals of our village lore, and we his family and kinsmen, basked in the pride of his glory. As a reward, the village elders gave Grandfather the head of the Python to feast upon, while the menfolk shared the rest of the meat, roasted in the open fires underneath the full moon, amidst dancing, drumming, and celebratory songs. It was said that when Grandfather ate the great reptile's head, he ingested its ancient wisdom, knowledge so powerful that it knocked him out for several days, until everyone feared he might never recover.

But recover he did, on the fifth day, when the moon was so swollen it hung low on the skies like an overripe fruit ready to burst. The first word Grandfather spoke on opening his eyes, was that the villagers should start harvesting their farmlands without delay; because in three days, he said, the heavens would darken at noonday and the sun shall be hidden from our eyes, bringing misery to our hamlets. Grandfather's eyes had been chalk-white as he spoke, the dark pupils swallowed behind his sockets. No one doubted his words, as they knew he now spoke with the voice of the oracle as a result of the wisdom received from the great reptile's head.

People started harvesting their corn cobs, *Akidi* beans, spinach and *Ugu* leaves, peppers, and even their cassava and yam tubers, the two king-crops that generally took longer to harvest. It wasn't much to boast about, since we were a riverine community and depended more on our fishing than our farming. Still, every morsel yielded from the soil was something to value and the villagers worked like soldier-ants to harvest every single seed from our farms. And on the third day, just as Grandfather prophesied, the skies went black in the middle of the day as the ferocious swarm of locusts descended on our village in their fearsome multitudes, devouring everything in their path.

The locusts remained for just a day and a night, but by the time they finally departed after the villagers had chased them away with a cacophony of noises, shrieks, drums, clashing metal pots, clapping and war songs, they had reduced our farmlands to brown barrenness. Everybody knew that, but for Grandfather's prediction, we would have lost our entire crop to the pestilence and faced famine and starvation. And our hamlet soon filled with the offerings from our grateful villagers, ranging from chickens to Palmwine kegs, goats and even a couple of *Akwete* calico wrappers.

From that terrible day of the locusts, Grandfather became the village's wise Seer, and everyone came to him for advice, and to settle family quarrels and neighbourly disputes. Once in a while, after that first spectacular prophecy, he would receive visions from the oracles, but not frequently. But when he spoke, people listened, and when he told us to treat Black Queen with respect, with greater respect than we accorded him, everybody heard his words, and everybody obeyed.

Crawling her winding flow along the contours of our village, Black Queen was as beautiful as she was terrifying. Her water-skin was as black as ebony and glistened as if greased with palm-kennel oil. She was so black that on still moonless nights, when the sky god enjoyed the secret pleasures of his rotund silver-wife, one could easily mistake her for the wide asphalt road that led to Onitsha town, save for the soft sighs she made as she glided her wet and meandering course along the sandy shoreline. Most days, her flow was steady, smooth and serene in her spectacular, shimmering blackness, and my skin never ceased to break out in goosebumps whenever I viewed her undulating waves each morning I visited with my family for our ablutions. Even the numerous fishing boats dotted along her black expanse, could never dent her menacing dark allure. I remember I used to be so terrified of Black Queen that I would refuse to bathe in the river like the rest of the villagers. Even when my mother invited me to try the smaller backwater enclave Black Queen had carved for our people before the birth of our ancestors, the encircled pond where the older women bathed in some privacy, I still recoiled from her cold and unfathomable embrace. Her black, shimmering surface filled me with so much terror that I would keep my eyes shut as I filled my clay-pot with enough water to wash my body in the safe privacy of our hamlet. The only time I felt safe was when I accompanied Grandfather to her shores to offer sacrifices to her. The bowl of cooked food always felt warm and comforting in my hands, and the tantalising aroma never failed to make me wish I were as important as Black Queen, so that I could get offered such delicious sacrifices.

Grandfather said Black Queen used to be married to the sky god, *Amadioha*, he of the thunderous voice and fiery lightning eyes. Theirs was a union of harmony and peace until the sky god betrayed her love and married two fat brides on the same day, the Night-Queen, *Ọwa,* with her cold, silvery sheen, and the Day-Queen, *Awu*, with her blazing golden rays. In fury, Black Queen appealed to the Earth-Mother, *Anά,* for refuge. *Anά* welcomed her like a daughter and gave her the piece of earth in our village, where she curved her long twisty route into the hard soil.

In revenge, the sky god pelted both the Earth-Mother and Black Queen with his hard rain-spit and lightning strikes from his blazing eyes. And on dark windy nights, when *Amadioha*'s thunderstorm caused Black Queen to rage and foam, her wave-fists raised in fury at her philandering sky lord, the villagers quaked inside their dark huts as her waves crashed in deadly combat against herself and the unfortunate villagers who lived nearest to the shorelines. Thankfully, Black Queen's fury was always short-lived and her benevolence, steadfast.

Grandfather told us all these wonderful tales during the numerous story sessions held underneath the silvery glow of the pregnant Night-Queen, just before she gave birth to her litter of glittering stars. The blaze from the open fires would warm our faces as we listened with hushed breaths to Grandfather's raspy sing-song voice, the aroma of roasting sweetcorn cobs from our farmland tantalising our tastebuds. He said that in the old days, our people used to sacrifice the most beautiful virgins to appease Black Queen, since it was known that she loathed beautiful women. She viewed them as rivals, eternally fearful her fickle husband might snatch them from earth as wives, giving birth to new moons or suns in the endless skies. Grandfather said that as long as Black Queen received her virgin sacrifices, her rage never harmed the villagers and she rewarded us with more fish than we could consume, enough fish for us to sell to the other land-locked villages who craved the wonderful gift given us by our river deity.

However, with the arrival of the gun-wielding police force in our local government, our villagers ceased the practice of human sacrifices to Black Queen, substituting virgins with cows, sheep and chickens, although it was whispered that on some secret occasions, a lost stranger, some female albino, a dwarf female, or an accursed witch from the neighbouring villages, were sacrificed in the deep of night to appease Black Queen. This was to mitigate the terrible effects of her anger over the cessation of human sacrifices, as she had taken to sporadically drowning young women from our village who were foolish enough to venture far from the beach for their ablutions.

Grandfather told us that during the rainy season, Black Queen raged and wept for her lost love, her spuming waves crashing against the beach and flooding the red mud-huts dotting the shoreline. The villagers have long learnt to evacuate their huts in those dire months to give her the privacy to mourn. Fishing was generally abandoned for farming and hunting during those few months of supernatural grief, thereby enabling our people to feed off both the land and the river. Listening to Grandfather's tales, my heart would quiver with a masochistic combination of thrill and terror. I wanted to hear more about our fearsome and powerful river deity, yet the more I heard, the more I quaked. I was ashamed of my cowardice and irrational fear, coupled with the relentless teasing and bullying by my siblings and village children. But my terror of Black Queen was greater than my shame, and it stayed with me through those unforgettable days of my childhood, till I sprouted into the young marriage-age woman that I am today.

Grandfather is now dead, and his wonderful stories have died with him, together with the wisdom that had guided our village through the long years of lively serenity. I doubt if anyone remembers his warnings to treat Black Queen with respect, certainly not the greedy villagers who now follow the lead of the fat one they call Eze, the stupid village boy who somehow managed to mould himself into a man of importance in the big city of Lagos, another riverine place like our village, but from what I've heard, much larger and more important than our tiny, remote village. I knew Eze when he was a bare-feet, bare-chested runt, with snot dripping down his dirty face and mosquito bites crusting his skin with sores. But now, he's worshipped by the villagers like a deity, just because he freed them from their servitude to Black Queen and brought them easy wealth and the freedom to drown themselves in the fiery drinks supplied by Eze's friends, the Chinese bosses.

It all started on the day Eze drove into the village with a group of men, men with black skin like us, but dressed in the white people's black suits, white shirts, and knotted ties. They were accompanied by two camouflage-coloured jeeps crammed with men in military uniforms and evil-looking long guns slung low across their shoulders. All the strangers wore dark sunglasses and it was impossible to read the truth in their eyes as they spoke to our elders. Eze, the snot-nosed kid of our childhood days, was their spokesperson.

I remember that fateful day as if it were carved into my skin with lightning strikes. It was on a Friday afternoon and the midday sun rode high in the sky, while the air was somnambulant with the aroma of cooking foods, Hammattan dust, and that peculiar musky smell of Black Queen, which could only be experienced, but could never be truly described. The happy thrills of the village children fought for dominance over the bleating of the goats and the lazy, gossipy chirps of the womenfolk, while occasionally, the mechanical sound of a passing bus at the sole village asphalt road, reminded us that we were part of the twenty-first century. I recall that I had just finished hanging the laundry on the high cassava stalks that formed the ringed fencing of our hamlet, when I heard the incredible sounds of several motor-vehicles rumbling down the dust-path that led to our compound. In the days when Grandfather lived and prophesied, that path had been constructed by the one-score age group, to accommodate the myriad of visitors that trooped to our compound to seek his wisdom. But since he slept with the ancestors, the path had ceased to see much traffic, save for the villagers, some stray *Ekuke* mongrel dogs, and the occasional bicycles and three-wheeled barrows.

So, the sight of the convoy of motor-vehicles driving into the dust-path on that bright Friday afternoon quickly sent the entire village population outside our hamlet. They congregated in their hordes, children, women and adults, curiosity layering their sweaty faces. I joined my father, his four wives and my twenty-three siblings, both womb-siblings and half-siblings, as we all joined the rest of the villagers surrounding the unexpected and unannounced strangers in our midst.

Eze spoke at length, cracking jokes and laughing loudly at his own jokes. When he had finally tired of hearing his own voice and sweating under his heavy *Agbada* flowing gown, he invited the elders to inspect the metal boxes the strangers had brought along with them. The men with the long guns quickly surrounded the boxes, their guns cocked, and pointing threateningly up at the sky. But one of the strangers, most likely their leader, and the fattest and loudest of the visitors, dismissed the uniformed men with an imperious wave of his ringed hands. He was dressed in a black three-piece suit and darker sunglasses, and sweated profusely under the scorching heat, his white handkerchief glued to his broad face. The two massive wristwatches adorning each fleshy wrist, winked brightly in the midday blaze as he urged our elders to draw closer to the open boxes.

I heard the elders gasped audibly when they saw what was contained inside the metal boxes. Soon everybody surged forward to get a view of the mysterious boxes. I also looked, and what I saw caused my eyes to goggle. There were six great metal boxes filled with countless bundles of *Naira* notes, in fact, more money than our entire village had ever possessed in our lifetime. As people gasped in awe, the obese leader began to speak in a voice that was as stentorian as his superior face. He explained to the villagers that the money was the first instalment for the commercial deforestation and sand-mining agreement our government had signed with the Chinese foreign investors.

People looked at him with perplexed frowns, shoulders shrugging indifferently, as his words made no sense to any of us. Moreover, he spoke in formal English grammar, instead of the pigeon-English which most of the villagers understood. Seeing our baffled expressions, Eze quickly took over from the stranger. Speaking in our local dialect, Eze explained that the deal, which involved the large-scale felling of the trees in our lush forest, as well as the industrial collection of the fine, white sand along our beaches, would be beneficial to our community in the immediate and long term. He said the deal would ensure we would no longer need to rely solely on fishing for our livelihood, and could start replacing our red-mud huts with cement houses, complete with shiny corrugated sheets for our roofs, instead of the old thatched eyesores in the village. Eze even threw in the possibility of electricity, stating that the Chinese miners would be building their own secluded village near our village, as well as a larger, enclosed quarters for their local workers. Our young men, of course, would be given priority in the recruitment drive, thereby, bringing further wealth into our village. The money boxes, lease money for our lands, forest and beaches, would continue to arrive every month as long as the village community did not cause any unrest or disrupt the project.

Eze's words were like nectar to the entire village and in no time, large jars of palm-wine were brought out to celebrate the deal. My father and our entire clan were amongst the people celebrating the lucrative deal with Eze's companions, with a big ram butchered and roasted under the open flames in our hamlet to mark the great event. I also joined the dancing women in the merriment, lured by the prospect of electricity and the brightness I had seen a few times when I visited the large city east of our village, with its big houses, wide roads, colourful shops, and electric-bright nights. I still nursed the old contempt I always had for Eze from our childhood days when he used to spy at me washing my body behind my mother's hut. But, if he was going to bring us the miracle of electricity, then I was ready to forget his pervy lechery and let bygones be bygones.

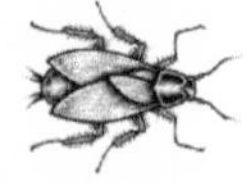

A year after the elders accepted Eze's money boxes, another group of visitors arrived unexpectedly in our village, this time in a delegation that comprised of both men and women, including a young white man with hair the colour of the Day-Queen, *Awu.* Just like Eze's delegation, the new group of strangers arrived in motor-vehicles, albeit without the armed, uniformed men. Once again, they parked their two vehicles outside our hamlet and within minutes, a crowd of villagers surrounded them, mainly women, children and the elders, since most of the adults were absent, busy working at the Chinese mining sites.

The new visitors were led by a young man who introduced himself as Chudi. I did not think his age surpassed my twenty years by more than eight years, yet, when he spoke, he spoke with the authority of an elder. He spoke the white man's language from the nose, just like the yellow-haired white man in their group, yet, he also spoke pigeon English like a native. Chudi was tall and lean, his close-cropped hair a deep black colour, just like his eyes, which fixed me with intensity as he addressed our community underneath the roasting heat of the Day-Queen's rays.

Chudi and his group begged us to reject the deal Eze had brought to our village. They said the deforestation and sand-mining were dangerous to our village and the earth's climate and would bring floods and devastation to us. They said the normal functioning of the ecosystem was being ruthlessly destroyed by the unethical activities of the Chinese miners, in cahoots with our corrupt government. Chudi and his companions used miniature toy trees and several props, including plastic animals, to explain the dangers posed to our environment by the large-scale felling of trees and sand-mining, which was going on even as they spoke. The deafening sounds of heavy lorries and sawing machinery in the background failed to drown out their desperate pleas.

I remember that Chudi spoke with passion and urgency, his deep voice coaxing as he urged us to fight for our heritage and preserve our children's future. His eyes seemed to return to my face several times as he spoke, as if he felt that mine was the one face in the crowd of uneducated villagers that was connecting with his words. To my shame, I confess that it wasn't so much his words I connected with, but rather, his voice; the deep, resonate tone that sent delicious shivers coursing through my body, making me wish I could hear the special music of his voice for the rest of my life. I kept staring at him like a python-hypnotised fool, smiling when he smiled, frowning when he frowned, and nodding when he nodded.

A handful of the village youths who were off work for the day, shouted Chudi down, while the women sang mocking songs, shaking their stupendous bottoms rudely at him. The children, encouraged by the adults, snatched their props and threw fistfuls of sand at them. Everyone could see they had no gun-toting soldiers to protect them, so there was no need to fear them, not even with the red-skinned white man in their entourage, who looked about to faint in the boiling midday heat. Nobody wanted to hear Chudi's words. The villagers called him a snake, with a forked tongue that spoke falsehood — *Black Queen is as she has always been; our village has changed for the better as any fool can see. Why, even the route to the river is now clear, easy and safe for the villagers to use, all thanks to the felling of the trees by the Chinese bosses. Nobody fears the aggressive Chimpanzees and deadly Cobras, which have mostly vanished from the forest with the deforestation project. Clearly, Chudi and his group belong to a different, envious community, who resents our good fortune and unexpected wealth. Our children's futures are very secure, thank you very much, and good riddance to your crazy garbage.* The villagers screeched their angry thoughts in loud voices.

They were right. Our village was indeed thriving, with new cement houses springing up every week in the lush landscape. Even my father had demolished several of the huts in our hamlet, to build an impressive cement-block bungalow for himself and his four wives. The rest of the children still continued to occupy the old huts. We now had a couple of drinking bars in the village, where the menfolk went to drink and enjoy the sudden wealth that flowed from the forests and beaches into our village coffers. Papa Li Wei's new grocery shop now offered us amazing foodstuff like nothing we had ever seen save on the big outdoor cinema the Chinese bosses screened for us once every month. Canned drinks, packet noodles, soft white loaves of the sweetest bread, even cakes and biscuits, were now everyday treats for us. Yes; Eze had told us half-truths, but it didn't seem to bother anyone. The Chinese bosses didn't bring our village electricity as he'd promised. Instead, the bright lights blazed only at the two local bars, the chief's house, Papa Li Wei's grocery store, and of course, Eze's house. The rest of us remained in darkness, except on those nights when the Night-Queen, *Ọwa*, hung pregnant and heavy in the skies, and blessed our lands with her bright glow.

I saw the defeated and hopeless look in Chudi's eyes as they turned to depart from our village after their abortive mission. It touched something in my soul. Suddenly, in his words, I heard the wisdom of my late grandfather, and in that minute, my heart feared the vengeance of Black Queen as never before. I didn't need anyone to tell me what I could already see, what I knew like a mother knows her child; that the villagers had ceased to treat Black Queen with respect, the great respect Grandfather had demanded in the days he walked the earth. The elders no longer sacrificed animals to her since the arrival of the Chinese bosses and their metal boxes of *Naira* banknotes. The workmen dumped all their building waste inside her black bowels, while the debris from the murdered trees ruined her once dark beauty, giving her a dull, murky sheen. When I went to collect water for my bath, I found her surface layered with assorted cans, bottles, plastics, bread wrappings, discarded clothing and cardboard papers.

One day, I caught one of my younger half-siblings chucking his empty Cola can into the river as I filled my bucket with water. I cuffed his ears and warned him to be more respectful of Black Queen. The lout ran home and reported me to his mother, who slapped me, resulting in a big fight between her and my mother. Papa was angry with me when he found out what I had done.

'Are you the river's keeper, you foolish girl?' he shouted at me, his eyes red with rage. 'Did Omambalu tell you it's unhappy because of the stuff thrown into it, eh? What do you think rivers are meant for, if not to carry away rubbish? Do you want to go and tell our Chinese bosses not to throw things into the river, and to take their money and go away so our village can starve and suffer as in the past?' Papa hissed loudly. 'Let this be the last time I hear that you've hit any of your siblings because of the river, do you hear me?'

I heard him. Everybody heard our father, and from that day, my half-siblings and the rest of the clans-children took joy in provoking me by throwing every kind of rubbish into Black Queen whenever I was around, calling out teasing insults and laughing at my scowls. One of the idiots even made it a point of duty to piss into the river whenever I arrived with my bucket, waiting for me to hit him as I itched to do, so he could get me into trouble with our father. I couldn't believe how quickly everyone had forgot Grandfather's teachings and my sense of betrayal on his behalf was great.

Still, I couldn't blame them entirely in all fairness; after all, they saw the adults disrespecting Black Queen on a daily basis, and figured she was now fair game for all. Even the shoreline villagers no longer accorded her the privacy to mourn her lost love as they used to do in the past. Their houses were now built with strong cement blocks, instead of the red mud and straw roofing of old, and they could now climb to the decked roofs of their homes to take refuge when Black Queen flooded their houses in her grief.

Black Queen was now a dead queen, her once smooth skin decayed into putrid rottenness by the polluted poisons that consumed her former glory. She chugged along pathetically, slow and clumsy, humiliated and hopeless, just like a once beautiful woman limping on amputated limbs. If Grandfather lived, he would weep for her ruined beauty, the death of her glossy blackness and the shameful proof of her disrespect littering her filthy surface. So, as Chudi and his group spoke to us on that unforgettable afternoon, I recognised the wisdom in their words and prayed with everything in me that the others heard as well. As I watched them drive away in their dusty Land Rover Discovery, I knew with a feeling of embarrassed excitement, that my heart also yearned to hear the secrets of Chudi's heart.

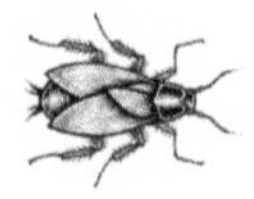

Chudi made several trips to our village after that first futile visit, sometimes with his friends, and at other times, by himself. When he came alone, I knew he came mainly to see me, even as he tried to sway the villagers to his mission. Despite the difference in our social and academic status, our hearts quickly recognised themselves as equals. He didn't mind that my education ended after my third year in the village secondary school, while he had two university degrees to his name. He called me his beautiful treasure and said that my eyes were precious opals, my braided hair, strings of black pearls, and my soul, a priceless diamond, pure, clear, and bright. His words were like music I had never heard, wondrous poetry unlike anything ever spoken by man or the gods. And as our relationship blossomed, I started to believe that I was indeed a beautiful and precious stone, nestled snugly in the hands of a master jeweller. Chudi started to bring me books to read, what he called African classics — Chinua Achebe, Wole Soyinka, Ben Okri, Credo Mutwa, and many other amazing works by geniuses blessed specially by the gods of words and the ancestors of imagination.

When Chudi asked my father for my hand in marriage several months later, I knew that all my yearnings had been granted by my ancestors. The womenfolk cautioned me about marrying "the crazy one" as they affectionately, yet, contemptuously called Chudi. They warned me I was making a great mistake by leaving the safety of our village for the big city, with a book-crazy man whose mind bordered on lunacy. I know my mother would have urged me to reconsider if my spinster status hadn't become a bother to her. My siblings said they always knew I would end up marrying someone as crazy as I was, recalling my irrational fear of Black Queen and my refusal to bathe in her cool waters as everyone else in the village did. Even the fat lout, Eze, decided to save me from my insanity, doing me the favour of offering to make me his second wife. He flashed his two Chinese companions as enticement and proof of his elevated status, his beer-bloated flesh reeking of perfume overdose and stale sweat.

I did little to hide the scorn in my eyes and my voice as I coldly declined his proposal and bowed my way out of his companions' presence. I liked the Chinese bosses even though I hated what they were doing to our village, and especially to Black Queen. They were always polite and smiling, bowing to us and offering our children treats and gifts. In fact, some of them already spoke our tongue with impressive dexterity, and even ate our chilli-heavy dishes without blinking. The village rumour mill even had it that one of the bosses was planning on making the skinny hog, Adaku, his bride, the poor man. We heard that the Chinese liked their women small and skinny like Adaku, but we all feared that this time, they had struck a bad bargain. Everyone said Adaku would soon eat her betrothed out of hut and hamlet in no time and still remain as bony as a stick.

When Adaku was a child, the villagers used to curse her parents for being stingy with her meals, especially since she was their only child. It wasn't until the witchdoctor confirmed that she was an *Ayọmuwa*, "a returned", one of the reincarnated souls with unfinished business, that people began to pity her afflicted parents. The witchdoctor said Adaku was the reincarnate of Ugodi the widow, who had died of starvation and swore that in her next incarnation, she would eat till there was nothing left in the world to eat. Ugodi the widow also swore to remain skinny no matter how much she was fed, so as to torture and shame her family and remind them of how badly she'd been treated in her former life. But worst of all, she had returned with a vengeful curse, ensuring her new parents would have no other living child apart from her, to ensure no other mouths competed for her food. Adaku's mother and stepmother had both experienced so many spontaneous miscarriages since her birth, that her father had finally resigned himself to the sad reality of witnessing the end of his bloodline, since such returned souls were generally known to die at a young age. My mother said she thought Adaku was marrying the Chinese boss because he was the only man rich enough to afford her hunger.

Yes, I liked the Chinese bosses a lot, and under normal circumstances, wouldn't have minded living side by side with them in our village. But Chudi and his friends from the environmental NGO had filled my head with such terrifying knowledge that I now knew the Chinese activities in our forests and beaches were a slow poison, a simmering plague waiting to devastate not just our village, but the broader universe in the long run. I wondered if I was the only one to notice Black Queen raged more frequently than before, grieving for her lost love both during the rainy season, the dry season, and even the dusty Harmattan season. She had never behaved with such randomness and fury in Grandfather's days, yet, it was as if our people's memories had died on the day Eze brought his metal boxes of blood money into our village square.

Grandfather visited me for the first time in the week I was about to have my traditional marriage to Chudi. It happened strangely on a clear bright morning when our hamlet teamed with clanswomen gossiping about my upcoming marriage, while the children played as was their habit in the sandy and dusty terrain, chasing lizards and grasshoppers while fighting, crying, singing, laughing, or shouting for the sheer stupidity of it. I was feeling inexplicably sad, dreading the prospect of leaving the familiarity of my people and my village for the big city of Onitsha where Chudi lived. Of course, I loved my fiancé and was looking forward to being with him for the rest of my life, but still, a part of me feared the unknown and the total permanency of my separation from my family.

Needing solitude to work through my emotions and thoughts, I wandered into Grandfather's old hut, located right in the centre of the hamlet, where his grave mound was raised, to watch over his family and keep us from harm. Everybody went to visit Grandfather's Grave-hut whenever they had a burden or question in their hearts, and I was lucky and thankful that the hut was empty of supplicants that morning as I wandered into its gloomy cocoon.

With deep reverence, I bowed low before the elevated mud-grave, placed the bottle of Coca-Cola I had bought for him from Papa Li Wei's shop, before sitting on the hard floor by his grave-mound. I folded my legs under me and clasped my hands together, as I lowered my head in respect. Grandfather had slept before the arrival of the bosses and their wonderous foods, and I always made it a point of duty to bring him different treats from the white man's world to sample whenever I visited.

The Grave-hut was peaceful, silent, and blissfully cool as ever. It was the only place in the hamlet and possibly, the entire village, guaranteed to be almost chilly regardless of the scorching sun, and I sometimes went in there just to get away from the heat instead of communing with Grandfather. But, today, my comfort was the last thing on my mind. I just wanted to share my worries with him and seek his advice. I knew that he would visit me later in my dreams to give me the answers I sought, just as he was known to do since he slept. Numerous villagers claimed to have had visitations in their dreams, and I knew they spoke with truth, because I too had experienced the same dream-visits from Grandfather, just like my family and clans-people.

In no time, I was baring my soul to Grandfather, tears trickling down my cheeks as I spoke in hushed tones, fearful of disturbing his sleep, just in case he was yet to rise up in the realm of the ancestors, seeing as it was still somewhat early in the morning. I must have spoken for several minutes before I became suddenly conscious of an unsettling quality in the air. The chilly air became colder, like the iced drinks from Papa Li Wei's freezer. I shivered, wrapping my arms around myself. Just then, the bottle of Coca-Cola I'd placed on Grandfather's grave mound trembled, tottered, and before my incredulous eyes, fell to the floor, shattering the bottle in a million sharp fragments and wasting the precious dark drink on the now-damp soil.

As I scrambled to my feet, Grandfather materialised right before my stunned gaze, right in front of the wooden door, blocking my escape route. For, my first instinct after my initial scream was to run, a desperate flight bred from the terror thuds in my heart and the terrified swelling of my head. I was shaking, my mouth quivering with whispered gasps that could only repeat one word with idiotic repetitiveness...*Ghost! Ghost! Ghost!* That was until I saw something that stunned me and killed my terror. I saw a great river of tears crawling down Grandfather's cheeks like the former gentle flow of Black Queen's waters. In all my life, I had never seen my grandfather cry, not even as he lay dying from the painful venom of the snake-bite that stole his life, a snake believed to be the child of the great python Grandfather had killed in the forest, now come to avenge its murdered parent. But now, my dead grandfather stood before me, crying silently, the tears flowing in an endless river with countless tributaries.

'Grandfather...Big Papa...why do you cry?' I managed to whisper, my eyes wide with confusion, and my heart twisted with soul-crushing pity. Grandfather's ghost, so solid and real, just like a living human, merely shook his head, his movement laborious, and pathetic. Then in a blink, just as its appearance had occurred, he vanished, right before my incredulous eyes. With his vanishing, my terror returned, and I fled the Grave-hut on feet as fast and light as the antelope's, my heart pounding louder than the masquerade drums. In my blind terror, I almost crashed into my little sister, Ifedi, the one affectionately nicknamed *"Onye-ajuju"*, meaning, "The Questioner", she of the countless questions in our childhood days, and even into our adulthood.

Grandfather used to say that there were two kinds of questioners in the world. First were the questioners that asked questions to elevate their minds, seek enlightenment and truth. The other were the questioners that asked questions just for the sheer bloody-mindedness of it, simply to be awkward and troublesome. My sister, Ifedi, sadly fell into the second category. Though Grandfather had answered her uncountable questions about Black Queen in our childhood days, she and her band of hoydens persisted in littering the river with their empty drink-cans, biscuit wrappers and even their soiled period pads, a new-found luxury purchased from Papa Li Wei's shop. Still, despite her recalcitrance, I loved Ifedi the best of all my siblings because she was without malice, just exceedingly playful and mischievous.

Without catching my breath, I soon began to spill my terrifying experience inside Grandfather's Grave-hut, my body pouring with sweat of terror, made worse by the blistering heat. Ifedi listened with wide-eyed awe to my story before reverting to her default modus operandi.

'Are you sure you didn't fall asleep while meditating and dreamt it all?' she asked, peering intently into my eyes as if seeking lunacy or idiocy.

'No, I didn't. I tell you, I saw Grandfather as clearly as I'm seeing you now,'

'And you insist he said nothing, absolutely nothing, eh? So, why do you think he appeared to you then?'

'If I knew, do you think I'd be asking you about it?'

'Do you think we should tell Papa about it?'

'No,' I shuddered. The last person I wanted to hear about it was our father. I knew he would cuff my ears for spreading lies and frightening the children in the hamlet with my tale of hauntings. Everyone would be terrified to visit the Grave-hut if they believed it was now haunted, even as we all loved and revered Grandfather. Dream haunting was the acceptable type of haunting in our community, not the real, visible ghost haunting. 'No, don't tell anyone about this, Ifedi; you swear?'

Ifedi nodded. 'I swear on Grandfather's grave. But, do you think he'll visit you again?'

I shrugged. 'I don't know. He didn't say anything, but there must be something worrying him at the ancestors' realm and causing him not to rest, as well as the tears. I'm thinking I should go back to the Grave-hut and see if he'll appear again and maybe say something this time,'

'Aren't you afraid?' Ifedi's eyes were wide with anticipated fear, as if she were already seeing Grandfather's ghost.

'I am, but I'm not, if you get my meaning,' I looked into a space beyond her curious face, seeing Grandfather's beloved face and the ubiquitous bowl of peanuts all ready for our Tales-by-Moonlight underneath the Mango tree in my happy childhood years. In the gentle midday breeze, I heard his raspy voice weaving magic and bliss into our souls, and suddenly, an overwhelming sense of loss washed over me. *If only Grandfather would come back again…if only I could see him just one more time as a living person and not as a ghost.*

'Do you want me to come with you to the Grave-hut?' Ifedi offered generously, though the terror in her eyes told me it was the very last thing she wanted to do.

'No, it's alright,' I smiled, seeing the relief in her eyes. 'I think he wants to talk to me alone. I'll return again tomorrow morning and see if he'll appear. But remember, not a word to anyone, okay?

'Okay,' Ifedi hugged me tightly before skipping off, no doubt, to re-join her group of rowdy teenage girls. I stood at the same spot for several minutes, lost in a world of memories and yearning, a lost world of innocence and happiness, a paradise that was created by Grandfather and was painfully lost when he slept. In that second, I knew that I would give anything and everything to see my grandfather one more time, even if it meant seeing him as a ghost.

The next morning, just as I expected, Grandfather's ghost appeared once again. And just like the previous day, he shattered the bottle of Coca-Cola I offered him, wasting the drink just as before. I was starting to think that Grandfather didn't like this particular white man's drink, and made a mental note to bring him something different in future. This time, Grandfather cried black tears, tears so dark they resembled the black colour of Black Queen's waters in her former glorious days, before the Chinese bosses and our government and village accomplices, ruined her spectacular beauty.

'Grandfather…please tell me why you cry so sadly?' I pleaded, this time my voice stronger, louder. He opened his mouth to speak, but nothing came out of it, no sound, not even a whisper. And yet, the black tears wouldn't stop drowning his face in a black flood of grief. When he vanished, I again sought the company of my sister and narrated my latest haunting.

'Do you think you should maybe take him something sweet to cheer him up, so he can stop crying and talk?' Ifedi asked, reaching into her pocket and coming up with a bar of chocolate. 'Here, you can have my chocolate, and don't forget to tell Grandfather that I gave it to you, so we can share whatever blessings he gives you; you promise?'

'I promise,' I hugged her, thinking my sister was very wise despite her air-headedness. The next morning, when Grandfather appeared to me for the third and final time, I wished I'd never returned to that Grave-hut that was now starting to be the saddest place on earth for me. This time, the chocolate bar didn't just shake on his grave, it flew right off the mound in a violent hurl, smashing into the mud-wall just as Grandfather materialised, howling terror into my heart. His face dripped blood, a riverful of blood-tears that coated his body with fire. He glowed as he'd never glowed in the past, finally looking like the true ghost that he was. And from his wide mouth issued forth the most bone-chilling howl ever heard by human ears, shrieks that curdled my blood and froze my limbs. I didn't need to ask him any questions as in the past, because this time, he answered my unspoken thoughts.

'Leave…. everybody leave now…danger…Black Queen…leave…leave…lea…'

By the time he vanished, I too was howling, my body drenched in terror-sweat as I stumbled out of the Grave-hut and rushed into Papa's new bungalow, hyperventilating between my tears and snivels. In no time, I was telling Papa and all gathered, including my mother, stepmothers, visiting clanswomen and adults, as well as some curious children who had followed my howls into the bungalow, everything that had occurred inside Grandfather's Grave-hut.

Papa listened to my incoherent babbling, his face growing more thunderous as I spoke, while the other adults all made horror-signs, casting the evil over their shoulders with their clicking fingers and hissing lips. When I was done, I wished I'd never spoken. Despite the fact I was engaged to be married in just a couple of days, Papa thrashed me till the women had to restrain him and remind him my body mustn't be too blemished for my upcoming marriage rite. He screamed and cursed me instead till my ears rung into near-deafness.

'Didn't I warn you about that blasted river, you stupid, crazy girl, eh?' Papa's shouted with rage-reddened eyes. 'Now, you decide to use your Grandfather's sacred name to impose your lunatic fiancé's will on us. It's a good thing you're getting married next tomorrow and leaving our village, hopefully for good. Leave my sight and don't let me see you again till the day your husband takes you and your crazy lies away from my hamlet. Go!'

I left, nursing my bruises and my pain. *What did I expect after all, that anyone would believe me, that anyone would pay heed to Grandfather's dire warning?* Grandfather had said that Black Queen's grudge was deep and her spite, deadly; just like the fury of every scorned woman. Now, with every hour that passed as I prepared for my marriage day, I sensed her grudge growing, her sighs louder, and her reek stronger, almost overpowering. And something deep within my soul dreaded the day her spite would finally spill. Like the doomed people in one of the books Chudi gave me to read, the foolish ones who loved and feasted with careless abandon beneath the boiling rage of their mountain-deity in a doomed city called Pompeii, our villagers sang, drank, and danced their days and nights away alongside the simmering rage of their abandoned and betrayed deity. A cold voice in my head told me that our day of reckoning was not far, that Black Queen would make us pay for our fickleness and gross disrespect.

It happened exactly ten moons later, on the day I gave birth to our first son, Ikemefuna, meaning, "May my strength never be lost", named after my beloved grandfather. I heard the news first from my husband's lips, and then I saw it on the small television set in my hospital room. On the bright screen, I saw the terror that had blighted my childhood and ruined my sleep, Black Queen's terrible, terrible rage, as her long-suppressed spite finally crashed into our village, her surging tidal waves wreaking appalling devastation on the land and its faithless people. The stunned newscaster, a young man around the same age as my husband, said that nobody, not a single soul in our village survived Black Queen's rage, not even the Chinese bosses and their local employees. He called it a tragedy of biblical proportions.

The news cameras beamed the apocalyptic images of our Armageddon from their hovering helicopters, sharing with the world the total annihilation of my history and my roots. Icy shivers broke my skin in goosebumps, hard tears quaking my body, pain and horror killing my soul. My family had been wiped off the face of the earth as if they never existed, my parents, stepmothers, siblings, half-siblings, cousins, aunts, uncles, in-laws and extended clansmen; my sweet sister, Ifedi, with her riverful of unfinished questions, swallowed in a blink, her questions never again to be heard or answered. And poor Adaku, whose great appetite will forever remain unsatisfied into her next reincarnation; all gone, all dead. And my village, the place my ancestors and I had lived, laughed and cried, sang and danced for countless generations, had ceased to exist. In a blink of an eyelid, my past and the very source of my existence, Grandfather's Grave-hut, Papa's proud new cement bungalow, our bustling hamlet and neighbouring compounds, were all expunged from the annals of mankind, soon to be reduced to the realms of lore and folktales — *once upon a time, there lived a little village called Ukari, swallowed up by a long river called Black Queen…oh sweet Jesus, have pity!* There was now nobody to tell our story, nobody to remember us, our songs, our lore, our festivals and our culture. There was no one to dream for us and hope for our future. In a blink, it was over, wiped away as a teacher wipes the alphabets on the black board of life. I was the last of our community, the sole proof that our ancestors once existed.

And as I stared at the screen with shell-shocked horror, hot tears streaming down my cheeks, my stunned eyes staring disbelievingly at the still surging waves of our raging river deity cascading waves of vengeance on my vanquished village, a sad insignificance shrouded me in sudden, weary hopelessness. A great mind, a male genius, had once written that mankind was nothing but mites to the gods. The deities were immortal, he wrote, eternally trifling with us foolish humans for their merriment and spite. Black Queen had vented her deadly spleen on our feckless villagers, ignoring centuries of faithful service and loyalty by my people, forgetting the reverence of so many ancestors long gone, the same ancestors whose bloods flowed in the veins of those she had so coldly annihilated. And all for her foolish pride and our monumental stupidity, greed, and ignorance.

Chudi hugged me close, his arm wrapping my shoulders with love. The haunted look on his face fought with the anger raging in his eyes. Over and over, he cursed softly under his breath as he watched the horror unfolding on the television screen. I knew what he was thinking, what was causing his despair. *If only the villagers had heeded his warning, none of this would have happened.* Perhaps, he also thought that it was a good thing he'd married me and taken me away from the village before the disaster struck. Either way, nothing mattered anymore.

The tears continued to flow down my cheeks unchecked as I clutched my new son close to my chest, fearing Black Queen might yet snatch him away as well, should I relax my grip or my guard. I never trusted that deity and now, I have less reason to trust her. I guess the deities reflect the humans they spawned, selfish and fickle, spiteful and vengeful, but yet so beautiful, and so, so terribly flawed.

SNOW ANGELS

Sarah Pinborough

It was February when the snow fell - the same day the nurses moved Will from his bed at the far end of the dormitory and into the smaller, private sanatorium on a different floor of The House. I was eleven years old. I hadn't seen the sanatorium and I didn't want to. No one who was taken from the bedrooms ever came back, and even as children we knew why. Death lived that way. Dying was, after all, the business of The House; it was what we'd gone there to do. None of us left watched as they took Will away. It was better to imagine that he'd never been there in the first place; just a vague shadow or shape, or a ghost of a boy who'd once lived.

The world outside the window had been smothered in grey for days, and as the temperature dropped frost cracked across the glass and breathed its white onto the lawns where the nurses would let us go out and sit or play if we were feeling well enough and the weather was mild. Finally, as Will was ushered away to die somewhere "other" stillness trickled through The House and thick white flakes drifted in clouds from the sky. Poor yellow Will was forgotten in the glory of that sight.

According to Sam, who'd been considered something of a math and science prodigy before cancer had gripped him and squeezed his difference into a less acceptable shape, it hadn't snowed in England for more than thirty years. Sam was fourteen and had been a broad and handsome boy with an easy grin when he first arrived. Now his glasses slid too often down his thin face, as if the tumor in his head was somehow hollowing out his cheeks as it ate up his clever brain.

"At least I think it hasn't," he said. Small frown lines furrowed across his forehead under his sandy hair. By the time the snow came I'd been at The House for more than a year and I'd stopped talking to Sam so much. His smile was too often lop-sided and his sentences drifted away unfinished or suddenly ended with a burst of expletives. It didn't really matter whether he was right or wrong — although an idly curious check years later proved him right — what mattered was that none of us had seen such a thing beyond old photographs and films when we'd had our brief flirtations with normality, and been healthy and at school and had families that weren't ashamed of us. In our short, dark and over-shadowed lives, the arriving snow was something of a gift. A miracle that changed the world into something new — something in which perhaps we belonged as much as everybody else.

There were twelve children in The House that day, and in both the girls' dorm and the boys' thin fingers clutched at the windowsills and wide eyes stared outside. Our breaths coated the glass with rotten steam as we watched, afraid that if we looked away for even a precious second the sky would suck the white treasure back.

We needn't have worried. Over the next few days the cold snap showed no sign of relenting. More freezing snow was driven our way from the Arctic, carried on angry blasts of icy winds that howled across the stretches of water that divided the warm from the cold. The world had changed outside the window. Everything was white.

Even the nurses showed vague signs of humanity beneath their clinically efficient exteriors. They smiled without stopping themselves mid-expression and their eyes twinkled and cheeks flushed with the glow and excitement of the chill. Perhaps it gave them a small lift in the deathly monotony of the duty they had been given. The nurses shared The House with us, but we were two separate tribes and I'm not sure either really "saw" the other; the dying children and the healthy adults. Only when the snow came was there any sense that the blood that flowed through their veins was barely different to our own.

On the morning the nurses came to clear Will's possessions away I found Amelie in the playroom. She was kneeling on an old couch and peering out across its back through the chipped sash window. She looked thinner. Her large red sweater swallowed her tiny frame and my heart ached. My world had changed when Amelie arrived with her long, blonde hair and sharp blue eyes. Her laughter was infectious and alive, and even as she rapidly got sicker, that laugh never lost its vibrancy. Dying with Amelie made dying easier, even with the knowledge of the tears, the sleeping, the pain and the fear that came before the final move to the sanatorium. I loved Amelie Parker with the whole of my damaged being, and in all the years that have passed since I don't think that love has ever really let me go.

"Isn't it beautiful?" Her cheekbones cut lines through her skin as she smiled. "We should go outside."

"To the garden?" I looked out at the sea of white and grey. It was cold and my back ached where my kidney was eating itself, but my feet itched to find out what the snow felt like beneath them.

"No," she shook her head. "Past the garden. Lets go out and walk along the river and around the park." Her eyes sparkled. "What do you think?"

"Yeah." I grinned. "Let's do it. Just us."

"Of course just us." She tossed her hair over one shoulder in a gesture that had first made my stomach flip two months earlier on the day she'd climbed out of the back of the ambulance. Now my stomach just tightened. The spun gold had slipped away over the intervening weeks and although she washed and brushed it every day she felt well enough, Amelie's glory was now dull, lank and lifeless. Sometimes she would hold the ends and stare at it sadly, but mostly she smiled defiantly at the world, and I'm sure that in her mind her hair was always the color of the sun.

"Let's do it." She climbed down from the couch and took my hand. "While we still can."

Her palm was dry, as if the skin was flaking away, and although I know that in that moment Amelie was simply referring to the fleeting life the snow and ice was likely to have rather than our own predicaments, those words still haunt me.

We were both sick, - Amelie had spent the three days of the snowfall in bed with a hacking cough - but neither of us was in any hurry to die, and so we layered ourselves up in all the warm clothes we could muster. With our coats done up tight, we ventured outside. We weren't the first to explore the snow, but I was the healthiest amongst the children and Amelie the most determined and we were the first to go beyond the confines of the small garden and the safety of The House's proximity.

We shuffled past the snowman Sam had attempted the day before. It was barely more than a ball of compact white, scarred with dirty streaks. The older boy had drifted back inside within ten minutes of being out, his mind confused and stabbing pains attacking his eyes. It wouldn't be too long before Sam was headed to the sanatorium. He was becoming too erratic and unpredictable. He was nearly just another empty bed to haunt my dreams. Our numbers were dwindling, and by rights I should have had my turn in the sanatorium months before, but my body just kept on living despite the fire in my back.

Amelie coughed once, a long and loud sound that racked her chest, and then as her fragile lungs adjusted to the icy air we stepped through the small gate that separated our world from the one beyond. Somewhere behind us a nurse or two probably stared disapprovingly out of the windows, but none would come and fetch us back in. We were here to die. No one treated us; they just medicated our pain and waited. It didn't matter much to that other tribe at The House whether we did our best to stay alive or otherwise.

We stood at the start of the path that wound a circuit along the river and around the field and simply stared. Before us was an ocean of white that met with grey on the horizon, the colors so similar that it was hard to see where the land ended and the sky began. I squinted against the harsh gleam that glared from the powdery surface and beside me Amelie lifted one hand to her forehead as if we truly were adventurers peering out over alien lands.

"Come on." Her giggle cut into the empty silence, and we trudged carefully forward. The snow had compacted into ice and I could see echoes of the footprints that had beaten it down trapped like fossils in the glistening surface. The ice glittered and as I looked the more colors I could see hiding in its shards; purples and blues and pinks and hints at shades in-between. I sniffed, and so did Amelie. It was the only sound other than our crunching feet and the the occasional twisting whistle of the wind. My ears stung with the cold, but my heart was lifted by the quiet.

With the ice in places too slick to keep our unsteady feet gripped, we slowly made our way to the edge of the field, arms held out slightly for balance, and then stepped onto the snow. Amelie gasped. Her face shone, and for a second it was almost as if she had a whole lifetime ahead of her.

"It's so soft!"

My feet sunk through the cold white that crumpled beneath my weight, and I pulled my gloves off to slide my fingers into the wet surface. Beside me, Amelie crouched down so that the hem of her coat was dipping into the snow and scooped a small handful into her mouth. She grinned and poked her tongue out, and I watched the white dissolve into the hot pink before doing the same back.

We didn't speak but giggled and gasped and held the almost-whole-almost-nothing substance in our fingers until our hands were red and raw. We didn't play with it, or roll it into balls and throw it at each other. Those things didn't come to mind as perhaps they would have with other children. Maybe because it had been a long time since we'd run and laughed and played, and to do that again might break us from the inside out with the memories of all that was lost, or perhaps it was just because our bodies were too tired from the simple fight to stay alive. Whichever, we simply touched the snow and tasted it and smelled it. Our wide eyes drunk in the strange grey view as if it were something to be savored and stored safely away for reliving in the terrible days ahead.

In the distance a blot of darkness came through the gate from the far field and started on the slow walk around the path, a dog bounding ahead. Amelie stood up and we both smiled, willing the animal with its soft fur and wet tongue to come our way. The figure behind paused, and even from the hundreds of yards between us, I was sure I could see the person stiffen. A whistle sliced through the air, and the sheepdog immediately turned and headed back to the owner. Together they disappeared back through the gate, as if even from this distance our diseases would somehow be catching. We watched them go and Amelie's smile fell.

"Let's go and look at the river," she said, eventually.

The grey shifted to a deeper hue and shrunk closer to frozen earth, as if the sky above had felt the darkening of our moods. We turned and headed to the river bank where trees rose up like the bones of ancient hands, gnarled and greedy and keen to grasp at anything that would stop the cold ground dragging them down to be forgotten forever. Barely any hint of brown gasped from the empty branches lost beneath the snow and frost. The temperature dropped and my hot breath turned from steam to almost crystal as we crossed the path to stand overlooking the uneven river and the empty tundra that days before had simply been English fields. My lungs felt raw in the sudden cold.

A few feet from the steep bank,Amelie paused and we stood in silence as the snow began to fall again. Heavy flakes appeared directly above us. They winked into existence at the edge of the grey, and within seconds the sky was falling towards us like drifting ash. I tilted my head up and felt each one land like the kisses of the dead brushing against my skin. More and more tumbled down until the wind caught the excitement and sent the storm whirling in a frenzy across the open spaces. I gasped, the snow and cold air fighting to fill my mouth and lungs first.

Amelie simply smiled, and as the increasing flakes settled quickly on her head and coat, I thought she would be lost in the blizzard that gathered force around us. The wind bit at my exposed ears and cheeks and I stepped up beside Amelie in the small protection of a naked tree. Amelie stared at the river, ignoring the flakes that sat like glitter on her long eyelashes and clung to her skin. I followed her gaze, squinting against the snow that blew in every direction as if we were the center of a maelstrom.

The river hadn't frozen entirely but was covered in a slick sheen as ice fought to conquer the surface. The dark fluid beneath maintained supremacy over the white that had conquered the rest of the surrounding world, the water like a gash across the pale skin of the land. Amelie looked up, her eyes widening. She dropped her head, a flush blazing from her cheeks, and stared at the river again.

"Can you see it? Can you see them?" she laughed, but both the sound and the words were muffled by the heavy air as if the blizzard were trying to create a void in the small space between her and I. I frowned and stared. My eyes stung and for a fleeting second I thought I may have seen a flash of purples and blues dancing brightly on the dark, freezing surface; a swirl of colors that were almost shapes in their own right, casting black shadows behind them. I blinked and looked up, forcing my eyes to stay open. All I could see was the tumbling alien snow.

Amelie laughed again, and jumped slightly with excitement. "But they're beautiful! Aren't they beautiful?" She turned and grabbed my frozen hand. The heat in it burned.

"I can't see. What are you looking at?"

Her eyes shone, the blue so sharp it was as if all the ice in the field had been condensed into those tiny irises. Her cheeks were too flushed for our surroundings, too red against the absence of color.

She gasped again and her eyes darted this way and that, following something beyond my sight and hidden by the falling snow. I wondered which of us the storm was mocking and decided maybe both. I shivered, suddenly aware of the deep chill that had sunk into my bones as fingers of pain squeezed at my spine.

"Let's go inside." Over my shoulder, even the forbidding structure of The House was almost lost in the grip of the blizzard. The snow consumed everything it touched in the relentless onslaught, and I knew with a shiver that if we stayed out here much longer, it would devour us too and we would be lost forever. My feet were numb in my shoes and I stepped back slightly, pulling Amelie with me.

"It's too cold. I'm tired."

Her feet stayed planted as she stared, but her thin frame swayed.

"Just two more minutes," she whispered, a beatific smile on her beautiful face. "Please."

As it was, a quarter of an hour passed before the energy slumped from her shoulders and she turned to me with sad eyes and let me lead her back across the field and through the gate to the safety of our world, where children politely waited to die. We didn't speak but went to our separate dormitories, dazed and blinded by the blizzard that had held us in a white embrace for most of the afternoon. Back in the brightness and warmth of the building my teeth rattled, shaking barely a flicker of warmth into my thin face and it took an hour soaking in a bath before the jaws of the freezing cold released their grip on me. The nurses glared balefully as I shuffled past in my dressing gown but said nothing. I didn't expect them too.

It was still snowing when night finally swallowed what little muted light the day had held. As The House slipped into slumber and took me with it, I dreamed that Death came in a white coat and smothered me while his black eyes glittered purple and blue reflections of something beautiful and terrible that was out of sight. I screamed in my nightmare, but his unflinching fingers burned and then froze my skin as he pulled me upwards out of the mess of sheets and blankets. Behind him, two nurses waited patiently by the door, one pointing towards the corridor where the elevators were and the other holding a small cardboard box. I struggled, desperate to stay in my bed, not to be dragged to the sanatorium, and around me Death's hands stretched and twisted, each digit hardening into wood until the sharp branches of the skeletal tree by the river had grown from his pale wrists and entangled me.

I woke up scratching madly at my own hot, wet skin.

The shivers and cold sweats grew worse, and by the morning my fever was raging and my throat burned as if every snowflake I had allowed to land on my tongue was a shard of glass embedded there. The nurses brought pills and hot drinks, and muttered quietly amongst themselves about the *stupid boy and girl and what had they been thinking, especially her being so close to the*…and then they'd glance around and down at me, and from behind my haze I could see them wondering if I'd heard and the shutters would close over the parts of their eyes that mattered.

I slept most of the day, and then forced some soup through the barbed wire of my insides and took more aspirin that would ease the flu that the nurses were allowed to treat, but give my ailing kidneys more to worry about.

No one spoke to me, but in my more lucid moments, while the heat and infection raged through my body, I could see curious glances darted my way. I knew then how Will and all the others before him had felt as the slow isolation began. I knew what the quiet watchers were thinking. They thought the sanatorium would be welcoming me next and there was a relief in each of them - even poor confused Sam - that it wasn't their turn quite yet.

They stayed well back and flinched each time I coughed germs out at them. I knew these things without looking because I would have done the same. When I closed my eyes all I could see was falling snow against the crimson dark backdrop. Finally I slept.

The House was still when Amelie woke me. Her face shone in the half-light like the glaze that had been forming on the river, and her long hair hung in lank matted strands. There was barely a hint of blonde left. Her hand was hot on mine.

"I want to go out," she whispered. "I want you to see. *I* want to see."

She licked her lips and her mouth trembled.

"It's the middle of the night."

"It's nearly dawn. I can't sleep. Please."

"Amelie…" I let my sentence drift off. I didn't want to get up. I didn't want to go out. The snow still held a mystery in it, but the cruel cold frightened me. Across the room, Sam stirred in his sleep and barked out a word that meant nothing but was spat fresh into the world with a vehemence I'd never heard from the boy with the easy grin. At night, the cancers ruled our sleep. I looked at Amelie's burning face and knew that I loved her more than I feared the cold grip of the blizzard.

"Okay."

Her fragile smile was almost worth it. I pushed back the covers and shivered, but my skin was cooling. Unlike Amelie's, my fever had begun to break somewhere between dusk and now, and although my limbs ached and my back was on fire, I knew the worst of that particular illness was over.

We moved like silent ghosts through the dark house, and wrapped ourselves up in coats and scarves housed in the rarely used cloakroom and turned the old-fashioned key in the back door. The lock clicked loudly. For a second the falling snow paused as if to welcome us. The cold air crept into the house carrying a handful of flakes on its wings, and as they came in to melt and die on the stone floor, we pulled the door closed and stepped out into the drift.

This time Amelie didn't hesitate or waste time giggling and laughing and clutching at handfuls of the elusive white that now sat several inches high over the frozen ground. Instead, she took my hand and led me out through the garden and across the field to the riverbank. By the time we reached it, The House was a lifetime away and looked like a dark dead thing pasted against the night. My hair was soaked from the relentless snow, and my shins were damp from where the icy wetness had crawled up my jeans above my shoes. My skin tingled with the cold and I flinched with every breath drawn in against my ragged throat.

Equally wet and surely as cold as I, Amelie simply smiled as we reached the slope and stood in the shelter of the frost-gripped tree that had plagued my dreams. The sky was slowly creeping from black to midnight blue, and the snow fell like stars or diamonds forever tumbling against it. I looked at the river. It had lost the battle with the ice since our last visit, and streaks and lines of crystals cut like fractures across the hard sheet of the surface.

"They'll come," Amelie whispered. "I know it."

We stood like that as the sky shifted above us, the blue fading to grey as dawn broke. My body numbed and my skin burned with outrage as the cold tortured it with bitter kisses, but I stayed staring at the river and wondering what I was doing here, knowing in my heart it was simply for the love of the dying, feverish girl beside me.

When the sky and the horizon blended into the same shade, becoming one endless vision of deathly grey, Amelie suddenly laughed and clapped her hands to her mouth.

"They're here!" she said, and jumped up and down on the spot where she stood while my own legs screamed if I even tried to bend them.

"They're here," she repeated, and her whisper escaped in a mist. As she looked upwards, I stared at the river. At the center of the frozen water streams of purples and blues twisted on the surface. Flashes of sparkling lights came from the air above and the water below simultaneously, as if the colors were reflecting from within the ice rather than on the crackled surface. The snow paused, hesitant, as the unnaturally bright colors grew denser. They spiraled and flashed too vividly against the grey that had swallowed the world to be part of it, and yet each of the mad hues had been distilled from the ghosts of colors that lived at the edge of each flake of snow, just out of sight, but held fast in the molecules.

My breath stopped. I was aware of Amelie's joy beside me, but my own moment had locked me in so completely she might have been miles away. I slowly looked up, dragging my eyes from the dazzling array on the river to the sharp white of the endless sky. I gasped. Hazes of colors stretched across the sky right above our heads, their purity made clearer against the backdrop of emptiness and I wondered if somehow these were the northern lights dragged to us upon the wind. The numbness in my feet crept away. With an imperceptible sigh the blizzard came again, and as the snow launched itself around us, whipping around our slim frames, the colors pulled in on themselves. Faces formed in the flying streams, sharp eyes and beautiful smiles that danced and flew in the wind.

"Aren't they beautiful?" Amelie's dull hair rose up around her head as the cold air rushed through it, fingers made from icy flakes curiously teasing each strand. Her words barely reached me, the snow thick between us as the creatures in the sky whirled around, examining us. The snow felt like butterfly wings on my skin despite the urgent power of the breeze. For a moment, I thought she was right. They were beautiful. They were angels — snow angels, come to share something wonderful with us. I stared in awe until the air shifted and the moment changed. The angels separated, darting this way and that across the sky before coming back.

Amelie continued to laugh with delight beside me, but my heart froze. The lights in the angels eyes hardened. The glittering smiles stretched and yawned wide, and I was sure sharp teeth of black ice flashed from within. And then they rushed at me.

The blizzard was suddenly hard against my skin and snow stung my eyes. I flinched. The wings that beat at me were sticks, not feathers, and as I raised one arm to protect my face the wind forced it down. I squeezed my eyes almost shut, but even through the haze of attacking white I could see the cruel laughter in their eyes and feel their cold breath burning my skin; rotten water dragged from the pit of a stagnant frozen well. Tears streamed from the corners of my battered eyes and the monstrous creatures licked them away.

My feet tried to pull me backwards, but I was stuck on the riverbed, held in place by the snow and the wind and the whirling beings that tore at my skin with greedy fingers. They spoke in whispers that I couldn't quite make out, the words like freezing water in my ears. They sucked the air from my lungs, leaving only an icy void inside me, and through the madness I thought I saw something terrible and dark waiting just behind them — a creature hungrier and meaner and with no mercy, that lived in the blackness hidden just beyond the light.

I don't know how long I stood there. When the wind eventually fell, letting the lifeless snow simply drift to the ground, every inch of my being stung. My fingers and face tingled. My insides were made of ice. Amelie turned and half-collapsed on me, but the smile stayed stretched across her thin, pale face. It was only as we reached half-way across the blanketed field back to The House, my legs barely carrying me, and with Amelie leaning weakly on my arm, that I realized my back no longer hurt. It ached, yes, but it didn't burn. Something had changed.

I think I knew what would happen. It snowed for a further two days, during which time Amelie's fever grew worse. There were unspoken whispers about the sanatorium as she lay listless and sweating in her bed. For my own part, my throat raged and my voice died, but even though the nurses kept me confined to the dormitory and filled me with hot drinks, I could see their immediate concern for me had passed. The boys drifted back over to my side of the room, even poor Sam who would barely see the thaw before they wheeled him upstairs with blood pouring from his nose and his eyes gazing in two different directions.

It was on the second morning that the alarm went up. As with everything in The House, it happened quietly. There were no screams or shouts, simply a shift in the atmosphere. A hurriedness in the nurses' movements. It was seven o'clock in the morning. Amelie's bed was empty, only her thin pathetic outline left in the damp sheet.

I knew where she was. I let them search The House before squeezing the painful words "the river" out from my swollen throat. The snow had stopped, and when I stepped outside the sun shone bright against an azure blue sky, promising a return to normality. We crunched across the field, my small boots following in the remains of Amelie's last footsteps, their outline barely visible unless you'd known where to look.

She sat frozen on the side of the riverbank. Her hands were wrapped around her knees, and she wore only her nightdress. Her feet were bare. The nurses and I paused a short distance away, and I'm sure I heard one of them let out a tiny gasp. It wasn't that she was dead. We were all used to death, and seeing her sitting there in the thin cotton I knew it couldn't have taken her very long to slip from one state to the other, and for that my breaking heart was glad. Her death we had all been expecting ever since we'd stepped into the cold February air. That didn't make the nurse pause, or my mouth fall open.

It was her hair.

It hung like spun gold down her back, glorious and healthy, the color it must have been before she started dying in earnest and The House claimed her. It was beautiful. Magical. And by all rights, it just couldn't *be.* Her head was tilted backwards, as if she'd been staring at the sky when she died, and a smile danced on her mouth, her lips pink against cheeks that had lost their pallor and become fuller and flushed. She looked radiant, but as I stepped closer, I thought I saw crystals of blue and purple fear at the edges of her eyes, and there was the shadow of something dark behind them as if in the final breath she'd seen something unpleasant and unexpected.

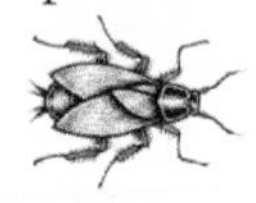

All the children in The House died apart from me. I watched them go in turn and saw how they hated me as my body grew stronger as theirs weakened. After a year, the doctor's ran more tests and found the tumors on my kidneys had shrunk to nothing. They could do nothing but let me out. My childhood, such as it was, continued in foster care. My parents didn't want me back. I had been defective once, and could be again. They weren't prepared to take the risk.

As it turns out, they were right. Six months ago, just after I turned thirty-five, the pain came back. Governments had changed and cancer treatment was back on the menu. Not for me though. Too aggressive, is what the doctors said. In their eyes I saw the ghosts of the nurses and the elevators to the sanatorium.

Most days now I'm too weak to get out of bed. At best, I sit in the chair by the window and gaze out over the fields and countryside. I thought I was ready. I thought I'd made my peace. But last night the first blizzard in twenty-three years came across from the cold lands. By this morning the world had faded to grey.

The snow still falls. I can feel its purpose, and I think that if I close my eyes a little, I'll see the colors hiding in it. It's beating at the door and sounds like wings, sometimes butterfly, and sometimes something heavier and meaner, and they fill me with fear and make me wish for Amelie in equal measure.

I think I'll go outside. Maybe take a seat. And perhaps I'll see a hint of spun gold before the darkness comes for me.

MAW

Priya Sharma

The sea brought the container in on the highest tide that Little Isle had seen in thirty years, beaching it on the rocks at the base of the cliffs.

Magnus and his sons found it first. They'd been following the trail of dead seals and fish along the beach.

The ferry had been cancelled because the sky over the other islands and the mainland was wild, but the driving wind and rain had paused over Little Isle, making it a bright spot in the darkness.

Hildy, Magnus' wife, gave him a pointed look when he suggested a day of roaming to the boys, before saying, "Back for lunch time, okay? You have a homework box for days like this."

Days when they were cut off and they couldn't get to primary school on the next island.

The sea was now in retreat. The air smelt swept clean. Water collected in the ripples on sand and reflected the blue sky overhead.

Donald, Magnus's younger son, saw the dead seal first. Magnus squatted down beside it. Its neck was badly bruised and one of its eyes had gone. A flipper was missing.

"What happened to it, Dad?"

Magnus rolled it over. His cursory post-mortem was inconclusive.

"I don't know."

They followed the curve of the beach, and there lay mackerel, herring and ugly monkfish, dull eyes wide in surprise at their fate. Some were whole, but most were in torn up, the clumsy dissection revealing guts and flesh already starting to rot.

"Shame. What a waste."

They picked their way through more seal carcasses. These had fared less well. Most were missing great chunks. Some looked bitten down to bone, the edges black and high.

"Rank." Peter covered his nose.

"It's nature." Magnus loved his sons too much to coddle them. "We all end up like this."

Magnus meant rotting, not chewed up. Donald screwed up his face.

They found pieces of oars too, beaten and worn. A rowing boat with a hole in its hull. A length of fearsome looking chain. The ocean bed had been dredged and deposited on the shore.

After a quarter of a mile, the soft ascent of beach onto land was replaced by vertical columns of rock. The container was in the cliff's shadow.

Donald was about to run to it but Magnus grabbed the hood of his coat and hauled him back. Peter, who was ten, stayed by his father's side, frowning.

"What is it, Dad?" Peter whispered.

"A shipping container. Take Donald and go straight home. And not up the cliff path either, it'll be slippery. Go back the way we came."

Two figures approached them from the opposite direction. Magnus was relieved to see it was just Jimmy and Iain. His sons walked away, looking back. Jimmy waved at them. Magnus watched them go and then turned his attention back to the container.

"They don't normally drop off ships, do they?" Iain asked.

"No, not usually."

Magnus had authority on Little Isle because of his knowledge of plumbing, plastering, and mechanics and because his grandfather was John Spence. Plus, he'd worked on the mainland port when he was younger, amid acres of decks stacked high with these identical steel boxes. That was the year before he'd married Hildy.

"That's odd." Magnus went from one end of the container to the other, kneeling to inspect it "No twist locks."

Iain looked blank.

"There should be each corner. They lock each container to the one below it, or to the deck."

Jimmy picked up a pebble.

"Don't."

Iain was too late. It hit the container's side with a dull thud rather than the clang Magnus expected. The stone that had survived endless beatings by the sea shattered into jagged shards. Jimmy's gaze darted to Iain and then Magnus's face, awaiting reprimand. Iain shook his head, then turned to Magnus.

"Are they watertight?"

"Should be."

"What if it's full of bodies?" Jimmy said. "Immigrants."

"Don't be daft."

Iain's embarrassment didn't register with Jimmy who put his ear to the container.

“What can you hear?” Magnus asked gently. Jimmy’s was everyone’s to look out for, not just his younger brother’s responsibility.

“I can’t hear what they’re saying.” Jimmy closed his eyes.

“Oh, for God’s sake.”

“What?” Jimmy was on Iain, fast and fierce. “For God’s sake what?”

“Hey, hey, it’s okay.” Magnus soothed him. “Come and help me look for something. Can you do that?”

“Yes.” Jimmy looked deflated, as if the unaccustomed anger had taken it out of him. His focused shifted to somewhere beyond Magnus.

“I’m looking for something called a CSC plate. It’s a metal rectangle. So big.” He held up his hands to demonstrate. “It has writing on it. Normally it’s on the doors.”

They circled the container, climbing up and down the rocks, or leaping from one to another. Nothing. Magnus lowered himself between two boulders to inspect the underside.

“What do you see?” Iain called.

“A load of barnacles. This hasn’t come off a ship recently.”

Barnacles, inside their carapaces, looked like closed eyelids or mouths. *Barnacles don’t have hearts.* His father had told him that.

I must remember to teach the boys, Magnus thought.

He ran his fingers over the jagged colony that was interrupted by limpets, their shells marked with starburst ridges.

Iain reached down to help him climb out.

“Can we keep it? They found one of these on Hesketh Head. It was full of quadbikes. That would be something, wouldn’t it?”

Magnus put his chin on his chest, considering Iain’s suggestion. “The police called them looters.”

“Didn’t catch them though, did they? We don’t have to keep it for ourselves. We could use it for everyone.”

“Maybe you’re right. We’re owed a bit of luck.” He lifted his eyes skyward. “Here comes his lordship. Well, that’s fucked that idea then.”

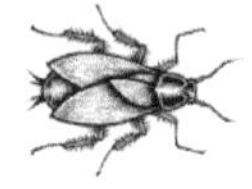

“Simon.” Magnus gave him a curt nod.

“How’s Hildy?”

“Fine.”

“Give her my regards.”

"Will do."

"Did that wash up this morning?" Simon gestured towards the container.

Magnus didn't reply, so neither did Iain.

"There's no CSC plate on it. We looked." Jimmy kicked at a dead fish and then wandered away when Simon gave him a bemused smile.

"Have either of you been able to get outside contact?"

"No, everything's down," Magnus replied. "The storm's still out there."

"We'll let the coastguard know when the radio's back up."

"So that's it. You've decided without a word to anyone."

Magnus willed Simon to say *It's my island* so he could have a go at him but Simon didn't oblige.

"What's there to decide?"

"You have no idea what's in there."

"Whatever it is, it isn't ours."

"Look at it. It's been in the ocean for God knows how long. The insurance will have already been paid out on it."

"It might be someone's personal things."

"Or there might be a load of laptops."

"So you're planning to sell stolen goods?"

"You can't decide for everyone."

There were distant figures on the beach. The islanders that couldn't get to work on the bigger islands were out to see what the storm had washed up.

A fish flopped around in a shallow rockpool at Magnus's feet. It was barely covered by the water. Magnus flipped the mackerel onto the sand and then seized it. He put his thumb in its mouth, snapping the head back at a sharp angle. The sudden motion ripped the gills from its throat and blood pulsed from its arteries onto its silver stripes. Magnus let it drip, holding the fish fast in its death throes.

"Was that necessary? Wouldn't hitting it on the head be kinder?"

"Ignoramus."

Bleeding kept the flesh from rotting, otherwise it clotted in the body where bacteria could breed.

Magnus flung it to Simon who fumbled with it, getting blood and brine on his jacket.

"Take it home. Make some fucking sushi or something."

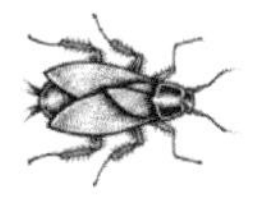

Magnus left the gawping crowd that was gathering on the beach. Simon talked to them from the vantage point of a rock. Cormac had joined him. He was Simon's manager which made him the second most important person on the island. He was also Magnus' cousin. Their shared genes were apparent in their size.

Magnus went back to where coarse grass overtook the sand and up the hill. He crossed the sodden earth and made his way to the church. It was the same path his granddad favoured. Stern John Spence transformed into historian and story teller, just for him.

St Connaught's stood out against the scoured sky. Faith had arrived in a row boat bringing a crucifix and conviction to Little Isle. All that remained of the church was stone. Windowless, roofless, doorless, grass had sprung up within. Spiders' webs sagged with raindrops.

Magnus and Hildy had brought Simon to the ruined church when they were children.

"Posh, aren't you?" Cormac towered over Simon, who was still wearing his school uniform, even though it was the summer holidays. All the children had gathered on the makeshift football pitch at the end of the village. "Are you a frog, like your mum?"

"She's *French*." Simon's accent was cut glass.

Cormac snorted, as he'd seen he adults do when they were talking about her.

"She's a snob, that's what." Simon's mother had only visited the island once. The islanders had mistaken her shyness for snootiness and her eating disorder for Parisian chic. "And so are you, turning up for the summer and then buggering off. You don't belong here."

"Let him alone." Magnus stepped in.

"Or what?"

"You'll get another share of what I gave you last time."

The two boys squared up to one another. Simon was incidental to old enmities. The other children looked on, too scared to take sides. Except for Hildy. Strong, desirable Hildy was the only one who wielded enough power to end it. She got between them, thumping them both.

"Stop, you idiots." Cormac laughed but Magnus still cut a fighter's pose. She pulled at his sleeve. "Let's go."

They went up to the cliffs to show Simon the puffins and the gulls' nests on the precipices. Seals basking on the rocks below. There was a whole fleet of trawlers out on the glistening water. The three of them spent the long holidays roaming. Little Ilse was rough, green fields and granite hills sculpted by glaciers.

"What's that noise?

Hildy was about to answer Simon but Hildy put a finger to his smiling lips to hush her. The roaring got louder as they approached.

Magnus stood close to Simon, enjoying his surprise. There was a whirlpool out on the calm sea. Its pull was mesmeric, the downward spiral of all that water into the depths.

"It's Maw." Magnus felt a swell of pride.

The maelstrom was a conspiracy of complex tidal flows in a narrow straight. Water forced itself up from a stone pinnacle on the seabed, opposed to the surface stream, so create a downward vortex. The swirl was visible below the glassy surface.

"Wow."

"It's clearer when there's a high wind or standing waves. You think it's loud now. Just wait 'til the tides are right. You can hear Maw roaring from miles off."

At St Connaught's they found a nest of mice in the shadow of the stone altar. It had become nature's temple.

"I found a crow skeleton here once. And a snake's skin." Magnus had never seen Hildy so shy. She pulled a sketchbook from her rucksack and passed it to Simon. "Look."

He leafed through the pages. "These are brilliant."

She gave Simon a broad smile.

"I like drawing too, but I'm not as good as you."

"Will you show me yours?"

"Look, here", Magnus pointed to the wall above the altar.

Simon squinted at the weathered markings. "What are they?"

"Fish jumping into a boat." They leapt high, pouring themselves onto the deck in an arc.

"How can you tell?"

"My grandfather said. He died last year. He knew everything. Our family have always lived here."

Simon flushed. His father had purchased the island only two years before.

"He didn't mean anything by that." Hildy nudged Simon.

Magnus hadn't finished yet. "Guess what this is."

Above the fishing boat was a figure falling into a spiral.

"A man going to hell?"

"It's Maw."

Magnus recited his granddad's teachings. "He's been given to Maw as a gift and Maw will give us the sea's bounty in return."

Magnus checked in on Mairi on his way home, just like his dad used to. Andrew Spence called her *the old woman*, even though she wasn't that much older than he was.

He'd would sit with her, sometimes for up to an hour at a time. Magus would peep into the single roomed cottage through the door that was always propped ajar to *let the weather in.* Sometimes Mairi would scream and shout at his dad, other times they'd sit in silence.

"Hello."

"I've been waiting for you." Mairi sat on a stone bench outside. "Come and sit, John."

"It's Magnus, Mairi, not John."

She turned her lined face to him. She was pushing seventy now, he reckoned. She'd been more muddled of late. He wondered whether he should talk to the doctor when the radio was back up.

"Of course you are." Her voice was strong and certain now, which unnerved him. "Have you seen it?"

"What?"

"The bloody great container down on the shore."

Her eyes were as temperamental as the sea, sometimes clear aquamarine, sometimes grey and chilly.

"Yes."

"Maw sent it."

The comment alarmed him less than her mistaking him for his granddad. Mairi was known for it. She'd lived alone from a young age. A bit touched. She'd been visited by a psychiatrist once, after which she learnt to keep her stranger pronouncements to herself.

"That bay over there," she jabbed with her finger, "used to be full of trawlers. Everyone had work. All because of John Spence."

There'd been crops of barley, oats and potatoes that thrived on seaweed fed beds. Lambs, sweet on salt laden grass. There were farmers, shepherds and weavers, but the island only flourished because the fishermen were kings.

John's re-energisation of the industry brought a row of shops, two pubs, a new church and a primary school. The only thing that remained of this golden time was the new church. The school had shut years ago, despite the protests.

"We've turned our backs on Maw. We won't be forgiven easily. To think, we have the blood of marauders and conquerors in us. We sailed to Byzantium. And now we're diminished with each generation by the milksop messiah, taxes and fishing quotas."

History marked the land. Cairns and gold torcs buried in the earth.

"I still send Maw boats."

An old tradition. The islanders once gathered on the shore at harvest festival and sent out wicker and wooden boats, laden with gifts for Maw's Maelstrom. Priests came and went over the centuries, either smiling indulgently or shaking their heads.

The sea is hungry.

The sea has blue hands.

The little boats contained the choicest fish, the finest prawns, a cake, or a piece of fat marbled lamb. A baby or man carved from soap.

"We put boats on the water last year." Magnus repeated, wondering if Mairi had heard.

"Yes," she spat, "and we were the only ones. A can of sardines and a loaf might be good for the five thousand but not Maw."

She seized Magnus' hand.

"You and I need this place. We can't survive anywhere else. Not for long. It's why you came running back with your tail between your legs. Same for your dad. You shouldn't have let them take him away."

Magnus turned his face from her. He'd looked after his dad for as long as he could after his mother died. *Poor Andrew, so young to have dementia. You've done a grand job*, the nurse had said, *but he's getting worse. He needs care from trained nurses now.*

Magnus took a job on the docks over on the mainland so that he could visit his dad's nursing home each day. The trained nurses were hard pressed and didn't have time to dab the crusted cornflakes from his dad's shirt.

His dad hated cornflakes.

Dementia stripped his father of sense, self and dignity. It took the meat from his bones and hollowed him out, as crafty and insidious as cancer.

The sea, the sea needs little boats, the sea, there are men in the water, blue hands, blue hands, blue hands. They're so hungry.

He'd gripped Magnus' wrist so hard that he'd left bruises.

Hungry hands. Why did you do it, Dad?

It's Magnus, Dad, not John.

I saw you. I heard her crying. Why would Mairi give up little Brid?"

Then he pushed Magnus from him, weeping into his sleeve. Magnus was relieved when his dad died and he could go home.

"How did Granddad do it, Mairi? How did he turn this place around? Were those freak years of fishing just luck?"

Her eyes were the silver of needles.

"Fool. Ingrate. All you do is complain. You're weak. Only John had what it took, the bastard. What are you willing to sacrifice for what you want?"

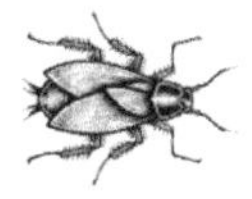

There was nothing to be done but leave the container. The rumble of thunder closed in. Night brought in the tide. The islanders took shelter.

Magnus watched the waves from the window until it was too dark to see out. The cottage was built from granite blocks, hunkered down against the hill to withstand the onslaught of wind and rain.

Peter and Donald lay on their bellies in front of the fire, playing cards. Hildy occupied the table, her sketchbooks spread out.

Magnus lay on his side on the sofa. He was aware of Hildy's voice but it didn't reach him. His mind drifted.

"Hild," he rolled on to his side, "do you know if Mairi ever had a baby?"

"You're not listening."

"Sorry. What did I miss?"

"Nothing important." There was the angry clatter of pencils on the table. "I've no idea about Mairi. I've always kept clear of the spiteful old crow. When did you see her?"

"On my way back from the beach."

"I wondered why you were so long."

"I couldn't bear to listen to his lordship holding court about how we have to tell the authorities about the container."

"He's right. We can't keep it."

"Why not?"

"Because-"

The lights died. The chair creaked as Hildy got up. Husband and wife went around the room lighting candles.

"Can't we live somewhere that the electricity always works?" Peter threw down his cards.

"Because it's much more fun here."

Quiet candlelight and their voices made the cottage timeless. When Magnus was Peter's age the power often went out. Three generations sat close, mending nets and listening to John Spence. Magnus wished such fond memories for his sons too.

"It's not fun here. It's boring."

"That's enough." Magnus' temper was a lit flare.

"Boys, I'll get the lanterns out. Early bedtime. You can read for twenty minutes."

"Mum!"

"Shift when your mum tells you." Magnus saw Donald flinch. He tried to lighten things with a joke. "Or the blue men will get you."

Magnus listened to their tread on the stairs and then the creak of floorboards above. He picked up the photo frame on the table beside him. It was of his grandfather and his crew in front of *Maw's Teeth*, the trawler named against all counsel. It was the first catch after John Spence had gone to London and insisted the Ministry of Fisheries retest the waters that had been depleted for years. He made a nuisance of himself until they did. A month later the fleet sailed after two years in dock. The sea was teeming.

It was a time of plenty. The deck was piled with fish, white in the monochrome snapshot rather than silver.

Now the fish were gone, the sea was empty and the Fisheries' team came each year to check and left shaking their head sadly.

When Hildy returned, Magnus sat ramrod straight and half cast in shadow.

"Mags, don't be mad at the boys, not when it's Simon you're angry at."

"I won't be disrespected by my own sons."

"That sounds like something your grandfather would say."

"What's that mean?"

"That he was a fearsome bully."

"Don't talk about him like that."

"No, nobody can say a bad word about John Spence. How exactly was Peter being disrespectful?"

"These are my choices about our way of life."

"*Our* choices, not just yours."

That was why he'd wanted Hildy. She wouldn't be cowed. Free spirited Hildy had been a prize.

"Peter's just a boy. He just wants to be like his friends on Big Isle."

"That bloody generator." Magnus didn't want to be reasoned with. The generator was old and unpredictable. Sam the Spark would be up there with his bag of tools.

"There never seems to be a good time for us to talk about anything anymore. Promise me you won't get angry."

"Why would I get angry?"

"Because everything makes you angry."

Magnus sat back.

"Donald's been telling me about his nightmares. They're about the blue men and the Cailleach."

The blue men lived in the straight and reached for sailors with outstretched arms. The Cailleach had a list of pseudonyms and occupations but on Little Isle she was a witch who washed her linens in Maw's Maelstrom.

"Why didn't he tell me?"

"Because he's scared of disappointing you. He knows how much you love the old tales."

"They're just stories. My granddad taught me them when I was younger than Donald is. And Peter wasn't bothered by them."

"Yes, he was. And just because we all learnt about them as kids it doesn't mean they have to." She shuddered. "I used to wake up screaming."

Magnus had chronicled the dreams. Only those bred from old stock had them. Magnus used to wake in a sweat after the Cailleach bundled him up with her washing and chucked him into the whirlpool. The blue men pulled him down. They were always waiting in the undertow. Their teeth were pointed. The pain of drowning was like a knife.

"I'm not trying to hurt your feelings."

"Why's everything's so hard?" Magnus blurted out.

"What do you mean?"

"This place is dying. Our boys will be gone soon."

Peter would go to high school on the mainland as a boarder. Magnus wouldn't see him from one weekend to the next. Donald would follow before he knew it. How time fleeced you.

"They're going to school, not Australia."

"They'll stay on there when they've finished to find work."

"So? They should be free to do as they please. Hell, we could even move too."

"I hate it over the there. Too many bad memories." He meant the loneliness of the docks and his father's slow death.

"The world's bigger than that. We could go anywhere."

No. The boys would go and he couldn't follow. Mairi was right. He was only alive when he was on Little Isle.

The lights went back on.

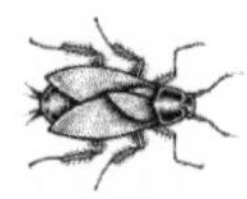

When Magnus opened his eyes it was light, to his relief. He'd been waking earlier and earlier of late, the fluorescent hands of his bedside clock marking the slow progress of the night.

When Magnus slipped from the bed, Hildy rolled over, searching for him from her dreams. She snorted and settled into the warm patch on the mattress that he'd just vacated.

That one's so sharp she'll cut herself, his grandfather had said before he died. *She'll cut you, more likely. Are you sure you want a girl that's so headstrong?*

Yes, Granddaddy.

Well, just don't marry her. He cuffed Magnus' head.

Magnus pulled on the clothes he'd left on the bannister the night before. Peter's door was closed but Donald's was open. His pyjamas were rucked up to reveal spindly legs. He whimpered and shifted. Magnus knelt beside him. Donald's curls were soft and loose, the same as Magnus' were before his grandfather took the shears to them.

Girlishness. What's your dad thinking?

"Mummy?"

"Hey, little man."

Magnus waited until Donald settled and then went downstairs.

He tried the radio but all he got was static. Outside the light was still thin and grey. The storm had blown over but Magnus could see another front out on the water, waiting.

There came a tap, tap, tap.

Iain was at the kitchen window. Jimmy stood beside him, grinning.

"Mags, come quick. They're trying to get the container open."

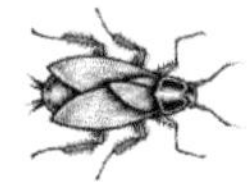

The night had brought another massacre. The beach was littered with sea birds, flight curtailed. The tide line was thick with their carcasses.

The storm and tide had been merciless. It had thrown the birds about. Feathers were matted with blood. Heads made strange angles with their bodies. Guts were revealed, auguries that Magnus couldn't read.

He recognised the fallen, even in pieces. The black guillemot's monochrome plumage and their shocking red feet. The large angular wings of the gannet, tipped in black. The puffin, comical with its painted eyes. A variety of gulls. And his favourite, the storm petrel. His grandfather would tell him how whole flocks of these tiny birds would feed in the wake of the trawlers. Their feet would patter on the water's surface and they held their wings in a high V shape, as if trying to keep them dry.

Flies rose from the dead as gulls and corvids landed to feat on them.

Magnus stumbled on the rocks in his rush to reach the container. He could see the shower of sparks from the welding rod as he pushed through the crowd.

"Oi! What are you doing?"

Niall flipped back his visor and mopped his forehead with his sleeve. "What's it look like?"

"It's not yours."

"It's not yours either."

"It belongs to everyone."

"It belongs to whoever can get the fucking thing open."

"Check it out, Mags." Isla stepped in. "Niall's been at the same spot for twenty minutes and the paint's not even blistered. Go on, show him."

Niall pulled off his glove and slapped his palm against the spot that he'd been trying to cut. Magnus reached out with a tentative fingertip to check for himself. The metal was like ice.

"I thought I'd made myself clear." It was Simon, standing shoulder to shoulder with Cormac. "I told you all to leave it alone. We don't know what it is. It might be military. There could be something dangerous in there."

"Then it's something they'll pay to get back," Niall countered.

"The military don't pay ransoms." Cormac rolled his eyes. "They'd take it by force."

"As soon as the radio's working, we're calling it in." Simon was adamant.

"You're full of shit." Everyone turned to look at Magnus.

"Less of that." Cormac stepped forward.

"What, you and Simon are best buddies now? I remember when you picked on him every chance that you got."

Cormac flushed.

"We're not fourteen anymore." Simon shook his head. "Cormac had an interview, just like you. He was the better man for the role. Is that why you're so sore?"

"No, it's you. You want to be *part of the community. For all of us to work together.* What's in there could help fund wind turbines to replace that shitty old generator."

"I've applied for a grant for that. I told you."

"You're full of *ifs* and *when*. Nothing's guaranteed.

And you're ignoring my point."

"Which is?"

"That you don't listen to any idea that runs contrary to your own. Everything's fine as long as we all do what we're told."

"You mean I ignore *you*. You're bitter because you don't get a personal invitation to meetings. That you don't get the last word in everything. If bother to listen you'd understand." Simon paused. "What exactly *is* your problem with me?"

"You're blind. More and more of us leave each year. You're not one of us. You don't understand. Your rich daddy bought this place for a song. And your stuck-up mother didn't even want to live here."

Simon's face was a mask.

"My mum was painfully shy. She didn't come back here because she didn't feel welcome. She was anorexic. She spent most of her life after I was born in and out of clinics being fed through nasogastric tubes. Little Isle was all Dad and I had left. I care about it as much as you do."

"Refurbishing a few cottages and building a kiln isn't going to save us."

"And who made you the mouth of the people?" That was Cormac.

"I know the art world. My mother was a dealer. I have connections through college. I can make this happen. People will come. They'll need housing and feeding." Simon was talking to everyone now. "We'll bring back farming. Rare breed sheep. We can start dyeing and weaving again."

All the colours of the landscape in the warp and weft.

"That's not sustainable industry. The other islands are developing halibut farms."

"Which is exactly why we need to be different."

"What we *need* is to be rid of you. Form a community council and a development company. Flog that big house of yours for capital. Attract people with business ideas and young families."

The sky was getting darker. The air smelt of iron. Their anger was calling in the gale. Clouds were as unreliable as the sea, just being water after all. Now they were in scud formation, black and loaded with rain. Magnus felt the gustfront on his face, the cold downdraft a harbinger.

"And you'd be in charge, of course. The problem with you is that you need to feel important. Most of us are keen for this to work. And Hildy will be a massive draw when her book deal is announced."

"What?"

"She's not told you? Maybe you should show more interest in your wife." Simon's laugh was bitter. "You never liked me, not really. Hildy's a diamond. Did you know that I persuaded her to apply to St Martin's, when I did? She turned down one of the most prestigious art schools in the country *to stay here with you*. She made me promise not to tell you. All you've done is hold her back-"

Magnus was a juggernaut. He barrelled Simon over. He felt a satisfying crunch as he landed on the man. They made a furious knot. It came down to who was bigger. At least here, in the muck and brawl, Magnus was the better man.

Hands gripped his arms. Jimmy and Iain hauled him off. Cormac pulled Simon to his feet. The rain was coming down hard.

"I'm not sleeping with your wife, you stupid sod." Simon wiped his bloodied nose. "She's too good to cheat. In fact, she's better than both of us put together."

Magnus deflated. He felt Iain's grip slacken, then he threw another punch at Simon.

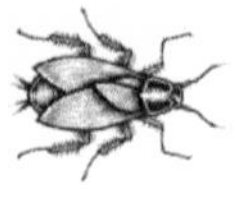

"Where have you been all day?"

Hildy was sat in the hall chair, facing the front door. Magnus' hair and coat were dripping. He bristled at her tone. She threw him the towel that had been folded on her knee. He kicked off his boots and started to pat himself dry.

She followed him into the kitchen, picking up his soggy shirt and trousers and throwing them into the washing machine. He pulled warm clothes from the clothes maiden that she'd left in front of the radiator.

"Where are the boys?"

"At Jack and Helen's."

"Why?"

"So we could talk properly. Why have you been fighting with Simon?"

"He had it coming. I don't want that man in this house. I don't want you to ever see him again." Magnus sat on the kitchen stool, his mouth rucked up. "You and Simon have already done a fair bit of talking. What's this about you getting a place at a posh college when we were kids?"

"Mags, that was such a long time ago."

"Well, it's news to me."

"Your dad had just been diagnosed with Alzheimer's. Your granddad had died few years before. I didn't want to leave you."

"Didn't stop you applying though."

She tilted her chin at that, all remorse gone.

"My chance at that's long gone, so you've no need to worry."

"Yet here it is, another reason for Simon to insult me."

"How exactly has Simon insulted you?"

"He's robbed me of the chance to provide for my family."

The washing machine drum started to gain speed. The spiralling clothes made Magnus' stomach churn.

"Simon offered you good work on restoring the cottages and knitting."

"Men don't knit."

"Of course they do. All the men here used to. You learnt from your dad."

Knitted cables represented fishing lines and nets, knot stitches added together to form fishes. Each fisherman had a unique pattern so that their sea mauled corpse could be identified from their sweater if washed ashore.

"I want to make nets, not jumpers for rich boys."

"What's the difference between selling them jumpers or oysters? You heard Simon. He can get you a hundred quid for each one from a boutique in London. You have real skill. You could even teach it."

"It's not proper work!"

"There. There it is," she hissed. "That's what you *really* think of what I do. Dabbling with paints. *Not proper work*. I cook, clean and I take care of the kids and then I sit down at night and work while you stride around like a king, doing fuck all. Well, it's my dabbling that's been paying the bills and clothing our sons."

"That's not fair. And art college isn't the only thing you've been keeping secret from me." He had another reason to take the high ground. "Simon loved telling me all about your book deal. Why exactly does he know and I don't?"

"He promised not to say anything. It was him that sent my book to a friend of his in publishing. That's why he knew. They want me to write and illustrate a whole series of books. If Simon's plans work I'll have my own studio at the big house, beside the classrooms."

"I bet you will."

"You're being ridiculous. There's no room here to work properly. And I tried to tell you last night but you weren't listening. You started going on about Mairi. What is it about her and the men in your family?" Hildy didn't wait for an answer. "The worst bit is that I've been waiting for you to be in a good mood to tell you, so that I can pretend you're genuinely happy for me. If you spent as much time looking for a job as you do moaning about everything we'd all be a damn sight better off. If you don't want to work for Simon get on the ferry each day and go work somewhere else."

"Why should I? We could have a life *here*. Simon's destroying what's left of us."

"Listen to yourself. It's always about Simon. Your issue with Simon is that he went off to university and came back with new ideas that don't involve you."

Magnus stared at the floor. The words wouldn't come. Something was rising inside him.

"Sea fishing's dead. There aren't the stocks left. Get over it. Everyone laughs at you because they know all those stories you tell are hand-me-downs. You've never worked on a boat in your life and you bleat on about making nets." She followed him to the door. "And while we're at it, your grandfather was a tyrant. He trampled over everyone, including your mum and dad. He gave them a dog's life."

"He loved this place. He sacrificed everything for it."

What? What exactly had he sacrificed?

"You don't want a job or a future. You want the past."

Magnus couldn't help it. The past persisted in his blood. He craved what was lost. Lighting a candle and carrying it in a cow's skull through the byre and out into the black night of the new year. Stargazy pie. Gifts launched on the tide. A time when men ruled the seas and themselves and life was easier to navigate.

"All that crap about wanting things to be better for the boys. The problem with you is that you want them to live the life you want for yourself."

The problem with you is that you want to be important. The problem with you.

Simon and Hildy had talked behind his back. They'd talked and laughed.

"I love you, Mags. There's only every been you but I don't know how much more I can take. I need you to think about this. I'm telling you so that we can try and change. I'm telling you because if things don't change I'm going to leave."

"Leave? The island?"

"I'll take the boys somewhere, just until we both work things out." She started to cry. "I'm not trying to punish you. I'm trying to save our marriage."

Peter and Donald had been born at the cottage. Magnus had cut the cords tethering them to Hildy. Every inch of the squalling babies was his from the fine down on their backs to their screwed-up faces. They made him immortal. Part of an unbroken line. His heart had flipped and flopped in his chest. Fear and awe gnawed at him. It was his duty to remake the world for them.

Nothing would part him from them.

"Say something. Anything. Tell me you'll fight for us."

The swell inside him threatened to wash him away. He would pummel Hildy with his fists. He would snap her neck. This body that he promised to worship would fall before him. Beautiful Hildy. Strong Hildy. The mother of his sons. She held out her arms to him.

"I have to go out."

"Not like this-"

"No." He backed away from her, pleading on his face. "Let me be for a little while."

At the door he turned back, "I'll make it right, I promise, no matter what it takes."

The beach was clear as the tide was coming in. As Magnus approached he could see that a figure was crouched beside the container. When it stood, he could see it was Mairi.

She stood up, paint dripping from the brush as she slapped it against the container's side. She made a clumsy spiral with a shaking hand. Red stood out against the blue paint.

"Mairi."

Her nightdress flapped around her legs. Her bare feet were covered in dark smears of paint.

"You must be freezing." He took off his coat and put it around her shoulders.

"It won't stay."

The spiral was fading. It was *sinking in.* She turned to him, crying.

"What's happened to you?" He clutched her head in his hands.

One side of her mouth drooped. She looked like a lopsided doll. He recognised it as a stroke. It wasn't paint on her feet. They were bloodied from cuts and abrasions.

"Come on, let's get you to my place."

She pulled away, intent on daubing more marks. BRID. The word faded fast.

"Who's Brid?"

"You dare ask me that, John Spence?"

"I'm Magnus, not John."

Herring gulls gathered on the rocks around the container, more and more coming in. Some of them landed on the container's top edge. A pair faced off, screaming at one another. Their wings made acute angles with their bodies in furious symmetry. Then they flew at one another, intent on blood. Red stained grey and white feathers. The other gulls piled in, finishing off the weaker one.

"I should be young and beautiful. I used to run ahead of the lightning. Now it hurts when I get up in the morning and it's all your fault, John."

"Mairi, we need to get you inside." He reached out for her.

"No, you don't touch me. I'm not Mairi. I'm the Cailleach. You've tricked me before, you devil. I used to summon the wind and fly down to visit my brother, Maw, in the water. You, with your silky promises and kisses. Then it was too late. You made me just a woman. You stained my plaid. It'll never white again."

"What about Brid?"

"You know! Our little Brid," she keened. "I hate you. I hate you and your family, John Spence. Little Brid was the only good thing to come from you." Spittle landed on Magnus' face. "You're a damn liar. You said she wasn't real because she came from me. That she was bound for Maw. She was just a baby, and I let you do it."

"Do what?"

"You know," she wept, "you know."

Magnus did know. John Spence was a determined man.

Beneath the wind and waves there was the sound of their breathing and a click.

The container door was open.

"Will you kiss me, John?" Mairi's voice was full of self- loathing. "Will you love me, like I love you?"

Magnus leant down. Her lips were dry and withered. Her breath was sour. Her fingers fluttered around his face.

He picked her up. She was like dry kindling in his arms. The old woman's eyes were paler than he'd ever seen them. She rested her head against his chest and sighed.

She needed to be air lifted off the island to a hospital. How long would it be before the storms cleared and they could radio for help? He knew Mairi wouldn't want that. She wouldn't want to leave, not for anything.

The tide was closing in, faster than he'd ever seen, and another weather front directly behind it. Scud clouds were just the messenger. They hid the vast heights of the thunderhead above them. The air crackled with energy and the wind rose. Lightning discharged from cloud to cloud, not as a zigzag but a vein. The closing rumbling became a crack. Rain poured through.

Mairi wasn't a fallen goddess or an elemental trapped in flesh. She was an addled old woman, touched in the head. It didn't matter though. Maw had sent the container and now the tide was coming in.

MEAN TIME

Paul Tremblay

The old man's name began with an R, I think, yeah, but definitely a capital R. Mom told me to stay away from R. Dad said R was harmless but I shouldn't encourage him. Sherry, the semi-goth teen who lived on the floor below us and spent her afternoons listening to the Smiths and Kelly Clarkson told me R spent too much time in his pockets and that he smelled like what she imagined a burning jellyfish would smell like. Sherry was wrong. R smelled like chalk. He had countless chalk sticks in his pockets and dust was all over his hands and his brown wool suit. The smears looked like letters tattooed on his lapels and sleeves. R used his chalk to draw lines on the sidewalks and streets. Or arcs, not lines. Arcs would be a more accurate description. Whatever. R walked backward, all hunched over, tip of chalk pressed against the cement or brick or cobblestone, and he drew until the stick disintegrated into dust. R drew his looping arcs and lines from *Gracey's Market* to *Wilamenia's Flower Festival* then to *Frank and Beans Diner* and on and on, to points A then B, and to C, then to D, past the alphabet and to points we'd have to name with alphas and epsilons. The first time I worked up the courage to ask him the obvious, he gave me an obvious answer. R used the chalk to find his way home because even in our small city he was afraid he would get lost. We all lived in a city that was smaller than most towns, so I'd heard. All our apartment buildings, libraries, markets, salons, and restaurants were crammed together, like space was something to be shared intimately with everyone. So, that first day, after I asked him what was what, after he told me what was what, we shared our space quietly, uncomfortably, then, he said, "Well, okay, little one, in the mean time, I have more errands to do." Back then I didn't know meantime was one word, so I imagined it as two. Later, I tried following him in the afternoon, as he backtracked over his loops and lines, reliving his previous paths, but he walked too fast for me, and I lost him and the chalk path in the maze of alleys between *Gorgeous George's Peach Pit* and *Dolly Lamas Liquor Mart.* I tried restarting on the path but I couldn't follow the intersecting arcs he'd drawn earlier, and never found the beginning or the end. The chalk lines faded overnight, washed away by light rain, according to Mom. Dad liked to try and scare me and told me the night scrubbed it all away. Sherry said the students who dropped out of trade school cleaned the streets and sidewalks at night. Didn't matter where the lines went because R was always back out there the next morning and for all the mornings after that. Each day I asked him clever variations on the theme of why he drew the chalk lines. He'd give me the same afraid-of-getting-lost answer, followed by the same mean time quip. I grew frustrated with his consistent ducking of my questions, or maybe I was frustrated because his weirdness which had once been cool and exciting had become boring, rote, part of the scenery I so desperately wanted to alter or affect in some way. So, one morning, after he left *Missy's Galaxy Meat Emporium*, I erased his chalk line, rubbed out about half a block, made my own gap in his path. It was cloudy, I remember that, and the yawning gap made me feel anxious, like something big was indeed missing, or wrong. If I had a piece of chalk in my hand, I would've fixed what I'd done right away. Instead I stood and waited for R to retrace his steps. Which he did. He stopped at the end of his line, did a classic double take, looked around the city, down at the clean clear line behind him, the one that just suddenly ended in the middle of the sidewalk, in the middle of nowhere. R dropped his bags, round fruits rolled away, spheres suddenly loosened from their strict orbits, and the stuff prepackaged in boxes stayed where they fell. R fumbled in his pockets, pulled out chalk sticks and they dribbled out of his fingers, crashed to the sidewalk and broke into jagged pieces. I started crying and I told him I was sorry, that I could fix it for him. I grabbed one of the chalk pieces and drew a rough line over the gap to where I thought it was supposed to go, but I wasn't sure anymore, and I think I made the wrong connection. I dropped the chalk and ran home to my apartment, watched him from my bedroom window, the shade pulled over my head behind me. R spent the rest of the afternoon walking the city, following those lines, never really getting anywhere. He disappeared into alleys and I thought he'd finally found his way home, but he'd reappear a few minutes later. I watched him until my parents came in and found me asleep and curled up in the windowsill.

AFTERWORD

Allow me to share a revelation that came to me during the Christmas holidays in 2020. The world was knee deep in a coronavirus pandemic and families tried their best to make the most of a season that is usually full of joy and festivities. But not in 2020. No, this year was different. While lying on the couch, midday, half drunk, flicking mindlessly through TV stations, I suddenly found myself in a state of despair when an Attenborough documentary grabbed my attention… visual images of our beautiful planet struggling and an old man, who has dedicated his life to showing us this planet, stood there talking to the camera with a harrowing tone about how we, as a species, are on a road to ruin.

At first, I thought: *what can I do? I'm just lying here, surrounded by consumerism, gaining weight…* and then it occurred to me; every single human on this rock we call home has a role to play in the fight against the biggest challenge our species has ever had to endure. And so, an atom of an idea began forming…

Like most semi-responsible people I know, I always tried to do my bit. I'm not a litter bug and do call them out when I see them in action. I try to recycle responsibly by washing my glass jars out before listening to them smash into pieces when they enter the bottle bank and ultimately, I do my best to be mindful of my impact on the world I live in. But the idea that was forming in my head kept growing and before I knew it, I was questioning everything. If every semi-responsible person I know is like me and trying their best, then why is David telling me the planet is on its way out? Now I look around, I see my four-year-old son and pregnant wife playing a game. Smiling and living in the moment and this is where that aforementioned atom exploded and evolved into a full-on purpose — every single human on this planet, must do more! So, I asked myself, how can *I* do more? Well, what tools do I possess that can maybe make a difference? And now we arrive at the reason you're holding this book…

I've published a few horror fiction books and through this I've been lucky to make friends with some great writers. One of which is Tim Lebbon. I sent him a message on WhatsApp asking how he'd feel if I asked him to recycle a story for a charity anthology… thankfully his reply was very enthusiastic and from there the vision for the book you are holding was complete, a revelation, if you will.

Fast forward ten months and here I am writing this afterword with a sense of imposture syndrome and crippling anxiety. I look back on that nugget of an idea and am amazed that it is now an anthology packed with some amazing writers — all of whom answered the call and for this, I am forever grateful because their willingness to help me with this anthology showed me that people do care about the world we live. And I believe, if you dig deep into every human on this planet, you'll learn they care too. Earth is our home and it must be protected at all costs. If you're reading this, you too have made an effort. This book isn't a celebration of horror fiction. No, this book exists because horror writers are for climate action and by using what they had at their deposal they want to contribute to saving our home. By buying it, you get some fantastic stories to keep and treasure, but more importantly, the proceeds from the sale of this book will go towards Climate Outreach — a charity dedicated to communication of climate action.

So, dear reader, my final thought is this… look after your planet, do the best you can, future generations are relying on the choices you make today and if we as species can mobilise and unite, humanity might just have a chance.

– Seán O'Connor
Dublin, Ireland.
October 14th, 2021

ACKNOWLEDGEMENTS

Without the following humans, *Revelations* would not exist: Tim Lebbon, Ellie Lebbon, Gemma Amor, Clive Barker, Laird Barron, Ramsey Campbell, Richard Chizmar, Tananarive Due, Philip Fracassi, T.E. Grau, Joe Hill, Gwendolyn Kiste, John Langan, Sarah Langan, Joe R. Lansdale, Josh Malerman, Adam L.G. Nevill, Nuzo Onoh, Sarah Pinborough, Priya Sharma, Paul Tremblay, Sadie Hartmann, Phil Stokes, Sarah Stokes, Laurel Choate, Katherine Wilcox, Kristin Nelson, Alexander Cochran, Kenneth W. Cain, Boz Mugabe, Chuck Verrill, Jeremy Wagner, Jarod Barbee, and Stephen King. Every person listed here has either a minor or large role in the creation of this anthology and have my eternal gratitude.

COPYRIGHT & PUBLICATION HISTORY

Field of Ice, Gemma Amor, © 2021

The Wood on the Hill first published in *The Dark Fantastic by Douglas E. Winter* by HarperCollins, © 1967

Fear Sun first published in *Innsmouth Nightmares: Lovecraftian Inspired Stories* by PS Publishing, © 2015

No Name In It first published in *Imagination Fully Dilated Volume II* by IFD Publishing, edited by Elizabeth Engstrom, © 2000

The Tower first published in *Hides the Dark Tower* by Pole to Pole Publishing, edited by Kelly A. Harmon and Vonnie Winslow Crist, © 2015

Carriers first published in *Ghost Summer: Stories* by Prime Books, © 2015

The Guardian, Philip Fracassi, © 2021

Low Hanging Clouds first published online in the *June 2011 Edition* of the Eschatology Journal, © 2011

Dead-Wood by Joe Hill, first published in *Subterranean Press e-newsletter, February 2005* and subsequently in *20th Century Ghosts* in 2005 by PS Publishing and in a later edition published by HarperCollins, © 2005, 2007

Jude Confronts Global Warming by Joe Hill, first published online in *Subterranean Press Magazine, Spring 2007*, © 2007

Summer Thunder, from *The Bazaar of Bad Dreams* by Stephen King. Copyright © 2015 by Stephen King. Reprinted with the permission (US) of Scribner, a division of Simon & Schuster, Inc and Hodder & Stoughton (UK). All rights reserved.

The Maid from the Ash: A Life in Pictures first published in *Weird Whispers* by Nightscape Press, © 2020

Inundation first published online in the *Lovecraft eZine*, © 2016

Love Perverts first published in *The End is Nigh — The Apocalypse Triptych 1* by Broad Reach Publishing, edited by John Joseph Adams and Hugh Howey, © 2014

In The Cold, Dark Time first published in *Cosmic Interruptions* by SST Publications, © 2018

The Evolutionary first published in *Last Exit For The Lost* by Cemetery Dance, © 2010

Teenage Graveyard Nightwatchman first published as *The Givens Sensor Board* in *Lost Signals* by Perpetual Motion Machine Publishing, © 2016

Call the Name first published in *The Gods of H. P. Lovecraft* by JournalStone, edited by Aaron J. French, © 2015

Black Queen , Nuzo Onoh, © 2021

Snow Angels first published in *The British Fantasy Society Yearbook* from The British Fantasy Society, © 2009

Maw first published in *New Fears 2* by Titan Books, edited by Mark Morris, © 2018

Mean Time first published in *In The Mean Time, Hardcover Edition* from ChiZine Publications, © 2010

ABOUT CLIMATE OUTREACH

Climate Outreach work with people and organisations who want to communicate climate action, to ensure their messages are tailored to their audiences: resonating with their values and identity and presented by people they trust in the most impactful way possible.

Our three key aims are to:

1. Build and sustain cross-societal support for climate action in nations critical for global decarbonisation.

2. Overcome political polarisation in countries where it is impeding action on climate change.

3. Turn climate concern into climate action on key behaviours, policies and corporate responsibility.

We are proud of the impact we're having. Highlights of our work include: driving climate conversations across society; finding ways to talk about climate change across the political spectrum; changing the way millions of people see climate change; accelerating understanding of how to mainstream low-carbon lifestyles; working with local partners in countries around the world; and working to ensure a just transition is at the heart of our path to net zero.

www.climateoutreach.org

Lightning Source UK Ltd.
Milton Keynes UK
UKHW011848250422
402051UK00008B/568/J